Use of Force

USE OF FORCE

A THRILLER

Brad Thor

EMILY BESTLER BOOKS
—
ATRIA

New York   London   Toronto   Sydney   New Delhi

EMILY
BESTLER
BOOKS

ATRIA

An Imprint of Simon & Schuster, Inc.
1230 Avenue of the Americas
New York, NY 10020

First Emily Bestler Books/Atria Books hardcover edition June 2017

EMILY BESTLER BOOKS / ATRIA BOOKS and colophon
are trademarks of Simon & Schuster, Inc.

For information about special discounts for bulk purchases, please contact Simon
& Schuster Special Sales at 1-866-506-1949 or business@simonandschuster.com.

The Simon & Schuster Speakers Bureau can bring authors to your live event. For
more information, or to book an event, contact the Simon & Schuster Speakers
Bureau at 1-866-248-3049 or visit our website at www.simonspeakers.com.

Manufactured in the United States of America

10 9 8 7 6 5 4 3 2 1

Library of Congress Cataloging-in-Publication Data is available.

ISBN 978-1-4767-8938-5
ISBN 978-1-4767-8940-8 (ebook)

For Duane "Dewey" Clarridge
Keeper of the midnight's watch.
Godspeed.

Citius venit malum quam revertitur.

Evil arrives faster than it departs.

PROLOGUE

ITALIAN COAST GUARD HEADQUARTERS
MARITIME RESCUE COORDINATION CENTER
ROME

An explosion of thunder shook the building as Lieutenant Pietro Renzi, dressed in his Navy whites, answered the phone in front of him.

"Mayday. Mayday," a voice said in heavily accented English. "My latitude is N, three, three, four, nine."

Renzi snapped his fingers to get his colleagues' attention. "Three, three *degrees*?" he asked.

"Four, nine," replied the caller.

This was exactly the kind of call Renzi and his team were worried about tonight. North African refugee smugglers were subhuman. All they cared about was money. Once they had been paid, they put their passengers into unseaworthy boats, tossed in a compass and a satellite phone preprogrammed with the emergency number of the *Guardia Costiera*, and pointed them toward Italy.

Rarely did they provide them with enough fuel to make the journey. Rarer still, did they consult weather forecasts. Swells as high as fifteen meters had already been reported tonight, and the storm was only getting worse.

"Thirty-three degrees, forty-nine minutes north," Renzi repeated, confirming the caller's position.

"Yes."

"And beneath that? I need the number beneath."

"Please," the man implored. "I do not have much battery."

"Sir, calm down. I need the number beneath."

The man read the numbers from the screen: "One, three. Dot four, one."

Renzi entered the full coordinates into his computer: 33°49'N– 13°41'E. The distressed vessel's position appeared on the giant screen at the front of the operations center. The boat was 120 nautical miles from the island of Lampedusa, Italy's southernmost territory.

"Please, please, you must help us," the caller implored. "There is much water inside the boat. We are sinking."

"Sir, please. We will send rescue, but you need to be calm. How many people are onboard?"

"One hundred and fifty persons. Many women. Many children. *Please* hurry. We are in danger. We are *sinking*."

An Italian Coast Guard helicopter was out of the question. They were too far away and there were too many people.

Lieutenant Renzi studied the screen at the head of the room. It showed ships and boats in the central Mediterranean Sea. He searched it for one close enough to help effect a rescue.

There was nothing. Seasoned captains had already fled the storm's path. It would take hours to get any type of vessel to them.

"Hello?" the man said. "Hello? Do you hear me, please?"

"Yes, I still hear you."

"The waves are very high. All the people are sick. We need your help."

"Sir," Lieutenant Renzi repeated, trying to reassure the man, "we are sending a ship to rescue you, but you must stay calm."

"Okay. Okay."

"Now, how many flotation devices do you have?"

"Flotation devices?" the man replied.

"Life jackets," said Renzi. "How many *life jackets* do you have?"

There was a pause as the man shouted out a question in his language to the people on his boat. When he came back on the line, his response chilled Renzi to the bone: "We have no life jackets."

CHAPTER 1

S cot Harvath wasn't supposed to be here. The CIA was forbidden to conduct operations inside the United States—especially the kind he was about to undertake. Desperate times, though, called for desperate measures.

The seven-day Burning Man event was an extreme, weeklong summer solstice festival held on a flat, prehistoric lakebed three hours outside Reno, Nevada. Outrageous costumes were encouraged—as was "tasteful" nudity. Costumes ran the gamut from Mad Max to Carnival in Rio.

As fit as he was, he could have gotten away without wearing much of anything. That wasn't his style, though. It also wouldn't have made sense for his assignment.

Instead, the five-foot-ten-inch Harvath, with his sandy brown hair and his glacierlike blue eyes, wore a Continental Army coat and a full face of Cherokee war paint, obscuring his handsome features.

As the wind kicked up again, he pulled a pair of steampunk goggles over his eyes and wrapped a keffiyeh around his face. Clouds of the fine alkaline dust that covered the playa were swirling everywhere. Visibility was dropping.

"Fifty meters," a disembodied voice said over the device pushed deep into his left ear. He kept walking, scanning from left to right.

Burning Man took place in a temporary "metropolis" built in the Black Rock Desert, which was called Black Rock City. With more than seventy thousand attendees, BRC was twice as dense as the City of London.

Seen from above, the festival was laid out in the shape of a giant letter C, or two-thirds of a circle. It looked like a blueprint for the Death Star with a good chunk blown away.

It was a mile and a half across, and a quarter mile out from the center of the C was the "Man"—a giant effigy that would be set on fire Saturday night.

There were no accommodations in Black Rock City, only what you hauled in (and hauled back out) yourself. "Burners," as attendees were known, spent months in advance planning elaborately themed camps and villages. Only the ultrarich showed up on Day One, usually via helicopter, to luxury, turnkey camps that had already been constructed for them.

Almost as controversial as the camps of the ultrarich was something called Kidsville. It was one of the largest camps at Burning Man and was for families with children—an interesting choice at such an adult festival. Nevertheless, this year, there were about a thousand kids in attendance.

An army of volunteers, augmented by private security, had screened each vehicle as it entered the festival. Occasionally, the volunteers were assisted by undercover law enforcement.

The massive flow of traffic, in addition to the laid-back atmosphere of the event, made it impossible to do anything thorough. It was more security "theater" than anything else.

Local and state law enforcement patrolled the festival, as did Park Rangers from the Bureau of Land Management. But as long as you weren't openly doing drugs or providing alcohol to minors, it wasn't difficult to stay off their radar. They had their hands more than full. It was no wonder Burning Man had caught the attention of terrorists.

The voice spoke again in Harvath's ear. "You should be able to see it now."

He stopped walking, raised a bottle of water to his mouth, and used the opportunity to look around.

Banners and tent flaps blew in the wind. There was a makeshift bar called 7 Deadly Gins, something called Camp Woo Woo, another place called No Bikini Atoll, and an enclave named Toxic Disco Clam. Just beyond was the blue RV.

"I see it now," said Harvath, tossing the water bottle.

"Hey!" a woman behind him complained, but he ignored her and kept moving. He had come too far to let Hamza Rahim escape.

Through the dust, the evening air was redolent with the smoke from bonfires and burn barrels. Music thumped from every direction. Hidden out of sight, diesel generators rumbled their low growls, powering turntables, sound systems, and massive light shows. Dancers on the playa spun flaming orbs on long chains. Rolling art exhibits, brightly lit from end to end, spat fire into the night sky.

He did a slow loop around the camp that contained the blue RV. Everyone seemed to be congregated in a large tent, content to party and wait out the dust storm happening outside.

After a group of bicycles covered in synchronized LED lights passed, Harvath approached the RV.

It was dark inside. He tried to peer through several windows, but the blinds were drawn. A sunshade covered the windshield.

Pressing his ear against the door, he listened. *Nothing.* If there was anyone inside, they were being very quiet.

He tried to open the door, but it was locked.

Removing a set of picks, he looked over his shoulder to make sure no one was watching. No one was. Within seconds he had the door unlocked, had affixed the suppressor to his Sig Sauer pistol, and had slipped inside.

Even through his keffiyeh, the RV smelled terrible—like stale cigarettes and a toilet that didn't flush well. After he peeled off his goggles, it took a second for his eyes to adjust.

Plates of half-eaten food sat on the table. Dishes were stacked in the sink. A white plastic trash bag, overflowing with garbage, was tied to one of the drawer handles. The upholstery was torn, the carpeting was stained, and there was playa dust covering everything. Hamza Rahim lived like an animal.

Noticing something on the floor, Harvath bent over and picked it up. *Pieces of electrical wire.* His heart rate went up.

As far as anyone at the CIA knew, Rahim had been sent to Burning Man for preattack surveillance. His job was to gather intelligence and feed it back up the chain. Harvath's assignment was to snatch Rahim and break his network by any means necessary. The wires, though, suggested the CIA's intelligence might have been dangerously off target. Raising his pistol, Harvath crept toward the rear of the vehicle.

The first thing he checked was a small closet. It was filled with junk. Across from it was a set of bunk beds—both of which had been slept in. *Bad sign*. Rahim was supposed to be alone.

Beyond the bunk beds was the master area. That bed had also been slept in.

There was only one place left to search: the bathroom.

The door to it was shut. Taking up a position to the side, Harvath slowly tried the knob. *Locked*.

He listened for any sound, but all he could hear was the thump of the dance music pulsing outside.

Stepping in front of the door, he raised his boot and kicked straight through the knob, shattering the lockset and leaving a hole where it used to be.

As the hinges were on the outside, the door was meant to swing away from the bathroom into the RV.

Harvath took one hand off his pistol and reached for the door. That was when it exploded.

CHAPTER 2

A Middle Eastern–looking man inside the bathroom kicked the door open and threw the contents of a large plastic cup where he thought Harvath would be standing.

The highly corrosive cocktail of drain cleaner and household bleach missed Harvath and splattered across the wall and window blinds to his left.

Harvath answered the attack by slamming his pistol into the bridge of the man's nose.

Immediately, his adversary's knees went weak and began to buckle. Harvath swept in behind him, wrapped his left arm around his throat, and demanded, "Where's Hamza Rahim?"

The man, who must have seen Harvath peeking in the RV's windows or heard him as he came in, struggled.

Harvath struck him again, this time in the side of the head. "Where is he? Where's Rahim?"

The attacker continued to resist, so Harvath pointed his pistol at his left foot and pressed the trigger.

The resulting scream was so loud, Harvath had to cover his mouth for fear the man's cries might draw attention. "Tell me where Rahim is or I'll shoot the other one."

The man clawed at Harvath. As he did, Harvath noticed that he was missing two fingers on his left hand. Harvath's worst fears were confirmed. *This guy was a bomb maker.*

Harvath now had even more questions, but his eyes, nose, and throat were burning from the poisonous cloud of gas the man had created with his bathroom bleach bomb. They needed to get the hell out of the RV.

With his left arm still wrapped tightly around the man's throat, Harvath jabbed the pistol suppressor into his back and pushed him toward the front of the RV. They had only made it halfway when someone appeared at the door.

The figure was dressed in what looked like a monk's robe with a featureless mask made of chrome. The figure also had a weapon, and before Harvath could react, he began to fire.

Harvath used the bomb maker as a shield until he had to drop his lifeless body and dive for cover. Rounds from the attacker in the chrome mask continued to chew up the vehicle.

Harvath wanted to return fire, but he couldn't see because of the toxic cloud. He couldn't even breathe.

Shooting out one of the rear windows, he raked the broken glass with his weapon and leapt out, landing hard on the ground.

His instincts told him to roll under the motor home for concealment, but he knew chlorine gas was heavier than air. If any of the fumes were leaking out, they would pool beneath the vehicle. He needed to move away from the RV, fast.

Spraying the front of the motor home with suppressed rounds from his Sig Sauer, he scrambled behind a nearby pickup, hoping the dust storm would help hide his movement.

At the truck, he pulled his goggles back up around his eyes, tightened his keffiyeh, and tried to catch his breath. His lungs were burning. How much was playa dust and exertion versus how much was chlorine gas, he had no idea. All he knew was that his chest hurt like hell.

"Rahim's not alone," Harvath coughed over his radio. "There was someone else in the trailer."

"Who?" the voice replied.

"A bomb maker. They're not here to scout. They're here to *attack*."

"*Jesus*. Did you get them?"

"The bomb maker's dead," Harvath said, "but Rahim's on the run. Dressed in a brown robe with a chrome faceplate. Get the drone up."

"It won't survive the storm."

"I don't care. Get it up. *Now*."

"Roger that," the voice responded.

Inserting a fresh magazine into his weapon, Harvath issued a final command before rolling out from behind the truck. "Tell the extraction team to split up. We have to find Rahim."

"And when we do?"

"Take him out."

With that, Harvath ended his transmission and began moving.

Mike Haney was a smart guy. The CIA had snapped him up two years ago. Before joining its secretive paramilitary detachment known as the Special Operations Group, he'd been a Force Recon Marine. Harvath knew he could count on him.

The extraction team was made up of four additional, highly experienced former military personnel: Navy SEAL Tim Barton; Delta Force operative Tyler Staelin; Green Beret Jack Gage; and Matt Morrison, who, like Haney, had also been a Force Recon Marine.

While Haney ran everything from the large tour bus they were using as their base of operations, the extraction team was a couple of blocks over in a heavily modified, six-person golf cart.

Though Black Rock City was designed for pedestrians and bicycles, they'd been able to get the cart in by providing documentation "certifying" one of the team members as disabled.

Beneath one row of seats was a storage area just large enough to hide Rahim and smuggle him out. Under another was the hidden compartment they had used to smuggle in their weapons.

Using spray paint, Christmas lights, and pool noodles purchased on the way in, they had "decorated" the cart. It looked like shit, but none of them cared. As long as it did its job, that was all that mattered.

Rahim couldn't have gotten far. Unscrewing the suppressor, Harvath returned his weapon beneath his coat and moved from tent to tent.

Near an art installation of public telephones advertising "Talk to God," he gave a description of Rahim's costume and asked if anyone had seen his "friend."

A woman wearing a motorcycle helmet and not much else said she had, and pointed down a road to the left. Harvath thanked her and took off.

Clouds of dust were still blowing through Black Rock City, but visibility was getting better. Harvath relayed his position to Haney and told him to have the extraction team members start closing in. As soon as he relayed his instructions, though, he saw a robed figure up ahead with a chrome faceplate.

Quickening his pace, Harvath tried to close the distance between them. The man weaved through one camp after another, slipping between parked vehicles, tents, and stacks of supplies. He was careful not to get caught in any open spaces. Someone had taught him good tradecraft.

"Where's my drone, Haney?" Harvath demanded as he leapt over a pallet of bottled water and kept moving.

"Inbound. Thirty seconds."

"This guy's gonna be gone in thirty seconds. Hurry up."

"Got him," another voice said over Harvath's earpiece. He recognized the voice. It was Staelin, the Delta operative who was teamed with Barton the SEAL.

"Where are you?"

Staelin gave his position.

"You're still two blocks away," Harvath replied. "You've got the wrong guy."

"Bullshit. I'm looking right at him. Brown monk's robe, chrome faceplate."

CHAPTER 3

"Stay on him," Harvath ordered, not sure what the hell they were up against, or whom he was even following at this point. "But don't let him see you."

"Roger that," Staelin replied.

"Haney—" Harvath began, but he was interrupted.

"Overhead now."

He pulled a small infrared beacon from his coat pocket and clipped it to his lapel as he kept moving. "Got me?"

"Stand by," Haney answered, as he used the drone's infrared camera to search for Harvath's strobe. Finally, he came back over the radio and said, "I've got you."

"There's a robed figure up ahead of me," Harvath stated. "Same bearing. Moving like he's late for a job interview. See him?"

Haney paused before replying, "Negative. I don't see anything."

"What do you mean?"

"I *mean*, I don't see him. The drone's not picking him up."

Suddenly another voice broke in. It was Morrison, the other Marine who was moving with Gage, the Green Beret. "I have eyes on."

"What's your position?" Harvath asked.

When Morrison gave his location, Haney said, "You're not even close to Harvath or Staelin. You guys are chasing three different targets."

Shit, thought Harvath. *How many of these guys are there?* "Everybody, strobes on," he ordered.

A chorus of "Roger that" flooded the radio as the men activated their infrared devices, visible only to the infrared camera aboard the drone. "Strobes on."

Based on the wire clippings and the presence of the bomb maker, something bad was in the works. *But was it in the works for tonight? Or were they just getting the lay of the land, perhaps waiting for two nights from now, when there'd be the biggest concentration of Burners in one spot?* There was no telling. All he knew was that at least one of them was armed. And if one was armed, the others probably were too.

Getting back on the radio, Harvath instructed Haney to fix the other two figures on the map. In his mind, he tried to picture the layout of Black Rock City. *Where the hell were they headed?* And even more important, *did Rahim have even more operatives out there?*

The most pressing question, though, was *What had he interrupted? Were the men in the process of planting a bomb? Had they already planted a bomb? Or did they have something totally different in mind?*

When Haney's voice came over his earpiece moments later, he didn't have good news. "I can't see them."

"Is it the weather?" Harvath asked, though his gut told him that wasn't the answer.

"Negative. Whatever they're wearing, it's masking their heat signature."

Damn it. More tradecraft. These guys knew how to avoid infrared surveillance. Harvath's worst fears were being confirmed.

"Based on their direction of travel," he asked, "what do you think their target is?"

Haney studied the festival map on the console in front of him. "It could be anything."

"Think like them."

"I *am* thinking like them," Haney replied. "But every one of these theme camps reeks of symbolism."

Staelin's voice interrupted the transition. "Our guy just doubled back and took a hard left. Headed west now."

Moments later, Morrison stated, "Our target just took a shortcut through two camps. Now headed east."

Up ahead of Harvath, the hooded figure he was following paused and looked around, as if checking his position, and then began moving north. *They were all changing direction.*

"Where are they headed, Mike?" Harvath asked as he continued after his target. "Come on. Figure it out."

"I'm telling you," Haney replied. "It could be anything."

Just then, Morrison interjected, "I know where my target is headed. We need to take him *now*."

"Slow down," cautioned Harvath. "Where's he going?"

"*Kidsville.* The family camp."

The urgency of the situation instantly took on new meaning. They had to act.

Passing through another camp, Harvath saw a roll of duct tape. Grabbing it from the tent pole where it hung, he picked up his pace and kept going.

"Is anyone close enough to see if they're buttoned down?" he asked.

Suicide bombers were known for employing what was called a "dead man's switch." It was a button that when depressed armed their device. If a bomber was shot or somehow incapacitated, simply releasing the button would cause their device to detonate.

There was also the chance of a "chicken switch." It was a fail-safe that attached the bomber's vest to a cell phone. If the device failed to go off at the designated place and time, a handler could trigger it remotely.

The chance that either technology, and possibly both, was present made the situation much more dangerous.

"Negative," Staelin replied. "I can't see anything. Our target has his hands under his robe."

"Same with ours," said Morrison.

Except for the split second he had a weapon pointed at him, Harvath hadn't seen the hands of the man he was chasing either.

Tackling multiple potential suicide bombers wasn't part of this assignment. It was supposed to be surveillance of a terrorist planner, followed by a snatch and grab. Once they had him out of Black Rock City, they were to fly him to a prearranged location for interrogation. Any heavy lifting was Harvath's responsibility. Everyone else was supposed to be support.

Harvath didn't know much about the men he was working with, but what he did know was that they were men of honor. They did the right thing, no matter what.

"Gut check," Harvath relayed over the radio. "If anyone wants out, now's the time."

"Negative," came the replies.

Harvath laid out his plan. "Assume they're carrying weapons. Assume they're all wearing vests. And assume they're buttoned down. If they come off that switch, it's over. So when you go kinetic, you each take a hand and focus on it like a laser. Understood?"

"Roger that," the men answered.

Haney knew Harvath was operating without a partner. That meant he was going to have an even harder job. He'd have to get his target's hands under control by himself. "I can be to you in less than five minutes," Haney offered.

Looking up ahead, Harvath figured out where his target was headed. It was the biggest of the luxury camps—the one die-hard Burners resented the most—called Crystal Sky.

It was packed with wealthy and powerful executives from Silicon Valley. A successful attack inside Crystal Sky would reverberate across the tech industry and feed headlines worldwide.

"Stay on the drone," Harvath ordered. "And have Langley get word to law enforcement. If there are more of them out there, we've got to find them fast."

Once Haney had confirmed, Harvath hailed Morrison and Staelin. "Your teams are clear to engage. Take them down."

From the Crystal Sky stage, he could make out a speeded-up version of "Super Freak" by Rick James. The robed figure in front of him cut out into the crowded street and headed for the camp entrance. Two hundred yards more and he'd be inside.

Harvath had no choice. It was time to make his move.

CHAPTER 4

The biggest challenge for Harvath was making sure that the robed man didn't see him. If he did, it would be game over. Knowing the terrorist's target, though, gave him an advantage.

The dust storm had begun to slow. As it did, visibility continued to improve. Harvath moved though the throng, careful to stay out of the man's line of sight.

People were being pressed tighter together as they approached the entrance. Inside the camp, it looked like a mosh pit, punctuated by glow sticks and LED jump ropes. Phosphorescent jellyfish appeared to pulse through the air above the dancing crowd.

With his eyes glued to the man, Harvath willed him to act. *Show me your hands, you son of a bitch. Do it. Let me see them.*

As if answering his silent prayer, the crowd suddenly surged forward and a drunk Burner bumped into the robed figure. The terrorist stumbled forward. His left hand appeared from beneath his robe. Steadying himself against the person in front of him, the man quickly returned his empty hand to hiding. That was all Harvath needed to see.

Threading himself through the crowd, he slid into position at the terrorist's five o'clock, took a deep breath, and, ignoring the pain in his lungs, sprang.

He punched the man just behind his ear while grabbing for his right hand, which was wrapped around a switch.

Immediately, the terrorist's legs buckled and he went down. Harvath went with him as people began to scream.

"Dead man's switch!" he yelled into his radio so Haney and the rest of the team would know.

Landing in the dust, Harvath began elbowing the man in the face. Once the chrome faceplate cracked, he could see the man's face. It was Rahim. He delivered two more crushing blows, shattering the man's nose.

A handful of Burners, unaware of what was going on, tried to pull Harvath off him. He kicked one in the gut and followed up by sweeping another's leg.

Instead of dissuading them, it only doubled their resolve to break up the fight. The idiots had no idea what they were doing.

Regrouping, they steeled themselves and moved forward. Harvath did the only thing he could.

Pulling his Sig Sauer, he fired three shots into the air. Instantly, the crowd scattered.

Rahim stirred and Harvath elbowed him again. Not knowing how much time he had, he dropped his pistol and grabbed the roll of duct tape he'd snatched.

Using his teeth to help loosen the edge of the tape, he wrapped Rahim's hand as tight as he possibly could around the dead man's switch. Even if the terrorist had wanted to let go of it, it would have been impossible.

Once he had it exactly as he wanted it, he wrapped the tape around several more times. Over his earpiece, he heard Staelin and then Morrison report that they had neutralized their targets.

Pulling his knife, he sliced open Rahim's robe. It was lined with a space-blanket-like material, which was probably what had helped reduce his heat signature. His suicide vest, though, was unlike anything Harvath had ever seen. The terrorist had enough high explosive strapped to his chest to bring down an entire building.

Harvath searched for a chicken switch, but there wasn't one. "Thank God," he said as he relieved Rahim of his pistol and reclaimed his own.

Falling back on the ground, he took a moment to catch his breath. Then he announced, "Target neutralized." *They had done it.*

The moment, though, was short-lived. His mind began swirling with all the things they had to do. Staying here would allow local law enforcement to find him. He'd lose Rahim and the terrorist would be put beyond the CIA's reach. His assignment wasn't done yet. He still needed to get them out of the desert and interrogate them.

"Haney," Harvath said, pushing himself up off the ground. "I'm headed west with Rahim. Tell the plane to get ready, then grab the cart and come get us. Hurry up."

Yanking the terrorist up onto his feet, Harvath dragged him toward the edge of Black Rock City and their ride.

Inebriation was an amazing thing. Just as they got moving, a new round of emboldened Burners tried to get in their way.

When Harvath gestured at his prisoner's suicide vest, they reacted as if it was a costume. When he drew their attention to his gun, though, they seemed to get the message. He had been seriously considering squeezing off a few more rounds when they all took a step back. Shaking his head, he shoved Rahim forward.

As the Crystal Sky DJ moved from Rick James to George Clinton, Harvath filled his seared lugs with another deep breath of air.

It was at that moment that an additional suicide bomber detonated his vest in the center of Black Rock City.

CHAPTER 5

Ravshan Tursunov's rough hands rubbed a yellow lemon peel around the edge of his porcelain espresso cup.

He'd told the ignorant Italian waitress "No sugar," but she'd brought it anyway. He tossed the cubes, like a pair of brown dice, into the cobbled street.

Sugar was one of the many things he'd given up. Bread, rice, and pasta too. The doctor had been adamant. For the transformation to work, he'd been required to shed forty pounds.

As an observant Muslim, there were few vices left available to him. Coffee was one. And even though ISIS forbade them, cigarettes were another.

He had become a connoisseur of both. With the money he was being paid, he could more than afford to.

In his native Tajikistan, the only thing worse than the coffee was the cigarettes. That went double for Syria. Both countries, though, were now behind him.

The tiny café, three blocks up from the water, was one of the best-kept secrets in the city. And while he didn't care for the waitstaff, the barista was the Michelangelo of coffee.

Both the Russians and the Americans had taught him never to visit the same location twice. There were certain things in life, though, worth making an exception for. This was the exception. Besides, no one knew him here.

Looking at his reflection in the glass door of the café, he still didn't even know himself. Blepharoplasty and canthoplasty had softened his eyelids and made him look less Eurasian. Rhinoplasty had narrowed the bridge of his nose, adjusted his dorsal hump, and tightened the tip.

Otoplasty improved the shape of his ears by reducing his earlobes, while cheek and chin implants gave his face more distinguished, angular features.

A neograft addressed his male pattern baldness and gave him a full hairline. Vaser liposuction helped him vaporize the remnants of the spare tire around his middle.

In short, the Pakistani surgeon had done an amazing job. There was very little scarring, and in less than two weeks, he'd been ready to sit for his new passport photo. The trip to Lahore had been worth it.

Now, such as it was, he was finally in Europe.

The suicide bombing in America was all over the news. From where he sat on the terrace, he could see the TV inside. Cell phone cameras had captured the aftermath. Festivalgoers were covered in blood. Many wandered around in a state of shock. Others writhed on the ground in agony. Multiple people had lost limbs. Even more were dead. *But not nearly enough*.

According to witnesses, there had been one enormous explosion. *There should have been four.* Something had gone wrong.

The target, and the method of attack, had been his idea. He felt he should have been more involved. His superiors had other plans. They didn't want to risk smuggling him into the United States. They wanted him focused on Europe. That was where they needed him the most.

But what if the U.S. cell had been penetrated? What if the Americans were working their way up the chain?

Though the thought had been haunting him all morning, he didn't want to think about it anymore. He had too many of his own problems. Chief among them was the loss of his chemist.

He was still infuriated by the incompetence. The ship never should have sailed—not with that kind of a storm barreling down on it—and certainly not without lifeboats or, at the very least, life jackets.

For the smugglers, though, it was a risk they had been willing to take. All that ever mattered to them was getting paid. That's why they always demanded the money up front.

As far as Tursunov was concerned, they shouldn't have been paid until arrival—especially for someone as valuable as Mustapha Marzouk. How they were going to replace him at such a late date was still beyond him.

Turning his attention back to the street, he removed a pack of Treasurer cigarettes from his blazer pocket and lifted its aluminum lid. The cigarettes had gold foil tips and looked like thin works of art. Placing one between his lips, he struck a match, and then inhaled deeply.

So much had been invested, he thought to himself. *So many things had been set in motion. Too many to pull out now.* The burden of the operation weighed heavily on his shoulders.

Shaking his watch from under his sleeve, he checked the time. It was almost nine o'clock.

Exhaling slowly, he placed a few coins on the table, sipped what was left of his espresso, and exited the terrace. He wanted to get a feel for the pickup location before his ride arrived.

Reggio was the toe of Italy's boot. To its east was the Aspromonte mountain range and to the west was the Strait of Messina, which separated the Italian peninsula from the island of Sicily.

Under certain weather conditions, an optical phenomenon known as the Fata Morgana took place, and people could be seen walking in Sicily as if they were only meters, rather than miles, away.

Today, though, there was no such illusion. It was sunny and the temperature was already climbing.

As he walked, Tursunov admired the city's exotic palm and lush magnolia trees. Reggio was known as the "City of Bergamot." The name came from the fragrant, nubby green citrus, with its lemon yellow interior, grown exclusively in the region and used to flavor perfumes and Earl Grey tea.

It was a port city with a thriving fishing community, but it was just as driven by agriculture from the surrounding countryside. From spring through fall, tourists flocked to its beaches and azure water.

In a rundown neighborhood, several blocks from the Castello Aragonese, was a pastry and gelato shop with a narrow bar called Ranieri. It sat next to a vacant lot, beyond which was a burned-out building that had been left to rot.

Graffiti was spray-painted across several buildings. Bars covered the windows of others. Cigarette butts littered the sidewalk like dead moths under a neon beer sign. Tursunov added his to the pile and entered through the rear door.

A heavyset man in a wrinkled shirt stood behind the bar, doing a half-assed job of polishing glasses. He had dark circles under his eyes and several days' growth of beard. He looked as if he hadn't seen a bed or a bathtub in weeks.

Tursunov grabbed a stool at the end. He wanted to sit with his back to the wall and watch the doors that were open onto the street.

The faded interior had seen better days. Decades-old sports and rock band posters were thumbtacked to the walls.

The bartender didn't greet him. He seemed angry to already have a customer. Pausing his glass polishing, he cocked an eyebrow in the stranger's direction.

"Negroni," Tursunov stated, as he placed a copy of the *Gazzetta di Reggio*, open to the classifieds, on the bar.

The barman looked at him, looked at the paper, and then went back to polishing his glass. After a moment, he set the glass on the shelf behind him and got to work on the cocktail.

Tursunov would have preferred another coffee, but had been instructed to order the Negroni. That and the newspaper had been passwords.

Missing an ingredient, the barman yelled back toward the kitchen. Tursunov could make out the Italian word for orange, *arancia*, but not much else.

Shortly, the bartender's wife emerged with a cup of fresh peels. She looked Tursunov over, but didn't acknowledge him. A cigarette with a half-inch of ash dangled from her mouth.

Setting the cup on the bar, she withdrew an iPhone from her stained apron and thumbed out a text message as she headed back toward the kitchen.

Three minutes later, a black Mercedes with dark windows rolled to a halt outside.

CHAPTER 6

Tursunov had flown into Italy a day early to get his bearings. If everything was in order, he would fly out tonight. It all depended on how long the meeting took.

The two men who picked him up from the bar were big. Tursunov was just under six feet and weighed one-eighty. These men had to be at least six-foot-three and more than two hundred pounds each. He was being sent a message. *Don't try anything.*

They asked for his phone and when he turned it over, they placed it in a special bag that prevented sending or receiving any signal. He half expected to be blindfolded, but they didn't bother. After checking him for weapons, they seated him in back of the Mercedes and then navigated their way out of town.

While the two men up front listened to the radio, Tursunov watched the countryside change as they corkscrewed through the foothills and dense forests of the Aspromonte Mountains.

There were groves of olive trees, as well as bergamot. Oak trees were everywhere. The higher up in elevation they climbed, pine, beech, and Sicilian fir began to appear. It was a rugged and beautiful landscape. The roads, though, soon became deserted.

They were headed into one of the most dangerous territories in Italy. Known as the stronghold of the *N'drangheta*, or Calabrian Mafia, Aspromonte was an area avoided by tourists and Italians alike.

Most of the southern tip of Italy was poor, but Aspromonte was strikingly so. Earthquakes, rockslides, and the iron fist of the N'drangheta had taken their toll. The Mercedes drove through one abandoned village after another—each in a greater state of disrepair than the one before.

Tursunov had thought they'd be headed somewhere near the capitol of the N'drangheta, a village on the eastern side of the Aspromonte range called San Luca. Instead, they ended up outside a small hilltop town on the western side named Monterosso.

Pulling off the main road, they followed a small dirt track that ran along a shallow stream. After crossing a narrow bridge, the path widened.

Here and there, Tursunov could make out caper bushes and stands of prickly pear cactus. Up ahead was a crumbling stone farmhouse.

It must have been an amazing structure at some point—solid, with two-foot-thick walls and a soaring roofline clad in ochre terra-cotta tiles. Bougainvillea tumbled from an old arbor. Swaths of jasmine still clung to parts of the old house.

The driver pulled up in front and turned off the engine. Tursunov didn't wait to be asked. He was eager to stretch his legs, and climbed out.

It was warm here, warmer than it had been in Reggio. Tursunov looked up into the blue sky. It was force of habit. He had survived three drone strikes. The last one just barely. His wife, though, hadn't been so fortunate.

Every day, he regretted having suggested that she come to Syria with him. It shouldn't have mattered that other fighters had brought their wives. It shouldn't have mattered that because of his stature, ISIS was providing him with a house. It shouldn't have mattered that they were childless and it was just the two of them. It shouldn't have mattered that she wanted to escape Tajikistan as much as he did. He should have left her behind. If he had, she might still be alive.

He closed his eyes. The sun was almost directly overhead. He felt the warmth on his face, heard birds off in the tree line. A breeze stirred and brought with it the scent of rosemary. For a moment, he tried not to think—to just be still. But as soon as the moment began, it ended.

Out on the road, he heard two vehicles approaching. Taking a deep breath, he opened his eyes. *Back to reality*.

Removing a cigarette from the pack, he placed it in his mouth and leaned against the Mercedes. As he struck a match, he watched two navy blue Range Rovers come into view, trailing a cloud of dust behind them.

They were flashy cars, especially in this part of Italy. That was probably on purpose.

Near the top of the driveway, one Range Rover peeled off toward a large outbuilding. The other rolled up next to the Mercedes and parked.

A beefy bodyguard climbed out of the front seat and opened the rear passenger door.

A petite, Gucci-clad foot was the first thing Tursunov noticed. It was followed by a small, manicured hand, above which rested a very large gold watch. Antonio Vottari had arrived.

At five-foot-five-inches tall, he was known throughout Calabria as La Formícula, or "the ant." He was the nephew of one of the N'drangheta's most powerful crime families. His brutality was legendary.

The man allegedly lived for revenge. It was said to be the only thing that got him out of bed in the morning.

Tursunov looked him over. He was in his early thirties, thin, with pale skin. His eyes were black, like a crow's. His steep nose resembled a beak.

He wore an expensive suit, likely custom made. His cufflinks matched the gold of his watch. His hair was combed with so much oil that it looked wet, as if he had just climbed out of a pool. Even through the cigarette smoke, Tursunov could already smell his cologne.

When Vottari moved, he did so like something out of the jungle. His dark eyes never left Tursunov's. He seemed aware of everything around him—every person, every stone, every blade of grass. Each step he took was deliberate, confident. This was his territory. He was the alpha. You lived or died at his pleasure.

Within a fraction of a second of the Calabrese getting out of his car, Tursunov knew how he was going to kill him. Business, though, would have to come first. Smiling, he extended his right hand. "It's good to see you, Signori. Thank you for meeting with me."

"Let's get started," Vottari replied, returning his grasp.

"As you wish. Do you have everything?"

"We have enough."

Tursunov looked at him. "Excuse me?"

The Italian jerked his head toward the outbuilding. "Come. This way."

Tursunov didn't know what he meant by having *enough*, but he fell into step alongside him anyway. Two bodyguards took up the rear, while the rest stayed with the vehicles.

The path was overgrown with weeds. As they walked, Tursunov looked up into the sky again. *This is Italy*, he reminded himself. *There are no drone strikes here.*

But if there were, a voice in his head countered, *waiting until everyone was inside the building would be the perfect moment.*

Tursunov felt a twinge of paranoia building at the edge of his mind and shut it down. He needed to remain in control.

At the door to the outbuilding, Vottari motioned at his cigarette. "No smoking inside."

The Italian was being overly cautious. Nevertheless, Tursunov complied. Taking a final drag, he dropped the cigarette to the ground, and crushed it out with his heel.

Exhaling the smoke from his lungs, he stole one more glance skyward, and then followed the man inside.

The walls were built of concrete block and the building appeared to have been used to house livestock.

"Don't worry," Vottari said, suddenly reading his mind. "Sheep. No pigs."

In Islam, contact with pigs was forbidden, as was contact with alcohol. It was obvious the Italian knew it. Vottari was fucking with him. It was why he'd sent him to a bar and told him to order a Negroni. And it was also why Tursunov was positive that they were at a pig farm.

He'd have to rethink the little Mafioso's death. He'd have to come up with something much more painful and drawn out.

"Come. Come," Vottari said, waving him forward. Three wooden crates, all painted olive green, were displayed on a long table. Their tops had been pried off and some of the packing straw removed.

Tursunov studied the markings on the first crate before removing its contents and assembling the pieces.

"Not your first time," the Italian remarked.

Before joining ISIS, Tursunov had served in both the Tajik military and an elite police unit—facts that were none of Vottari's business. So he ignored him.

Moving to the second and third crates, he examined their markings and assembled the contents.

"Where are the rest of them?"

The Italian grinned, "You don't trust me?"

Tursunov looked at the clumps of what he was certain was dried pig shit covering the floor, and smiled back. "Where are the rest of them?" he repeated.

"You'll get them when I get my money. Half now, half on delivery."

Tursunov shook his head. "We agreed that I would be allowed to inspect all the merchandise. *Before* delivery."

Vottari snapped his fingers and one of his men handed Tursunov a tablet.

"What's this?"

"Pictures of the rest of your merchandise."

Tursunov angrily swiped through them.

"You can clearly see all the markings and serial numbers," the Italian stated.

"This is not what we agreed to."

"It is within the *spirit* of our agreement."

Tursunov thought for a moment and stated, "Thirty percent."

"My friend, this isn't a negotiation."

"This isn't a business relationship either," he replied, handing the tablet back. "We'll take our money elsewhere. Good luck selling those."

"*Pazzo,*" he chuckled to his men. *Crazy.* But Vottari liked crazy. You had to have balls to be this crazy.

He let Tursunov walk all the way back to the farmhouse before sending one of his men to return him to the outbuilding.

When Tursunov came back in, Vottari said, "The merchandise you requested was very difficult to get. Only a fool would bring all of it together in one place. If something were to happen to it before I received my money, that would be very bad."

Tursunov didn't respond. The Italian hadn't asked a question. He had made a statement. People weakened their hands by feeling they had to fill uncomfortable silences.

"Forty percent," the Italian offered. "And you allow me to change the delivery location."

"Change it? Why? Where to?"

"Someplace safer. Not far from where we agreed."

Safer? Tursunov didn't like it. Vottari was changing all the parameters of the deal. "Twenty-five percent."

"*Molto pazzo!*" the Italian exclaimed, smiling. "Thirty percent and I'll throw in two cases of these. No charge."

He nodded to one of his men, who retrieved a smaller crate from the back of the Range Rover and brought it over for inspection.

Tursunov lifted the lid. *Fragmentation grenades.* His plan didn't call for them, but better to have something and not need it than need it and not have it. "Deal."

Vottari shook hands with Tursunov, but didn't let go. "Remember," he cautioned, "all of the merchandise leaves Italy. Take it to France. Take it to Germany. Take it to the moon. I don't care. But if I find out you didn't, you and your people are dead. *All* of you."

Tursunov smiled right back and replied, "The last thing I and my people want is any trouble, especially with you and your people."

CHAPTER 7

The small lockkeeper's house, only a short drive from D.C., sat along the Chesapeake and Ohio Canal. It was a squat, two-story structure, built of local stone painted white.

Its shutters and door were painted robin's-egg blue—the genesis of its nickname.

Unlike other lockhouses in the C&O National Historic Park, which could be rented for overnight stays, the "blue lockhouse" was closed to the public. And for good reason. It was owned and maintained by the Central Intelligence Agency.

One of the Agency's numerous safe houses, it had been used extensively during the Cold War for debriefing high-value Soviet defectors. Today, it was being used for a very important, very quiet meeting.

When Harvath rolled up, he saw three heavily armored black Suburbans parked in front. Even in casual clothes, the detail agents posted outside gave off a serious don't-fuck-with-us vibe. Intensity was an important prerequisite for the job.

Even more important were experience and ability. Terrorists the world over would have loved nothing more than to get their hands on the two people inside.

Parking his Tahoe in the grass, Harvath shook hands with the lead agent—a man named Haggerty—and chatted with him for a few seconds.

Haggerty had gone to Notre Dame, which Harvath, as a University of

Southern California grad, always explained wasn't the man's fault. It was obvious that his parents hadn't cared much for him.

It was good-natured ribbing born from a storied college rivalry. Haggerty was confident about the football team Notre Dame was fielding this year. So confident, in fact, that he wanted to place a wager on the game against USC.

After reminding him of the Code of Federal Regulations banning gambling in the federal workplace, Harvath smiled and agreed to a hundred dollars.

"Cash," Haggerty clarified. "None of that Bitcoin crap."

Harvath laughed and they shook hands. Turning, he climbed the three slate steps to the lockhouse and knocked.

"Come in," a voice replied. "It's open."

Harvath entered to find the CIA Director, Bob McGee, and the Deputy Director, Lydia Ryan, at a weathered wooden table in the living room.

McGee was in his early sixties. He had dark wavy hair, which was rapidly going all gray. His most distinctive feature, though, was his thick mustache. You didn't see a lot of those in Washington, and even fewer in government.

Ryan was a gorgeous woman. She was the five-foot-ten product of an Irish father and a Greek mother. She had long black hair and deep green eyes.

Both McGee and Ryan had come from the clandestine service side of the CIA. They were smart, seasoned, no-bullshit people. The President had chosen them specifically to clean out the dead wood at Langley and bring the Agency back to its former glory.

"There's coffee in the kitchen," Ryan said as Harvath stepped inside.

Walking back to the kitchen, he grabbed an enamel mug from one of the cupboards and poured himself a cup.

Returning to the living room, he joined McGee and Ryan at the table. It was covered with files.

They had been meeting like this a lot—outside CIA headquarters, on nights and weekends. The less people knew about what they were up to, the better.

Like a ruptured appendix, terrorism had exploded, gushing its poison in all directions. Attacks were on the rise everywhere, especially in Europe, and now in the United States as well.

Losing territory and suffering defeat after defeat, ISIS had become like a cornered, wounded animal. In desperation, it had lashed out, calling for attacks on Americans whenever and wherever they could be found. They were sending a very clear message—nowhere was safe.

In return, the American President had sent a very clear message of his own—there wasn't a rock big enough for ISIS to crawl under or a hole deep enough to slither down. Wherever its members tried to hide, the United States would find them. *All of them.* America would hunt its enemies to the very ends of the earth. And it would be relentless in doing so.

The problem, though, was that not everyone in the U.S. agreed with the President. Some saw his approach as too antagonistic. They worried that he was giving the terrorists exactly what they wanted, that he was playing right into their hands. They wanted less cowboy and more samurai—wise, patient, striking only when absolutely necessary and then slipping back into the night.

Then there were those who didn't want any strikes at all. They claimed that hitting back only perpetuated a cycle of violence. They cautioned that if we didn't stop, neither would ISIS. The already bad situation would only grow worse.

Many felt that the President didn't appreciate their opinions and hadn't even bothered to take them into consideration. But those who knew him—that small circle with whom he kept counsel—knew that wasn't the case at all.

The President didn't like waging this battle, but it was a just war. The use of force was not something he took lightly. His greatest desire was peace. He wanted nothing more than the security of the American people. He saw the safety of Americans at home and abroad as his number-one responsibility as commander in chief. It was the duty he placed above all others.

He also was privy to something his fellow citizens were not. Every morning, he received an intelligence briefing, which laid out how truly dangerous organizations like ISIS and Al Qaeda were.

They were fanatics who believed that they had been chosen to rule the earth. For that to happen, they had to subjugate America and her allies through jihad. Anything less than total commitment to this goal was an act of defiance against God himself.

The fundamentalism that drove them was a cancer. It infected almost everyone it touched. And yet the people best positioned to remove the cancer lacked the courage and the desire to do so. No matter how many atrocities were committed in the name of their religion and their God, the Muslim world was wholly incapable of combating the problem.

With so little cooperation, the President had been left with few choices. And those choices only narrowed as many of America's allies were overwhelmed with resource shortages and tidal waves of radicals on their own soil.

While the President respected those American voices that disagreed with his position, he could already see over the horizon. He could see what was coming if the United States didn't act.

Like Israelis, Americans would find themselves in a state of constant siege. Beaches, restaurants, trains, buses, night clubs, grocery stores, schools, playgrounds, dog parks, movie theaters, sporting events, parades, shopping malls, even the places where they worshipped, nothing would be off-limits.

And as the attacks mounted, a frightened population would demand that something be done. There would be armed guards and security checkpoints everywhere—and even that would not be enough to deter America's enemies. The terrorists would strike as Americans dropped their children off at school or stood in line waiting to step through a body scanner at the latest Broadway show. It simply wasn't possible to keep *all* of America safe *all* of the time.

The calls to do more, though, would only grow. Finally, the bureaucrats and politicians would step in and attempt to regulate terrorism away. At that point, America would take a very dangerous turn. As Ben Franklin was alleged to have said, those who would trade a little liberty for a little security deserve neither and will lose both.

That, in a nutshell, was the President's greatest fear. So he decided to act.

Despite using much of his political capital to push through a dramatic increase to the FBI's budget, the Bureau was drowning. It had active investigations in all fifty states, but still nowhere near the resources it needed to see each investigation through to its end. The terrorists were coming at them too quickly—from everywhere and every walk of life. There simply were too many cases, too many leads, and not nearly enough agents.

The President had been left with only one course of action. A course that, if made known, would very likely lead to his impeachment.

Looking at Harvath, McGee said, "Let's talk about what happened at Burning Man."

CHAPTER 8

Harvath was operating on a black contract. Technically, none of what he was doing should ever see the light of day. But in the age of hackers and leaked documents, he went to extraordinary lengths to make sure he put little, if anything, in writing.

Administrations changed, as did opinions on what the CIA should or should not be doing. What was justified in the weeks and months after the September 11 attacks might take on a different light when re-examined from some point in the future. As far as Harvath was concerned, the best way to avoid being judged by history was not to be a part of it to begin with.

Harvath understood the President's position. He had deep feelings about individual liberty. He also cared about keeping Americans safe.

He had seen the utter barbarism of groups like ISIS and Al Qaeda up close. He had witnessed what they had done to their victims, including women and children.

One of the most painful moments of his career was rescuing the kidnapped son of an Iraqi policeman, only to have the little boy die in his arms. The torture the child had been subjected to was beyond horrific.

There were only so many dark corners in a person's mind to hide such experiences. It was why, from time to time, Harvath needed to be alone with a couple of six-packs or a bottle of bourbon. Long runs and pushing heavy stacks of weights brought him only so much relief.

It wasn't the healthiest way to deal with things, but unfortunately the human mind didn't have a Delete button. Sometimes, if only for a little while, he just needed to forget.

It was a terrible burden to drag around, but it was part of the job. Without someone to hunt the wolves, the sheep would never be safe. The wolves were multiplying too quickly. The sheepdogs were being over-run. It was a matter of survival.

So when the President had decided to alter America's rules of engage-ment, Harvath had agreed to go along.

Those new rules of engagement were what had placed him at Burn-ing Man, operating without official sanction. There just weren't enough fingers and toes at the FBI to plug all the leaks springing from the terror-ism dike.

Whenever possible, the CIA shared its intelligence with the Bureau. Too often, though, that intelligence was placed on the back burner. It wasn't their fault. They were being forced to drink from a fire hose.

With the President's quiet encouragement, Langley had begun to de-velop, plan, and execute more operations on its own. Depending on your point of view, Burning Man had been either a spectacular success or a spectacular failure.

Listening to Harvath's debriefing, McGee and Ryan both saw the op as a success. Had the other bombers been able to detonate, many more people would have been killed and injured.

No one, not even Harvath, had known it was an active plot until mo-ments before it had gone off. Even if they had shared their mountain of intelligence with the FBI, it would have taken too long for them to assign a surveillance team to Hamza Rahim.

"Once the plane lifted off from Black Rock City Airport," Harvath said, wrapping up his report, "I went to work on them. You know the rest."

Yes, they did. Rahim had been extremely uncooperative. Harvath had quickly ratcheted up the pressure, playing on the would-be bomber's fear of being returned to his native Egypt.

Harvath convinced Rahim that not only did their jet have the capac-ity to make the flight, but also that the Egyptians would gladly accept him and help get the information he wanted out of him.

Rahim knew all too well how the Egyptians operated. He had been viciously tortured by their secret police before. He had no desire to experience it again. No matter what the Americans had in store for him, it couldn't be worse than going back to Egypt.

So, he had slowly begun to cooperate—revealing how the attack had been planned, financed, and why he had returned to the RV.

To avoid detection, the materials for the suicide vests had been smuggled in separately and assembled on site. The bomb maker, though, had become nervous. Rahim was concerned that he might be having second thoughts and was worried he'd be captured after the attack.

It was a business decision—no more, no less. The bomb maker was a loose end that had needed tying up.

Rahim and the other cell members had been transferred to a secret facility in Colorado for further interrogation. As soon as the handoff was complete, the jet had flown Harvath and his team to D.C., where they had gone their separate ways.

Though Harvath was renting a place in Boston, to be closer to his girlfriend and her family, he hadn't officially given up his house in Virginia. It was along the Potomac River, close to George Washington's Mount Vernon estate. Most of the furniture was gone, but he'd left just enough behind to make it livable.

If nothing else, it was good to be "home" and to shower off the playa dust and toss all of his clothes in the washer.

He'd been in the midst of arranging to return to Boston when he had gotten the call about a meeting at the blue lockhouse. He figured the main point would be deciding what to do next about the ISIS plotters who had tasked Rahim with the attack.

"So what's next?" Harvath asked. "The refugee camp where the cell members were recruited?"

McGee shook his head. "We're putting somebody else on that."

"*Somebody else?* Why?"

"This is why," the Director replied, as he opened a file, removed a photograph and handed it to him.

Harvath studied the photo.

"His name is Mustapha Marzouk," said Ryan, taking over the briefing. "He was a graduate student in chemistry from Tunisia.

"Three years ago, during a raid on an ISIS compound by a CIA-backed rebel group in Syria, a laptop was found. At first, no one thought anything of it. It wasn't password protected and all the drives were empty. But then we started drilling down on it and discovered over 146 gigabytes of hidden material.

"Among the more than thirty-five thousand files were all the usual things you'd expect to find on a laptop at an ISIS stronghold—justifications for jihad, military manuals, terror videos, et cetera. Then came the interesting stuff—document after document showing that the laptop's owner was researching weapons of mass destruction."

From the minute she had mentioned chemistry, Harvath had begun to develop a bad feeling. "Let me guess. The laptop's owner is Mustapha Marzouk."

Ryan nodded. "Correct. For three years we have been looking for him. Syria. Iraq. Libya. Tunisia. We even followed an alleged sighting in Somalia. Everything, though, has turned up empty."

"So why are we talking about him now?"

"Over the last several months, we've been picking up chatter about an impending series of attacks, culminating in something very big, some-where in Europe."

"Any clue as to what that *something very big* is?"

"The laptop contained a thirty-page fatwa from an obscure, jailed Saudi cleric justifying the use of chemical and biological weapons."

Harvath felt a chill sweep over him.

Ryan opened the folder in front of her and read from the Islamic ruling. "If Muslims cannot defeat the unbelievers in a different way, it is permissible to use weapons of mass destruction. Even if it kills all of them and wipes them and their descendants off the face of the Earth."

For a moment, Harvath was at a loss for words. "I'm guessing the Saudis didn't pick him up for unpaid parking tickets."

"No, they didn't. He was turning into a problem. They decided to act before he developed any more of a following. The damage, though, has already been done. Mixed within the chatter have been references to the same fatwa, from the same obscure cleric."

"So you want me to find this Mustapha Marzouk. Is that it?"

"Not exactly," replied McGee as he removed another photo and handed it to him. It showed a bloated corpse with chunks of flesh ripped away.

"Mustapha Marzouk is dead. The Italian Navy fished his body out of the Mediterranean yesterday. Near the island of Lampedusa. They're not sure if he drowned before or after the sharks got to him. Not that it makes much difference.

"We had his fingerprints from the laptop. Despite his having spent several days in the water, they were still able to ID him. He was on a smuggler's boat, packed with migrants, headed toward Sicily. The boat went down in a storm Tuesday night."

Harvath handed the photo back. "For three years, this guy has been a ghost bouncing around the Middle East, North Africa, and Somalia—then he suddenly hops on a boat to Italy? Why?"

"That's what we need you to find out. We think whatever he was planning, it's ready to go operational."

"When do you want me to launch?"

"ASAP," McGee replied. "We've got a plane standing by. All you need to do is tell it where to go."

"Let's start with whatever intel you've compiled."

The Director slid a stack of files toward him. "These don't leave this room."

"Understood."

"What else do you need?"

At the top of his list, he needed to call Lara. He wouldn't be back to Boston anytime soon. He was also hungry. Looking at his watch, he said, "Let's order some food. We're going to be here awhile."

CHAPTER 9

Always prepared, McGee and Ryan had brought their encrypted laptops. Whatever information Harvath needed beyond the files, they were able to retrieve via a secure link back to Langley.

Slowly, he developed three different plans. The first two were immediately shot down. They weren't crazy about the third one either. As capable as Harvath was, it put him in very hostile territory, without backup. It was, though, their only viable option. Reluctantly, McGee agreed, but with one condition. He wasn't sending Harvath into that hellhole alone.

Removing his cell phone, he stepped into the other room to get the ball rolling on all of the things Harvath had asked for. Ryan was left sitting at the table. She cleared her throat.

Harvath looked up from the folder he was studying.

"I was hoping for a better time to tell you this," she said. "I'm leaving the Agency."

He didn't believe it. "You're kidding."

"No. I'm serious."

"Does the President know?"

She nodded.

"McGee?"

She nodded again. "It was their idea."

He closed the folder and set it on the table. "I don't understand. You were tapped to help fix it. How do you walk away from that responsibility?"

"I'm going to head the Carlton Group."

Harvath was stunned. "*My* organization?"

Ryan raised an eyebrow in response.

The Carlton Group *had* been Harvath's organization, or more appropriately, it had been the organization he had spent the last several years working for. It was a private intelligence organization, founded by one of the founders of the CIA's Counter Terrorism Center.

Reed Carlton, a legendary spymaster with more than thirty years in the business, had gotten fed up with all of the bureaucratic red tape at Langley and had left to start his own company.

When a previous president had cut Harvath loose, Carlton had recruited him. He had become Harvath's mentor, teaching him everything he knew. And then, he took the collar off and unleashed him on America's enemies.

Theirs was a formidable pairing. Harvath was an apex predator and Carlton was one of the greatest strategic thinkers the intelligence world had ever known. Together, they were unstoppable.

The Old Man, as Harvath referred to him, had always envisioned Scot as his successor and had groomed him to one day take over the Carlton Group. The only problem was that Harvath wasn't interested in that job.

He loved being in the field. If the truth be told, he was addicted to the action. He had also met someone.

With Lara and her little boy, Marco, he had a real chance for a family— something he had always wanted.

When Lara received a major promotion, cementing her need to remain in Boston, he had had a choice to make. And choose he did. He chose to walk away from D.C.

The Old Man had encouraged him to go, but had also refused his resignation. "Let's see what happens," he had said.

Harvath continued to take contract work from the Agency—the best part being that he could say no.

As far as he was concerned, he had the three necessary ingredients to happiness: something to do, someone to love, and something to look forward to.

With the revelation that Ryan had taken the position meant for him, he felt a ripple of guilt. He knew he had let the Old Man down.

Nevertheless, he had made the right decision for himself and his own future. He was sure of that.

"Congratulations," he offered.

"Thanks."

"But why now? And why the push from McGee and President Porter?"

Ryan leaned back in her chair. "It's complicated."

"It's always complicated."

"I don't know that I should go into it."

"Go into what?"

She took a deep breath and exhaled. "He's not well."

"Wait. The Old Man isn't well? What's wrong?"

"It's being kept quiet, but he's starting to forget things."

Harvath looked at her. "As in dementia?"

She nodded. "He has Alzheimer's."

It was like getting hit in the chest with a hammer. "How long has he known?"

"What difference does it make?"

"Lydia, *how long*?" he repeated.

"The diagnosis came right before you decided to go to Boston."

Harvath's ripple of guilt turned into a wave. "He never told me."

She managed half a smile. "He didn't want it to influence your decision."

"How bad is it?"

"He's having trouble retaining new information, but all the old stuff is right at his fingertips."

"Will it get worse?"

She nodded again. "It typically starts with difficultly retaining new information. Then, as it moves through the brain, symptoms get more severe. Confusion about times, dates, places, and events are common, along with disorientation, and deepening suspicion of friends and family. Behavior changes are often seen, and eventually there's more serious memory loss, which can be followed by the inability to speak, swallow, or walk. None of it's pretty."

Smiling, Ryan added, "He's a tough son of a bitch, though. He doesn't want anybody feeling sorry for him."

"Why you, though?" Harvath asked. "Why would McGee and President Porter want to lose you at CIA?"

"Because the reforms at the Agency aren't going as well as we'd hoped."

"Meaning?"

"*Meaning*, it's like turning a battleship around."

"But you knew it would take time," he stated. "McGee has already fired a ton of deadweight."

"Which is a good start, but it's not enough," she said. "Not with how quickly the threats are mounting. There are some absolutely terrific people at CIA, but nowhere near the numbers needed to reverse the broken culture. That's still years off."

"What's the Carlton Group's role in this supposed to be?" Harvath asked.

She thought for a second about how best to frame her response. "If the CIA needs a total gut rehab, the Carlton Group is the home we're going to live in while it's being done."

The Old Man had always believed, and Harvath had agreed, that the CIA needed to be burned to the ground and rebuilt in the model of its predecessor, the nimbler Office of Strategic Services. With all of the bureaucratic calcification in Washington, though, he had doubted whether he'd ever live to see it happen.

He knew that anyone who tried to carry out such a mission was going to get overwhelming pushback—or worse. "You're going to tick off a lot of people."

"That's why it's being kept quiet," she replied, "along with Reed's diagnosis. I'm telling you because I think you should know."

Harvath appreciated her being straight with him. Reed Carlton had been more than just a mentor. He'd been like a father. "What can I do?" he asked. "Does he need anything? Do *you* need anything?"

The list was miles long. The task she had taken on Herculean. There was one item, though, right at the top. "The Carlton Group needs its own Special Operations Group."

Harvath wasn't surprised. Covert operations were a vital part of national security. One of the most counterproductive things the CIA had ever done was put its operatives in embassies around the world. Too many of them began to think like State Department employees. They brought their families along on each two-year rotation, focusing on the next promotion, while the Ambassador, not the Chief of Station, had final say over what ops they could and couldn't conduct. It was poisonous.

In an environment controlled by the State Department, diplomacy came first. Espionage, depending upon the steel of a given Ambassador, came a distant second.

The stories of good men and women in the clandestine service missing out on big intelligence wins because of State Department fears were legion. Trolling diplomatic cocktail parties, running low-risk recruiting operations, and waiting for foreign walk-ins all had their place, but so too did complicated, high-risk operations that offered potential windfalls. As long as Foggy Bottom was calling the shots, Langley was operating with one arm tied behind its back.

If the Carlton Group was going to be a leaner, meaner version of the CIA, it would need its own Special Operations Group.

Based on the amount of work the Agency had been feeding him, Harvath wasn't surprised. What did surprise him, though, was that Ryan was raising the issue with him.

"Why are we talking about this?" he asked. "The Old Man isn't hoping I'll lead one of the teams, is he?"

Ryan shook her head. "No. He's hoping you'll lead the entire thing."

Harvath couldn't believe his ears. "You're *both* losing your minds."

She put up her hands. "Now's not the time. Right now, you need to focus on what Mustapha Marzouk was up to. We'll talk about everything else when you get back."

•   •   •

They worked for several more hours, refining Harvath's plan and making several final preparations.

When he stood up to leave, McGee and Ryan accompanied him outside. It had been a long day. He needed a drink and some time to process.

More important, he wanted to pay a visit to the Old Man. Ryan, though, cautioned against it. "See him when you get back. He'll still be here. Don't worry."

She was right, but he did worry. There were few things he could think of worse than having your entire mind taken from you. *It was heartbreaking.* Part of him felt like he should apologize for letting the Old Man down—as if doing so might help reverse his Alzheimer's. It was stupid and he knew it, but that didn't stop him from feeling it.

Another part of him just wanted Carlton to know he wasn't alone. He was one of the best men Harvath had ever known. He deserved better.

Ryan seemed to be able to read his thoughts. Instead of a handshake, she put her arms around him and gave him a hug. McGee shook his hand and wished him good luck.

As they turned back to the lockhouse, Harvath's mind turned to what lay in front of him.

Had he been paying better attention, he might have sensed the figure hidden in the woods. Two hundred yards away, a man was snapping photos of him with a long-lensed digital camera.

CHAPTER 10

The Catholic pilgrimage trail known as the Camino de Santiago was a vast network of routes across Europe. They culminated at Santiago's massive Romanesque cathedral, where the remains of Saint James the Elder—one of the twelve apostles, and patron saint of Spain—were buried.

Tursunov could have picked any religious building, but this one was special. From his position on the Praza do Obradoiro, he noted the masses of tourists. The body count would be exceptional.

But it wasn't just the cathedral's popularity that had appealed to him.

While researching his Burning Man attack, he had come across something remarkable. Black Rock City was laid out in such a way that its central axis pointed directly to the Cathedral in Santiago. He knew this wasn't an accident.

His mother, a follower of the mystical strain of Sufi Islam, had always encouraged him to see the hand of the Divine in all things, everywhere. It was as if Allah himself was directing him.

James was also known as Santiago Matamoros, or St. James the "Moor-slayer."

By the time King Alfonso the Second of Asturias died, the Moors already controlled most of the Iberian peninsula. A popular myth held that in return for allowing his Christian kingdom in northwest Spain to continue enjoying its autonomy, the neighboring Islamic Emirate of Córdoba demanded the reinstitution of the "Tribute of One Hundred Virgins"—an annual payment of fifty virgins of noble birth and fifty of common birth in return for the promise of Muslim forces not to invade.

Alfonso's successor, Ramiro the First, though, refused to pay, and both sides readied for war.

According to legend, on the night before the battle, St. James appeared to Ramiro in a dream, reassuring him that he would be victorious. The next day, at the Battle of Clavijo, Ramiro invoked the name of St. James and with his men slew more than five thousand of the Moorish forces.

It was claimed that St. James, riding on a white horse, with a white banner and a long silver sword, rode among Ramiro's men, cutting down every Muslim soldier who appeared before him. Hence, St. James became known as Matamoros, and there were paintings and statues of him performing his abhorrent deed all over the city.

The attack on the cathedral that held his bones, and more important, his name, would be an undeniable victory for the Islamic State and Muslims around the world. Tursunov had planned its timing very carefully.

More than 250,000 pilgrims visited the cathedral every year. August was considered peak season. He was pushing things by waiting until the end of the month, but it had been important to attack at Burning Man first. The Americans were reactionary. In light of a successful attack in Europe, they would have hardened targets, possibly making it too hard to strike. It had been better to catch them by surprise. Now it was time to surprise the Europeans.

Tursunov had attended the "Pilgrim's Mass" only once, but it was enough. Like everyone around him, he had filmed the entire thing with his camera phone.

Based on his estimates, the service at the high altar catered to just over a thousand worshippers, all tightly packed into the pews.

He would have loved to collapse the Cathedral of Santiago de Compostela, but with its sweeping arches, barreled ceiling, and soaring columns, its structural DNA eluded him.

He didn't have the engineering expertise of a bin Laden. His experience came from his service in the Tajik Army, followed by a career in the Special Operations Unit of the National Police Force. Neither had called for taking down churches. He was much more conversant in things like artillery and blowing doors off hinges. Even so, he had tried to improve his knowledge.

Using the Christian churches and heavily columned archeological sites of ISIS-held territory, he had conducted experiment after experiment.

And while the structural DNA of the sites continued to elude him, something more dramatic was revealed. With each test, they learned how to build better bombs. In particular, their martyrdom vests took a huge leap forward.

As the technology improved, so did their understanding of how best to maximize the effects. Whether indoors or out, they developed a whole new approach that would accelerate the lethality of their attacks.

With these advancements, he had pushed for a new way of structuring personnel. There was no need to create one operational cell. He wanted multiple small cells, with each believing it was acting alone.

If one was captured, the operation would still be able to continue. In fact, authorities might even drop their guard, believing that they had successfully interrupted the entirety of the plot.

It meant more work, more cutouts and double-blind intermediaries, but Tursunov's ability to strategize on a higher plane was what had earned him his position as the senior ISIS commander for Europe. His brothers in America would have been smart to follow his lead.

Opening a new package of Dunhill cigarettes, he placed one between his lips and lit it. Closing his eyes, he inhaled and tried to picture how everything would unravel inside.

The highlight of the Pilgrim's Mass was the flight of a massive brass incense burner. Suspended high above the main altar, the cathedral's *Botafumerio* was controlled by a series of ropes, the pulling of which caused it to soar to amazing heights as it released its sweet-smelling smoke.

Tursunov imagined the quiet titter of excitement as the red-robed *Tiraboleiros*—the men charged with lofting the frankincense-packed censer—walked past the faithful and made their way toward the altar.

Once there, the lead Tiraboleiro would light the Botafumerio and it would begin to release its heavy aroma.

Once the other Tiraboleiros were ready, the chief would give a signal and they'd pull on the ropes in unison, dramatically launching it heavenward.

As it swung back and forth in a hypnotic, pendulous motion that seemed poised to touch the walls of the cathedral itself, its intoxicating smoke would fill the air. So effortlessly would it swing, and so wonderful was its heady perfume, that the entire spectacle would seem to provide a way to commune with the Divine. As the organ played, a nun would sing.

Exhaling, Tursunov opened his eyes and glanced at his watch. They were seconds away.

Inside, the organ would be building to a thunderous crescendo as the lead Tiraboleiro reached out to capture the swinging Botafumerio. Tursunov counted down from ten as he took another drag from his cigarette.

Looking up, he fixed his eyes on the glazed windows adorning the structure's western facade.

Three seconds later, the entire city shook as a series of explosions rocked the cathedral—sending shards of stained glass, chunks of flaming stone, and pieces of bone, blood, and human flesh in all directions.

CHAPTER 11

When news of the attack on the cathedral in Santiago de Compostela broke, the CIA had accelerated Harvath's timetable. More than four hundred people had been killed, ninety-two of them American. Four hundred more people were wounded, including more than one hundred Americans. The numbers were still climbing.

Though the Spanish had only begun to gather intelligence, McGee and everyone back at Langley were already convinced. Santiago de Compostela was the kickoff of the series of attacks they had been worried about.

And if that attack was just the beginning, things were going to get much, much worse. They needed to get ahead of this fast, or many more people were going to die.

"In case nobody's on record yet," Matt Morrison stated from the front passenger seat, "this is a really bad fucking idea."

The five-foot-eleven, thirty-one-year-old former Force Reconnaissance Marine from Cullman, Alabama, kept his head on a swivel as he peered through the tinted windows.

Next to him, driving, was his fellow Force Recon Marine, Mike Haney. The forty-year-old Marin, California, native stood six feet tall.

In back of the white Toyota HiAce panel van, Harvath—a Southern California native—leaned against his plate carrier and manipulated the feed from the 360-degree camera mounted to the roof. Across from him, five-foot-ten, thirty-nine-year-old Tyler Staelin, the Delta operative from downstate Illinois, read a Brad Meltzer paperback.

Trailing a block back in a blue Land Cruiser were Navy SEAL Tim Barton and 5th SFG Green Beret Jack Gage.

They were all wearing civilian clothes with baseball caps, sunglasses, and keffiyehs. Even though they were all tanned, they didn't really blend in. The point, though, was to minimize how much they stood out.

Harvath hadn't intended to drag his Burning Man team along with him, but McGee had insisted.

Libya was one of the most dangerous places in the world. It had gone from the wealthiest country in Africa, with the highest life expectancy on the continent, to a failed state.

These days, instead of rule by a ruthless dictator, local militias with shifting allegiances held sway. Your best friend in the morning could be your worst enemy by the afternoon. That made it difficult to conduct business and practically impossible to gather intelligence.

The key to success was to stuff your pockets with carrots and carry the biggest stick anyone had ever seen. Fortunately, McGee was able to provide Harvath with access to both.

As a new government of "national accord" was struggling to unite Libya from its capital in Tripoli, the CIA and U.S. military had been providing cover and breathing room by helping to hunt and kill Islamic militants. The last thing they wanted was for Libya to become another Caliphate or pre-9/11 Afghanistan.

In its multimillion-dollar game of whack-a-martyr, the CIA paid for actionable intelligence, which the United States Africa Command then used to carry out drone strikes. There was enough to keep everyone busy.

But with so much at stake, no one—especially Libya's fledgling government—had time to deal with the smugglers. Paying off their local militias, they ran their businesses with virtual impunity.

For one smuggler, though, that was about to change.

Harvath had made it his mission to understand how they operated. What he learned made him want to kill all of them.

The smugglers employed two types of vessels: decommissioned, no-longer-seaworthy fishing trawlers and inflatable rubber boats. A decent-sized trawler could cram anywhere from 300 to 600, sometimes even 1,000 migrants looking to be smuggled to Italy. The rubber boats could only take 100 without sinking, but even so, they always tried to squeeze more on board.

Migrants came from all over Africa and the Middle East. From places like Niger, Mali, Sudan, and Syria. They handed over their life savings in hopes of making it to Europe and starting over in a better place.

None of the vessels they were loaded into had lights, flare guns, or safety equipment. Bottles of water and cans of tuna, if offered at all, were sold by the smugglers for a hundred dollars apiece. Rarely was enough fuel provided to make the trip—just enough to sail beyond Libyan territorial waters.

Of course the smugglers didn't do any of the actual transporting themselves. Instead, they selected one or two passengers—often at gunpoint—handed them a satellite phone and a compass, and then sent them out into the open ocean.

In case of emergency, which was "smuggler speak" for when your boat runs out of fuel or falls apart and begins to take on water, the satellite phone had been preprogrammed with the emergency phone number for the Italian Coast Guard.

Even though the Europeans were operating a massive interdiction operation in the Mediterranean, they didn't have enough assets to be everywhere. Under good weather, the smugglers were launching ten to fifteen boats a day, up and down the Libyan coast. Under bad weather, they still launched, though fewer boats.

Passengers along the route died from drowning, hypothermia, disease, starvation, shark attack, rape, beatings, and even murder.

Harvath had read harrowing accounts of people being reduced to eating toothpaste and drinking urine to stay alive, of women thrown overboard because observant Muslim men suspected them of menstruating and therefore being "unclean," of people being packed so tightly in sweltering holds belowdecks that they all suffocated. The inhumanity of the smugglers, and even some of the passengers themselves, was on par with barbarity he had only seen in war.

And at the very top—the worst of the worst—was the man he had come looking for, Libyan smuggler Umar Ali Halim.

Plenty of Halim's customers never even saw the water, much less a boat. He was notorious for splitting up families, selling women and children into the sex trade, or forcing them into his own private harem.

Anyone who resisted—be they husbands, mothers, fathers, it made no difference—was dealt with on the spot. They were savagely beaten, sometimes even to death, as a warning to the others.

Gang rape, lashings, being folded in his "flying carpet"—a board with metal hinges in the middle meant to shatter the victim's spine—and other methods of torture, spoke to Halim's depravity.

In his line of work, Harvath saw killing men like Halim as a public service. It needed to be done and required a willingness that not everyone possessed.

He knew that there were people who objected even to the thought of what he did for a living. Every once in a while, he wished he could get them an up-close view of animals like Halim. Maybe then they'd better understand not only what he did, but also *why* it was necessary.

Harvath had voiced that desire to a handful of people, one of them being Reed Carlton. He still remembered the Old Man's response, "Everyone else wants to be appreciated. Not you. You're not looking for thanks. You want to be *understood*. That's what makes you different."

He hadn't thought much about it at the time. Probably because he didn't feel "different." He figured everyone else felt the way that he did. The whole "It's a dirty job, but somebody's got to do it" thing.

But people did feel different. Not all of them, but enough. Not long ago, he remembered a colleague saying, "While most of us are trying to come up with a plan on how to get out, you're trying to figure out how to stay in."

It was true. He had no desire to get out. He believed in what he was doing. And though he loved the idea of having a family, he didn't want to give up his career.

That was probably the biggest difference he saw between himself and guys who were looking to pull the rip cord. They had families. They wanted a life beyond slinging a weapon for a living. Those who stayed in usually did it because they needed the money or didn't know what else to do. Harvath, though, wanted to have his cake and eat it too.

"Really bad idea, exhibits D, E, and F, coming up on our right," said Morrison, as they passed three more men in a pickup truck with a .50 caliber machine gun mounted in its bed, known as a *technical*.

The Libya Liberation Front was a brutal, local Islamist militia that provided protection for Halim and his smuggling operations. Even more unpalatable for Harvath and his team, though, was the fact that the Libya Liberation Front was aligned with Ansar al-Sharia, the Al Qaeda–linked group behind the attacks on a U.S. diplomatic outpost and CIA annex in Benghazi.

They only numbered in the hundreds, but they had access to a ton of firepower. The last thing Harvath wanted was to tangle with them. It wouldn't end well. Get in. Get the job done. Get out without being seen. That was his plan.

But as experience had taught him, things rarely went as planned. That was why McGee had made everything conditional on Harvath's bringing the team.

Turning the corner, Haney piped up, cutting off Morrison and interrupting Harvath's train of thought. "Approaching target," he called out. "Three hundred meters. Left side."

CHAPTER 12

The Europeans had chosen not to project force into Libya. That was their choice, but as far as Harvath was concerned, it was a mistake.

Libya was in their backyard. The smugglers were pumping massive numbers of refugees into their countries. Hidden among those refugees were terrorists who were massacring their citizens.

It didn't seem like a difficult calculus. Why have a military—complete with special operations units—if you weren't willing to use it to take out threats to your nation? Fortunately, the United States didn't feel that way.

From attacks on American tourists, embassies, and interests abroad, to attacks on its own homeland, the more terror was left to grow unchecked, the worse it was for everyone. Europe's problems today would only grow to become America's tomorrow.

U.S. President Paul Porter had laid down a marker. If America's allies couldn't, or wouldn't, handle the metastasizing threats within their sphere of influence, the United States would.

He understood that, like his own FBI, European intelligence agencies were overwhelmed. Nevertheless, their reluctance to get more aggressive was concerning.

By clarifying his position, Porter was putting allies on notice that America would not sit idly by. In other words, if you see us operating in your neck of the woods, don't be surprised *and* don't say we didn't warn you.

Harvath liked and admired many of the European teams he had worked with over the years. He understood that an overwhelming bureaucracy had hamstrung them. Nevertheless, their nations were in a fight for their lives. They needed to ask themselves some very difficult questions—and to do so quickly—beginning with *who were they and what exactly were they prepared to do?*

It was the same question their enemy had already asked, answered, and was acting upon.

If the Europeans had decided to go on the offensive in Libya, they would have started by focusing on the most accurate, most readily available intelligence. That was what Harvath had done, and the Italian Coast Guard had tapped into some of the best.

In addition to a satellite phone, most smugglers provided Italy-bound migrants with a GPS device. There were plenty, though, who didn't.

Far too often, the Coast Guard's Maritime Rescue Coordination Center in Rome received distress calls from terrified migrants who had no idea of their precise location, rendering a rescue next to impossible.

Even when a caller had access to GPS, the center still needed to verify their position. The slightest deviation from the caller's actual location could mean the difference between life and death.

Fortunately, the Rescue Coordination Center had access to an outside verification source.

Abu Dhabi–based Thuraya was one of the largest satellite telecommunications companies in the world. Because of Thuraya's excellent coverage of the Mediterranean, Libyan smugglers bought all of their satellite phones from them.

When the Italian Coast Guard received a migrant distress call, the first thing they did was contact Thuraya's emergency 24/7 hotline. In turn, Thuraya would do a quick search and provide the phone's GPS location.

That cooperation had helped save tens of thousands of lives. Sometimes, though, the Italian Coast Guard was unable to get to a sinking vessel quickly enough.

Such had been the case when the distress call from Mustapha Marzouk's trawler had gone out six days ago. It too, the CIA had learned, had come from a Thuraya satellite phone.

Harvath, though, wasn't interested in the phone's position when the call had been made. He wanted to know who had purchased the phone in the first place.

While the CIA or their Italian counterparts could have requested the information from Thuraya, they doubted the Emirati company would comply. It was decided that the best, and quickest, way to access the data was to go take it.

Thuraya's encrypted servers proved no match for the NSA, which soon delivered the information the CIA wanted.

Of the 150 passengers on Mustapha Marzouk's doomed fishing boat, only three had survived.

After they had been found, clinging to a piece of wreckage, and pulled from the water, they all identified Umar Ali Halim as the smuggler who had sent them out into the impending storm.

Halim's hideous reputation was well known by Italian authorities. What wasn't so well known was his location.

The migrants he smuggled knew nothing about Libya. He changed embarkation points daily. Often, his men ferried the migrants out to their boats, which were already waiting for them a mile or more offshore. None of them could identify where they had been held or where they had specifically departed from. That's why Harvath had wanted to focus on the satellite phones.

The phone used in Mustapha Marzouk's case had been part of a bulk purchase. The purchaser didn't try to hide his location, nor did he bother to travel from Libya to the Emirates to pay cash and smuggle back the devices.

Instead, the purchaser sat eleven kilometers southwest of the highly dangerous port city of Zuwara, clicking on the satellite company's Buy button and running everything through a PayPal account flush with cash.

The NSA had pinpointed his Internet usage as the same location the phones had been delivered to.

It was a hole-in-the-wall electronics shop advertising cell phones, digital cameras, and laptop computers.

"Pull over," Harvath ordered.

Haney did as instructed.

They observed the store as Harvath gave their communications gear a final check, then, grabbing a black messenger bag, he opened the door and stepped out.

It was the kind of hot, dusty street he had seen countless times over countless deployments. Squat buildings made of concrete block sat side by side. Sun-bleached awnings hung over faded, hand-painted signs in Arabic. In the little shade they provided, stacks of cheap crap sat for sale. There was sand everywhere. The entire town looked one breeze away from being swallowed up by the desert.

Whether it was the heat, or time for the midday Qailulah, few people were about. Even so, he didn't want to draw attention to the shop by leaving a vehicle idling out front. "Find someplace close to park," he said.

Glancing into his side mirror, Morrison replied, "Don't be long. I don't like this place."

"Don't worry," Harvath stated, as he slid the door closed. "I don't want to be here any longer than we have to."

CHAPTER 13

Entering the store, Harvath took it all in. It looked as if it had been a small grocery or maybe a pharmacy at some point.

The walls were lined with empty metal shelves. In the back sat an empty soda cooler alongside an old freezer chest covered with ice cream advertisements. The cracked linoleum floor had been designed to look like alternating tiles of blue and white marble.

The temperature inside wasn't much better than out. An air-conditioning unit above the door in back sounded like it was ready to die. The place smelled like milk that had gone bad months ago.

What few electronics the store offered were laid out in a long glass display case up front. A lean, bearded man in his thirties sat behind it. He wore a green polo shirt and dirty jeans and was doing something on a computer.

He should have been surprised, or at the very least intrigued, to see a Westerner wander into his shop. But if he was either, he didn't let on. In fact, he barely looked up from what he was doing.

"Ah-salaam-alaikum," Harvath said, greeting the man as he walked up to the counter and set his messenger bag down on top of it.

He waited several moments, but the man remained focused on his computer and didn't reply. Harvath rapped his knuckles on the display case and drew out the word *"Marhaba?"* in Arabic. *Hello?*

There was an edge to the clerk, a toughness. Harvath had picked up on it the minute he walked in. *Former soldier? Militia member?* Maybe he was just a local thug. Harvath couldn't tell. But there was definitely something.

Shutting down his computer, he stood slowly and faced him. *"Shen tebbee?"* he demanded. *What do you want?* His upper left front tooth was black, dead.

"Nibi ma'loumat," Harvath replied. *I want information.*

"Abie 'illiktruniat, la ma'loumat." *I sell electronics, not information.*

Harvath smiled. *Sure you don't.*

"Shen tebbee?" the man repeated, gesturing angrily at the handful of cell phones, digital cameras, and laptops in his glass case.

Unzipping a pocket on his messenger bag, Harvath withdrew a sheet of paper and set it in front of the shopkeeper. On it were strings of numbers.

"Shu hadha?" the man asked. *What is this?*

"Thuraya satellite phones," Harvath replied in English. Raising his finger, he pointed at him. *"Your* satellite phones."

The man slid the paper back across the counter and said, *"Ma bíhki Inglízi."* *I don't speak English.*

Opening the main compartment of his messenger bag, Harvath withdrew two ten-thousand-dollar stacks of cash and set them on the counter. *"Wáyn hu Umar Ali Halim?"* *Where is Umar Ali Halim?*

Upon mention of the smuggler's name, the shopkeeper's icy demeanor turned to stone. But as it did, Harvath saw a brief flicker of something else slip across his face—*fear.*

"Ana mish mohtam," he answered. *Not interested.*

Harvath withdrew two more stacks of cash and set them next to the others. "That's forty thousand dollars, U.S.," he said. *"Araba'een-alf."* *Forty thousand.*

As the man eyeballed the money, Harvath repeated his question. *"Wáyn hu Umar Ali Halim?"*

When the man didn't respond, Harvath added two more. *"Sitteen-alf."* *Sixty thousand.*

There was still no response.

Harvath upended his bag, dumped the remaining money on the counter, and pushed it toward him. *"Maya-alf."* *One hundred thousand.*

Staring the man down, he demanded once more, *"Wáyn hu Umar Ali Halim?"*

The shopkeeper had had enough. *"Barra nayiek,"* he replied. *Fuck off.*

Pushing the money back, the shopkeeper pointed at the door and added, in English, *"Now."*

So much for the language barrier, Harvath thought.

He was about to respond when Staelin's voice came over his earpiece. "Boss, we've got a problem. Exhibits D, E, and F just pulled up outside your front door. Looks like they're getting ready to come in."

Damn it. That was the last thing he needed. The Libya Liberation Front was in Halim's pocket. As soon as the shopkeeper opened his mouth, it'd be game over. There was only one thing Harvath could do.

Grabbing the man by his shirt, he pulled him forward and head-butted him as hard as he could.

Instantly, the shopkeeper's knees buckled, and he crumpled to the floor. As he did, Harvath pulled a syringe of ketamine from his messenger bag and leapt over the counter.

Pulling the cap off the needle, he jabbed it into the man's thigh and depressed the plunger.

Ketamine was created as a powerful battlefield anesthetic, but was best known as a horse tranquilizer. When injected into humans, it caused muscle paralysis in less than a minute. Too much of it, though, sent users into a hallucinatory state called the "K-hole."

Stuffing the cash back into his messenger bag, Harvath removed a set of plastic restraints, flipped the shopkeeper onto his stomach, and flex-cuffed him.

"How much time do I have?" Harvath asked over his radio.

"All three are getting out of the truck. You've got maybe sixty seconds," Staelin replied.

"Tell Gage and Barton to bring the SUV around back. I'm going to be coming out plus one."

Rolling the shopkeeper back over, he grabbed him by the collar, slung his messenger bag, and dragged the man across the floor toward the rear exit.

Immediately, he realized the heavy security door was locked.

Harvath ran his hand along the top of the frame, hoping to find a key, but there was nothing there.

"Forty-five seconds," said Staelin.

He patted the shopkeeper down and checked his pockets. *Nothing. Where the hell was the key?*

Staelin continued his countdown. "Thirty seconds."

Maybe it was under the counter. Maybe it was inside the register. There wasn't time to tear the store apart. Harvath needed to come up with a Plan B.

"Tell me exactly what you're seeing," he ordered, as he rapidly scanned the store.

"Three men with AK 47s. Mix of fatigues and street clothes. All three carrying sidearms in holsters."

"Body armor?"

"Negative," Staelin replied. "No radios either. One guy's talking on a cell phone."

"Anyone else in the truck?"

"Negative. At your door in fifteen seconds."

"Roger that. Zero comms," he ordered, calling for radio silence.

Dragging the shopkeeper over to the ice cream freezer, he flipped up its lid. Instantly, he figured out where the terrible smell had been coming from. With the lid open, it was worse than spoiled milk. The inside of the chest smelled like death.

He could only imagine what it might have been used for during and even after the revolution. The bottom of it was covered with several inches of moldy, black sludge. Squatting, Harvath heaved the shopkeeper over his shoulder, dumped him inside, and closed the lid. There was only one place left for him to hide.

As he took cover, he removed a suppressed H&K VP Tactical pistol from his bag and did a press check to make sure a round was chambered.

Harvath didn't know why the three men were about to enter the electronics shop and he didn't care. The Libya Liberation Front members were bad actors.

He had no reservations about what he was about to do.

CHAPTER 14

H arvath had positioned himself between the soda cooler and the
wall. The interior of the cooler was pitted with rust. One spot had
been eaten away just enough to allow him to see the front door.

The first Libyan to enter the shop had a thick, jet-black beard. He carried his AK by its wooden pistol grip, letting it dangle at his side. The second man was tall and skinny, and held his weapon in both hands.

The third man, though, was the one Harvath was most interested
in. He was the one talking on his cell phone. But because of the narrow
doorway, his two comrades shielded him.

"Hello?" the first man called out in Arabic. "Anyone here?"

No one's here, Harvath whispered to himself. *We all went to Hooters for
wings and dollar beers. Come back tomorrow.*

When no one responded, the bearded man called out again.

The sputtering of the air-conditioning was the only reply.

Turn around and leave, Harvath whispered. *Just turn around and leave.*

None of the men moved.

Finally, the bearded man told the skinny militiaman to see if anyone
was out back.

Bad decision, thought Harvath as he began applying pressure to his
trigger. As soon as Skinny got two feet from the rear door, all he had to do
was look to his left and Harvath would be in full view.

Skinny, though, never made it that close. Halfway across the floor,
there was a noise.

Everyone in the shop heard it and everyone froze—including Harvath. He didn't need to hear it again to know what it was—*the shopkeeper*. He had dosed him too hard and pushed him into the K-hole.

Because ketamine caused excessive drooling, sometimes even vomiting, Harvath couldn't have risked gagging him or slapping a piece of tape over his mouth. He might have choked to death.

When the second moan sounded, Skinny made a beeline for the ice cream chest.

The only upside was that Harvath could see the third man now. He was still holding his cell phone in one hand, but had his pistol in the other. It was time for Harvath to act.

Dropping low, he leaned out from behind the soda cooler and fired twice in rapid succession.

There was an explosion of pink mist as the man with the cell phone took both rounds to his head and dropped.

Before he had even hit the floor, Harvath swung around and put two rounds into the man at the ice cream chest. They were sloppy, but did the trick. One round went up through the man's jaw and into his brain, the other tore straight through his throat.

Swinging his weapon back toward the front door, he saw that the man with the jet-black beard now had his weapon in both hands and was bringing it up to fire. Harvath fired first.

The first round entered just below the man's nose. The second entered just above his left eyebrow. He dropped like a bag of wet cement.

Coming out from behind the cooler, Harvath quickly shot each of the militia members point-blank in the head to make sure they were dead.

Picking up the cell phone of the last man through the door, he disconnected the call he had been on, removed the battery, and tucked the device in his pocket.

He then radioed his team as he looked behind the counter for the shopkeeper's keys. "Tangos down. Staelin, I need you in here."

"Roger that," he replied.

Harvath found the shopkeeper's phone as well as the key to the security door as Staelin entered.

"Nice shooting," he remarked as he looked at the bodies near the front.

"Open up the rear door," Harvath said, tossing him the key. "Tell Gage and Barton I need both of the spare gas cans, plus a road flare."

"Where's the SAT phone salesman?"

"In the freezer. Now get moving. I want to be out of here in three minutes."

Staelin did as instructed while Harvath gathered up the militia members' weapons. All three of them had been carrying Glocks. That wasn't a weapon you saw every day in these parts. In fact, several years ago, a cache of American Glocks had gone missing from a training camp not far from here. Harvath didn't have time to think about that now, though.

Despite the heat, two of the men had been wearing camouflage jackets. Removing them, he set them on the counter and then stripped the men of anything that could be used to identify them.

Tim Barton came back inside with Staelin. The former SEAL Team Six member from Tacoma was in his early thirties and only stood about five-foot-six. But what he lacked in height, he more than made up for in width. He was a devoted weight lifter and was built like a fireplug. He had reddish-blond hair, a bright red beard, and was a bit OCD.

In one sense, it was an asset, because Barton would double- and triple-check every piece of gear and everything he did. But he was also a clean freak and carried tons of extra hand sanitizer on ops. His teammates busted his balls over it all the time.

"Where's the package?" Barton asked, tossing Harvath the road flare.

Harvath nodded toward the freezer.

The SEAL lifted the lid and exclaimed, "Jesus Christ!" as he turned his head away from the stench.

Harvath accepted the gas cans from Staelin and instructed him to help pull the shopkeeper out of the freezer and get him to the SUV. Unscrewing one of the caps, he then began splashing gasoline everywhere.

It didn't need to look like an accident. It just needed to slow the local militia. Once he and his team had gotten hold of Umar Ali Halim, he didn't care what the Libya Liberation Front was able to figure out.

Wrapping their keffiyehs around their faces, Barton and Staelin pulled the shopkeeper out of the rotten-smelling ice cream chest, carried him outside, and tossed him into the cargo area of the SUV.

Barton then hopped into the backseat, pulled out his hand sanitizer, and kept an eye on him.

Six-foot-three Gage from Edina, Minnesota, remained up front with a wad of chewing tobacco in his cheek and the engine running.

Staelin returned inside.

"Libyan lightning?" he asked, playing on an old arson joke.

Harvath nodded. "Fire sale. Everything must go. Put this on," he said, tossing him one of the camouflage jackets.

"Are we taking that technical with us?"

Harvath nodded again and put on one of the jackets himself. After dumping the militia members' sidearms in his messenger bag, he slung one of the AK-47s and sent Staelin outside with the other two to fire up the truck.

When it was running, he announced. "We're good to go. Ready when you are."

"Stand by," Harvath replied as he opened the second gas can and soaked the corpses.

This was supposed to be the easiest stage of their operation, but it had gone sideways, fast. It wasn't a good omen.

What can go wrong, will go wrong, he reminded himself. Then something else came to mind. Once Murphy, of the infamous Murphy's law, had you in his sights, he wasn't usually content to just let you off with a warning. He tended to stick around and make sure things got much worse. Harvath, though, tried to push the thought from his mind.

Striking the flare, he tossed it into the center of the room. As the fire leapt to life, he backed out of the shop.

But as he did, a very bad feeling about what lay in front of them began to take hold in the pit of his stomach.

CHAPTER 15

Paul Page wasn't a particularly attractive individual—not on the outside, and definitely not on the inside.

He was in his late fifties, with a receding hairline and gray eyebrows that formed distinct peaks when he was angry or surprised. As a purveyor of global intelligence, rarely was he ever surprised.

He was a hard, calculating man who enjoyed Kentucky bourbon, Maryland crab cakes, and D.C. call girls. The word that best described him, though, was *forgettable*.

His ability to melt into the background had been an asset as a CIA officer—right up until the moment he'd been "let go."

He hated the term *let go*. *Cut loose* was another he couldn't stand. He'd been cut loose all right. As if he were an astronaut in the middle of a space walk, Langley had uncoupled his umbilical cord and let him drift off into the cold darkness of space.

Snatching the terrorist Imam off the streets of Milan had been his idea. He had planned it down to the tiniest detail. In retrospect, would he have done things differently? *Probably*. But he had never expected to get caught.

He had picked the team himself. They were good people, people he knew from his years at the Agency. They were hard workers. *He* was a hard worker. Creating fully backstopped covers was a pain in the ass and took shitloads of time—a year at least. They hadn't had that luxury.

When the Imam popped onto the CIA's radar, Page's superiors had encouraged him to act quickly. He had made a judgment call. Ironically, no one on his team had given him any pushback.

They all traveled under their real names, used their own cell phones, and checked into their hotels with their loyalty program numbers so they could get rewards points. As long as the government was picking up the tab for the trip to Italy, why not? It wasn't like they were skimming money out of petty cash.

What he hadn't seen coming was that the intelligence about the Imam might be faulty. The thought hadn't even entered his mind.

The thought hadn't entered the minds of the Egyptian interrogators they were using either. After grabbing the Imam and rendering him to a black site in Cairo, Page and his team had gone back to the United States and waited for him to spill his secrets.

As it turned out, the Imam didn't have any. He wasn't involved in terrorism at all.

That was a problem.

It was a problem because during the year he spent in Egyptian custody, he had been beaten, tortured, and even raped—repeatedly.

Eventually, Egyptian Intelligence realized the CIA had made a massive mistake. The Imam was moved out of the black site and placed under house arrest.

In that house, though, was a telephone. And as soon as he was alone, the Imam called every friend and family member he had.

At first, they were overjoyed to hear his voice. Then, they were outraged as he described what had happened to him. Right away, they began reaching out to journalists.

The story spread like wildfire. The public was outraged. The CIA looked every bit as monstrous as the Egyptians. Not long after the story broke, the Italians launched an investigation.

Because Page's team hadn't bothered to take the batteries out of their phones while in Italy, much less use untraceable burner phones, the Italian authorities were able to re-create their every move. In the nine days they spent stalking the Imam, staking out his home and mosque, they had left a distinct trail of digital breadcrumbs.

The Italians issued warrants for Page and his entire team. Naturally, none of them complied.

A trial was held in Milan. In absentia, Page and his fellow CIA operatives were all found guilty. Prison sentences were handed down, as was a judgment that each operative pay one million Euros to the Imam and five hundred thousand Euros to his wife.

With the verdicts in place, the Italians issued new arrest warrants and entered red notices with INTERPOL. If any of the convicted CIA operatives ever set foot in Europe again, they would be arrested on the spot.

It was considered one of the most embarrassing moments in the Agency's history and the blame-storming began immediately. The President wanted blood. The Intelligence committees wanted severed heads on pikes outside the Capitol Building. Everyone on Langley's seventh floor ran for cover.

As they cowered under their desks, they conspired to come up with an appropriate human sacrifice. It didn't take long for them to arrive at a name—his.

Page was expendable. Hell, everyone who worked at the Agency was expendable. But after years of dedicated service, he expected better. He expected someone in leadership to stand up and defend him. Of all people, he expected his mentor, Reed Carlton, to come to his defense.

That, though, hadn't happened. Instead, Carlton sat on a board of review and voted against him. Carlton called the operation "misguided and unprofessional."

Page was stung by the critique. Yes, he had made mistakes. Yes, Carlton had pulled him aside in the past and had warned him about his behavior. But this was different. Nevertheless, Carlton had chosen to put the precious Agency ahead of their friendship. That was unforgiveable in Page's book.

Though he was well liked and had many other friends at the CIA, there was nothing any of them could do to save him. The decision had been made by the CIA Director himself. The angry Potomac gods downriver needed to be appeased. They would not be denied their pound of flesh.

Without the career that had defined him, the lesser of Page's angels took over. He began drinking heavily. His marriage (his second) fell apart. His wife left him. He burned through his 401(k). He came inches away from suck-starting his Walther pistol.

Then, one of his old friends from the Agency had dropped an opportunity in his lap. A big, golden opportunity.

An American company looking to do business in several Russian satellites needed highly sensitive intelligence. With that intelligence, the company would have a strategic advantage over its competition. The contract it was chasing was worth more than a hundred million dollars.

It just so happened that Page's friend had access to the intel that the American company was looking for. As an active CIA employee, he couldn't deal with the company directly. Page, though, could.

And thus Page Partners, Ltd.—a global, private intelligence-gathering service geared toward multinational corporations—was born. Paul Page interfaced with the clients and kept the money flowing, while his pal inside the Agency kept the intelligence flowing. It was a lucrative, not to mention illegal, match made in heaven.

But while Page seemed to have everything he could want—an expensive downtown apartment, a new Mercedes, a flashy wardrobe, and money to burn—there was something missing. Something he wanted above all else. *Revenge*.

When the bell rang, he set down his copy of the *Washington Post* and stood to answer the door.

He took a deep breath. This was a historic moment—something he had been waiting years for. If everything worked according to plan, this was the beginning of the end for Reed Carlton.

CHAPTER 16

"Couldn't find a garbage can outside?" Page asked as Andrew Jordan pushed past him into the kitchen and emptied the remnants of his sack lunch onto the marble counter.

Jordan was a jowly man in his midforties, with perfectly combed blond hair and an ill-fitting suit. The knot of his tie was poorly tied, but his brown shoes were polished to a high shine. He was a study in contradictions.

Holding up a crushed can of Coke Zero, he tilted it admiringly in the light as if he were showing off the Hope Diamond. Then he tossed it to his friend and covert business partner. "Merry Christmas."

Page caught the can in his left hand. "What's this?"

"Open it."

"What do you mean *open it*?"

"I mean *open* it."

Page looked at him, then gripped the can at the top and the bottom and began to pull. There was something inside. Lifting it to his ear, he shook it and heard something rattle.

Jordan smiled. "I thought about hiding it in the apple core, but this was cleaner."

Page turned the wrinkled can upside down over the counter and out came a micro SD card.

"If anyone had searched me," Jordan continued, "all they would have gotten was practice."

The CIA man was obviously pleased with himself. Page, though, was beyond pleased. If what he had was legitimate, a whole new era had just dawned. "You took a big risk doing this."

"*Everything* I do is a big risk."

Page grinned. The CIA had no clue what was going on right beneath their noses. Jordan was not only a pro at beating the regular polygraph tests, but he was also a pro at spotting coworkers ripe for recruitment.

The key to successfully stealing intelligence from within the CIA was making sure no one ever noticed anything was missing.

It was akin to being an art thief. Only a fool would attempt to steal the Mona Lisa. The security alone rendered it pointless.

The smart thief aimed his sights lower, on lesser pieces of art people weren't paying close attention to.

And unlike the art world, in this one Page didn't have to leave forgeries to cover up his crimes. All he had to do was make a copy of the original. As long as no one noticed, he was home free.

In fact, even if someone did notice, he had created such a complicated trail that it would take two lifetimes to trace it back to him.

"Where's your computer?" Jordan asked. "You need to pop that card in and see what's on it."

Page disappeared to his study to retrieve his laptop. He was gone less than two minutes. When he returned to the kitchen, Jordan had already pulled a four-hundred-dollar limited-edition bottle of Dom Pérignon from the fridge, peeled off the foil, and was loosening the wire cage from around the cork.

"Sure, help yourself," Page quipped, as he set his laptop on the counter.

"If you don't think what I brought you is worth celebrating, I'll buy you an entire case to replace this. Where do you keep the champagne glasses?"

Page tilted his head toward the cabinet above the microwave and fired up his MacBook.

It took a moment to boot up, but once it did, he attached an SD card reader, inserted the card, and clicked on the icon. Several folders appeared.

"Which one should I start with?" he asked.

There was a pop as Jordan wrenched the cork out of the bottle. "The one marked *Burning Man*."

Page did and instantly regretted it. It contained photo after photo of dead bodies, people missing limbs, and thick rivers of blood.

The carnage made his stomach churn. "I don't want to look at this."

"Keep going."

Page relented and scrolled through until he came across pictures of a man with a face full of war paint, beating another man.

"Those are the money shots," Jordan said as he handed him a glass of champagne. "Wait'll you get to the video."

"What's in the video?"

"Click on it."

Once again, Page complied. The feed was shaky, taken on a camera phone by someone quickly backing away from the chaos.

Several men in the crowd could be seen rushing the man with the war paint, who pulled out a pistol and fired into the air.

"Where'd all this come from?"

"Nevada Park Rangers," Jordan replied. "The people at Burning Man were apparently very cooperative. The Park Rangers handed the footage over to the FBI. We got copies from them.

"From what we've been able to figure out, there were four suicide bombers at the festival. Three were interdicted."

"By whom?" Page asked.

"CIA contractors."

"Working *with* the FBI?"

Jordan shook his head. "The Bureau had zero idea they were there."

"That must be causing a little consternation."

"Are you kidding me? The FBI Director hit the roof. And when the CIA Director asked him to keep quiet, he hit it again."

Page's eyebrows peaked in surprise. "McGee asked the FBI to hush it up?"

Jordan nodded. "Yup."

"This is a huge clusterfuck for the Agency. What does it have to do with Reed Carlton, though?"

"The guy with the war paint? He's Carlton's golden boy."

"What's his name?" Page asked.

"Scot Harvath. SEAL Team Six guy. He's got a pretty impressive background."

"How impressive?"

Jordan took a sip of his champagne. "Click on the folder marked *Personnel Records.*"

Page opened the folder and skimmed the documents. There were copies of Harvath's service records, his SF-86 Top Secret clearance questionnaire, the photo attached to the green badge he was issued to come and go at CIA headquarters, even prior tax returns showing the Carlton Group as his employer.

Page was impressed. "You weren't kidding. This is damn good stuff."

"It gets better. Click on the last file. The one marked *Blue Door.*"

Page did. The first photo showed a small lockkeeper's house along what looked to be the Chesapeake & Ohio Canal near D.C. "Is this what I think it is?"

"Keep scrolling," Jordan instructed.

As he moved through the pictures, he saw shots of the Director of Central Intelligence, Bob McGee, arriving with his security detail. He was followed by Deputy DCI Lydia Ryan. Last but not least, Scot Harvath arrived.

The best pictures, though, were the ones right at the end. In those, you could clearly see all three, standing together and chatting, followed by an extremely friendly good-bye.

While Page had made mistakes years ago in Italy, he wasn't a stupid man—not by a long shot. As he went back through everything Jordan had collected, he analyzed each piece.

He knew Carlton. More important, he knew how Carlton's mind worked. He knew that no matter what the situation appeared to be, Carlton was always ten steps ahead of everyone else.

There would only be one chance to take him down. If he failed, Carlton would come after him with everything he had. Page, though, didn't intend to fail.

And he didn't care whom he burned in the process. He wasn't going to let anyone—not Bob McGee, not Lydia Ryan, not even whoever this Scot Harvath was, stand in his way.

"So the CIA knew about a potential terrorist attack and didn't inform the FBI?" he asked.

"Not just the CIA," replied Jordan. "The Carlton Group too. Harvath's the linchpin in all of this. Imagine the lawsuits from the victims and their families if this was made public."

Page already *was* imagining it. It would be devastating for both organizations. "This has all got to be irrefutable. Are you going to be able to get me the rest of what I need?

"I'm already working on it," said Jordan. "Don't worry. I'll get it."

Raising his glass, Page saluted his colleague. "In that case, to revenge."

CHAPTER 17

The safe house was better than Harvath had expected. The property sat along the coastal road, en route to the Tunisian border. It had a motor court with a high wall, no neighbors, and an unobstructed, 360-degree view of the surrounding terrain.

It was sparsely furnished. There was electricity and running water. A rooftop deck, surrounded by a lattice parapet made of concrete, provided decent concealment for use as a sniper or observation post.

While Barton and Gage cleaned up and then secured the shopkeeper to a chair in one of the ground-floor bedrooms, Mike Haney drew up a roster for guard duty. Staelin and Morrison pulled first shift.

Morrison grabbed his rifle and a bottle of water and headed to the roof. Staelin took his rifle and his Meltzer book and headed to the motor court. Harvath collected his backpack and the phones he had gathered up at the electronics shop and walked upstairs to the second floor.

The home's master bedroom faced the ocean and had a wraparound balcony. Stepping outside, he saw a small table and chairs. He dragged them over to where he could get the best signal and then removed a laptop and satellite phone from his pack.

Once a connection was established, he attached his laptop to the SAT phone, removed the SIM cards from the cell phones, and uploaded their information back to the CIA. In particular, he wanted to know with whom the third militia member was talking when he walked into the shop and if any sort of alarm had been raised. With the help of the NSA, it wouldn't take long.

All of the phones had been locked. The lock on the shopkeeper's phone was controlled via fingerprint. All Harvath had to do to open it was place the man's finger on the sensor.

The address book was full of contacts, but there was nothing, at least not by name, for the man they had come looking for—Umar Ali Halim.

The smuggler could have been listed under an alias, or it was possible that the shopkeeper dealt with an intermediary. While it might have looked like a bust, Harvath's search of the phone did turn up something—something he anticipated would be very useful.

With a plan beginning to form in his mind, he fired off a quick email to the CIA. In it, he included pictures of the Glocks that he had stripped from the dead militia members, serial-number side up.

Then, repositioning his chair, he put his feet up and tilted his head back. He had been at this game long enough to know to grab rest whenever he could find it.

The late afternoon sun was warm on his face. Below, waves from the southern Mediterranean Sea rolled onto the beach. Harvath tried not to think about the dead bodies, from sunken smuggler vessels, washed ashore here, or the dozens of Christians ISIS had beheaded up and down the coast. For the moment, all that mattered was that he could close his eyes without fear of someone putting a knife to his throat or taking a shot at him.

As he listened to the waves, he breathed in the scent of the ocean— a mix of salt and seaweed and fish. He had spent most of his life around the water. No matter where he traveled, or how dangerous the assignment, he always found the smell familiar. It was a constant the world over.

There weren't many things that had been constant in his life. As a SEAL himself, his father had been gone more than he had been home.

And until Lara, his track record in the relationship department had been anything but stellar. The relationships had been fun, but few had been serious, and fewer still had shown any promise of surviving long term.

What he had with Lara and her little boy was the closest he'd ever come to creating a family of his own. Outside of his career, it was the thing he wanted most in his life. It was why he had rented a house and had moved almost everything he owned from Virginia to Boston.

He had encouraged Lara to come to him, but then she'd been offered the promotion of a lifetime. She couldn't replicate her position in Alexandria or D.C. He had encouraged her to take it. That left him with only one option if he wanted things to work—him going to her.

With the Old Man's blessing, that's what he had done. He picked and chose which CIA assignments he wanted, went away and did them, and then came home. Langley cut a check to the Carlton Group and money appeared in one of his multiple bank accounts.

He would have been happy to continue the arrangement in perpetuity, but based on what Lydia Ryan had told him, the Old Man had other plans.

It pissed Harvath off and made him smile at the same time. Reed Carlton was inscrutable. No matter how sure you were that you had him figured out, he was always running multiple different angles you had never even considered. He was the spy master's spy master. He had seen America through the Cold War and beyond.

As technology boomed, life became easier. As life became easier, Americans grew softer. As Americans grew softer, the threats arrayed against the United States grew more deadly. Weakness encouraged aggression.

And when the aggression arrived, America had turned to hard men like Reed Carlton to strap on their armor, climb into the arena, and run a sword through it. But now, Reed Carlton could no longer strap on his armor.

That was a hard fact for Harvath to come to terms with. The Old Man had been one of those few constants in his life. He was also the epitome of the warrior. Warriors died in the arena, in battle, on their feet.

Once again, Harvath was reminded of how cruel it was for a man as brilliant as Reed Carlton to lose his life to a disease known for robbing victims of their minds. Of everything he had given to his country—his courage, his patriotism, and his loyalty—it was his genius that had served America without equal.

Now, his mind was being stolen from him. But it wasn't gone yet. His wife was in a nursing home, and before he joined her, he intended to not only set the chess board, but stack the bench of American chess players as deep as he could as well.

To do it right, though, he needed Harvath onboard. That was why he had asked Lydia Ryan to intercede. It wasn't hard to see.

The Old Man loved him like a son, but Harvath knew he loved something more: his country.

So now, here he was—a world away with the weight of the world where it shouldn't be at this moment, on his shoulders. This was the last thing he should have been wrestling with. He couldn't do anything for the Old Man if he returned in a flag-draped box.

He needed a few minutes to decompress, to rest. And then he'd need to focus on his assignment.

He adjusted himself in his chair, turning his face ever so slightly to track the sun as it began its descent toward the horizon. He slowed his breathing and synchronized himself with the ebb and flow of the waves below.

He was about to drift off when he heard Mike Haney step onto the balcony.

"The shopkeeper's coming out of the K-hole."

CHAPTER 18

Haney was one of the most squared-away Marines Harvath had ever worked with. Handing him a cup of fresh-brewed coffee, he offered to monitor the laptop for message traffic from Langley while Harvath went downstairs. It was the best offer he'd had all day.

Grabbing the shopkeeper's phone, he stepped back into the house and descended the stairs.

Down the hall was the bedroom where the shopkeeper was being held. Jack Gage sat in a chair outside the door. In his hand was the cup he'd been spitting tobacco juice into.

"Everything good?"

"Livin' the dream," the large man deadpanned, raising his dip cup in a toast. He was known for his dry sense of humor, as well as being stone cold under pressure. The saying in the Special Operations community was that the difference between Gage and a walk-in freezer wasn't the temperature, it was the beard.

"Is that coffee?" he asked, eyeballing Harvath's cup.

"Libyan style."

"Hot, tasteless, and totally fucked up?"

Harvath grinned. "I was going to say *Kareem*, no sugar, but never mind. It's in the kitchen. Go grab some."

Gage got up from his chair and Harvath stood aside to let him pass. Then he knocked on the bedroom door and let himself in.

Barton was sitting on one of the beds. He had a towel in front of him and was cleaning his Sig Sauer pistol.

In the center of the room, the shopkeeper was bound to a chair with a hood over his head.

Harvath dragged Gage's chair in from the hall and shut the door. Walking over to a small dresser, he set up his iPhone to record the interrogation.

After positioning himself in front of the shopkeeper, he motioned for Barton to go stand behind the man.

Once he was there, Harvath started recording and nodded for Barton to remove the man's hood.

The shopkeeper was groggy. His head rolled and he blinked his eyes as he tried to adjust to the light and figure out where he was.

Harvath slapped him a little bit to help him come around.

"Come on, Fayez," he ordered. "Wake up. Let's go."

He had learned the man's name from accessing the social media accounts on his phone.

Slowly, the shopkeeper began to emerge from his stupor.

"Fayez, look at me," Harvath commanded. "Look at me."

When he didn't obey, Harvath slapped him a few more times on each cheek. Finally, the man made eye contact with him.

"Where is Umar Ali Halim?"

As his mind returned from wherever it had been, and he realized what was happening, the man began to thrash in his chair.

"*Laa. Laa,*" he sputtered in Arabic. *No. No.*

"Look at me, Fayez."

When he didn't comply, Harvath grabbed the shopkeeper's lower jaw and twisted his face toward him.

"I offered you a lot of money. You could have cooperated. So now here we are. This can be easy, or it can be very painful. Where do I find Umar Ali Halim?"

"I don't know who—"

Before the man could finish his lie, Harvath drew his hand back and delivered a cupped slap to the side of his head.

Instantly, the shopkeeper saw stars and his ear began to ring.

"Where do I find Umar Ali Halim?"

When he didn't answer, Harvath nodded and Barton hit him the exact same way on the other side, from behind.

The shopkeeper tried to turn around, but Barton grabbed the back of his head and forced him to face forward.

"Who's this, Fayez?" Harvath asked, holding up the man's cell phone so he could see. On it was a picture of him with a young woman and two little boys. "That's your wife, isn't it? Those are your sons?"

The man tried to look away, but the flash of recognition, followed by fear, was enough to confirm Harvath's assumption.

"Have you ever called her from this phone?" Harvath asked. "That's all I need to find her."

The shopkeeper didn't answer, but the same flicker of fear raced across his face once more.

Turning the phone back around, Harvath began scrolling through the call logs. "Fayez, let me explain something to you," he said. "When we left your store, I set it on fire. It's completely burned to the ground. And if you don't tell me where I can find Umar Ali Halim, I'm going to go after your family. I'm going to kill them and then I'm going to burn your house to the ground."

The man's gaze intensified and his body tensed as he pushed against his restraints. Harvath had seen the behavior enough times to know that this was when they swore and spat at you, and he made ready to dodge any projectile saliva.

Instead, the shopkeeper leaned forward and challenged him. "I don't believe you," he hissed.

Harvath smiled and nodded to Barton, who put the hood back over the man's head.

Harvath then stood and left the room.

CHAPTER 19

Forty-five minutes later, Harvath walked back into the room, carrying his laptop and satellite phone. Crossing over to the window, he opened it up and then placed everything atop the dresser and slid it over.

Once he had a strong signal and a clear picture established, he grabbed the shopkeeper's chair and dragged him over, so that he could watch what was about to unfold.

Harvath didn't need to signal Barton to remove the man's hood. He snatched it off himself.

The shopkeeper shut his eyes against the light. Harvath grasped him by the back of the neck and pushed his face forward toward the screen. "Open your eyes," he demanded. "Watch."

Slowly the man's eyes adjusted and he focused on the screen in front of him.

Through Facebook's facial recognition program, the NSA had identified the shopkeeper's wife in record time. From there, they were able to pinpoint her cell phone and to leaf out her entire relationship tree.

Placing a headset on, Harvath gave the order to begin. The animated globe spinning on the screen was replaced by a live feed from a Reaper drone already in flight.

The drone had been launched from a covert U.S. base just across the border in Tunisia.

Harvath wanted to bring the drone in over the port city of Zuwara. As soon as the shopkeeper realized what he was looking at, he'd know exactly where the drone was headed.

Despite the Reaper's amazing speed, the minutes would pass like hours as a sense of dread built within him. As he watched familiar buildings and landmarks pass by underneath, he'd agonize that his family was that much closer to death.

But, because of its airport, the CIA wanted to avoid Zuwara entirely. Instead, they decided to fly the drone in via the desert. Harvath wasn't happy.

The desert offered nothing but sand and rocks. The shopkeeper could only guess what he was looking at.

As the drone neared the edge of Al Jmail, though, he began to pay closer attention. There was a soccer field, a gas station, a bank. Harvath watched the shopkeeper. He recognized all of it.

Near Al Jmail's center, the drone slowed and went into a wide elliptical orbit overhead. The ruins of the burned-out electronics shop were not hard to discern. Harvath instructed the drone operator to zoom in on the scene.

If the shopkeeper thought Harvath had been lying to him, he was now fully disabused of that notion.

The detail captured by the drone's camera was astounding. After scanning across the smoldering rubble of the electronics shop, its roof having fully caved in, the drone's camera switched to the faces and license plates of those gathered outside. It was an incredible piece of technology.

Just as incredible, though for different reasons, was the shopkeeper's cell phone. Harvath had disabled the fingerprint sensor and was able to dip in and out of it at will.

Opening up the call log, he held it up for the shopkeeper to see. "Your wife has called you multiple times. Do you think she has heard about the fire?"

The man's jaw tightened.

"Speaking of your wife," Harvath continued. "Let's go see what she's doing."

Activating the microphone, he instructed the drone operator to proceed to "Target Bravo."

Like a telescope being collapsed, the camera lens zoomed back out and the drone took on a new heading.

The NSA had pinpointed the shopkeeper's wife to a property outside Al Jmail. Harvath knew they had the right spot just by the shopkeeper's reaction once the drone had arrived overhead and began to circle.

"Zoom in," Harvath instructed.

The operator did, and the home could be seen as clearly as if they were floating fifteen feet above it.

Financially, the shopkeeper appeared to be doing well. There was evidence of recent construction on the house. There was a healthy garden, much greener than his neighbors'. There was even a large play set, the kind you saw in suburban backyards across the United States, for his children.

Harvath was about to comment on it, when movement caught his eye. "Zoom in," he instructed.

A woman, presumably the shopkeeper's wife, had just opened a door from the house to let the two boys play. Their timing was perfect.

Harvath looked at the man and said, "This is your last chance, Fayez. Tell me where I can find Umar Ali Halim."

The shopkeeper stared at the laptop, speechless, his eyes moist. It wasn't the answer Harvath was looking for.

Hailing the drone team, he requested a readout of the Reaper's weapons package.

The screen split in two and a digital rendering of the drone's underbelly appeared next to the live feed. The Reaper was carrying a contingent of highly accurate air-to-ground Hellfire missiles and a pair of five-hundred-pound laser-guided Paveway II bombs.

"Arm Hellfire missiles," he said.

On the weapons readout, the Hellfires were highlighted in red, followed by the word *Armed*.

When the shopkeeper finally broke, he spoke so softly Harvath could barely hear him.

"Riqdalin," he whispered. "Umar Ali Halim lives near the village of Riqdalin."

CHAPTER 20

Tursunov chose a small hotel in the twelfth arrondissement near the Gare de Lyon. It was in the eastern part of the city, north of the Seine. There were lots of tourists and plenty of turnover. It was an easy neighborhood to disappear in.

He had begun his morning as he always did. After conducting a partial ablution, he had directed himself toward Mecca, had prayed, and then begun his exercises. The Americans and the Russians had been sticklers for physical fitness. In the quiet of his room, he had carried out thirty minutes of intense push-ups, sit-ups, chin-ups, and dips.

When his workout was complete, he had showered, dressed, and left the hotel. Near the train station was a café with an outdoor table that allowed smoking. He had taken a table and ordered *un serré*—a shot of the blackest coffee you could get in Paris.

Unwrapping a pack of Gauloises, he had lit his first cigarette of the day and drew the smoke deep into his lungs. The nicotine relaxed him and helped him focus.

He had been taught that like his body, his mind was also a weapon. It was yet another area in which his Russian and American instructors agreed.

Both countries had taken an active interest in counterterrorism measures in Tajikistan. As an elite operator, he had been invited to travel abroad and train with their Special Forces units. He had grabbed the opportunity with both hands.

He learned as much traveling to Russia as he did traveling to the United States. He hadn't spent much time outside Tajikistan before that. They had been eye-opening experiences.

Instead of developing a greater appreciation for and deeper commitment to his homeland, he began to loathe the Tajik government. Everything was corrupt—from the President, with his grand palace in Dushanbe designed to look like the American White House on steroids, to his own command structure within the National Police Force.

As he had exhaled a trail of smoke into the air, his eyes had tracked the people moving up and down both sides of the street. He had seen a police officer chatting with a grocer. He had wondered if it was about money.

In Tajikistan, everyone was on the take—even the cops. But while they took just a little, the politicians took a ton and lived like royalty.

Everything was based on a pecking order. You knew where you stood based on your license plates. The president had 8888. His family was just beneath him. The numbers, along with a person's status, dropped from there.

Tajikistan was such a poor country that just to make ends meet, street cops resorted to shaking down citizens by "arresting" their cars if they didn't have the right safety equipment onboard. Tajiks would have to bribe the officers on the spot, or face an even steeper payment when they went to retrieve their vehicles from the government impound facility. He hated Tajikistan.

The more corruption he saw, particularly from fellow Muslims, the angrier he became. It got to the point where he couldn't even stand to attend mosque with cops or politicians.

He had searched for good, pure men of faith. He had found them in a small religious center outside the capital. It was there that his introduction to true Islam began, and his passion to wage jihad in the name of Allah was ignited.

Removing a small map of Paris from his coat pocket, he established where he was and planned his route. There were a handful of sights he had wanted to see before his afternoon meeting.

After paying for his coffee, he headed west toward Notre Dame. As expected, in the wake of the attack at Santiago de Compostela in Spain, France had beefed up security at its major churches.

Security had also been stepped up at the Louvre museum and the Pompidou Center, the Musée d'Orsay and the Eiffel Tower. The French authorities were everywhere they should be, which was exactly what Tursunov had wanted.

Moving around the city, he took great pains to make sure he wasn't being followed. By the time he made it to the sprawling flea market north of Paris, it was late afternoon.

There was still a sea of people milling about. Their faces were a mix of white, brown, and black—European, North African, sub-Saharan. The smell of roasting meats, of shawarma and kebabs, wafted through the air from food carts out on the street.

He had committed the shop's name and location to memory—the matchbook cover with the information long since discarded.

It was in a section, deep within the market, that was a maze of tiny alleys and passageways. The sign above the door was made from hammered copper, weathered to a chalky-green patina—L'Ancienne.

When he opened the door, an electronic bell chimed, alerting the owner to his arrival.

The small shop looked like an Arab souk had exploded inside someone's garage. Hand-crafted pots and pans hung from beams across the ceiling. A pile of Persian carpets sat stacked shoulder high. Hookah pipes were organized in neat rows like a company of soldiers. There was clay pottery next to delicate side tables inlaid with mother-of-pearl.

Bolts of jewel-colored silk leaned against intricately carved wooden dressing screens. Dusty mirrors framed in polished silver hung alongside vintage Janbiya daggers from Arabia. Nearby hung ornate flintlock rifles clad with ivory from the time of the Ottoman Turks.

The store even smelled as if it came from another era—as if he hadn't stepped through a door in Paris, but rather through the flaps of a trader's tent somewhere along the ancient spice route.

An older man of Moroccan descent greeted him. He wore a crocheted prayer cap, thick black glasses, and walked with a limp.

Tursunov handed him a business card from a Dutch antiques dealer.

On the back was written the name of a nearby boutique hotel, Maison Souquet.

"Is it true that their rooms are named after famous courtesans?" the man asked.

"Yes, but their *hammam* more than makes up for it," Tursunov replied. The Maison Souquet was known not only for its private indoor pool, but for its *hammam*, or Turkish-style bath, as well.

Having presented the business card and responded correctly to the man's question, Tursunov's authentication was complete.

"*As-salāmu 'alaykum,*" the man offered. *Peace be upon you.*

"*Wa 'alaykum al-salaam,*" Tursunov replied. *And unto you peace.*

The man stepped past him, locked the door, and turned the sign so that it read *Fermé.* Closed.

He pulled the draperies across the front windows, then stepped back and embraced his guest.

"Welcome to Paris, brother."

Tursunov returned his embrace. "Thank you, brother."

"I am Abdel."

The man was nervous. Tursunov smiled. "Abdel El Fassi. Yes, I know you."

"And you knew my brother," he replied. "Aziz. You fought together for the Caliphate in Syria."

"We did. Your brother was a great warrior. A lion."

Abdel beamed with pride. "Will you take some refreshment?"

A meteor could be screaming toward the earth and the Arabs would still want to stop to take tea.

"Is everything ready?" Tursunov asked.

"Yes. The Paris operation is ready."

That was a relief, but only partially. "What about the new chemist I need?"

The Moroccan forced a smile. "Let's take some refreshment."

Tursunov didn't smile back. He didn't want refreshment. He wanted his chemist. "Is there something you want to tell me?"

Abdel shifted uncomfortably. "There is a problem."

CHAPTER 21

Abdel brewed a pot of Moroccan tea for them. It was a staple of the Maghreb and a cornerstone of daily life for its people—at home and abroad.

It combined green tea with spearmint leaves and sugar. The host poured it with great panache from several feet above the glass.

Not only did it provide a dramatic presentation, but it also aerated the liquid and created a foamy, white head likened to the prophet Mohammed's turban.

Because the ingredients were left to steep, the flavor of the tea changed over time.

Traditionally, a guest was offered three glasses—each more flavorful than the last. It was considered extremely impolite to accept anything less than all three.

The two men took their tea Bedouin style, on a rug in the middle of the floor. Abdel set out a plate of Moroccan cookies filled with almond paste, known as Gazelle's Horns.

After their first glass, Tursunov got down to business. While he had been placed in charge of all European operations for ISIS, Abdel was the terror organization's point person in France. He was highly thought of. A methodical man. A good thinker. A planner.

"You communicated that you had found me a chemist," said Tursunov.

The man nodded.

"What's the problem then?"

"The chemist may be under surveillance."

"So find me another one," the Tajik ordered.

Abdel shook his head. "There isn't time."

The Moroccan was right. "Why do you suspect surveillance?"

"Over the last few days, several members of his mosque have been followed."

"Followed by whom?"

Abdel shrugged. "No one knows."

"How were they followed?" Tursunov asked. "On foot? With vehicles?"

"Both."

Coordinated surveillance, thought the Tajik. *Not good*. "Tell me about the mosque. Is it considered a problem?"

"All mosques in France are considered a problem."

"But why would authorities be surveilling this one?"

The Moroccan removed his glasses and polished them on his sleeve before putting them back on. "French intelligence monitors all mosques."

"Mosques, yes," replied Tursunov. "Mosque members, no. Not unless they suspect something."

"I think we should assume French authorities suspect something."

This was a problem the Tajik neither wanted nor needed right now. He needed razor-sharp focus on their pending operation. Nevertheless, it raised a critical question. "Is there any connection between this mosque and the brothers you have recruited for the operation here in Paris?"

"None," Abdel replied with a shake of his head. "One team is from Roubaix, in the north of France near the border with Belgium. The other comes from Marseille, in the south. They have no connection with Paris."

"So the only connection is you."

The Moroccan paused. "What are you suggesting?"

Tursunov brushed his question aside. "How did you find this chemist?"

"Brother, if you think that—"

"Answer my question."

"I find it very insulting—" Abdel began, but the Tajik cut him off again.

Tursunov was leaving nothing to chance. He had fought alongside

Abdel's brother, but that was a lot different from having gone into battle with Abdel.

The ISIS hierarchy had selected the Moroccan to oversee operations in France. He hadn't been Tursunov's pick. Organizations, no matter how noble or devout, made mistakes. He, on the other hand, survived by avoiding them.

"Answer my question," he repeated.

The Moroccan looked at him. He was disappointed by his distrust. Finally, he said, "He is my nephew."

Tursunov had been right to question him, but it was obvious the man was insulted.

Before he could say anything, Abdel added, "You bled with his father in Syria."

The Tajik was confused. "Aziz?"

Abdel nodded. "Yes. Your chemist is the son of a lion."

"I don't understand. He never spoke of a son. Only a wife and daughter in Marrakesh."

The Moroccan poured them each another glass of tea. As he did, he recounted his brother's story. "The boy is from an earlier marriage. It was not a good match. His wife, Safaa, was beautiful, but not a good Muslim. Aziz was devout. He was also strict and they often fought.

"Much of her family lived in France. One year, she took her son for a visit and never returned home.

"She divorced Aziz from abroad, renounced her Moroccan passport, and took full French citizenship.

"Eventually, Aziz remarried. His new wife gave birth to a daughter and soon thereafter he took up arms for the jihad."

"Did he ever see the boy again?" Tursunov asked.

"He made only one visit to France. Its decadence repulsed him, and Safaa's family treated him quite badly."

The Tajik could only imagine what the experience had been like for Aziz. It was understandable that the man would keep such an embarrassing chapter of his life hidden. "How did you become connected with the boy?" he asked.

"He found me. Years ago, after he had moved to Paris and had begun his university studies, he walked into this very shop. For a long time, he had wanted to reconnect with his father's side of the family, but his mother had forbidden it."

"And you encouraged him, as a good and pious Muslim, to pursue jihad?"

"No," Abel replied. "As a good and pious Muslim, he came to that decision on his own. My job was to direct him. Younes is a smart, talented young man. He better serves our cause through his mind. Picking up a rifle or strapping on a suicide vest would be an insult to Allah and the gifts He has bestowed upon him. I merely made these truths clear."

"I see," said Tursunov, still concerned about the surveillance of the mosque and Abdel's connection to the chemist. "Has your nephew been involved in any previous operations?"

"None."

"How certain are you?"

"I am positive."

"What about his Internet searches? The videos he watches online? The message boards and the chat rooms he visits?" the Tajik asked.

"I have trained the boy myself," the Moroccan replied. "I would trust him with my life."

Tursunov paused and then said, "Good. Because you are about to trust him with all of our lives."

CHAPTER 22

Diverting the Reaper north of Al Jmail, they found Umar Ali Halim's compound right where the SAT phone salesman had said it would be.

Set in the barren desert outside Riqdalin, the only glimpses of vegetation came from humble, family-owned farms with neat rows of irrigated agriculture.

Locals grew modest quantities of dates, almonds, grapes, watermelons, olives, and tomatoes—but only enough to live on. There wasn't enough arable land or fresh water for much else.

As the drone circled above, it fed back a series of images. Double doors, large enough to drive a truck through, secured the entrance. A ten-foot-high wall surrounded the rectangular compound. There was a main house, a guesthouse of some sort, what appeared to be a barn, a handful of vehicles under a sun shade, and a smaller structure without windows.

Stacked stones framed two outdoor animal pens. A handful of men milled about carrying rifles.

From Afghanistan to Somalia, everyone on Harvath's team had hit targets like this before. They could almost do it in their sleep.

But Harvath had a rule about walled compounds: never go over a wall you could go through and never go through a wall you could go around.

He'd seen guys get shot off walls, fall off walls, and torque knees and ankles landing hard off walls.

One this size would require a ladder, preferably two. The first to put a sniper in place to watch over the courtyard, the second to get another team member up and over, who could then open the double doors from inside.

Special operations teams often used lightweight, collapsible ladders. The problem was that Harvath's team didn't have one, much less two.

Even if they had, he wasn't sure ladders were necessary. Halim was a smuggler and Harvath had yet to meet one who didn't have at least one alternate way in and out of his compound. It was just a matter of finding it.

Two hundred meters south of the compound was a large warehouse surrounded by chain-link fence, topped with razor wire. From what the phone salesman had told him, this was where Umar Ali Halim housed his "customers" before they were sent off in leaky, unseaworthy boats for the death cruise to Europe.

Mustapha Marzouk, the graduate student in chemistry from Tunisia, whose trail the CIA had sent Harvath to track down, had stayed in that very warehouse. He was sure of it.

When the Italians had interviewed the three survivors from the doomed fishing trawler, they had spoken of being kept in a long, metal warehouse-type building. It allegedly had large roll-up doors and ventilation fans at each end and was surrounded by razor-wire fencing—just like the images captured by the Reaper.

Harvath tried to remember all the details from the stacks of files he had gone through at the blue lockhouse back in the States. It was less than three days ago, but it already felt like weeks.

There had been so many horrible refugee accounts, he couldn't get through all of them. Many hadn't even been translated, only those the CIA felt had the greatest intelligence value.

The tales of torture and gang rape by Halim and his men were some of the worst Harvath had ever read. There were two details in particular, though, that he thought might prove helpful, but that he needed more information about.

As part of the operation, the CIA had assigned a handful of SSOs, or Specialized Skills Officers, to Harvath's team. SSOs were subspecialists in a wide range of areas. One such SSO was named Deborah Lovett, and she was based out of the U.S. Embassy in Rome.

Lovett was not only fluent in Italian, but she was well connected and had been working the Mustapha Marzouk/Umar Ali Halim investigation from the Italian side.

She knew the files backward and forward. Once the Reaper had located Halim's compound, Harvath had begun asking Fayez about its specifics. He had visited only a handful of times, dropping off phones or coming to deal with technical issues. He didn't know about secret ways in or out. So, Harvath had reached out to Lovett via text.

When her number came up on his satellite phone a short time later, he hoped she was calling with good news.

"What have you got?"

"I went back through all of the refugee interviews like you asked," she said. "The beatings usually happened inside the warehouse. They were a form of punishment, as well as a warning to the others. The rapes, on the other hand, happened outside. Apparently, Halim's men prefer privacy for those."

"What about the torture?"

Lovett could be heard flipping through her notes. "Victims were hooded or blindfolded and then taken someplace else on the property. It was described as dark, with a low ceiling and no windows. Sounds like an interior room or maybe something underground."

Harvath doubted it was something underground. In fact, it sounded as if it could have been the windowless structure he had seen in the drone footage.

Shifting gears, he got to the heart of why he had contacted her. "What about any passageways or tunnels? Anything about alternative means in or out of the compound?"

"No. Not, specifically. But I may have found something interesting."

"What is it?"

"About a year ago, Halim had raped a Sudanese woman at his compound. Unlike his men, who rape the refugees and then throw them back inside the warehouse, he brings the women to his bedroom.

"He has a big four-poster bed that was allegedly stolen from one of Gadaffi's palaces. He likes to tie women to it as he has his way with them.

"Apparently, the Sudanese woman fought back and he beat her, severely. She lost consciousness. He waited for her to come back around and then he raped and beat her again. She didn't remember much after that. Except for one thing—being dragged down a long hallway."

"Any idea *how long*?" Harvath asked.

"No."

"That doesn't help us much."

"Maybe this will," Lovett offered. "Another Sudanese refugee remembered the night the woman was taken and raped. There was a terrible storm. When she was brought back to the warehouse, her clothes were damp, but not soaked."

"Which means they probably dragged her outside in the rain, put her inside a vehicle, and drove her back to the warehouse."

"There's just one problem," Lovett replied. "It was Halim, not his men, who brought her back. And the pair didn't enter the warehouse through one of the exterior doors. According to the report, there's a small office at the back of the warehouse that's always kept locked. Halim stepped out of the office, dumped the Sudanese woman on the floor, and then disappeared back inside.

"None of them saw him again after that. A truck picked the refugees up the next morning, took them to the coast, and they boarded a boat that actually made it far enough to be rescued by the Italians."

It certainly sounded to Harvath like there might be a tunnel, just not connected to the main house. He thought about what Lovett had told him.

If it was raining, if the Sudanese woman was unconscious and couldn't reveal its existence, if the front gate was all locked up for the night, and if Halim didn't want to wake his men to take her back to the warehouse, he might have used the tunnel.

Those were a lot of ifs. Ifs got people killed. But ifs were a part of what he did for a living—a big part.

And, as he didn't want to go *over* the compound's wall, there was no other choice but to see *if* a tunnel existed.

CHAPTER 23

They waited until well after midnight to launch their operation. Harvath tried not to think of everything he was doing wrong.

One of the things they absolutely should have had before going in was a study of the people in and around the target called a pattern-of-life analysis. By observing a target over time, you could gain a lot of additional intelligence helpful in planning and executing a raid. Harvath, though, had decided to do without it.

The flat, barren terrain around the smuggler's compound offered no way to approach it without being seen. There was only one exception, and tonight was it. There was no moon. It was the only advantage they were going to get.

Harvath tried to reassure himself with the fact that while still a dangerous assignment, they weren't going up against a professional military or hard-core terrorist organization. Halim's men were likely to have very little training, and even less discipline.

What concerned him, though, was the Libya Liberation Front. They were trained, they were disciplined, and they were paid to "protect" Halim.

Based on the drone footage, there was no sign of them anywhere near the warehouse or the compound.

More likely than not, they were protecting Halim from rival smugglers trying to cut in on his business, as well as other militias that might want to shake him down for money and refugee women they could sell or use as sex slaves.

The big question was: *Were they being paid enough to come running if Umar Ali Halim was under attack?* Harvath already knew the answer.

Based on the contacts in the dead militia members' phones, the NSA had already intercepted a significant number of Libya Liberation Front phone calls.

The men's bodies had been pulled from the charred remains of the electronics shop. And even though they were burned beyond recognition, the bullet holes in their skulls made it clear that the fire wasn't the cause of death.

The militia was out for blood. That meant, whatever happened, Harvath's team couldn't let Halim or any of his men raise the alarm.

It would all come down to three key elements, perfectly summed up in the Delta Force maxim: surprise, speed, and violence of action.

All of Harvath's guys knew their jobs. The rules of engagement were simple. Anyone with a weapon was fair game. And that went double for anyone who tried to call for backup.

The one person the team was not allowed to kill was Halim. Harvath had been adamant about that. Only if there was no other choice was anyone allowed to put a bullet in him.

Though the moonless night gave them the advantage on their approach, two homes north of Halim's compound caused Harvath to conclude that they should come in from the southwest. There was no telling if the neighbors were on Halim's payroll. They couldn't take a gamble on whether they might tip him off to unfamiliar vehicles in the area.

They had chosen to bring the technical. If anything went down, Harvath wanted the extra firepower. Before leaving the safe house, they had done a full inventory of its contents and divided them up between the two vehicles.

In addition to the .50 caliber machine gun mounted in the bed, the Hilux pickup also contained five hundred rounds of .50 cal ammunition, a Russian KBP LPO-97 pump-action grenade launcher with three thermobaric rounds, an RPG-7 shoulder-fired rocket-propelled grenade launcher with two PG-7VL grenades, and one thousand rounds of 7.62 x 39mm ammunition suitable for feeding the three AK-47s they had taken off the dead militia members earlier that day.

For once, Murphy had paid the bad guys a visit. Harvath was happy to profit from their loss. The question now was whether Murphy would stay out of their way long enough so that he and his team could parlay this small advantage into a win.

One of the biggest things concerning Harvath was that even though they were all experienced operators, they actually had very little experience operating together.

Extra training would have fixed that, but with the clock ticking, the CIA couldn't invest in any. Part of Harvath's responsibility was figuring out how to make it work. It was why he had been chosen, and why he had been given this team. As had been drummed into him in the SEAL Teams, failure wasn't an option. He had to adapt and overcome.

Dosing the shopkeeper with another round of ketamine, they had departed the safe house.

With Haney and Morrison in the technical, Harvath, Staelin, Gage, and Barton had followed in the Land Cruiser.

Two miles out from the compound, they pulled off the road and into the desert.

The terrain was flat. There were no hills, no gullies, no stands of trees—no place to hide their vehicles. If not for the pitch darkness caused by the absence of the moon, it would have been like putting up a billboard announcing their arrival.

They had pulled the fuses for their taillights back at the safe house. Killing their headlights and instrument lights, they now carefully piloted the vehicles with only their night vision goggles to see by.

Once they got as close as they dared, they stopped and turned off the engines. Overhead, the Reaper monitored the smuggler's compound and kept Harvath apprised of any movement.

His plan had been to hit the compound while Halim and his men were asleep. The only movement the drone had picked up was more than an hour ago. A man had stepped out of the guesthouse, smoked a cigarette, and returned inside. Since then, there had been nothing else. So far, so good.

Climbing out of the vehicles and gathering at the rear of the technical, they quietly gave their equipment a final check.

On such short notice, the CIA had done an admirable job. In addition to getting them into Libya, it had secured the safe house, arranged their primary vehicles, and provided a decent array of gear.

In addition to helmets and night vision goggles, there were six suppressed M4 rifles, all complete with red dot sights and infrared lasers.

In the sidearm department, it had been a grab bag, but no less impressive. Harvath still had his H&K from earlier, Gage and Staelin had called dibs on the two 1911s, Barton had chosen the Sig Sauer, and Marines Haney and Morrison had each snatched up a Beretta 92.

Despite most of the equipment being second-hand, the communications gear was top-notch. It was all cutting-edge, fully encrypted, and the absolute best available.

With the drone as their only backup, Harvath had insisted the team up their combat load. As a result, they had all stuffed their chest rigs with as many extra magazines as they could carry.

Once everyone was ready, Harvath gave the signal and they crept soundlessly toward the compound.

CHAPTER 24

G age was the team's designated marksman. And though Harvath
had submitted a detailed equipment list ahead of time, not everything he had asked for was available.

In particular, Gage had requested a SOCOM MK-13 sniper rifle in
.300 WinMag. He wanted a powerful weapon with a solid round that
would take care of business in any situation.

But when they arrived, there was no sniper rifle with their gear. Either
someone hadn't gotten the message, or they just weren't able to get their
hands on one. Gage would have to make do with what he had.

Just before the team reached the fence at the back of the warehouse, he
peeled off. He did a quick sweep for scorpions and any other potential surprises, then lowered himself to the ground and settled in behind his rifle.

With their overwatch in position, Harvath radioed the drone team for
a SITREP.

"Negative movement at the compound. Negative movement at the
warehouse," came the response.

"Good copy. Roger that." Harvath replied, as he then signaled for the
rest of the team to approach the fence.

Along with the gear the CIA had provided, there had been a small
breacher's kit. It should have included bolt cutters, or at the very least a
pair of Channellock cutting pliers. Instead, all they had was a Leatherman tool.

Harvath took one look at the gauge of the fence and waved Morrison forward. Handing him the Leatherman, he motioned for him to get to work.

The fence was fabricated from heavy, galvanized steel. With such a small tool, it took a ton of force to cut through the links. It was a bear of a job. At least once, Harvath could have sworn he caught Morrison mouthing the words *Fuck you* at him. He smiled and continued to scan the area for threats.

There were no guards and no foot patrols. In all likelihood, Halim either didn't have the manpower, or didn't think it necessary to post an around-the-clock watch. *Big mistake.*

When Morrison had opened a hole large enough for them to slide through, he handed the Leatherman back. Harvath offered him a fist bump, knowing the young Marine's hands had to be killing him. Instead of responding in kind, Morrison gave him the finger. Off to his right, Haney suppressed a laugh.

On Harvath's command, one by one they climbed through and took up positions at the rear of the building.

The large roll-up door was locked with a heavy padlock. Even if he'd had a pair of bolt cutters, he wouldn't have bothered. There was no telling exactly who was on the other side, or how much noise it would have made.

Instead, their objective was a pedestrian door on the north side of the structure.

With confirmation from the Reaper that the coast was clear, Harvath snuck a peek around the corner of the building and then led his team forward.

At the pedestrian door, he gave the command for everyone to stop, and then he tried the knob. He had lost count of how many times he had been in some of the world's shittiest, most dangerous places and doors had been left completely unlocked. That wasn't the case here.

Letting his rifle hang against his chest, he removed a set of picks from the breacher's kit and went to work on the lock. Twenty seconds later, he had it open. Pulling back the door, he stood aside to let the team pour in.

The first thing they noticed was the smell. Even the large, industrial fans spinning above the doors couldn't circulate it out. It smelled like despair.

The odors of vomit and urine mixed with sweat and blood. More than one hundred people slept on the rough concrete floor. Some had blankets. Most did not. A trench drain ran down the center.

Toward the other end of the structure, several people were coughing. The coughs were deep, wet. Harvath and his team could only imagine the illnesses being suffered, shared, and incubated here.

Closing the door, he glanced down at the lock. It was keyed from this side as well. If there were ever a fire, the building would be a deathtrap for those caught inside.

The team moved quietly through the open space, sweeping their weapons from side to side. Considering how unpalatable the conditions were, they weren't surprised not to find any guards.

The people sleeping on the floor had paid enormous sums of money to escape their home countries and be smuggled into Europe. They had traveled thousands of miles from places like Gambia, Nigeria, Senegal, and Sudan. Others had come from places like Iraq and Syria.

Some were sick. Many were malnourished. And even with the horrors that had been visited upon some of their fellow refugees, none of them were going to run. They had come too far to turn back now.

In the back corner of the building was the office. As the team cautiously approached, Harvath noticed a young woman leaning against the wall. She was gaunt, her skin sallow. A piece of fabric lay draped over her shoulder. Beneath it, an impossibly small baby breastfed.

She stared up at Harvath, her eyes unblinking, almost lifeless. He didn't know how well she could see him in the dark, but she seemed to know he was there. He raised his finger to his lips and instructed her not to make any sound.

Unwrapping an energy bar he had brought with him, he placed it in her hand. Nearby, was a half-empty bottle of water. He moved it closer so that she could reach it without disturbing the baby.

He wished he could do more, but already Haney was signaling that the office door was locked and that they needed him to come open it.

Harvath left the mother and baby to rejoin his team.

The office door was solid—even more solid than the one they had entered the warehouse by. It reminded Harvath of the security door at the electronics shop. Removing his picks, he got to work.

This lock was tougher to defeat, but not impossible. As soon as he had beaten it, he nodded at Haney, who signaled the team and then counted backward from three with his fingers.

On the Marine's mark, Harvath eased the door open and Haney button-hooked inside, followed by Morrison and Staelin. Harvath and Barton brought up the rear.

It was a small room, stacked with supplies. There was a metal desk with two chairs atop a faded Persian rug. Tattered binders were jammed haphazardly into a cheap, wooden bookcase. A ten-gallon bucket stood in one corner like an umbrella stand, but instead of containing umbrellas, it contained prayer rugs.

Along the far wall were several tall filing cabinets. Taped to the wall above them was a nautical chart of the Mediterranean. In it, several small pins had been stuck.

Harvath examined the map as Morrison and Barton moved the desk and chairs in order to pull back the rug. *Nothing said smuggler like a trapdoor.*

The team's hopes were dashed, though, when all they found underneath was the same battered linoleum tile that covered the rest of the office.

Taking his eyes from the map, Harvath looked down at the floor beneath his boots. The tiles here, as best he could tell through the gray-green of his night vision goggles, looked less worn than the rest of the others.

Crouching, he ran his fingertips across the top of them. At first, he didn't feel anything. Then on his second pass, as he moved his fingers more slowly, he felt it.

There were two extremely fine grooves. Waving Haney over, he showed him what he had found.

It took them five minutes to discover the release mechanism. Once they did, there was a click, and the center filing cabinet popped out a quarter of an inch.

It was on wheels, and by grabbing hold of the top, they were able to pull it into the room and reveal a small passageway behind.

Radioing Gage, Harvath stated that they had found what they were looking for and to meet him at the warehouse door.

He wanted his full team there for what they were about to do.

CHAPTER 25

Morrison studied the wire connected to the filing cabinet release. He wanted to make sure it wasn't attached to a signaling device that might somehow alert Halim and his men that they were coming.

"We good?" Harvath asked after several seconds.

The Marine nodded, but then added with a smile, "You go first."

Harvath rolled his eyes and, taking point, led his team into the passage.

There was a short flight of stairs, after which the stone tunnel widened, but not by much.

They moved slowly, at times having to duck or turn sideways to make it through. Helmets scraped against the ceiling. Elbows scraped against walls.

They maintained strict silence even though each of them—especially the larger guys—wanted to utter a few choice words.

At the end of the tunnel, Harvath signaled for the team to stop. Hammered into the wall was a series of metal rungs made out of rebar. It reminded him of a sewer ladder.

Looking up, he saw the outline of a trapdoor. Using hand signals, he relayed what he wanted done.

As the message was passed down the line, he transitioned to his pistol and spun the suppressor onto its threaded barrel.

He tested his weight on the first rung, and, once confident that it would hold, he began climbing.

With each step, he kept his eyes glued on the trapdoor above him. He hated trapdoors. They were often obstructed with rugs or tables, and could be a pain in the ass, if not impossible, to open. Worse still, all of your guys had to follow you up the ladder one at a time. But the closer he got, the less he thought it was going to be a problem.

Based on the length of the tunnel, he had a good idea of where they were beneath the compound. The smell of animal dung confirmed it.

Placing his ear against the trapdoor, he listened. If there was anything or anyone on the other side, they weren't making any noise.

Wrapping his arm through the uppermost rung, he steadied himself as he raised his pistol and applied pressure to the door. It wasn't locked or obstructed. To his surprise, it moved.

Before raising it any farther, he scanned the frame for booby-traps. He'd seen more than his fair share over the years. He had left a few as well.

They weren't hard to build. One of the simplest required nothing more than a grenade, a piece of wire, and half a Coke can.

Seeing no indication that it was rigged, Harvath opened the trapdoor the rest of the way.

A cascade of moldy wood shavings being used as animal bedding fell down into the tunnel. The smell of dung was even stronger now.

As Harvath scanned the small barn, he saw four goats staring back at him. The minute they made eye-to-night-vision-goggle contact, they started bleating.

They were loud. It sounded like someone had just tripped a burglar alarm. Harvath had to act fast.

He had come ready to kill Halim's people, but not a bunch of goats. It wasn't their fault they were here. Besides, the suppressor on his H&K could only muffle his shots to a certain degree. There was no such thing as a true "silencer." Those only existed in the movies.

Quickly scanning the barn, he saw several sacks of grain suspended from the ceiling. They had been hung out of reach of the goats, as well as any bugs or rodents.

Hopping out of the opening in the floor, he drew his knife and slashed open the nearest sack. Grain spilled out and began piling up beneath. The goats went right for it, and immediately quieted to eat.

Harvath looked down into the hole and signaled for his team to hurry up and climb out. As they did, he cut down the rest of the sacks. He needed the goats to be quiet long enough for them to get out of the barn.

Approaching the door, he opened it just wide enough to peer outside. They were in the northeast corner of the compound. Directly across from them was the guesthouse, beyond that was the main house, and directly to the right was the structure with no windows. Piled next to it was a bunch of wooden crates and empty pallets.

"It's a good thing you left the goats alone," Gage whispered, as he joined him at the door. "They hate it when you drag their girlfriends into these things."

Harvath chuckled and stood aside so he could take a look.

"See the building to our right?" he asked as Gage peered outside.

The Green Beret nodded. "Good view of the courtyard."

"Think you can get up on the roof?"

"Let's find out."

Harvath reached out to the drone team again.

"Negative movement in the compound," they replied.

With Morrison and Barton keeping an eye on the goats, Harvath counted down from three and opened the door. Gage headed for the building while Staelin and Haney covered him.

Once there, he quietly leaned several of the pallets up against the wall and then hopped on top. Harvath braced for the dry, sun-bleached wood to splinter under the big man's weight, but it didn't happen.

Pulling himself up with his massive arms, he swung his legs over the parapet and soundlessly belly crawled to the other side.

"In place," he radioed a few moments later.

"How's it look?" Harvath asked.

"Like church on a Monday. Quiet and empty."

From his perch, Gage had a clear view of the guesthouse, the main house, and the front gate. If anyone appeared with a weapon, or if there were any "squirters," bad guys who tried to make a run for it, Gage knew he was free to engage.

The first thing Harvath wanted to make sure of, though, was that the Green Beret wasn't perched atop a nest of Halim's men. Giving the signal, he sent Staelin and Haney to check it out.

One of the number-one rules in taking down a target was: *Don't run to your death*. With their weapons up and at the ready, they moved purposefully across the courtyard, scanning for threats as they went.

At the door, Staelin waited for Haney to squeeze his shoulder—the signal that he was ready to go. When he did, the Delta Force operative tried the handle. It was unlocked.

Opening the door, Staelin stepped aside to allow Haney to sweep in and then followed.

They both radioed back the same message: "Clear."

Staelin then stated, "Jesus. This guy Halim is a sick bastard. It looks like a medieval torture chamber."

"Everything but an iron maiden," Haney added.

"Stand by," Harvath replied.

He wasn't surprised to learn that the windowless building was where the smuggler indulged some of his most vile psychopathy. Rumor had it that Halim had been a commander in the Soqur Al-Fatah, or Hawks of Al-Fatah.

They were the most feared of Gaddafi's death squads. Their unit traveled the country, hunting down insurgents. They used shipping containers, painted with a black crescent moon, to imprison and torture suspects into providing information on their networks. Wherever they went, people disappeared and shallow, mass graves followed.

Only in a unit like Soqur Al-Fatah could a psycho like Umar Ali Halim have found a home and been paid to hone his exceptionally evil penchant for inflicting pain on his fellow human beings.

Harvath signaled Barton and Morrison to open the last bag of grain and join him at the door.

When they did, he asked for a final SITREP from the drone team back in Tunisia and Gage up on the roof. Once they had reported back the all clear, he ordered everyone to get ready for phase two.

Staelin and Haney were closest to the main house, so they would go for Halim. Harvath, along with Morrison and Barton, would hit the guesthouse, where Halim's men were believed to be.

With a final check of weapons, comms, and gear, everyone was good to go. Harvath, having transitioned back to his suppressed rifle, once again counted down from three.

This was why they had come all the way to Libya. It was now *game on.*

CHAPTER 26

Both assault teams slipped out of their respective buildings and headed toward their designated targets.

On Harvath's team, Barton took point, Morrison covered the rear, and Harvath was in the middle.

The guesthouse reminded Harvath of buildings he had seen across North Africa—cinderblock construction, small windows, wooden door with iron hardware.

Approaching the entry, Gage whispered over the radio, "Knock, knock, motherfuckers."

At the door, Barton waited for Harvath to squeeze his shoulder. When he did, the red-bearded SEAL tried the handle. It was unlocked. As he opened it, Harvath swept inside, followed by Morrison. Barton closed the door and brought up the rear.

It was a narrow hallway with a door to the left and a door to the right. *Dealer's choice*. Harvath could choose either one.

He had been on countless raids throughout the Muslim world. He knew what to look for in situations like this. *Shoes*.

Glancing to his left and his right, he saw men's shoes stacked up outside both doors. There were no women's or children's shoes. That was a good sign.

Harvath chose the door with the larger pile and cut to the left. Morrison cut to the right, and Barton—as planned—followed Harvath.

He tried the knob, but the door wasn't even fully closed. Whoever had entered last hadn't closed it all the way.

Harvath leaned gently against it, his rifle ready to fire. He braced for the squeal of metal on metal, thinking the old hinges would give him away. But the sound never came.

Pushing into the room, Harvath was almost clear of the doorway when one of Halim's men sat up in his bed, followed by two more. All three of them had their weapons not next to their beds, but in their beds.

Whether they had been awakened by the goats bleating and were just being cautious, or whether they always slept with their AK-47s, Harvath would never know. Nor would he ever care. Depressing his trigger, he engaged.

He felled the first two men with headshots. But as he engaged the third man, his shot went wide and hit the wall.

Reacquiring the target, he skipped one off the man's skull—giving him a Mohawk—and then put one right into his left eye, killing him.

By now, Barton had shoved into the room from behind him. Halim's men were throwing off their blankets and scrambling for their rifles. Barton took the right side of the room. Harvath focused on the left.

Harvath fired in controlled pairs—his shots now rock steady and deadly accurate. Barton was just as deadly, if not more so.

As soon as the job was done, Harvath sent Barton to check on Morrison. Once he had exited, Harvath walked the length of the room, delivering extra rounds to make sure there were no survivors.

At the end of the row of beds, he heard Haney's voice come over his earpiece. "Jackpot."

They had Halim.

. . .

After sending Morrison and Barton to cover the front door, Harvath moved through Morrison's room to make sure there were no survivors. There weren't. The Force Recon Marine was damn good at his job.

Exiting the guesthouse, Harvath headed to the main house while Morrison and Barton, covered by Gage, swept the rest of the compound.

Staelin and Haney had found the smuggler, alone, in his bedroom.

As Harvath entered, he saw Halim sitting, flex-cuffed to a gilded chair with a blood-soaked towel wrapped around his hand.

"What happened?" Harvath asked.

"He went for this under his pillow," Haney replied, holding up a Makarov PMM pistol. "So, I shot him."

"Good job. Go clear the rest of the house. I'll keep an eye on him."

From his pocket, Harvath removed one of the few pictures ever taken of Umar Ali Halim.

It was twenty years old, but the scar that ran from above his left eye, down through his eyebrow, over his nose, and across his left cheek was unmistakable. There was no question they had the right guy.

Halim was built like a wrestler, thick and muscular. He had short black hair, a close black beard, and a noticeable overbite that reminded him of Saddam Hussein's psychopathic son Uday.

Harvath could have turned on the lights, but he wanted to keep the smuggler on edge. The room was extremely dark. Being denied the ability to see was unsettling.

"Let's see your hand," Harvath said, as he slung his weapon and unwound the towel.

Even through his night vision goggles, he could tell that the injury was severe. There was a lot of blood and one of Halim's fingers had been blown almost all the way off. It lay on the towel, barely attached.

"It looks like your piano career is over," said Harvath.

Halim didn't respond. Instead, he brought his head back and spat a huge glob of spit in Harvath's face.

Drawing back his weapon, Harvath crashed it into the bridge of the smuggler's nose, breaking it. "Your modeling career isn't looking so good now either."

Wiping the man's saliva from his face, he chastised himself for not expecting it. North African and Middle Eastern men used spitting as a high-grade insult.

It wasn't the first time one had spat at him. They usually did it out of fear. It was their way of trying to assert dominance over a situation in which they had zero control. It had to be responded to quickly, which was why Harvath had broken the man's nose. The smuggler needed to know, right up front, who was boss and that Harvath hadn't come to play games.

He looked back down at the man's injured hand and touched it near the severed finger with his suppressor. The smuggler's body went rigid as a lightning bolt of pain shot through his body, and he let out a piercing scream.

Harvath carefully wrapped the towel back around it, making sure not to get any blood on his bare hands.

They were going to have to treat him before they started his interrogation. The easiest route to answers would likely be through the man's injured hand. But as far as Harvath was concerned, that would be taking it too easy on him.

Karma was a bitch and Umar Ali Halim deserved as much of his own medicine as could be forced down his throat. Harvath wanted to take him for a ride on his own flying carpet.

As Staelin had the most medical training on the team, Harvath wanted him to patch up the Libyan.

He was just about to hail him on the radio when he heard his voice in his earpiece: "Boss, we've got a problem. Need you in the courtyard ASAP."

CHAPTER 27

Once Morrison and Barton were done clearing the main house, he left them in charge of Halim and headed outside.

Staelin and Haney were standing by the awning where the smugglers' crappy vehicles were parked. On the ground, a Libyan lay flex-cuffed. He was in his late teens or early twenties and wasn't very big.

"Where'd you find him?" Harvath asked as he approached.

Haney nodded at the sedan closest to them. "Inside the trunk."

"He had these with him," added Staelin as he reached inside and removed an AK-47 in addition to a chest rack stuffed with magazines. "He was probably on guard duty and slipped into the car to take a nap. That's why the drone didn't see him. When you guys started shooting, he must have folded down one of the rear seats and snuck into the trunk."

"The dumbass even left his gear up front. But it probably saved his life. If he'd been holding a rifle when we popped that lid, he'd be a dead man right now."

"What about a phone? Was he carrying one?" Harvath asked.

Haney handed it to him, but it was locked.

"Stand him up," Harvath ordered.

Staelin and Haney got the Libyan on his feet.

Harvath held up the phone, pointed to the screen, and said to the man, "What's the password?"

"*Anna la 'atakallam 'Inglizi,*" the Libyan answered, feigning ignorance. *I don't speak English.*

Harvath nodded to Haney, who hit the man so hard in his stomach that it lifted him off his feet.

The man doubled over in pain.

Harvath gave him a minute to let it pass and then nodded again to Haney, who grabbed him by the hair and straightened him up.

"What's the password?" Harvath repeated.

The man only got halfway through his *I don't speak English* routine before Harvath drew his pistol and pointed it at his head.

All of a sudden, the man was fluent. "Two, two, three, seven," he said with a heavy accent.

Harvath entered the numbers. The phone unlocked. As soon as he saw the phone's activity, he knew they were in trouble. "Are there any keys in those vehicles?"

Staelin nodded.

Harvath raised the drone team, "Any movement in our area? Vehicles or individuals?"

"Negative movement."

He had a bad feeling it wouldn't stay quiet. Hailing Barton, he told him to come out to the courtyard to collect the new prisoner and bring him inside the main house.

"What do you want us to do?" Haney asked.

"Take one of these cars and bring back our vehicles."

"Then what?"

Harvath grabbed the Libyan by the back of the neck and pushed him toward the gate to open it for them. "I haven't gotten that far yet," he said. "Just get going."

"Roger that," the men replied. They chose an old LC70 pickup. As Haney fired it up, Staelin used the butt of his weapon to smash the taillights. The less attention they drew to themselves outside the compound, the better.

Turning the headlights off, they rolled out of the compound back toward where they had left the team's SUV and the technical.

As the little Libyan closed the gate, Barton appeared in the courtyard. Harvath handed him over and pulled out his satellite phone.

Back at the CIA, Harvath's call was picked up on the second ring. He gave a quick rundown of the situation, rattled off the telephone number of the cell phone he had taken off the Libyan, and told them what he was looking for.

He figured it would take Langley at least five minutes. They called back in three. The NSA had been patched in on the call. It wasn't good news.

"It looks like someone stepped on an anthill," the voice from the NSA said. "All of the Libya Liberation Front phones we're tracking are lighting up. The number you just sent us has sent text messages to at least six of the numbers we've been monitoring."

That was exactly what Harvath was worried about. "Understood. Keep an eye on them. Let me know as soon as they start moving."

"They're *already* moving," the voice replied. "You should think about doing the same."

Harvath thanked them and disconnected the call. Raising Gage, he said, "Company's coming, Jack. I want you up near the gate. You see anything but our guys, you shoot. Copy?"

"Good copy," he replied. "Shit's gettin' real."

"It's gettin' real, all right, but we're going to be long gone before *it* gets here."

Harvath was halfway across the courtyard, running the route to the safe house through his head, when the leader of the drone team hailed him.

"It looks like the Liberation Front is setting up a perimeter," the voice said. "There's already two roadblocks outside the town. You guys need to haul ass."

Block the exits, and then send in an assault team to clear out the threat. It was smart, and what Harvath would have done if the situation had been reversed. Whoever had trained them had trained them well.

Ending his transmission with the drone team, he radioed Haney. "Mikey, what's your status?"

"We're inbound to you. Thirty seconds."

"Roger that," Harvath replied, as he hailed Gage. "Jack, open the gates for them."

"Copy that," said the Green Beret.

Hurrying into the main house, Harvath checked on the status of the prisoners.

The little Libyan was lying facedown on the floor in the bedroom. Halim's flex-cuffs, which had secured him to the chair, had been cut away and a new set put on. An additional pair had been doubled up and pulled extra tight as a tourniquet to reduce the blood flow to his injured hand. The blood from his broken nose had slowed to a trickle. Each man had been gagged with a piece of duct tape.

"We all good to go here?" Harvath asked as he stepped into the room.

Morrison and Barton flashed him the thumbs-up.

Removing two hoods from his pocket, Harvath placed one over each of the prisoner's heads and gave the command to move out.

By the time they stepped outside, Staelin and Haney were already in the courtyard, engines running, doors open.

While Morrison and Barton loaded the two Libyans into the cargo area of the Land Cruiser, Harvath laid a map out on the hood and illuminated it.

According to the NSA and the drone team, militia fighters were headed toward them from all directions.

The only way to avoid contact was to stay off the main paved roads. Crisscrossing the desert was a series of dirt roads predominantly used by local farmers. They'd be tough as hell to follow, but Harvath had a plan.

Quickly indicating the route he wanted to take, he told everybody to mount up, and then he let the drone team know they were rolling.

Outside the gates, they slowed only long enough for Haney to pick up Gage, and then put the pedal to the metal.

They were going to punch right through the center of the trap. There was only one way it could go wrong.

CHAPTER 28

The woman looked at him as if he was crazy. "You want me to put a full package on Lydia Ryan? The Deputy fucking Director of the CIA. Are you nuts?"

"Keep your voice down," Andrew Jordan cautioned.

They were sitting at a small table in the back of the oldest bar and restaurant in town, the Old Ebbitt Grill. It was a popular spot for D.C. power players, just a stone's throw from the White House. And while Andrew Jordan didn't look it, he definitely considered himself a power player.

He was the hidden force behind Page Partners, Ltd. Without him, Paul Page would be nothing and would have nothing.

But unlike Paul, he had to keep a low profile. Every penny he made from his share of Page Partners, Ltd., was deposited into offshore accounts. From there it flowed into a series of shell corporations that invested in real estate and various foreign business ventures.

All of it stayed outside the United States, beyond the prying eyes of his employer, the Central Intelligence Agency. Nothing triggered an investigation faster than a report that you were believed to be living beyond your means.

To avoid getting flagged, he was extremely judicious with everything. He maxed out his retirement plans, had a mortgage below what he qualified for, drove a predriven car, vacationed modestly, and contributed generously to a handful of charities.

He had no vices, save one—from time to time, he liked to go out for a good meal. This time, it was dinner at the Old Ebbitt. With him was a contractor who did a lot of off-the-books work for the Central Intelligence Agency.

Unless someone from the Directorate of Operations had walked in, no one in the restaurant would have recognized either of them. And even then, it was highly unlikely they would have recognized the contractor. She was a discreet source whom Jordan had spent a lot of time quietly developing.

The woman's name was Susan Viscovich. She had been in Army Intelligence, then the NSA, and eventually had gone out on her own. She was in her late thirties, but took very good care of herself and looked ten years younger.

She had long blonde hair, which tonight she wore up in a tight bun. This was business. And from what she had just been told, it was dangerous business.

Leaning over the table, she lowered her voice and asked, "Why the hell would you want a full electronic surveillance package on Ryan?"

"I'm not at liberty to discuss that," he replied.

Picking up her wineglass, she leaned back in her chair and said, "Find somebody else."

"There is nobody else. You're the best."

Viscovich took a sip of her wine, but remained silent. She didn't want this job. No good would come of it.

"I'm willing to double your fee."

"I'll bet you are," she replied. Holding up her glass to get their server's attention, she signaled that she was ready for another one. "You?"

He nodded and Viscovich motioned for a full round.

There were a dozen large oysters in front of them. She chose one and added some mignonette sauce. Then, she raised the shell to her mouth, tipped her head back, and let it slide down her throat.

Jordan watched, his appreciation for how she consumed her oysters a bit too obvious.

"Is there a problem?" she asked.

"No, I was just thinking—"

"I know what you were thinking. Knock it off."

He held up his hands. "This is just business. That's all this is."

"You're damn right that's all this is."

Reaching down, she prepared another oyster and was about to eat it when she set it back onto her plate. "I understand why I get the kinds of jobs I do from you. It's not necessarily because they're hard, though most of them are, but rather because if I get caught, the Agency can deny any knowledge of me."

"Correct."

"And I'm okay with that," she stated. "But this is different. Why does the Agency want to run covert surveillance on its own Deputy DCI?"

"I told you it's—"

She raised her hand and cut him off. "Don't bullshit me, Andy. Not if you seriously want me to consider this job. And if that's what you want, you must have come here knowing that I'd expect an explanation."

He saw their waiter approaching and waited until he had set the drinks on the table and had walked away before responding.

"Ryan is leaving the Agency."

"Interesting," she replied, pouring what was left of her wine into the new glass and then taking a sip. "What do you care?"

"Have you heard of the Carlton Group?"

Viscovich smiled. "Everybody worth their salt in our game has heard of the Carlton Group."

"That's where she's going."

"Again, why do you care?"

Jordan loaded up an oyster with horseradish and cocktail sauce. "Because she's not going alone. She's going to be taking key people with her."

"Is that a crime?"

"It depends."

"Then why not bring in the FBI?"

"It's tricky," he said, as he raised the overloaded oyster to his mouth, slurped it back, and continued to talk as he chewed. "Ryan may be sharing some things with her new employer that neither they nor the FBI should be hearing."

Viscovich ignored the man's poor table manners and redirected. "So use your own people to surveil her."

"Therein lies our problem. Lydia Ryan has been at CIA a long time; everybody likes her. She's got friends everywhere. We can't do this internally."

"It sounds like you've got a pretty serious problem."

"Tell me about it."

Taking another sip, she swirled the wine in her glass and asked, "Who knows about your investigation?"

"It's a tight circle," he said as he loaded up another oyster. "And needless to say, none of what we have discussed here goes any further."

Viscovich rolled her eyes. "Give me a break. I know how this works. Is the Director involved?"

Without missing a beat, Jordan looked up from his oyster, smiled at her, and lied. "DCI McGee? Of course. He's running the entire investigation. One hundred percent."

"Good. From what I hear, he's a reasonable man. He'll understand I expect you to triple my fee,"

Jordan squinted at her.

"And," she added, "I want an official finding, signed by the Director, on his letterhead, authorizing me to do what you're asking."

He shook his head. "No way. He'll never go for it."

"Those are my terms. You either meet them, or I walk."

For several moments, he pretended to think about her demands. Finally, he said, "I think I can probably get McGee to agree to that. But for triple your fee, it's going to need to include another surveillance package."

"That depends. Who's the target?"

"Ryan's new boss," said Jordan. "Reed Carlton."

CHAPTER 29

Completely blacked out, Harvath's two-vehicle convoy pounded through the desert, using their night vision goggles to guide them.

Night vision goggles, though, depended on ambient light—something they had too little of.

Usually on an operation like this, the vehicles would have been outfitted with infrared headlights or some other sort of IR. But this wasn't a normal operation, and Harvath had known that even under the best of conditions, the dirt roads were going to be tough to follow. Fortunately, he had come up with a solution.

Keying up his radio, he had asked the drone team to "sparkle" the roads for him.

Onboard the Reaper was a powerful infrared laser that acted like a giant laser pointer. It not only helped illuminate their route, but it also helped direct them where they needed to go.

Light on the infrared spectrum was invisible to the naked eye and could only be seen with night vision. It was a very useful tool, which gave them an exceptional advantage.

The advantage, however, was short-lived.

Harvath's plan had been to stay on the desert roads until just south of the tiny fishing village of Abu Kammash, not far from the Tunisian border. There, provided no one was on their tail, they could cut back south

along the coast and pick up the road that would take them back to the safe house.

That plan was scrapped when the drone team alerted Harvath that his convoy had vehicles converging on it from multiple directions.

How the hell was that possible? "Off sparkle," he ordered.

"Roger that. Off sparkle," the drone team leader replied.

The effect was like someone turning off a streetlight. Their visibility instantly dropped. Staelin, who was piloting their Land Cruiser, had no choice but to slow down.

They went from doing more than sixty miles an hour, to less than twenty. Harvath, who was riding shotgun, leaned forward to get a better view through the windshield, but it was no use.

Behind them, Haney slowed the technical. Compared to how fast they had been going, they were now moving at a snail's pace.

"What are the hostile vehicles doing now?" Harvath asked over the radio.

"Same thing you are," the voice replied.

Harvath had been afraid of that. It looked as if they had night vision as well. It was the weak spot in his plan. And while he couldn't know for sure how the Libya Liberation Front had gotten their hands on such highly restricted technology, he had a pretty good idea.

A few years ago, American Special Forces soldiers had set up a secret training camp on an old military base in this part of Libya. It was called Camp 27 because it was at the 27 kilometer marker on the road from Tripoli to Tunis.

Its goal was to help train up a team of one hundred high-speed Libyan counterterrorism fighters. The United States had provided them with Glock pistols, M4 rifles, and other essential equipment, including night vision goggles.

Several months later, when no U.S. personnel were present, two local militias and a jihadist group sympathetic to Al Qaeda overran the camp. None of the American-supplied gear was ever seen again.

Harvath was willing to bet that the night vision the militia was using, as well as the three Glocks he had taken off the dead militia members at the electronics shop in Al Jmail, were from Camp 27.

Not that any of that information was of any help to him. Right now, they had to shake those vehicles that were barreling down on them.

Speaking with the drone team leader, Harvath said, "Can you turn the sparkle back on and lead them in a different direction?"

"Roger that. But are you sure you want us to leave you blind?"

"If you can get those guys off our ass, it'll be a fair tradeoff."

"Copy that," the drone team leader replied. "Adjusting course." Moments later, he added, "Sparkle in five, four, three, two, one. Sparkle engaged."

Without the powerful IR laser helping to guide them, trying to make it all the way back via the desert would take hours. They were going to have to risk a shortcut.

Harvath studied his map. They were just outside the town of Zelten. If they could get to the other side, they could pick up the coastal road and be home free.

"Let's pull over here," he said to Staelin. Behind them, Haney also pulled to the side of the road.

The dome lights had been deactivated, but nevertheless Harvath double-checked before opening his door.

It felt good to get out of the car and stretch his legs. Morrison and Barton hopped out too, but stayed near the rear of the SUV to keep an eye on their two Libyan prisoners.

When Harvath walked back to the technical, Haney was standing next to it taking a piss. Gage was busy packing a new wad of chaw into his mouth.

"When we get back to the house," the Green Beret said, "I'm ordering in pizza and a six-pack."

"Fuck that," Haney replied. "We're getting Chinese. And then we're going to the Holiday Inn up the street. I hear they've got an awesome cover band. Bomb Jovi."

Harvath couldn't help but laugh. Next to the action, one of the biggest things he missed when he was back home was the sense of humor so many operators had.

"Here's where I'm at," he said. "Using the IR from the drone is no longer an option. But without it, going the back roads under NVGs will take us all night.

"Even so, we can flip our headlights back on and press our luck through the desert. Maybe some farmer sees us and calls it in to the bad guys, maybe he doesn't. Or we can cut through this town up ahead, roll for the coast, and be drinking mai tais in under an hour. Thoughts?"

"Frankly," said Gage. "I think mai tais are elitist. But I like the idea of being home in under an hour. I say cut through town."

Harvath looked at Haney. While he respected everyone on the team, his was the opinion he valued the most.

"A lot more eyeballs and cell phones in town," he said, rubbing the stubble along his jaw. "Much higher potential for being spotted, even at four in the morning."

"True."

"We don't know what we're riding into. There could be some leave behinds. Who knows if every militia member saddled up and rode out? All it takes is one guy in a window or on a rooftop, and we're screwed."

Harvath was about to respond when Staelin walked up.

"Bad news," the Delta Force operative said.

"What is it?"

"We're starting to run low on fuel. There isn't enough to bounce all over hell and back."

"But there's an extra two—" Harvath began, then caught himself. They had used the extra cans of fuel to burn down the electronics shop. "Fuck."

"Yup," Staelin replied. "Exactly."

"So we've got no choice."

"Not unless you brought a siphon with you and want to suck the gas out of the technical."

There was some surgical tubing in the med kit, but nowhere near enough. "We could cut the fuel line or puncture the tank. Put something underneath it to catch everything."

"That sounds like fun," Staelin replied, as he turned and walked away. "If you need me, I'll be in the Land Cruiser."

Harvath turned back to Haney and Gage. "What do you think?"

"I think it's late," said Gage. "And anyone with any sense in that town is asleep. We keffiyeh up, we roll hard and fast, and nobody's the wiser."

"Mike, what do you think?" asked Harvath. Even though he was the leader, it was important to get buy-in from the entire team.

"I think there's no good answer. That's what I think."

"So is that a yes, or a no?"

Haney thought about it for a moment and then looked at him. "I don't want to miss Bomb Jovi, so I guess it's a yes."

Harvath smiled and turned to follow Staelin back to the SUV. As he was walking away, Gage imitated a goat and sang, "You give love a baaaaad name."

Back at the Land Cruiser, he spoke with Barton and Morrison. They both agreed with the plan, especially in light of the fuel situation. Neither wanted to court trouble, but they couldn't see a way around it either. All things considered, it seemed worth the risk.

Climbing back into the vehicle, Harvath double-checked his map and after a final check with the drone team that their ruse had worked and the sparkle was leading the militia vehicles away, he gave the order to get moving.

This was either going to be one of his best or one of his worst ideas ever. Only time would tell.

As Staelin got back onto the road and started rolling, Harvath looked at his watch. There wasn't much darkness left.

Quietly, he said a little prayer. All he asked was that they be allowed to get back to the safe house without any problems.

But something had attached itself to his vehicle. A little something called *Murphy*.

CHAPTER 30

Zelten was cut in half by the east–west road that ran to the border with Tunisia. The most densely populated neighborhoods were south of the road, and as luck would have it, that was the direction from which Harvath and his team were approaching. The road they needed to get to, which would take them to the coast, was on the north side of town.

The fastest and most direct route would have been to travel right through the center of Zelten. It would have also drawn the most attention. The dawn prayer, known as the Fajr, was only an hour away. There were going to be people making their way to local mosques.

Harvath decided to trade a little expediency for some added safety. They would loop around the west side of town to avoid as much as possible.

The road system, though, was medieval. Narrow, dusty streets sometimes ran for only a couple of blocks before looping back on themselves or dead-ending. It reminded Harvath of the maze of streets on the Greek island of Mykonos designed to disorient pirates. It was going to be a nightmare getting through.

They took their NVGs off and turned their headlights on. With their keffiyehs helping to disguise them, they moved quickly around the southern edge of the town.

If Zelten was a watch face, they were at about the eight-o'clock position when Haney radioed that they had someone on their tail.

"Everyone stay cool," said Harvath as he instructed Staelin to make the next right turn. "Let's see if this is for real."

The Land Cruiser made the turn, followed by the technical. It was one of the neighborhoods Harvath had wanted to avoid.

The houses, pockmarked and scarred from fighting during the revolution, were packed tightly together. Some were in better shape than others.

Parked cars lined the street. Electric lines were strung from one building to the next. There was no movement. It was quiet. *Very* quiet.

"He's still behind us," said Haney.

"Roger that," Harvath replied. Turning to Staelin, he said, "Take the next right."

The Delta Force operative obeyed and they headed down another crowded block of homes.

"How are we looking now, Haney?" Harvath asked, as he tried to get a good view with his side mirror.

"Not good. Still on my six."

Pointing out the windshield, Harvath told Staelin, "Take this next turn up ahead," and repeated the same to Haney over the radio.

"Roger that," they both replied.

As soon as they had made the turn, Harvath said, "Now floor it."

The big SUV's engine roared as it rocketed down the street—this one paved and complete with intermittent streetlights. Looking in his side mirror, he was finally able to see the vehicle tailing Haney. It was another technical.

Either this guy had just gotten lucky or somewhere someone had spotted them and had called it in. It didn't make a difference now. They needed to lose him.

"Three o'clock," Barton exclaimed from the backseat.

Harvath swiveled his head to the right. Paralleling them one road over was an additional technical. *Fuck.* "Make sure they don't box us in," he told Staelin.

The Delta Force operative nodded. "What do you want to do?"

He wanted to get the hell out of there, but with two tails and more likely inbound, that was impossible. He had to come up with an alternative plan, fast.

Keying up his radio, he announced to Staelin and Haney, "Left turn up ahead. Then the second right."

When the men acknowledged the directions, Harvath turned to Barton. "Hand me that Russian grenade launcher."

Once he did, Harvath double-checked to make sure it was loaded and then told everyone what he was going to do.

Suddenly, there was the crack of gunfire from behind. The militia was shooting at them.

"Contact rear! Contact rear!" Gage shouted over the radio, as he turned in his seat and began firing through the shattered rear window of their pickup.

"Don't slow down," Harvath ordered his team. "Left, then second right."

Arriving at the left turn, everyone braced as Staelin pulled the wheel hard. The tires screamed as the heavy SUV spun around the corner.

"Push it! Push it!" Harvath urged, and Staelin gave the Land Cruiser even more gas.

They had to be doing at least eighty. Next to them building facades whipped by. Then, an intersection. Had a car been passing through at the same time, it would have been a coffin-measuring festival.

There was a blur of more buildings and finally the next road.

"Right turn. Right turn," he announced.

Staelin applied the brakes, but only enough so as not to lose control in the turn. As soon as he was through it, he slammed the gas. Up ahead was their target—an Islamic cemetery.

"Get ready to jump," said Staelin.

Making sure his gear was secure, Harvath cracked open his door and then nodded.

When they reached it, Staelin slammed on the brakes and yelled, "Go! Go!"

Harvath hadn't even hit the ground before the Delta Force operative had once again put the pedal to the floor.

Jumping from a moving vehicle, even one that had just slammed on its brakes, was an invitation for a serious injury. It became an engraved invitation when you did it in the dark. As he hit the ground, Harvath rolled, and kept on rolling, until all his momentum was dissipated.

In Islam, the deceased are buried in a shroud and placed on their right side without a coffin, facing the Kaaba in Mecca. A small grave marker is used—usually less than twelve inches high.

Getting to his feet, he ran for the only cover available, a small row of date palms.

But Harvath hadn't come to the cemetery to hide—at least not totally. He had come to take out the two technicals that were following his team.

By the time he reached the trees, Haney had already raced by. Now came the gray pickup that was chasing him, with its heavy machine gun mounted in the back. A militia member with an AK-47 was leaning out the front passenger window, firing.

He had no idea where the second technical was, but it had to be close. Without wasting any more time, Harvath ran for the other side of the cemetery.

At the corner of the property was an intersection where three roads came together. It would give Staelin and Haney a greater opportunity to bring the technicals into his crosshairs.

As Harvath ran, he hailed the drone team and told them to get the Reaper back over his location. Killing the sparkle, they turned it around and set it on a heading for Zelten.

In the distance, Harvath could hear sporadic gunfire. "Haney," he demanded over his radio. "SITREP."

It took a moment for the Marine to reply. "Three blocks out," he finally yelled. "Still taking fire."

Switching his attention to the other vehicle, he said, "Staelin. SITREP."

"Four blocks away. No sign of—" the Delta Force operative began.

He was interrupted by Morrison. "Contact left! Contact left!"

From their direction, Harvath could hear another barrage of gunfire. He broke into a sprint.

At the edge of the cemetery was a rock the size of a Dumpster. What its significance was, or what it was doing there, was beyond him. All he knew was that it had an unimpeded view of the intersection and provided a perfect place to set up shop.

As he reached it, he relayed to the team that he was in place and ready for them to draw their tails into the kill zone.

"Coming in hot!" Haney immediately replied. "From the west."

"Roger that," Harvath answered, as he unfolded the grenade launcher's stock and flipped up its rear sight. Shouldering the weapon, he disengaged the safety, and positioned himself against the rock.

"Thirty seconds," Haney said over the radio.

Harvath took one last look around the area to make sure no one was sneaking up on him, and then made ready to fire. "Bring it."

The sound of gunfire got louder as Haney and his pursuer got closer to the intersection.

Soon enough, Harvath could see him flashing his high beams. The next thing he knew, Haney was in the middle of the intersection, and his truck had been sent into a spin.

It was at that moment that time seemed to slow down.

CHAPTER 31

It was called a bootleg turn. Dropping into second gear, Haney gave the wheel a quick jerk to the right, and then spun the wheel all the way to the left.

As Haney's vehicle fishtailed into a 180-degree turn, the men behind him had no idea what was going on.

Gage, who had already inserted his third fresh magazine into his M4, opened up full auto on the cab of the other vehicle. The rounds punched holes through the sheet metal and shattered the rest of the glass.

Both vehicles came to a stop, facing each other, fifteen feet apart in the middle of the intersection.

"Any time, Harvath," Haney said over the radio. Throwing his vehicle in reverse, he began backing out of the intersection as fast as he could.

Harvath's grenade launcher was loaded with high-explosive thermobaric rounds, which produced little to no shrapnel. Nevertheless, the minimum safe distance from detonation was thirty feet. As soon as Haney got to twenty-five, Harvath warned, "Going hot," pressed the trigger, and let it rip.

The fuse on a thermobaric round armed itself three meters after leaving the launcher's muzzle. In this situation, there was plenty of time for it to arm before hitting its target. Except for one thing—Harvath's aim had been off.

It wasn't like shooting a rifle. It was more like lofting a tennis ball the length of a long swimming pool and trying to land it in a wastebasket.

The round sailed over the militia technical and detonated in front of a building on the other side of the intersection.

"Damn it!" he cursed. Racking the weapon, he loaded another round and readjusted.

Before he could press the trigger a second time, the driver of the militia vehicle had already popped the clutch and was squealing his tires. Harvath fired anyway.

This round was on the money. It took off in a high arc from the cemetery and landed squarely in the bed of the militia technical.

It exploded hot and bright, melting the pickup truck's frame, killing all four people inside, and cooking off all of their ammunition.

Over the radio, Harvath could hear Haney and Gage cheering. But nearby, he could also hear the sound of automatic weapons fire.

Slinging the grenade launcher, he transitioned to his M4 and ran for Haney's technical.

As he ran, he scanned for threats and hailed Staelin. "Tyler, give me a SITREP."

The Delta Force operative's transmission crackled in and out and came in pieces. "Vehicle inoperable . . . Four tangos . . . Returning fire . . . One prisoner KIA."

One prisoner KIA? "Fuck," said Harvath as he increased his speed. When he got to Haney's pickup, he didn't bother climbing into the cab. Leaping into the bed, he pounded on the side and yelled through the broken rear window, "Move! Move!" as Haney peeled out.

Harvath had no intention of losing anyone from his team. He had to go in and pull them out before things got any worse.

The Reaper pilot didn't need to tell him a swarm of militia members were already headed their way. He knew it just as surely as he knew the sun would soon be up. Too much had gone sideways. They needed to regain the initiative.

"Corner!" yelled Haney. "Hold on."

Harvath did as he was told.

Haney hit the turn so hard, Harvath was almost thrown from the truck.

"Where the hell are you guys?" Staelin yelled over the radio.

"Inbound hot," Harvath replied. "Less than sixty seconds out. Coming in east of your position. Hang in there."

All of a sudden, he heard thunder. Except he knew it wasn't thunder. The militia technical had opened up its powerful .50 caliber machine gun.

Harvath didn't need to tell Haney to hurry. He'd heard it too. Dropping the hammer, he pushed the pickup as hard as it would go.

Thirty seconds later, Harvath pounded on the cab and yelled for Haney to stop. He had just caught a glimpse of the militia vehicle.

Jumping out of the bed of the truck, he yanked open the rear door and grabbed the RPG launcher from the backseat. As he loaded a grenade, he hailed Staelin over the radio. "RPG incoming. Take cover. *Now.*"

Running back to where he had seen the technical, he mounted the weapon, took a knee, and after checking his back blast area, sighted in his target.

The flashes from the monster .50 cal machine gun as it spat its rounds looked like lightning.

"Smoke-check that motherfucker!" Staelin shouted over the radio. "If you don't, we're dead!"

Harvath didn't wait. Pressing the trigger, he sent the 93 mm, single-stage HEAT warhead sizzling toward its target.

The militia member firing the machine gun never saw it coming. The grenade hit the technical, and it exploded in an enormous fireball.

Flaming pieces of wreckage littered the street, and a hail of razor-sharp shrapnel rained down as Harvath leapt back into Haney's truck. "Let's go!" he ordered.

A block down, Haney turned to the left. There was still the sound of sporadic gunfire.

He drove as close to it as he dared, then Harvath and Gage hopped out and moved to the battle on foot.

Locals peered out windows or stood in doorways to watch what was happening. When they saw the Americans, some retreated inside. Many simply stayed in place, as if rolling gunfights happened every day in their neighborhood.

As they neared the corner, Harvath asked for one more SITREP. Staelin radioed that there were two militia members remaining and gave their location. They had gotten onto the roof of a house. Every time Staelin and his team tried to move, the militia showered them with rounds. Harvath ordered him to sit tight.

When he and Gage got to the corner, he radioed Staelin and then counted down from three.

On cue, Staelin drew out the snipers.

As soon as the militiamen popped up, Gage stepped out from around the corner and, with Harvath covering him, shot them both.

But the moment Gage had gotten his rounds off, another sniper materialized in the window of a different building and fired.

The bullet entered the back of Gage's left shoulder. "Fuck!" he cursed, as Harvath grabbed him by his vest and yanked him back around the corner.

Harvath radioed everyone that there was a third sniper and for Staelin and his team to stay put.

"Where the hell did that guy come from?" Gage asked through gritted teeth.

"Second-story window across the street," Harvath replied. He hadn't seen the shooter until the flash had erupted from the end of his muzzle, and by then it was too late. "Can you still fight?"

Gage nodded.

Slinging his rifle, Harvath transitioned to the Russian grenade launcher and racked it, loading his last thermobaric round. "Just pin him down long enough for me to get off my shot."

"A hundred bucks says you'll miss."

Harvath shook his head and then pointed forward, signaling that he was ready to go.

Gage was in rough shape. He had trouble supporting his rifle with his left arm. It took him significant effort to raise it high enough. Finally, he signaled that he was ready.

Together, the two men swung out into the street. Gage peppered the building's second-floor windows with rounds from his M4. Harvath brought the pump-action grenade launcher up, sighted in the window, and fired.

The shot was perfect. It sailed right into the room where the sniper had been and detonated in a blinding explosion.

Glass, timber, and pieces of concrete erupted out onto the street. A pillar of thick, black smoke rose into the air.

"Time to go," Harvath said, as he transitioned back to his rifle, scanned for more threats, and began issuing orders over the radio.

He was relieved to see Staelin, along with Barton and Morrison, moving Umar Ali Halim quickly down the street. It must have been the little Libyan, the one who had ratted them out back at the compound, who had gotten killed in the exchange of gunfire.

Just beyond them, Harvath could make out their Land Cruiser riddled with bullet holes. The night sky was beginning to give way to morning. They needed to get moving.

Haney quickly backed the technical down the street to pick everyone up. It was a double cab designed to hold five people, but that was going to be pushing it for a team of men in tactical gear. With six shooters, plus a hostage, someone was going to have to ride in the back. Harvath and Barton both offered to do it.

Once they had all been loaded, Haney peeled out and began speeding them out of town.

As Staelin helped Gage pack his wound with hemostatic gauze up front, a call came for Harvath over the radio.

It was the drone team. They had good news, but they also had bad news.

The good news was that they were back overhead. The bad news was that an army of Libya Liberation Front members was headed right at them.

CHAPTER 32

"How many and from what direction?" Harvath asked.

"There's a three-vehicle convoy including one technical west of you out of Abu Kammash," the drone team leader stated. "A five-vehicle convoy is to your east from the port at Zuwara with two technicals. Finally, there's a seven-vehicle convoy approaching from your south. That one has four technicals, two of which are mounted with antiaircraft guns."

Shit. "How far out are they?"

"The convoy from Abu Kammash is a little over ten klicks out. The others are closer to twenty."

That was way too close as far as Harvath was concerned. They'd never be able to outrun them. Not with the piece-of-shit truck they were driving. And definitely not when it was loaded down with six shooters, two of whom were riding in the bed, all their gear, plus a hostage.

"I'll let you guys call it, but my preference is that you take out the Abu Kammash convoy first," said Harvath.

"Negative. We're not authorized to target Libyan militias."

"You've got to be kidding me. What do you mean you're not free to target Libyan militias?"

"Our agreement with the Tunisians is that airstrikes are only authorized when targeting Islamic militants."

Fucking politics. "Let me talk to your senior."

"I am the senior. In fact I specifically requested this op to make sure you guys got everything you needed."

"I appreciate that, but what I need right now is some CAS," Harvath replied, using the acronym for close air support.

"Don't worry," the drone team leader replied. "We're going to help navigate you out of this."

Harvath was worried. "What other armed assets do we have in the air that didn't launch from Tunisia?" he asked.

"There's another Reaper, west of Benghazi. But it launched from U.S. Naval Air Station Sigonella on Sicily."

"So what? How quick can we get it on station here?"

"Per our agreement with the Italians, only non-Libyans can be targeted in drone strikes launched from Sigonella."

The world had lost its mind. "The Tunisians and the Italians realize that the Libya Liberation Front is allied with Ansar al-Sharia, which in turn is linked to Al Qaeda, right?"

"Sorry, sir, I don't make the rules."

"Are there any U.S. Navy ships in the Mediterranean right now operating drones?"

"Yes, sir, but none that will be able to get an asset on station for you quickly enough."

"Give me the name of the nearest vessel."

The drone team leader confirmed his information and then replied, "It's the Nimitz-class supercarrier, the USS *George H. W. Bush.*"

Now they were getting somewhere. "Stand by," said Harvath as he pulled out his satellite phone and dialed the cell phone of the Director of Central Intelligence.

Back in the United States, it was just past eleven o'clock at night. Bob McGee answered on the third ring.

"Sorry to wake you," said Harvath. "I need you to make a phone call for me, fast."

He gave the DCI the details and secured his promise to cut out the U.S. Ambassador to Libya, as well as the Defense Attaché, even though that was protocol. They'd only get in the way.

Within sixty seconds of hanging up, McGee had the Secretary of Defense on the phone. The SecDef personally called the Commander of the Sixth Fleet, who conferenced in the Commander of Carrier Strike Group Two, which was responsible for the USS *George H. W. Bush*. Once they were all on the line, McGee explained the situation and what they needed.

Five minutes later, a phone rang at the Tunisian air base from which the Reaper tracking Harvath and his team was being piloted.

After authenticating the caller and listening to the Pentagon's instructions, the drone team commander replied, "Roger that. Right away."

Relaying the command to the drone pilot, he then turned to his Tunisian liaison and stated, "This drone is being removed from inventory and will not be returning to Tunisian soil. We're handing over control to the USS *George H. W. Bush*."

Within seconds, the drone banked and headed out to sea. As it did, Harvath's satellite phone vibrated. It was McGee.

"As soon as Strike Group Two has control of the drone, video to the base in Tunisia will be cut. They know what's going on, but it gives them cover. Once the drone gets beyond Libya's territorial waters, they're off the hook."

"But that's twelve nautical miles," Harvath replied, as he stared out from the back of the technical, expecting to see militia members behind them at any moment. "We don't have that long."

"Strike Group Two isn't going the full twelve. The second the handoff is complete, they're sending it back to you. In the meantime, you've got to figure something out, because you are on your own."

Harvath acknowledged the Director's update, made one more request, and then disconnected the call.

They were approaching the north side of Zelten now. With every building they passed, he saw people in windows and on rooftops—most of them with cell phones. *Not good.*

There was no question in his mind that the team's location and heading was being relayed back to the Libya Liberation Front.

Harvath wasn't one for ducking a fight, but he was a big believer that discretion was always the better part of valor. Gage was already injured. He didn't want to risk more injuries, or worse, if he didn't have to.

If they could make it out of town and into the sparsely populated area between Zelten and the coast, they might be able to find a place to hole up and avoid the Libya Liberation Front all together.

But without the drone monitoring the militia's progress, there was no telling how much time they had. If they were going to pull off and hide, they'd have to do it soon.

Getting on the radio, he relayed to the team what he wanted them to be on the lookout for.

Minutes later, he could see Zelten receding. So far, there were no vehicles approaching.

As the area's small farms grew farther and farther apart, Haney's voice came over the radio. Up ahead, he could see a small cluster of buildings surrounded by a low wall.

Harvath told him to head for it. He had a feeling those buildings might be their best, and only, opportunity for survival.

CHAPTER 33

Tursunov had eaten dinner in a small Moroccan restaurant near Notre Dame along the rue Xavier. It had come recommended by Abdel and was close to the last stop he needed to make before turning in for the night.

Walking up to the Pont Royal, he crossed the Seine and entered the enormous formal garden created by Catherine de Medici known as the Jardin des Tuileries.

Rolling out like a giant green welcome mat that stretched from the Louvre Museum to the Place de la Concorde, it was one of the most popular places in all of Paris to gather, stroll, and relax.

Statues by Giacometti, Maillol, and Rodin adorned the manicured grounds and crushed gravel walkways. It boasted two giant fountains. One of which—much like the cathedral in Santiago—had drawn his attention for a very special reason.

ISIS despised the French. They despised them for being the European embodiment of everything they saw was wrong with the West. The French were arrogant, libertine hypocrites who had outlawed all face covering, including niqabs and burkas.

The French not only pretended to desire Western ideals like democracy, free speech, and human rights, but they actively sought to impose them on the Islamic world through force. If that required dropping bombs on and killing Muslim people, the French were more than happy to do it.

ISIS had set its sights on France and was determined to attack it repeatedly. Tursunov had been told that they didn't care where he struck, as long as he was successful.

He knew they preferred that he strike Paris. It was the heart of the nation. And any successful attack there had the added benefit of not only damaging the French psyche, but also killing plenty of Western tourists, and thereby helping to damage the economy.

Very few would want to visit a city, or a nation for that matter, besieged by terrorism.

Paris presented the additional benefit of being awash with strangers. He could wander. He could linger. He could study the ebb and flow of people. He could take photographs. None of it would attract undue attention.

That had been important when selecting the Tuileries for his attack. But just as important had been an added, personal piece of symbolism.

His Sufi mother believed that symbolism was a reflection of the Divine and that numerology was one of its forms. The Holy Qur'an, when explored through the lens of numerology, contained incredible revelations—the atomic number for iron, earth's ratio of land to sea, the genetic code of the bee.

But one of its most fascinating revelations—made more than a thousand years before it would happen—was the date of man's lunar landing.

She had imbued in him a sense of awe and, most important, of respect for how Allah's hand guided all things.

It was this awe and wonder that had brought him to Paris, and specifically to the Tuileries.

Of the things he was most certain of, there was nothing greater than his certitude in the truth of his Muslim faith. His belief was consistently fortified by the wickedness and ignorance of the non-Muslim infidel.

A prime example was their devotion to the idea that the number 666 was somehow evil.

In their book, the "mark of the beast" was described as "six hundred threescore and six" or 666, but "six hundred threescore and six" was also the number of gold talents delivered to King Solomon in one year. Certainly they didn't believe Solomon to be the beast.

Yet, they never seemed to take their reasoning that far. They seemed content to accept 666 as evil and leave it at that. But the number wasn't evil. In fact, it was actually divine, and he considered it Allah's signature.

There was a host of reasons why. The angle between the North Pole and the plane on which the earth traveled around the sun was 66.6 degrees. The Tropic of Cancer was 66.6 degrees from the North Pole. The Tropic of Capricorn was 66.6 degrees from the South Pole. The Equator was 66.6 degrees from both the Arctic and Antarctic circles. The earth's average orbital speed was 66,666 miles per hour.

And as if he needed even more proof of Allah's design, the Dome of the Rock in Jerusalem, where the Prophet Mohammed ascended into heaven, was 666 miles from the Kaaba in Mecca.

Allah's signature was everywhere, and he always strove to let it guide him. That was why he had chosen the Tuileries. Not only was it popular and packed with people, but its round fountain was exactly 666 miles from the center of the Cathedral of Santiago de Compostela in Spain. Allah had sent him a message.

Reaching the fountain, he turned and looked to his east. Beyond the Place du Carrousel, he could see the Louvre's great glass pyramid. It was constructed of 666 rhombi and sat exactly 666 miles from the pilgrimage sanctuary of Lourdes. Turning to his west, he could see the Luxor obelisk 666 meters away at the Place de la Concorde. This was indeed willed by God.

Walking around the fountain, he made his way toward the rue de Rivoli and the Terrasse des Feuillants. Here, running for several blocks along the edge of the park, was the Fête des Tuileries.

The Parisian carnival had bumper cars, giant slides, trampolines, climbing walls, carousels, shooting galleries, a Ferris wheel, ice cream, doughnuts, crêpes, cotton candy, and even candy apples. It was popular with tourists and locals alike.

Tursunov had visited on multiple occasions. He wanted to make sure he chose the absolute perfect moment.

As he strolled through the crowded fairground, he smiled and whispered to himself, *"Allahu Akbar." God is the greatest.*

CHAPTER 34

The next morning, Tursunov rose well before dawn and said his prayers. After a quick round of calisthenics, he showered, shaved, and put on a set of fresh clothes.

Leaving the hotel, he passed by his café, but it was closed. He had to walk three more blocks before he found something that was open.

He ordered several shots of espresso to go, doubled up on the paper cup, and grabbed a free weekly magazine on his way out the door.

Outside, he lit his second cigarette as he headed toward the Metro. Abdel's nephew, the chemist, lived in Aubervilliers—a predominantly French-Arab suburb northeast of Paris. He wanted to ascertain for himself whether the young man was under surveillance.

Abdel had provided him with Younes's picture, address, and information about the mosque he attended. Under strict instruction, he did not let his nephew know that the man would be paying him a visit. Tursunov didn't want the chemist looking over his shoulder. If he were under surveillance, any unusual behavior would only heighten the suspicion of those who were watching him.

Arriving in Aubervilliers, he exited the station and started walking. It was a town that had seen better days.

The architecture at its center resembled that of any number of Parisian neighborhoods, but any similarity to the City of Light ended there.

Aubervilliers was dark. Its inhabitants were rough, its shops and restaurants down-market. The streets were dirty. Graffiti was everywhere.

Surrounding the town were ugly, concrete apartment complexes, built in the 1960s and '70s. Here, as in many of the suburbs, Paris hid its poor—particularly its immigrants.

Many of the immigrants were happy to have escaped the grinding poverty and hopelessness of their home countries. They had come in the same decades the ugly apartment complexes were built, grateful for the opportunity for a new life.

They gladly accepted the jobs most French didn't want to take—street sweeping, sewer work, menial labor jobs. This wave of immigrants, the bulk of which came from Muslim North Africa, appreciated how much better things were for them and their families in France.

They had hope for the future. Not only for themselves, but even more so for their children. *Liberté, égalité, fraternité* wasn't just a motto. It was a promise.

They believed that in France their children would experience more opportunity and achieve more than they could ever imagine. Their children wouldn't be Moroccans or Algerians. They would be free French men and women with all of the benefits thereof. Unfortunately, that wasn't how things turned out.

The immigrants' children found themselves with one foot in the old world and one in the new. Though born, raised, and educated in France, they were seen as outsiders and not fully welcome in French society.

While some pushed for greater access, others retreated into ethnic pockets outside the city, marginalizing themselves and their voices.

Without access to avenues of upward mobility, many angry young men turned to violence and criminal activity. Others turned to Islam.

With more than 70 percent of its citizens followers of the faith, Aubervilliers was often referred to as a "Muslim city."

It also had a reputation for being dangerous. There were certain areas in town that even police officers wouldn't enter without substantial backup.

Tursunov was wary of all these issues as he made his way to Younes's mosque.

Using a sophisticated system for surfing the web anonymously, he had studied Google Street View images of the area around the mosque.

It had been set up on a busy road in an old retail space that looked to be a former beauty salon. Across the street was a small café.

After familiarizing himself with the neighborhood, Tursunov entered the café and took a table near the window. It smelled like newspaper ink and dark roast coffee.

Once he had ordered breakfast, he opened up the weekly he'd picked up earlier and pretended to read as he watched the comings and goings at the mosque.

If French authorities were conducting surveillance, they were being very careful about it.

Though there could have been cameras in any of the upper-floor apartments along the street, there was nothing overt. Every person who passed by looked as if he or she belonged in the neighborhood. None of them stood out. None of them screamed "cop."

Having served as both himself, he could usually spot military or law enforcement personnel the moment he saw them. There was something not only about their bearing, but also about their eyes. They were always moving, always taking everything in. It wasn't normal.

Normal, everyday people were unobservant. Only those used to dealing with danger, or those expecting trouble, continuously swept their gaze from side to side. They were always searching for anything that seemed out of place or that might be a warning something bad was about to happen. It was a habit born of close calls and hard-won experience.

As the sunrise prayer service ended, Tursunov paid his bill and stepped outside to have a cigarette. As he lit the Gauloise, he leaned against the building and watched as the mosque emptied out.

There weren't many attendees—twenty at most. As the men reached the sidewalk, some lingered, but most said their good-byes and were on their way. There were still no signs of any surveillance that he could detect.

Tursunov watched as the last of the men exited the small storefront. He was concerned that Younes might have chosen to skip prayers that morning. Then he finally saw him in the doorway.

He and two other men were saying good-bye to an older man with a thick, gray beard who must have been the Imam.

The Tajik was struck by how much Younes looked like his father. Tall, the same intelligent eyes, the same broad nose. The resemblance was uncanny. The photo Abdel provided hadn't done him justice.

Younes and the two other young men embraced the Imam, stepped onto the pavement, and went their separate ways. Tursunov pretended not to be paying attention and continued to smoke his cigarette. He wanted to give any surveillance the opportunity to fall in behind the young chemist.

Once he felt he had allowed enough time, he flicked his butt into the street and headed off in the same direction.

He was careful to stay back and on the opposite side of the street. He didn't want to crowd anyone.

Two blocks away from the mosque, he was beginning to feel confident that the chemist wasn't being followed. But then a figure appeared from around the corner.

It was a man. He was dark-skinned and dressed like many of the men he had seen in Aubervilliers. On the surface, there was nothing to suggest anything out of the ordinary. There was something about him, though, that radiated *police*. He could sense it, even though the man was so far up ahead of him.

Younes must have sensed it as well, because at one point he turned around and looked back. Shortly thereafter, the dark-skinned man turned the corner and broke off. A block later, he was replaced by another cop. *The chemist was definitely under surveillance.*

That complicated things. *Enormously.*

The Tajik had to assume that in addition to following the young man, the French authorities were also listening in on his calls and reading his emails. They might have even bugged his apartment.

The big question was *why?* What had Younes done to draw such attention? Abdel claimed that he was clean, that he had not been involved with plotting any sort of jihadism. Was he correct?

Tursunov wondered if the answer might lie with the second cop on the surveillance team. He was lighter-skinned, with longer hair and a goatee. He could have passed for an Arab, but there was something else about him—something that gave Tursunov pause.

Making a right at the next corner, he broke off his pursuit and doubled back toward the Metro. He would wait until it was dark and come back then.

CHAPTER 35

The cluster of sand-colored, one-story buildings was just off the road. They were abandoned and in an advanced state of disrepair. In multiple places, the three-foot-high stone wall surrounding the property had crumbled.

Harvath, Barton, Staelin, and Morrison hopped out of the truck to quickly clear the structures. Once they were confident no one was there, they helped Gage climb out and directed Haney around back.

A thatched roof over a long covered patio had partially collapsed. Moving some of the refuse beneath it, they were able to make enough room to park the technical. Then they rapidly piled up garbage around it.

It wasn't the perfect camouflage job, but considering the circumstances, it would have to do.

Of the three buildings, the one to the north was the most secure. It had the thickest walls and an interior access to the roof.

After hustling the weapons and ammunition in from the truck, Harvath grabbed a length of tattered blue tarp from the pile of junk and climbed up to the roof.

It was flat and surrounded by a low parapet. In several places, pieces were missing. Whether that was by design or through neglect, the holes provided good spots for him to observe the road without being seen.

Crawling over to one, he raised a small pair of binoculars and peered out. There were no signs of any approaching vehicles.

Over his shoulder, the sun had cleared the horizon and was beginning its slow crawl into the morning sky.

Activating his satellite phone, he extended its antenna and waited impatiently for it to acquire a signal. Once it did, he sent a text back to Langley with his exact GPS coordinates.

Next, he punctured the blue plastic tarp with his knife and cut it in half lengthwise. Then, using pieces of concrete block to hold it down, he fashioned a large blue plus sign in the center of the roof.

Between that and the GPS coordinates, the drone should be able to pinpoint their location.

They had risked a tremendous amount in snatching the smuggler. If he didn't help them connect any dots regarding the drowned chemistry student and the impending attacks, Harvath was going to put a bullet right between his eyes.

Hearing something behind him, he turned to see Haney with the remaining rocket and RPG launcher. "Everything good downstairs?" he asked.

The Marine nodded as he set the gear down and joined him. "Gage is stable. Staelin tried to give him something for the pain, but Gage told him to fuck off. Says he can't fight if he's high."

Harvath smiled.

"Halim is also stable," Haney continued, "but in a lot of pain. Gage told him to fuck off too."

Harvath smiled again. "What about Barton and Morrison?"

"I've got Barton on the roof of the south building. Morrison is inside the one in the middle. In addition to their own weapons, they each took an AK and extra ammo."

No matter what needed doing, Haney was always on top of it. He was about to thank him when his satellite phone vibrated. It was a text from Langley.

"What's up?" Haney asked.

"Remember the Glocks the militia members were carrying at the electronics shop?"

The Marine nodded.

"I emailed the serial numbers to the Agency. DOD finally tracked the paperwork down. They were stolen from Camp 27."

"The Special Forces training base outside Tripoli?"

"Yup," said Harvath. "The one that got looted."

"Uncle Sam doesn't like when you steal from him."

"No, he doesn't. In fact, he gets very—"

Harvath was suddenly quiet. Picking the binoculars back up, he looked out through the hole in the parapet again. A multivehicle convoy was headed their way from Zelten. Keying up his radio, he notified the team.

Before he could tell Haney to head back downstairs, the Marine was already on his way.

Raising Strike Force Two's drone team on the USS *George H. W. Bush*, he updated them and asked, "What's the ETA on that Reaper?"

"There's been some complication with the handoff."

"We need that drone ASAP," Harvath replied.

"We're working on it. Stand by."

He wanted to tell them to hurry the hell up. Instead, he confirmed the transmission and told his team, "Weapons hot, but nobody shoots. Only if we absolutely have to."

They all hoped that the militia would just pass right by, but that wasn't the kind of day they'd been having.

The prior drone team had counted fifteen vehicles vectoring in on them. If there were four men in each, that could mean up to sixty fighters. Maybe more.

As the column got closer, Harvath counted ten vehicles. Half of them were technicals.

Of those, two were mounted with the massive antiaircraft guns he'd been warned about.

It looked like the convoy from Abu Kammash had linked up with the convoy pursuing them out of the south.

Keep going, Harvath said to himself, nodding his head down the road. *Nothing to see here.*

As the convoy rolled closer to their location, every muscle in his body tensed and adrenaline coursed through his veins. He was like a coiled snake, ready to strike.

Taking a deep breath, he willed himself to relax. Slowly, he got his heart rate under control. The SEAL mantra, *Slow is smooth and smooth is fast*, popped up from somewhere deep in his mind. *Be calm. Don't rush*, he reminded himself as he began to depress the trigger of his M4.

Near the entrance of the derelict compound, the convoy slowed. Fighters in the lead vehicle seemed to be trying to decide whether it was worth their time to check it out.

He could see the antiaircraft guns clearly now. If they were turned on the compound, they'd chew through it like a fat man going through a box of Thin Mints.

The militia must have decided the buildings weren't worth it as they picked up speed once again and proceeded past.

Harvath kept his finger on his trigger and followed the convoy with the suppressor on the end of his rifle. He didn't even take a breath until the last vehicle had gone by.

Once it had driven down the road, he radioed his team and said, "We're clear."

A feeling of relief washed over him as he set his rifle down and unkinked his neck. For a moment, he allowed his eyes to close. He was beginning to think that they just might make it out of this after all.

Then he heard Barton's voice over the radio. "Second convoy inbound," the SEAL said.

Opening his eyes, Harvath snatched up his rifle and looked. He already knew how many vehicles there'd be. He didn't need to count. Based on the math, this had to be the remaining five—including two technicals.

As they neared, he saw that he was right. It wasn't much consolation. The moment they pulled even with the compound, the two technicals came to a stop on either side of the entrance, turned on an angle to block traffic, and took up firing positions.

The other three vehicles were SUVs. One stayed outside the compound, a little farther down the road, while the other two slowly rolled inside and stopped. They were here to search the property. *Fuck*.

Harvath took a deep breath, exhaled slowly, and began applying pressure to his trigger once again.

CHAPTER 36

The militia members didn't seem keen to get out of their SUVs. Rolling their windows down, they pointed their guns out and waited. They were so close and the desert so quiet that he could hear them whispering to each other in Arabic.

Finally, one door opened. Then another. Out on the road, fighters had already climbed into the beds of the technicals, chambered the heavy machine guns, and pointed them at the buildings.

Harvath focused on the closest technical to him. Barton would take the other. Haney, Staelin, and Morrison would handle the men on the ground inside the compound.

There was still time for them to get back inside their vehicles and drive away. He knew, though, that they wouldn't.

There were eight of them. Slowly, they began to walk away from the SUVs and toward the buildings. That's when Haney gave the command to light them up.

As soon as they heard the word "Now" over the radio, the entire team began firing.

Harvath dropped the machine-gunner first, and then locked in on the ammo feeder standing in the truck bed next to him. He caught the man in the lower back as he was diving out and then lost sight of him.

Adjusting his rifle, he turned his attention to the windshield of the technical and pumped the cab full of hot lead.

Both the driver and passenger had been trying to get out and now fell to the ground dead.

When the ammo feeder popped his head up at the rear of the vehicle, Harvath was ready for him.

Pressing the trigger of his M4, he sent a round through his skull, just above his left eyebrow. There was a spray of blood across the tailgate as the man fell dead.

Sweeping his rifle toward the other technical, he saw Barton had already taken out its crew and had focused on a new target.

Out on the road, the remaining SUV was trying to make a run for it. Harvath added his rifle to the fight, sending round after round into the vehicle.

From downstairs, a round from Gage's M4 ripped through the air and entered the rear passenger side window, tearing through the back of the driver's head.

The fighter was killed instantly.

With no one controlling it, the SUV caught its tire as it veered off the side of the road and flipped over.

A fraction of a second later, Gage could be heard on the radio, "Enjoy the virgins, you assholes!"

Harvath and Barton remained on their rooftops to provide overwatch while Haney and Morrison patrolled out to the road to make sure there were no survivors.

They had checked the bodies around both technicals and were halfway to the overturned SUV when Harvath thought he noticed something in the distance. Raising the binoculars, he saw a string of militia vehicles coming back from the other direction.

And even at this distance, he could tell that two of them were the technicals with the antiaircraft guns mounted in back. The fleeing militiamen must have raised the alarm before Gage shot their driver and their SUV flipped.

Grabbing the RPG, he radioed for Haney and Morrison to get back to the compound as fast as they could.

His next transmission was to the USS *George H. W. Bush*. "Where the hell is my drone?"

"Ten minutes out," a voice responded. "Max."

"There's a convoy of technicals headed right at us. Two with ZU-2 antiaircraft guns. This is going to be over in less than five if you don't get that drone here *now*."

Ending the transmission, Harvath had a decision to make. The RPG-7 had a maximum effective range of five hundred meters. But that was for stationary targets. If the target was moving, the range was cut down to three hundred meters.

Once he fired, they'd know exactly where he was and where to shoot. Looking at the militia vehicles down in the compound and shot up out on the road, he came up with a plan.

It wasn't a great plan, but given how rapidly things were deteriorating, it was the best he had.

As Morrison and Haney came running back, Harvath had them stop at the bullet-ridden technicals only long enough to grab what they needed.

Barton leapt down from his roof and helped Staelin secure Halim in the bigger of the two SUVs. Morrison hopped into the smaller one and fired it up. Haney then brought their technical out of hiding and parked it alongside the rear of the far building.

When everyone was loaded, Harvath didn't waste any time. "Let's go!" he shouted, pounding on the sides of both SUVs. "Move! Move! Move!"

The vehicles sped out of the compound. Out on the road, they swerved around the perforated technical and headed in the opposite direction of the approaching column.

Back in the compound, Harvath and Haney took up their positions and readied their weapons. They were the leave-behind force. No matter what the militia decided to do, it was their job to wreak as much havoc on the convoy as possible.

Shouldering his RPG, Harvath looked over at Haney. The Marine, who had pulled an RPG from one of the technicals out front, was doing the same.

He flashed Harvath the thumbs-up, and then, over the radio, said, "Gage told me to tell you double or nothing you miss this shot."

Harvath just shook his head.

Normally, he was full of smartass rejoinders. Not now, though. His body was beat to shit from jumping out of the Land Cruiser, he'd spiked his adrenaline multiple times over the last eighteen hours, and he and Haney were severely outnumbered by an approaching force. He was saving all of his energy for the ass-kicking they were about to unleash.

As the convoy neared the compound, Harvath signaled Haney. Everything was going to be decided by what happened in the next thirty seconds.

CHAPTER 37

The column slowed as it approached. Then it came to a complete stop. The militia members could see the technicals blocking the road, the overturned SUV, and the corpses of their compatriots—all covered with bullet holes.

If they were paying attention, they would also notice that two vehicles were missing. It was decision time.

The compound was quiet. The only things moving were the flies on the dead bodies.

A militia commander rolled down his window and lifted a pair of binoculars to get a better look. With the right rifle, Harvath probably would have been able to take him out. But his focus wasn't the militia's command structure.

He wanted to knock out their technicals—first and foremost the two with the antiaircraft guns. Something easier said than done.

To their credit, these guys weren't stupid. There was plenty of spacing among all ten of their vehicles. They weren't bunched up on the road, bumper to bumper, unable to maneuver if they had to.

Two technicals with .50 cal machine guns were near the front and another was in the middle. The technicals with the antiaircraft guns were all the way at the back.

By coming to a halt, the convoy was now in RPG range, but just barely. Harvath wanted them closer. He wanted to stack the deck as much as he could in his favor.

So they continued to wait while the Libya Liberation Front tried to make up its mind.

What he had hoped for was that upon seeing the missing vehicles, the entire column would give chase. As they drove by, he and Haney would then pick them off, one by one, focusing on the two key technicals.

The second-best option was that they divided their forces, sending some to give chase and the others to inspect the compound. What they were doing now, though, was nothing. They were just sitting there.

Harvath could feel a headache coming on. He was hungry and caffeine deficient. He would have killed for a cup of coffee or an energy drink.

"Okay, fellas, what's it gonna be?" he said, as he watched the militia members. "Are we going to fight, or just stand around pulling each other's dicks?"

At that moment, the commander got out of his truck and started shouting orders. Up and down the line, militia members began getting out of their vehicles.

Haney looked at Harvath, who shrugged in response, before turning his attention back to the convoy. He had no idea what they were up to.

A group began to amass near the vehicles in the middle. They were armed predominantly with AK-47s, but some had M4s. Harvath didn't need to guess where those had come from.

When he saw other men begin to hop into the beds of the technicals, he knew they were in trouble.

The militia was going to send a team in on foot to check the compound while the rest of them, along with their vehicles, hung back. The technicals would provide overwatch for them.

"This isn't good," Haney said over the radio.

No, it wasn't. But they were going to have to deal with it.

"It looks like they're going to send in about twenty guys," replied Harvath. "That's nearly half their force. As soon as they're closer to us than they are to them, we let them have it."

Haney gave him the thumbs-up and got ready. This was their ambush. And while the militia members might not be fully cooperating by driving straight into it, they still had surprise, speed, and violence of action on their side. Harvath planned to leverage that to the hilt.

Within moments of being assembled, the assault force started moving. But much to Harvath's chagrin, they weren't moving alone. One of the technicals was moving with them. *Damn it.*

Harvath had to think fast. The moment he and Haney fired their rockets, that machine gun was going to rain a world of hurt down on them. And the closer it was to their position, the more accurate its fire was going to be.

They needed to find a way to take it out at the same time they took out the antiaircraft guns. There had to be something.

Harvath racked his brain, but he couldn't come up with anything. The antiaircraft guns had to be taken out first. If they began firing on their position, it was game over. The technical creeping up on them would just have to come second—an extremely dangerous second.

The assault force moved rapidly. If the compound was as empty as it looked, they needed to clear it and get back on the road. With every minute that passed, their quarry was getting farther away.

He watched as the Libyans came down the road, getting closer and closer with each passing second.

There was a withered crop of shrubs that he had decided on for his marker. Once they had reached that, it would be time to engage.

Perspiration ran down the back of his neck. His palms were slick with sweat. He rubbed them on his chest to dry them before readjusting his hands on the launcher. All the while, he never took his eyes off the fighters converging on the compound.

Eventually, he went from measuring the distance to the marker in meters, to feet. "Get ready," he said over the radio. "Almost there."

The technical passed the shrubs first, followed by the militiamen who were on foot. As soon as the last one had reached the marker, Harvath said, "Hit it!"

Simultaneously, he and Haney leaned out from behind the buildings they were using as cover, sighted in their targets, and fired their weapons.

CHAPTER 38

Before he even knew if he had struck his antiaircraft technical, Harvath retreated back behind the building, dropped his empty launcher, and began running toward the other corner. As he did, he transitioned to his Russian grenade launcher.

In one of the defeated technicals outside the compound, Morrison had found a handful of HEDP—high-explosive dual-purpose grenades.

Used for both antitank and antipersonnel assaults, as long as you got them near a target, they were highly effective.

He heard two explosions up on the road as the technical that was closing in on them then opened up with its .50 cal.

The gunner strafed the part of the compound where he had seen the rockets fired from. The heavy rounds sent bits of rock and cinderblock in all directions.

Now at the opposite end of the main building, Harvath leaned out and let loose. He fired all three rounds in his launcher, reracking it as fast as he could. And more important, he did it before the gunner in the technical could swing the heavy .50 cal in his direction and cut him down.

As he ducked back behind the building, he heard the rounds detonate. There was a massive explosion followed by a roiling fireball that curled up into the sky. He had scored a direct hit.

Slinging the launcher, he ran for the technical that Haney had parked behind the far building.

Out on the road, the other heavy machine guns mounted in the beds of militia pickup trucks began firing and chewing up the compound.

The tailgate to Haney's pickup had been lowered and Harvath leapt right into the back. Jumping up onto the top of the cab, he then grabbed the edge of the roof and pulled himself up.

"Haney," he yelled, as he did. "Don't shoot. It's me."

The Marine reached down and helped him over the parapet.

"Give me a SITREP," he said as he took a fraction of a second to catch his breath.

"You want the good news or the bad news?" Haney asked. He had to raise his voice to be heard over the gunfire.

Harvath signaled for him to get on with it.

"The good news is I hit my target. The bad news is you owe Gage two hundred bucks."

"Damn it," Harvath replied. "How many rockets do we have left?"

Haney pointed to the fully assembled RPG on the other side of the roof. "Just the one."

Harvath patted his chest rig. He had two HEDP rounds left.

"What are you thinking?"

Harvath began to speak, but was interrupted by the antiaircraft gun joining the fight. Even at a distance, it was earsplitting.

Its gunner was focused on the main building. The weapon's rounds tore through it like an angry child stabbing a gingerbread house with a screwdriver.

With the antiaircraft gun's maximum rate of fire of six hundred rounds per minute, the structure wouldn't last long. It wouldn't take them long to work their way down to the building they were on. Not to mention if one of them stood up and fired the RPG. They had to risk it, though.

"We've got to knock out that ZU-2!" Harvath insisted.

Haney gestured to the weapon. "Be my guest. But I don't want to be up on this rooftop when you do."

"How good are you with one of these?" he asked, unslinging the Russian grenade launcher.

"Good enough to be dangerous."

Harvath handed it to him, along with the two rounds from his chest rig. "I'll give you a head start. Whatever you do, make sure you take out both those other technicals."

"Roger that," Haney replied, as he loaded the weapon and picked up his M4. He stopped for a moment, put his hand on Harvath's shoulder, and then disappeared over the parapet.

Staying as low as possible, Harvath moved to the opposite side of the roof. He examined the RPG and made sure everything was in order. Setting it down, he then risked a glance over the parapet.

The technical he had taken out was a smoldering hulk, surrounded by bodies. Beyond it, the rest of the convoy was still in the same position. As the .50 cal machine guns sprayed the compound, the antiaircraft gun stayed focused on hammering the main building.

He had no idea why his first rocket hadn't taken it out, but it was his fault. He wasn't the kind of guy to blame his equipment. He owned the miss.

This time he would get it right. He had to. There wouldn't be another chance. If he didn't take out that technical, it'd be lights out for him and Haney.

Being atop the southernmost building gave him a slight advantage for sighting in his target. It also meant he was farther away. His aim would have to be right on the money.

Cocking the hammer, he raised the weapon and reminded himself to hold it firmly. Closing his left eye, he used his right eye to line up the RPG's front sight tip with the rear slide notch.

The moment he launched, he was going to draw enemy fire. He reminded himself to keep his weapon aimed at the target. If he scrambled for cover too soon, it could result in another miss.

Taking the weapon off safe, he double-checked his sight picture, exhaled, and began applying pressure to the trigger. There was no recoil with an RPG, but if he flinched or jerked the trigger in any way, that could also cause a miss.

It seemed to take forever for the weapon to engage. Finally, he heard the loud bang and distinctive *whoosh* as the warhead erupted out of the launcher and went sizzling through the air toward its target.

If the militia couldn't hear it over the gunfire, the gray-blue smoke trail headed right at them was unmistakable.

"C'mon, baby!" Harvath yelled. "C'mon!"

He watched as the rocket-propelled grenade sliced through the air at almost three hundred meters a second.

When it struck the antiaircraft technical, it did so dead-on. It was a perfect shot, followed by a spectacular explosion.

Harvath began running before the .50 caliber machine guns from the two surviving technicals could be turned on his position.

Reaching the far side of the roof, he leapt over the parapet and landed on the cab of the pickup below. Jumping down, he took off for Haney.

Using a pile of rubble for cover, the Marine took aim at the first technical and fired the Russian grenade launcher.

The round soared high into the air, landed right in the bed of the vehicle, and exploded.

It wasn't until Haney was preparing to take out the last technical that Harvath saw the second wave of militia members closing in.

The assault force this time was smaller. There were only six of them. They had used the withering fire from the technicals as cover and had flanked the compound.

Haney didn't even know they were there until Harvath yelled, "Contact left! Contact left!"

The Marine spun just as the final round left his grenade launcher. Dropping the weapon, he went for his rifle, but the Libyans had already begun shooting.

CHAPTER 39

Before Haney could even get his gun in the fight, Harvath was firing in controlled pairs. He dropped one militiaman, then another. "Get cover! Get cover!" he yelled at Haney.

Out on the road, the grenade landed short of the convoy and detonated. The remaining technical was unharmed.

The Marine fell back behind the rubble, propped his rifle up, and began to return fire along with Harvath.

Together, they took out four of the Libyans before the other two retreated behind the wall.

"Move right! Move right!" Harvath shouted, trying to get Haney to the more secure cover of the middle structure.

The Marine, though, was having trouble moving. Harvath looked down and saw his upper right thigh wet with blood. He'd been shot.

Suddenly, the .50 cal opened fire on their position. Seconds later, the Libyans behind the wall joined in.

Harvath and Haney were now taking fire from two directions. Any chance they had of making it to the middle structure was now gone.

As soon as the militia realized they had them pinned down, they'd send in a team to hit them from behind, or on their right flank, and finish them off. That was if the .50 cal rounds didn't eat away their cover first.

Poking his rifle out from around the rubble, Harvath fired at the two Libyans behind the wall.

He pulled the tourniquet from his chest rig and tossed it to Haney. "Get this wrapped around your leg. Now."

Then, poking his rifle back out, he fired several more shots, before focusing back on Haney.

"Have I mentioned how much I fucking hate Libya?" the Marine asked as he applied the nylon webbing around his upper thigh.

"You and me both," he replied, as he prepared to help cinch the tourniquet down. "On three, okay?"

Haney nodded.

Harvath tightened his grip, began the countdown, and then went early, pulling up as hard as he could on the word *two*.

The Marine roared in pain. Harvath secured the tourniquet and then fired off several more rounds toward the wall.

"I don't want to fucking die here," Haney said through clenched teeth.

"Nobody's dying here," Harvath reassured him. "Not on my—"

"Contact rear!" the Marine yelled, raising his rifle and firing behind them. One of the Libyans had split off from his partner and had tried to get the drop on them.

Haney shot the man several times in the chest until he slumped forward over the wall, dead.

At the same moment, rounds from the .50 cal shattered the rubble just above their heads, showering them with pieces of rock.

"We can't stay here," said Harvath as he swapped out his mag for a fresh one.

"Where are we supposed to go?" Haney grunted, as he tried to reposition himself.

"Over the wall. We stay low on the other side, we can move in either direction."

"And then what?" the Marine asked as another barrage from the .50 cal pounded into the rubble pile and sent rocks tumbling down on top of them.

"Let's get ready to move. Can you put weight on that leg?"

Haney half stood, but when he tried to put weight on his right leg, the pain shot through his body like an electric shock, and the leg buckled. "Fuck," he growled.

"That's okay," said Harvath. "We'll go with Plan B."

"What's Plan B?"

"We kill every last one of them."

The Marine shook his head. "Negative. I'll cover you. You go for the wall."

"And let you have all the fun? Jesus, you Marines are greedy."

"I'm serious."

"So am I," replied Harvath. "We fight together, or we go over the wall together. I'm not leaving you here."

"Don't be an asshole."

"Shut up and get ready to fight. That's an order."

Haney did as he was told. Swapping magazines, he made ready.

As he did, the hair suddenly stood up on the back of Harvath's neck. Whether it was something he heard, or something he sensed, he knew they were in trouble. "RPG!" he yelled. "Get down!"

The rocket crashed into the building just behind them and exploded, raining shrapnel and jagged pieces of cinderblock on their position.

Because Haney was unable to move quickly enough, Harvath had physically covered him and had taken the brunt of the fallout.

But before he could even brush off the debris, the Libyans launched another rocket-propelled grenade.

This one exploded even closer. A chunk of concrete hit Harvath's helmet so hard he saw stars.

"We've got to make for that wall," he yelled above the ringing in his ears, as he tried to regain his vision. "It's no good here."

He would have given everything he owned for a single smoke grenade to mask their retreat to the wall.

They didn't have one, though, and as far as Harvath could see, there was nothing he could use to create a diversion. He and Haney were going to have to fight their way out.

Even though it had only been a matter of minutes, it felt like they had been in this battle for hours. The only break in fire from the Libyans' .50 cal came when they were reloading.

At the rate they were going, Harvath half-expected them to melt the barrel, but that was hoping against hope for a miracle.

Judging the distance to the wall, he plotted the fastest course, and then, after filling Haney in, said, "When they stop to reload that fifty, we haul ass. Copy?"

Haney had serious doubts about Harvath getting them both across the open compound without getting shot. Nevertheless, the Marine nodded.

Seconds later, the machine gun fell silent and Harvath ordered, "Now!"

Getting Haney up onto his left leg, Harvath folded him over his shoulders and took off with him in a fireman's carry.

The Libyan behind the far section of wall popped up with his rifle and attempted to fire, but Haney was ready for him. His Beretta pistol was already in his hand.

He fired six rounds, two of which found their mark, striking the man in the stomach and lower jaw.

Out on the road, a handful of AK-47s erupted. The rounds popped and hissed all around them.

Harvath, his leg muscles already burning, focused on the wall and pushed himself to move faster. Haney fired back.

Weaving was out of the question. One wrong step while carrying his colleague and he could have easily blown out a knee.

They had barely made it a quarter of the distance, when there was a loud *pop* from the convoy and a blue-gray trail of smoke sped right at them.

"RPG!" shouted Haney.

Harvath immediately changed course and ran for a different section of wall. He only made it three steps before the warhead hit.

The force of the explosion threw both men to the ground. Harvath landed hard on his left side and once again saw stars.

When his vision finally cleared, he saw Haney's pistol lying on the ground a few feet away. Beyond it, Haney was facedown, not moving.

Harvath began crawling in his direction. As he did, he called out, but the Marine didn't respond. Harvath crawled faster.

Reaching him, he placed two fingers on his carotid artery and felt for his pulse. He was still alive.

Supporting his neck, he was about to roll him over so he could drag him to safety when the Libyans opened up the .50 cal on them again.

Harvath grabbed hold of the left shoulder strap on Haney's chest rig and pulled with all the strength he had.

The heavy rounds tore up the ground and carved a path right toward them. As the gunner adjusted his aim, they got closer and closer.

Harvath groaned as he doubled down and summoned every last ounce of energy he had. The wall looked like it was a mile away, but he refused to quit.

The earth shook around him and he prepared for the bullets that he knew were going to tear him up.

Suddenly there was a streak of orange in the sky. A fraction of a second later, there was an explosion, followed by another streak and another explosion.

He looked over his shoulder toward the road just as the team aboard the USS *George H. W. Bush* fired a third Hellfire missile.

The entire convoy was in flames. The Reaper had finally arrived back overhead. Their troubles, though, weren't over yet. Not by a long shot.

CHAPTER 40

E very morning as Lydia Ryan drove to Reed Carlton's home, she reflected on what an insidious disease Alzheimer's was.

After a lifetime spent in the espionage business, Carlton had amassed a wealth of experience. Every shred of it had come at great personal risk to him, as well as to the nation. That experience was invaluable. *He* was invaluable.

It pissed Ryan off to see what was happening to him. It wasn't fair, not with everything he had been through, all the scrapes and close calls. This wasn't how a man like Reed Carlton should go out.

Yet it *was* happening. A little more each day. Ryan had to remind herself that life wasn't fair.

Carlton had even told her to get over it. He was still in the fight and would be until the very end. In the meantime, he didn't want her around if she was going to be morose. They had a tough slog in front of them. If she couldn't be positive and optimistic, he told her, she could stay at the CIA and ride that sick pony into the ground.

He had a good sense of humor and she had grown to love and respect him dearly. She wished they had more time, but the clock was working against them.

As he was sharper and more focused first thing in the morning, she had adjusted her schedule to match.

Setting her alarm for 4:30, she was able to work out and get to his house by 7:00.

Always, the two dark SUVs of his security team were parked in the driveway. This morning, though, there was a third vehicle—a pearl-gray Mercedes van.

She rang the doorbell and was greeted by Carlton. He was always showered, shaved, and dressed before she got there. This morning he was wearing khakis, a green oxford shirt, and leather driving moccasins.

"Whose van is that outside?" she asked as they said their good mornings and he let her in.

Gesturing toward his study, he replied, "Nicholas is here."

Nicholas was the Carlton Group's IT wizard. He was a Soviet Georgian born with primordial dwarfism. As a result, he stood just under three feet tall.

He had been abandoned by his parents and raised in a brothel near the Black Sea. The things that had been done to him there were unspeakable.

Despite his small stature, his intelligence was off the charts. He had eventually turned snippets of pillow talk and the loose lips of brothel customers into a blackmail empire.

He had become known throughout the intelligence world as "The Troll." He dealt exclusively in the black market purchase, sale, and theft of highly sensitive, often classified, information.

Entering the study, the first thing Ryan noticed were Nicholas's giant dogs. Named Argos and Draco, the highly trained, fiercely loyal white Caucasian Ovcharkas were always at his side.

Upon seeing her, the dogs stood up and came over for some attention. She scratched them both behind their ears and ran her hands over their powerful shoulders.

"Me next," said Nicholas with a smile, as he gave the command for the dogs to lie down.

"Good morning," she replied with a laugh.

"Coffee?" Carlton asked her. Nicholas already had a cup.

"Yes, please."

It was Harvath who had brought Nicholas into the organization—something that wasn't an easy feat.

They had started out as bitter foes, and many in the Carlton Group, including Carlton himself, were highly suspicious of Nicholas. But over time, the little man had more than proven his loyalty and his worth.

He and Harvath had developed a deep friendship.

Though he had been happy for Harvath about his decision to pursue a life and family of his own in Boston, he had been profoundly saddened by his friend's departure. He had been the one person at the Carlton Group whom Nicholas felt he could fully trust.

"I didn't expect to see you this morning," Ryan said to Nicholas.

"Something's come up."

Carlton handed her a cup of coffee, and after thanking him, she asked, "What's going on?"

"Late last night," he continued, "a job order was opened on the dark web."

The dark web was a series of encrypted sites accessible only through networks using special software like the Tor Hidden Service Protocol. They allowed users to remain anonymous and beyond the reach of intelligence and law enforcement agencies.

From the most abhorrent pornography to the hiring of hit men, if it was illegal, and especially if it was morally repugnant, it was on the dark web.

"What kind of order was it?"

"A hack," said Nicholas.

"Okay," replied Ryan. "Of who?"

"You."

She laughed. As Deputy Director of the CIA, she was under constant threat of being hacked. In fact, she had stopped paying attention to the reports a while ago. The attacks and scams came daily. That's why the CIA had such a robust IT team, and she trusted them to do their jobs.

"So someone offered a bounty to hack me. What's new?"

"What's new," replied Nicholas, "is that it was a twofer. The contract was to hack you *and* Mr. Carlton."

That *was* new. It also told her that someone suspected they were working together. That had not been announced publicly yet.

"What are they looking for?"

"Everything," replied Nicholas. "Not only all of your previous correspondence, but they wanted code planted that would allow them to monitor everything going forward, undetected."

"Do we know who's behind it?"

"No," said Carlton, "and that's the problem. While state actors usually have their own hacking teams in-house, they also have been known to hire criminal hackers."

"Whoever this is," said Nicholas, "offered up a lot of money for the job."

"How'd you find out about it?" she asked.

"A broker I used to know reached out to one of my old aliases."

Ryan looked at Carlton. "Okay, so someone wants to hack us. It happens to companies every single day. It's probably even going to increase once it gets announced that I've left the Agency to come to work for you."

"True, but this one bothers me. I don't like the timing. I also don't like the amount of resources someone is willing to throw at this. The hack may only be a jumping-off point. I think we need to take this seriously."

She didn't disagree. "Okay. What do you suggest?"

"I think Nicholas should take the job."

She didn't disagree with that either, but the way he let the words hang in the air made her feel that there was another shoe still left to drop. Then it did.

"And I think we should let him actually carry out the hack."

CHAPTER 41

The ramp at the rear of the massive Air Force C-17 Globemaster cracked open and the last of the setting sun could be seen on the horizon.

When a small parachute attached to the rigging on the first High Speed Assault Craft was released, it began to pull the sleek HSAC down a set of rails running the length of the cargo hold.

As the long, gray boat was sucked out the back, the SEALs and their boat teams cheered. It never got old throwing huge pieces of equipment out of an airplane thousands of feet in the air.

They had lined up single file on either side of the ramp, flippers strapped to their thighs. After the second HSAC was launched, they began leaping out.

The air at seven thousand feet was much cooler than it had been on the ground at U.S. Naval Air Station Sigonella on the island of Sicily.

The SEALs and their boat teams were excited to get some action. From what they had heard, the Americans they were going into Libya to exfiltrate had seen some serious fighting.

It was the perfect night for a drop. The ocean was warm and calm. It was like landing in a bathtub.

As everyone climbed on board, the boat crews cleared the parachutes. Once everyone was accounted for and had taken their places, the crews fired up the powerful diesel engines and headed for the Libyan coast.

Back at the safe house, Harvath was on the roof when his satellite phone vibrated.

Reading the message, he turned to Barton and said, "Boats are on their way. Twenty minutes out."

•   •   •

After the Reaper had destroyed the militia convoy, Harvath had loaded Haney into the technical and taken off.

They were close to the coast. With the help of the drone, they had found an old beach road, which had allowed them to get back to the safe house without being seen. The rest of the team was already there.

The moment he pulled in, they rushed to the truck to help carry Haney inside, where Staelin assessed his injury. Harvath was exhausted and would have killed for some sleep, but he still had work to do too.

Strike Force Two had dispatched a new, fully fueled, fully armed drone to have on station above their location. It seemed unlikely that the remaining militia members knew who, much less where, they were, but it was good to have the extra firepower available just in case.

When he stepped into the safe house, the first thing he started working on was how they were going to get out of the country. None of their contingency planning had accounted for taking on the entire Libya Liberation Front.

Because the militia controlled this portion of the country and had eyes and ears everywhere, crossing at the border checkpoint into Tunisia was out of the question. So was trying to get out by airplane. They had been lucky just to make it back to the safe house. Going back out on the road would push that luck, probably to the breaking point.

You could only kick Murphy in the nuts so many times before he kicked back. That left only one way out—via water.

A boat extraction was a possibility he and McGee had discussed. It was an expensive, high-risk last resort, but there were no other options. Things had gotten too hot.

Once again, he got on his satellite phone and went directly to the DCI. McGee got the ball rolling right away.

When the DCI called back with confirmation, it came with one caveat. Because Haney and Gage were both stable, the powers that be at

AFRICOM and the Defense Department wanted to wait until dark. There was no use drawing undue attention by pulling up in broad daylight.

Harvath wasn't crazy about waiting, but he understood the reasoning. It was better to wait until dark.

With the added peace of mind of having the drone overhead, he assigned a new guard rotation, then went into the kitchen and started some coffee. He wasn't going to feel fully at ease until they had put Libya far behind them.

He prepared a quick bite and poured a cup of coffee, hoping it might improve his mood. It didn't.

Walking back to the bedroom where Halim as well as the satellite phone salesman were being held, he put his game face on and stepped inside.

"Who dressed his wound?" he asked, pointing at the smuggler's hand as he entered.

Morrison was in charge of watching the two prisoners. "Staelin did," he replied.

"We're not running a free clinic here," said Harvath as he pulled out his knife.

Walking over to the chair Halim was tied to, he slipped the blade against the man's wrist and drove it down and through his bandages.

Whether he had made contact with the injured area, he couldn't tell. What was obvious was how uncomfortable Halim was. As soon as the knife began to move, he winced and perspiration broke out across his forehead.

"Has he been given any pain meds?"

"Hell no," Morrison answered.

"Good," said Harvath as he began to peel away the bandages. Staelin had done a professional job. In fact it was too professional. Frustrated, Harvath yanked at the remaining pieces and the smuggler went into a spasm of pain.

Finally, he exposed the severed finger. It looked even worse in the light of day than it had under his night vision goggles.

"Whether you keep this finger or not is up to you. Do you understand me?"

The smuggler nodded.

Harvath held up his phone and showed him a university picture of Mustapha Marzouk—the chemistry student who was the owner of the laptop of doom. "Do you recognize this man?"

The smuggler shook his head.

"Look again," he ordered.

The man did.

"Well?" asked Harvath.

"I don't know him," the smuggler replied.

He was lying. Taking the tip of his knife, Harvath began poking at the exposed wound where his finger was barely attached.

Halim screamed in pain.

"Do you recognize this man?"

"Yes! Yes, I recognize him!" he yelled.

Harvath forced a smile. "Now we're getting somewhere. Who is he?"

"I don't know."

He began to bring the knife forward again.

"I don't know his name!" the smuggler cried. "I never know the names."

"But you recognize his face."

The man nodded.

"I can't hear you," said Harvath.

"Yes, I recognize his face!"

Harvath set the photo down where Halim could still see it. "You must see hundreds of new people a year," he said. "Maybe even thousands. Why would you remember this person?"

"Because he was a VIP."

"Bullshit," Harvath replied, going back in for the stump. "You're lying."

"No! No! No!" he cried. "Not lying. He was a VIP. His organization paid extra."

"Paid extra for what? To send him out in a storm and make sure he drowned?"

The smuggler lowered his gaze, but Harvath didn't buy his faux re-morse for a second. "What did they pay extra for?"

"For first class."

"*First class?*"

Halim looked up at him. "To sit on the top deck. To have food and water. To use the satellite phone if he wished."

"But not to have a life jacket," Harvath stated.

The man didn't respond. He simply cast his eyes back down.

"Who paid you? What organization?"

The smuggler remained silent. Harvath grabbed his arm by the wrist and jammed his knife into the man's stump.

Halim screamed and went rigid as the pain exploded throughout his entire body.

"Who paid you?" Harvath yelled.

"Daesh!" the man cried out, using the Arabic name for ISIS. "Daesh paid me."

Withdrawing the knife, he wiped it on the smuggler's shirt. Halim was on the verge of passing out. Harvath stepped away.

Leaning against the wall, he waited for the man to regain his composure. When he felt enough time had passed, he re-engaged.

"Why would you send a VIP into a storm like that?"

The man was slow to reply, but eventually said, "We thought they could make it."

"Bullshit. You sent them out like you always do, in a bad boat without enough fuel."

"No," the smuggler argued. "The boat wasn't the best, but it had extra fuel. We thought they could beat the storm."

"And then what? What was the VIP supposed to do then?"

Halim didn't want to answer the question. He averted his eyes. Harvath came off the wall, knife in hand.

"The Italians would put all of them in a refugee camp," he said, looking up, hoping to prevent any further pain.

The man was lying. He had a very distinct tell. "Bullshit," Harvath repeated. "You weren't paid so that he could end up in a refugee camp."

"I was," the man insisted, a little too quickly.

The tell was the icing on the cake. Harvath stepped forward and sliced the man's finger the rest of the way off.

Halim rocked in his chair, screaming. Harvath went back and leaned against the wall.

Considering the horror the smuggler had visited upon his victims, Harvath didn't feel a shred of remorse. Halim was evil incarnate. He deserved much worse.

When enough time had passed, Harvath once again re-engaged. For as big as he was, the man was a mess. He was shaking, his eyes were bloodshot, and perspiration and tears stained his face. He had lost a lot of his color.

"This is the last time I am going to ask this," he said. "What was the VIP supposed to do when he reached Italy?"

The smuggler refused to answer.

Grabbing his other hand, Harvath pressed his knife down and began cutting into the same finger. "What was the VIP supposed to do when he reached Italy?"

"A fishing boat!" Halim shouted. "Off the coast of Lampedusa."

"What about it?"

"It was supposed to pick him up and take him the rest of the way."

"Whose fishing boat?"

"I don't know."

Harvath sliced deeper into his finger and blood began to spurt out.

"The Mafia!" Halim cried.

"Give me a name," he demanded. "Or this is going to get a lot more painful."

CHAPTER 42

Leaving the bedroom, he stopped in the kitchen for a second cup of coffee. Unplugging his satellite phone from its charger, he carried it upstairs, along with his coffee, out onto the balcony.

It was at least fifteen degrees cooler at the coast than it had been inland. As he fired up the phone and waited for it to acquire a signal, he took a deep breath of the ocean air. It smelled and sounded exactly the same as it had yesterday. Despite everything that had happened, at least that hadn't changed.

There might have been a lesson in there somewhere for him, but at this moment he didn't have the mental bandwidth to grapple with it.

When the signal icon appeared on his phone, he relayed everything the smuggler had told him to Deborah Lovett, his CIA contact at the Embassy in Rome. She told him she'd get back to him as soon as she had something. After that, all he could do was wait.

He needed sleep, but with two cups of coffee in his system and so many things weighing on his mind, he was too wired. That wasn't like him.

Normally, he could calm his thoughts enough to slip into an almost meditative state that allowed him to replenish his strength. Today, though, had been anything but normal. He was still keyed up, expecting a fight. Until the boats arrived, he wouldn't be able to relax. Not even for a moment.

He felt fully responsible for his team, including their injuries. But, considering everything that had happened, it could have been much worse.

The bullet that hit Haney could have severed an artery or shattered his leg. It hadn't. And while Gage would have his left arm in a sling for a while, his wound could have been a lot worse too. All things considered, they'd been pretty fortunate to all be getting out of this alive. It was a testament to both their courage and their skill. Sometimes, shit just happened.

Unable to unwind, he put his mind toward what to do with the smuggler and the satellite phone salesman. Neither had any further intelligence value.

He thought about killing them. Halim certainly deserved it. And in his mind, Harvath could make the argument that the phone salesman deserved it too. He certainly wasn't going to cut them loose.

Listening to the sound of the ocean on the beach below, he let the pieces tumble in his mind.

As he did, an idea began to form. After making sure it was fully baked, he transmitted it back to Langley.

It was common knowledge that the locals, as well as the fledgling Libyan government, didn't like the human traffickers. Plenty of their boats had sunk only a few miles out to sea. When that happened, bodies washed up on Libya's beaches.

Harvath decided the best thing he could do was to leave their two captives right where they were—tied up in the safe house.

Once he and the team were safely away, the Libyan government could be tipped off. They could then "perp walk" the smuggler and his accomplice on TV. Rounding up one of the most-feared smugglers in the country would make them look strong and competent.

Freeing all the refugees locked up at his compound would further burnish their image as just and compassionate. And if they were smart, they'd vilify and undermine the power of the Libya Liberation Front by tying them to the monstrous smuggler.

By claiming that it was government forces that had clashed with the militia overnight and this morning while attempting to capture Halim, they'd look strong and brave.

It was a win, win, win that gave the new government everything tied up with a ribbon.

McGee liked the plan too, and felt a high degree of confidence that the Libyan government would go for it.

He also shared with Harvath that identifying the stolen Glocks from Camp 27 had turned out to be a big help in speeding up the earlier drone handoff.

This made the Defense Department, which was eager to settle that score, move faster. Also, once the Tunisians were informed of the evidence connecting the Libya Liberation Front and Ansar al-Sharia, they gladly took themselves out of the loop and allowed the attack to happen.

They were two small hash marks on a much larger balance sheet, but had just one of them been removed, there was no telling how things might have turned out.

• • •

When darkness fell and the High Speed Assault Craft with their knife-like hulls arrived off the coast, six SEAL Team members slipped over the sides and swam to shore.

Harvath was on the beach, waiting for them when they arrived and led them up to the safe house.

There, the SEALs passed out waterproof dry-bags for everyone to load up their gear, including the surveillance equipment Morrison had stripped from the van.

The SEALs then did a quick assessment and made plans for getting everyone out.

Harvath had his own ideas, but he kept them to himself. This was what these men were paid to do. If they wanted his opinion, they'd ask for it.

The biggest challenge was moving Haney, but the SEAL Team had come prepared.

HSACs, as long as they weren't getting pounded by waves in a surf zone, could come in very close to shore. The CIA couldn't have known when they chose the safe house, but the location had been perfect.

Using an inflatable stretcher that looked like some kind of tactical pool toy, they were able to carry Haney out of the house and down to the beach. Once everyone was assembled, they called in the boats.

Harvath and Staelin stayed behind with two of the SEALs to cover the rest of the team as they waded out chest-high in the water and climbed onto the boats.

When they were aboard, Harvath and Staelin followed. The two SEALs on the beach came next.

The newcomers were issued Mustang inflatable flotation devices and headsets, which were quickly put on and plugged in.

Blankets were offered, but none of Harvath's steely-eyed killers would be caught dead wrapped in a blanket. They had come into Libya like warriors and that was exactly how they were going to leave.

With all present and accounted for, the boat crews pointed their HSACs toward open water and slammed the throttles forward.

CHAPTER 43

It was after 9:00 p.m. when the chemist, accompanied by two other young men, also in prayer caps, exited the mosque in Aubervilliers.

Puffing on a Gauloise, Tursunov watched from across the street. The two young men were the same he had seen Younes with that morning. Now, instead of saying good-bye and heading home, Younes was walking off with them in another direction.

There were only two reasons Tursunov could think of for why the authorities would be following a young, unemployed Muslim chemist. One reason was terrorism. The other reason was drugs.

It wasn't until he saw the second cop following Younes that morning that the scales tipped for him. With his longer hair and goatee, that officer had drug detail written all over him.

Drugs and terrorism often went hand in hand. The Taliban made the bulk of their income from opium, and the cell that carried out the Madrid train bombing had financed its attack by selling drugs.

If Younes and his colleagues were involved with drugs, it was no wonder that the French authorities had taken an interest in them.

The surveillance team appeared about a block from the mosque. They were different players than Tursunov had spotted that morning.

Over the next six blocks, there were at least three different police officers who rotated in and out behind the young men as they walked. Tursunov also spotted a small Renault hatchback that had looped around the block twice, ignoring two perfectly good parking spots.

After another block, he could see where they were headed. Younes and his colleagues entered a crowded café and disappeared inside.

None of the surveillance team followed. The Renault hatchback double-parked several doors down. The first man from the rotation, who was now wearing a jacket and a ball cap, walked into a pharmacy and browsed near the window where he could watch the street. Tursunov decided to make his move.

Stepping into the café, he noticed that it was filled completely with men. There wasn't a single woman to be seen.

It was loud and smelled like urinal disinfectant. Soccer games were on all of the TVs. Many men were playing cards. Others were smoking sisha pipes.

Approaching the *comptoir*, he ordered a Coke. The North African behind the bar looked at him long and hard. It was obvious his customer wasn't from the neighborhood. He seemed to be deciding whether to serve him, or throw him out.

Removing a large roll of cash from his pocket, Tursunov peeled off a ten, set it on the counter, and then turned his back on the barman to study the room.

Off in a corner, Younes and his buddies had joined a group of other young North African men. Tursunov doubted any of them had just come from the mosque.

They sported gold jewelry and expensive basketball shoes. They were street thugs, probably gang members. It would not have surprised him if they had violent criminal histories.

He watched as the man who appeared to be the leader nodded at one of his lieutenants. The lieutenant withdrew three envelopes from inside his waistband and handed one each to Younes and his two friends. As he did, Tursunov thought he could see a pistol.

Neither Younes nor his colleagues opened the envelopes to see what was inside. As quickly as they appeared, they disappeared into the young man's pockets.

Tursunov was all but certain at this point that his hypothesis regarding Younes was correct. All he needed was a confession.

So, when the lieutenant stood up to go use the men's room, he decided to extract one.

Taking another sip of his Coke, he glanced at the barman, who was at the other end of the *comptoir*. His attention was on a newly arrived group of customers.

Back at Younes's table, the young men were engrossed in a serious discussion. None of them were even keeping an eye on the front, much less the traffic headed to and from the restroom.

Setting his Coke down on the bar, Tursunov collected his change and walked back to the men's room, eyeballing the location of the rear exit as he did.

As he opened the door, he saw one man at the sink washing his hands, and heard another man standing at one of the urinals.

The man finishing up at the lone sink looked at him in the mirror. The Tajik raised his hands like a surgeon and nodded at the water, indicating he needed to use the sink next.

Turning off the water, the man grabbed several paper towels from the dispenser and dried his hands as he exited.

Tursunov turned the water back on to mask the sound of his movements. Slipping across the dingy tiles, he quietly locked the door. Then, like a ghost, he materialized behind the lieutenant at the urinal.

The street thug was three inches taller, fifty pounds heavier, and a good thirty years younger than the Tajik. But if life had taught him anything, it was that there was no substitute for experience and treachery.

It had also taught him that a man was never so vulnerable as when he had his dick out.

Taking full advantage of the element of surprise, he drove the lieutenant's head right into the wall above the urinal.

Simultaneously, he pulled the man's pistol, a 9 mm PAMAS G1, from his waistband and drove the barrel into the base of his skull.

When the man tried to fight back, Tursunov slammed his boot into the back of the man's right knee, causing him to fall, face-first, into the urinal.

Grabbing a fistful of the man's hair, he forced him to remain there. "What were the envelopes for?" he demanded.

"Va te faire enculer!" the man replied defiantly. *Go fuck yourself!*

Tursunov knew some French, but not enough to carry out an interrogation. *"English,"* he demanded, as he moved the pistol to the man's temple, cocked the hammer, and released the safety. "What were the envelopes for?"

"Money," the man relented. *"Money."*

"Money for what?"

When the man didn't answer, the Tajik jerked his head back and slammed his face into the porcelain urinal, breaking three of his teeth.

"Money for what?" he repeated.

"Putain," the lieutenant cursed as blood gushed from his mouth. *Fuck.*

Tursunov jerked his head back again and the man yelled, *"Drugs.* It was for drugs."

Just as he had thought. "What kind?"

"Crystal."

"They sold you methamphetamine?"

"No," said the lieutenant. "Partnership. They cook. We sell."

"Who is *we?*"

"Mon bande."

"English," the Tajik growled, whacking the man's forehead on the urinal.

"Fils de pute!" he replied. *Son of a bitch.* "My crew sells it. My *gang.*"

Tursunov's mind was already turning, three steps ahead. Every gang had to deal with turf wars and competition.

"What gang is your enemy? Which one is trying to take your business?"

"Les GBs," the man sputtered. "The Ghetto Boys. From Saint-Denis."

That was all Tursunov needed to hear.

This time when he slammed the lieutenant's head into the porcelain, he did it hard enough to knock him out.

Letting go of his hair, he pulled a knife and slit the man's throat. Then, holding the lieutenant's index finger and using his blood as ink, he wrote the letters *GB* on the wall.

After washing his hands, he unlocked the bathroom door and left the café by the rear exit. He had just taken the first step in helping his chemist disappear.

CHAPTER 44

The trip took over four hours. They stopped once to refuel. Bladders full of diesel, with special beacons attached, had been airdropped over the water.

When they got within range of Malta, Harvath made a call. By the time they reached the drop point, several vehicles were already waiting for them.

It was on a secluded stretch of coastline, which was good for a covert insertion, but the rocks made it difficult to get in as close as they would have liked. Instead of wading into shore, they had to swim.

The warm waters around Malta were a particular favorite of great white sharks, which flocked there to give birth.

Harvath tried not to think about it as he helped swim Gage's stretcher into shore behind Haney's. Neither man was up to the task of swimming, and the last thing they needed was the scent of blood in the water.

Standing in the surf, ready to help bring the stretchers in, was a team of men. Harvath knew one of the faces well.

Dr. Vella was a slim man in his fifties. He was of average height with dark hair and glasses. He looked like someone better suited to picking stocks than running a highly fortified, top-secret interrogation and detention center a half-hour outside the capital of Valetta.

Nicknamed the "Solarium" because much of it existed below ground, it was one of the most efficient black sites on the planet. Harvath had rendered more than a few high-value targets to Vella for interrogation.

As Haney's floating stretcher neared shore, the doctor gave orders in

Maltese and his men took over. Wading into the waves they lifted it, carried it to the beach and up to a waiting black Suburban in which all of the seats had been folded down.

By the time they returned for Gage, he had already hopped off his stretcher and was wading in. He didn't need or want any further help.

With their cargo safely delivered, the SEALs returned to their boats and headed off to rendezvous with a ship from the Sixth Fleet.

Harvath stepped out of the water and shook Vella's hand.

"You look terrible," the doctor said.

"It's been a long couple of days."

"So I've heard," he replied, gesturing toward the vehicles. "I have two medical teams standing by. The sooner we get back, the sooner I can have your men looked at."

Harvath thanked him and, once all his guys and their dry-bags were loaded, climbed into the lead Suburban with Vella.

Vella had outfitted all of the vehicles with PowerBars and bottles of water. Harvath helped himself.

"There's hot food waiting at the farm," Vella offered.

The Solarium was built beneath a rustic farmhouse. When he took breaks from observing interrogations, Harvath liked to sit outside with a drink. Often, Vella would join him and the two would discuss all sorts of topics.

Sometimes, Harvath would just sit alone and enjoy the sights and sounds of rural Malta. It was one of the most peaceful and picturesque places he had ever been.

Tonight, though, all he wanted was a hot shower, a bed, and silence. He'd even be willing to take one of the isolation cells if it meant a solid eight to ten hours of uninterrupted sleep.

Leaning back against the seat, he wanted to close his eyes, but he willed himself to stay awake. Not until the Solarium. Then, they'd be safe and he could let his guard down.

He looked out the window and thought he recognized where they were. "This looks familiar."

Vella smiled. "You have a good memory. The last time you were here, we ate at a restaurant off this road. Very few people ever come back here. That's why I like it."

Harvath nodded. He didn't feel much like making conversation. He had been sent halfway around the world to piece together the itinerary of a dead ISIS chemist. Two of his team members had now been shot, and all he had to show for it was a single name, allegedly tied to the Sicilian Mafia.

Vella could tell Harvath was wiped out. He left him alone and they made the rest of the drive in silence.

Arriving at the farm, Haney and Gage were offloaded first and taken to the infirmary.

Because interrogations at the Solarium could be so intense, each prisoner was given a workup beforehand to try to identify any pre-existing medical conditions. There were also the occasional subjects who succumbed to strokes or heart attacks during the process.

When that happened, Vella's team couldn't simply summon the local ambulance service. They had to take care of things on their own. Therefore they had a fully equipped medical suite, as well as a team of highly paid medical personnel who quietly worked at the facility on a rotating basis.

There wasn't much, short of highly specialized or highly technical surgeries, that they couldn't handle.

The remaining team members were given room assignments and told to help themselves to dinner in the kitchen. Harvath stumbled back there, poured himself a large mug of coffee, and walked to his room. He wanted to grab a quick shower, change his clothes, and then check on Haney and Gage. As tired as he was, he couldn't turn in until he knew they were both okay.

Dropping his clothes in a pile in the corner of the bathroom, he turned the water on and waited for it to get hot. As he did, he looked in the mirror. His body was covered with bruises. Diving out of a Land Cruiser and getting knocked to the ground by RPG explosions had a way of taking their toll.

When the water was good and hot, he grabbed his coffee and stepped into the shower, afraid he'd fall asleep without it.

He let the water pound against him, and for the first time in a long while, closed his eyes.

Taking a sip of coffee, he tried, for just a moment, to push everything out of his mind. He wanted to not think of anything, to not be responsible for anything or anyone, for just ten seconds.

And for once, he got exactly what he wished for.

CHAPTER 45

Harvath stood under the water for a good ten minutes, drinking his coffee, and not thinking about anything.

When his mug was empty, he set it down, picked up a bar of soap, and scrubbed his entire body. Then, after rinsing off, he shampooed his hair.

Throwing the temperature control all the way to cold, he forced himself to stand beneath the icy needles of water for a full twenty seconds. It was like dropping two shots of espresso into his coffee.

Wide awake, he stepped out of the shower and retrieved a courtesy kit from the medicine cabinet. Inside, he found a comb, a razor, shaving cream, a toothbrush, and toothpaste.

After he was done in the bathroom, he pulled a set of clothes from his bag and got dressed.

Grabbing a bottle of water from the minifridge as he exited the room, he swallowed a couple of Motrin and headed down the hall toward the stairs that led to the infirmary.

The house always smelled like maple syrup to him, which seemed strange, as it was on a farm in the middle of Malta. No doubt it had something to do with Vella wanting to create a certain atmosphere outside the Solarium.

The doctor held Ph.D.s in both psychiatry and neurochemistry, and was obsessed with smell, particularly its ability to open up pathways into the brain.

In fact, Harvath had once watched him interrogate someone using "liquid fear." It was a synthetic pheromone he had created that triggered the "flight" portion of the famous fight-or-flight response. It was amazing to behold.

Upon arrival, everyone had been issued a key card. Harvath held his up to the reader that controlled the stairwell door. When it clicked, the door opened with a hiss, and he headed down to the Solarium.

The moment the door closed behind him, the maple syrup smell was gone. It was replaced by something colder, more institutional. The black site smelled like what it was, a prison.

As he passed the cell doors, they were all open. The Solarium was only a temporary detention facility. Anyone requiring a long-term hold was transferred elsewhere.

Everything was painted gray—the walls, the floors, even the ceilings. The only exceptions were the stainless-steel sink and toilet units in the cells themselves, and the bright white of the infirmary.

Walking into the outer office area, Harvath saw Vella in front of a large computer screen, chatting with one of the doctors.

The three men shook hands and Harvath asked, "How long do they each have?"

The doctor grinned. "Considering their luck, they'll both probably live to be one hundred."

"The rest of the guys will be sorry to hear that," Harvath replied. "Haney has a pretty wife."

Still smiling, the doctor shook his head and pointed at the computer screen. There were two digital X-rays up. "The wounds on both men were through and through. No bone fractures, and based on the rest of the tests, no vascular injury. We've got them on oral hydration and have started antibiotics and pain meds."

"How soon can they move?"

"I'd let them sleep tonight, but there's no reason they can't be on a plane tomorrow."

"Back CONUS?" he asked, using the military acronym for the Continental United States.

The doc shook his head. "U.S. Naval Hospital Sigonella is the closest American facility able to give them a full workup. If they're on Agency contracts, that's where they'll go. If they're at capacity, they'll turf them to Ramstein Air Base. Either way, they have to be cleared on this side of the pond before they fly home."

"Understood," said Harvath. "Have they been told the news yet?"

"I was just about to go in."

Grabbing a folder from a stack sitting on the desk, he replied, "Don't worry. I'll take care of it."

He walked down the hallway and entered the four-bed infirmary. Haney and Gage had been set up in beds right next to each other.

"They sent Harvath," said the burly Green Beret as he walked in. "The news must be terrible"

Haney chuckled. "Yeah, the human bullet magnet. That's close enough, Harvath. Neither of us wants to get shot again."

He was glad to see them in good spirits. Getting shot wasn't fun. He took the ribbing in stride.

Opening the folder, he said, "I've got good news and I've got bad news."

Both men looked at him, not sure if he was serious, or if he was kidding around.

Haney spoke up first. "What's the bad news?"

"You're going to lose the leg. The good news," he said with a smile, turning to Gage, "is that you'll just have to use your other arm to shave your back."

"Fuck you," they both said, laughing.

"In all seriousness," he continued, "the Agency is going to want to get you checked out at a base hospital in Europe before you fly back. Sigonella is the closest, so that's probably where we're headed tomorrow."

"What about you?" Haney asked. "Any update from Rome?"

"Not yet. We'll probably hear something in the morning. In the meantime, get some sleep."

•   •   •

Walking back upstairs to the kitchen, Harvath decided to get some real food in his stomach.

Vella had done a good job of anticipating what his American guests might like. There was a large vat of Texas chili on the stove, cornbread still warm in the oven, and cold bottles of Belgian beer in the fridge.

Harvath fixed himself a meal, grabbed a beer, and headed out to the patio. The rest of the team had already eaten and gone to bed.

It was a warm, quiet night. Flickering light spilled from old lanterns placed around the patio.

As he sat down, he realized he'd forgotten a bottle opener. Too tired to go back and get one, he made sure nobody was watching, and then used the edge of the table to pop the cap off.

Leaning back, he took a long pull and closed his eyes. Every muscle in his body was sore. A cold beer was exactly what he needed. If he never saw Libya or another shitty, third-world country like it ever again, it would be too soon.

He knew it was the fatigue talking. Taking another sip, he opened his eyes and leaned forward. He didn't want to fall asleep outside.

Though Vella had done a good job with the food, Harvath was too wiped out to finish. Carrying everything back inside to the kitchen, he then headed down the hall to his room.

When he got there, he drew the blackout curtains, kicked off his boots, and turned his phone all the way off—something he rarely ever did.

If a life or death situation arose, he didn't want to get that call. Not tonight. Someone else would have to handle it. All he wanted to do now was sleep.

Falling on the bed, he closed his eyes, and within seconds was completely out.

CHAPTER 46

When Harvath awoke, he felt worse than when he'd gone to bed. His body was stiffer and in more pain.

Grabbing a bottle of water from the mini-fridge, he swallowed several Motrin, turned on his phone, and returned messages. Then after a quick shower, he swung by the kitchen for a mug of coffee. Everyone else was already up.

Barton and Morrison were in the gym working out, while Staelin was outside in a pair of cargo shorts, working on his tan and reading another paperback, this time by Erik Larson.

It was the same hot sun overhead and same ocean off in the distance, but they were worlds away from Libya. Harvath didn't begrudge his team some leisure time. Especially not after everything they had been through. They had more than earned it.

Making his way to the stairwell, he waved his card in front of the reader, the door unlocked, and he headed down to the infirmary.

The overnight medical team had gone home and a new team had come on.

Harvath stopped briefly to speak with the doctor before walking back to check on Haney and Gage.

Part of the new medical team included an attractive nurse, named Olivia. When Harvath walked in, she was in the process of checking Gage's blood pressure.

"Speak of the devil," the Green Beret said as Harvath entered. "Harvath, tell this lovely woman how Haney and I threw ourselves in front of those bullets to save your life."

Harvath caught a smile, accompanied by an eye roll, from the young woman. She obviously knew a couple of liars when she saw them.

"Whatever you're giving them," he said to her, "you may want to let the doc know that it's affecting their memory—"

"One hundred men!" Gage continued. "When we ran out of ammo, we had to go after them with our bare hands."

Harvath ignored him and walked over to Haney. "How's the leg?"

"I think my modeling career is going to be okay," he replied.

Harvath smiled. "I'm glad you have something to fall back on."

"We still going to Sigonella today?"

Harvath nodded. It was one of the messages he had returned from his room. "They're working on getting us a plane. The doc says you're good to travel. Have you eaten breakfast yet?"

Haney pointed to an empty tray off to the side. "Omelets and fresh squeezed OJ. It's like being at the Ritz."

"Your tax dollars at work."

The nurse removed the blood pressure cuff from Gage's arm and asked, "Is there anything else I can get for you gentlemen?"

"I'm good," said Haney.

"If you see Cupid on the way," Gage replied, "tell him I'm going to need my heart back."

This time Harvath rolled his eyes. "Try ketamine," he told her. "I guarantee he'll stop bothering you."

Olivia was a good sport. Smiling, she reminded her patients where their call buttons were and left to report back to the doctor up front.

Harvath looked at his watch. "As soon as I have an exact time on the plane, I'll fill you in. And though I know I'm going to regret asking, is there anything you guys need?"

"There is," said Gage. "According to Haney, you owe me two hundred bucks."

Harvath shot Haney a look.

"A bet's a bet," Haney replied.

"You're going to a Navy hospital," said Harvath. "What are you going to spend two hundred bucks on?"

"What are you, my accountant?" Gage asked. "You've got a bag upstairs with one hundred grand in cash. Go peel off a couple c-notes for me."

"That's Uncle Sugar's money. I'll square up with you when we get home. In the meantime, leave the nurse alone. Copy?"

Gage winked at him in response and began bugging Haney, asking him how walking with a limp might affect his relationship with his wife.

"Tell the nurse to hurry up with that ketamine," Haney yelled after Harvath as he exited the infirmary and headed back upstairs.

●　●　●

They stayed at the Solarium for lunch and drove out to the airport an hour later. There, a Citation XLS was on the tarmac fueled and waiting for them. The midsize jet was just big enough to accommodate their team.

Haney took two of the seats facing each other so he could prop his leg up. Harvath and Gage sat facing each other across the aisle. Barton and Morrison took the two seats in the back. Staelin boarded last.

As such, he was left with the side-facing seat up near the cockpit, normally reserved for a flight attendant. And the minute he sat down, that was exactly how the team treated him.

As the jet taxied out onto the runway, the Delta Force operator checked the galley to see if any catering had been done for the hop over to Sicily. In typical CIA fashion, it was bare bones—no liquor, not even soft drinks—only small bottles of water. He accepted drink orders anyway.

When the pilots took off the brakes and the Citation began to roar down the runway, Staelin tossed Harvath, Haney, and Gage their bottles of water. He placed the two for Barton and Morrison on the floor. As the plane took off, the bottles rolled to the back of the cabin, where Morrison reached down and picked his up.

Barton did the same, but thoroughly wiped it off with his shirt before opening it and taking a drink.

After a few more shots at Staelin for being a lousy "stewardess," the team quieted down. Gage and Haney put their earbuds in, while Staelin opened his book.

As the Citation climbed into the sky and banked out over the Mediterranean Sea, Harvath closed his eyes. He had a lot to process. Not the least of which being what he was going to have to do once they landed in Italy.

CHAPTER 47

L ydia Ryan looked at both men with disbelief. There was no way the CIA would ever allow what they were asking for. Absolutely not.

"You want what?" she repeated.

"Access to the Malice source code," said Nicholas.

Malice was an ultra-top-secret program developed by the CIA's Center for Cyber Intelligence that allowed the Agency to skirt both the NSA and the FISA court, in order to intercept and trace encrypted Internet communications.

The program was so highly effective that the CIA had gone to great lengths to mask its existence. Neither the President nor the intelligence committees had ever been briefed on it. Only in the most extreme circumstances was it ever used.

She knew better than to ask how Nicholas even knew about it. She didn't want to know.

Instead, she directed her next remark to Carlton, "We're talking about the most valuable weapon in the Agency's hacking arsenal."

"I understand that," he replied.

"I don't think you do. This goes beyond anything they've ever developed. Beyond putting smart TVs into fake off-mode in order to listen in on people's conversations. Beyond hacking smartphones in order to capture audio and message traffic before it gets put through an encryption app.

"You're talking about launching the cyber equivalent of a nuclear-tipped missile, just because somebody looked at you sideways in a dark parking lot. And unlike a nuke, once a cyber weapon like Malice is loosed, it is out there for anyone to discover and turn back around on us.

"This isn't a fire-and-forget system. The moment it detonates, you have to send a team into the blast zone, right into the rubble, to physically recover it. Every device it has touched, every packet of data it has stowed away inside, all of it has to be accounted for. That's what you don't understand."

"I do understand," Nicholas countered. "That's why all I want is access to the source code. I don't want the entire missile. I only want its guidance system."

"So you can do what? Play Frankenstein? That could end up being even worse."

"Lydia, I know you don't like any of this."

"That's the understatement of the year," she replied.

"Which is why we *have* to do it this way."

"First you tell me that for your hack to be convincing, you've got to turn over all my personal emails, including ones that are a little *too* personal. Then, you drag Malice into this—something I shouldn't even be discussing with you."

"If there was another way to do this," said Carlton, "we wouldn't need to ask."

"There has to be."

"There isn't," Nicholas replied. "Believe me. For the last twenty-four hours, I've been trying to come up with one. Your personal emails, along with Mr. Carlton's, are the Trojan horse. They're the only means by which we can get Malice into the pipeline and figure out who ordered the hack."

"I can tell you right now that Bob McGee is never going to authorize this."

"You let me worry about Bob," said Carlton. "What I need you focused on is coming up with a plan to get Nicholas inside the Center for Cyber Intelligence."

"*Inside?*" Ryan repeated with a laugh. "You've got to be kidding."

"Malice can only be accessed from inside," Nicholas stated.

"You know you've got a bit of a reputation at the CIA, right? They'll go batshit if they see you in there."

"Which is why nobody can see him," Carlton clarified.

"Any other requirements?" she asked, turning to face him. "Maybe he can ride out of Langley on a unicorn."

The Old Man smiled at her. "If anyone can make it happen, it's you."

Ryan didn't smile back. Instead, she asked, "How much time do we have to put this together?"

"Nicholas needs to go in tonight."

Ryan stood up from the table.

"Where are you going?"

Walking out of the study, she replied, "To start a hot bath while I look for some razor blades."

CHAPTER 48

"I'm not riding in a fucking ambulance," said Gage as he looked out his window at the approaching vehicles.

"Yes, you are," said Harvath. "Haney too. That's an order. We keep a low profile and we don't cause any trouble. That goes double for the nurses. Understood?"

Gage nodded and Haney flashed him the thumbs-up.

When the jet came to a complete stop, Staelin opened the cabin door, extended the air stairs, and said, "On behalf of your anonymous flight crew, we'd like to thank all of you for flying Central Intelligence Airways this afternoon. We know you have a choice when traveling to far-away lands to interact with extremely bad people, and we appreciate your choosing CIA.

"Please check your seatbacks and overhead compartments for any weapons you may have brought on board and remember, you were never here."

There was a round of applause from the team, Staelin bowed, and they deplaned.

In addition to the ambulance waiting to take the two wounded team members to the Naval hospital, there was an older passenger van, and a black SUV with tinted windows.

Standing outside the SUV was Deborah Lovett, who had recently arrived from Rome. A tall, attractive woman in her midthirties with long blonde hair, she looked more like an Eastern European tennis star than a CIA case officer.

"Let's guess which vehicle is here for Harvath," said Morrison.

"A hundred bucks says he's kicking himself for using up all his ketamine," replied Gage.

Harvath shook his head as he helped retrieve bags from the plane's cargo hold. The air smelled like salt water and jet fuel.

Once Gage and Haney had been loaded into the ambulance, he told Staelin, Barton, and Morrison, who were on their way to base housing, that he would catch up with them in a couple of hours.

Picking up his bag, he walked over to Lovett and introduced himself.

"Do your friends want a ride?" she asked, after they shook hands.

Harvath looked over his shoulder and then back at her. "They're not my friends."

She smiled as he opened her door for her. Closing it, he was almost positive he heard Barton shout some sort of an insult his way, but it was drowned out by a pair of F-18 Hornets as they went screaming down the runway.

Hopping into the passenger seat, he asked, "Where are we headed?"

"To the SCIF," she replied.

SCIF stood for Sensitive Compartmented Information Facility—a secure room in which classified information could be briefed and discussed.

Lovett was dressed in a black pantsuit, and while it likely had been intended to showcase her professionalism and downplay her attractiveness, it failed. Harvath tried not to look at her and instead focused his eyes on the airfield beyond the windshield.

As they drove, she provided him with an update. "We received confirmation that the Libyans picked up Halim and the satellite phone salesman. They also liberated the refugees at the compound. The Red Crescent has them now."

Harvath was glad to hear it. "Any blowback from the firefights?"

She shook her head and he made the mistake of looking at her as she did. Once he locked eyes with her, it was difficult to look away.

Fortunately, she had to pay attention to where she was going and broke contact.

"Libyan government forces took credit for the losses that the Libya Liberation Front militia suffered," she said. "That's a good PR coup for them. Which, I heard, was your idea."

"Wasn't me," he replied. "I'm not that smart."

Out of the corner of his eye, he saw her smile.

"That's us up ahead," she stated as they approached an unremarkable two-story building whose only distinguishing features were the antenna arrays and clusters of satellite dishes on the roof.

Pulling into a parking space reserved for military officers, Lovett grabbed her credentials from the center console, a briefcase from the backseat, and, with a smile that displayed her perfect white teeth, motioned for Harvath to follow her.

He remembered being shown into a similar facility by a similarly attractive CIA officer at Al-Dhafra Air Base outside Abu Dhabi. She had turned out to be extremely good at her job. Harvath wondered if Lovett would prove to be as well.

Showing her ID to two Marines standing guard in the lobby, she led Harvath through a series of security doors and down a long hall.

Its walls were lined with pictures of aircraft and assorted commendations from American units that had been based at Sigonella over the years.

"Hungry?" the CIA officer asked as they arrived at a vending machine filled with plastic-wrapped sandwiches.

"No thanks," he replied.

Lovett bought a Diet Coke from the machine next to it and they continued walking.

Arriving at a door simply marked A7, she pressed a button and they were buzzed in.

He followed her into a small office where four Navy personnel sat working at gray metal desks. None of them looked up.

"Phone," she said as they approached the heavy metal door of the SCIF. Mounted on the wall next to it was an old wooden hotel mail sorter.

Harvath wasn't excited about leaving his cell phone in an office with four strangers, even if they were U.S. military personnel, but he understood the rules and slid his into the cubby next to Lovett's.

"Coffee?" she asked, nodding at the Keurig machine to their left.

"Actually, yes," he replied. "You good?"

"I'm fine, thank you," she replied, holding up her drink.

After walking over to the coffee station, Harvath brewed a cup of black coffee and added a shot of espresso.

Rejoining Lovett at the door to the SCIF, he smiled and said, "Good to go."

The CIA officer nodded, punched a code into the keypad, and then opened the door.

CHAPTER 49

SCIFs were designed to be immune to electronic eavesdropping and surveillance. The moment you entered, the first thing that struck most people was the silence. It was like walking into a tomb.

It was lit from overhead with strips of white LED lighting and smelled like compressed air. In the center was a chipped blue Formica conference table surrounded by gray faux leather chairs.

At the front of the room were three flat-panel monitors, as well as two workstations. Harvath and Lovett were the only people there.

Removing a laptop from her briefcase, she plugged it into a port beneath the conference table and motioned for Harvath to sit.

"What do you know about ISIS and its ties to the Italian Mafia?" she asked.

"Not much," Harvath replied. "Though I'd imagine there are some areas where their interests overlap."

"More than just some."

Once she had her computer powered up, she opened PowerPoint and an image of Roman ruins appeared on all the monitors.

Harvath recognized them immediately. "Palmyra," he said. "Syria."

She was impressed. "You know it."

"All too well."

On a recent assignment, Harvath had barely escaped from that part of Syria with his life. He had passed right through Palmyra.

What ISIS had done to that ancient city was as bad as what the Taliban and their RPGs had done to the Bamiyan statues of Buddha in Afghanistan.

"Across Syria, Iraq, and Libya, ISIS has overrun UNESCO world heritage sites, slaughtering archeologists and plundering everything they can get their hands on."

As she spoke, she backed her points up with slide after slide.

"They load the looted artifacts onto cargo ships headed for southern Italian ports. There, the Mafia usually purchases them with cash. Increasingly, though, we're seeing payment made in weapons.

"The Mafia then help smuggle the weapons farther north into Europe, where ISIS and other terror groups can carry out attacks."

Immediately, Harvath's mind was drawn to what had happened at the cathedral in Spain. "What about explosives?" he asked.

Lovett nodded. "The Italian organized crime groups are all interconnected. The Cosa Nostra, the Camorra, the N'drangheta—what one doesn't have, the other can get. They're supplied by an array of arms dealers from Ukraine, Russia, and other places across the Balkans and Eastern Europe."

"What about the name I gave you? The guy our Libyan smuggler, Halim, gave up?"

She took a sip of her Diet Coke and pulled up a new series of images, surveillance photos taken by Italian police. "Sicily is home to a highly organized, ruthless Nigerian criminal network known as the Black Axe. They operate with the permission of the Sicilian Mafia.

"The name you gave me, Festus Aghaku, he was a *tassista* for the Black Axe. It's Italian for taxi driver. His job was to meet the smuggling boats from Libya out at sea and sneak in high-paying customers before Italian authorities could get to them."

Harvath held up his hand and interrupted. "You said his job *was* to meet the smuggling boats from Libya. What's he doing now?"

Lovett advanced to her next slide. "He's dead."

The image showed a corpse inside an unzipped body bag. "What happened to him?"

"He drowned. The same night, the same storm, as your chemistry student, Mustapha Marzouk.

"The Italians have a handful of informants in the Black Axe. From what I've been able to gather," Lovett continued, "Festus Aghaku didn't want to go out that night, but he was forced to."

"Forced by whom?"

"The Sicilian Mafia. Allegedly, there was a VIP who needed to be picked up off the coast of Lampedusa. The Cosa Nostra didn't care about the storm. Festus Aghaku was a dead man if he *didn't* go."

"So what happened?"

"He went. The storm was much worse than predicted. The boat sank. He and two Nigerian crew members drowned."

"Do we know who the VIP was?" Harvath asked. "Did they mention Mustapha Marzouk by name?"

"No."

"What about where he was going once he reached Italy?"

Lovett shook her head. "They didn't mention that either. But they wouldn't have known his final destination. That's not how it's set up. The Black Axe runs the water taxi portion. That's it. Once the customer gets to dry land, the Cosa Nostra takes over. They then run the smuggling routes up through Italy and into the rest of Europe."

Harvath hated the Mafia. They thrived on human suffering. He didn't care if they were Italian, Nigerian, or Libyan. Profiting off other people's misery, they were nothing more than animals in his book.

The Sicilians were some of the most violent. They paid lip service to honor and respect while they trafficked in drugs, money laundering, blackmail, weapons, and terrorism. There was nothing honorable or respectable about how they made their livings.

"So who would have been in charge of getting Mustapha Marzouk to his final destination?" he asked.

The CIA officer advanced to her next slide. On it was a sixty-something-year-old man with dark, olive-colored skin, a prominent Roman nose, and a pair of green eyes saddled with heavy bags. His receding hairline had gone gray and boasted two prominent widow's peaks.

"Meet Carlo Ragusa. Anything and everything the Black Axe does in Sicily, it does because Ragusa allows them to. He's the one who sent Festus Aghaku and his crew into the storm that night. He's also the one who can tell you where Mustapha Marzouk was headed."

It was some of the best news Harvath had gotten yet. "Where do I find him?"

Lovett winced and clicked to her next slide.

CHAPTER 50

Tursunov checked out of his hotel late that morning and took the train out to Charles de Gaulle Airport.

There, he caught a taxi back into the city and, under a different passport, checked into Le Meurice, the grand luxury hotel on the rue de Rivoli.

It resembled a modern-day Versailles. Gilded mirrors. Silk draperies. Crystal chandeliers and velvet couches. He was offended by the opulence.

Opening the doors to his balcony, the cacophony from the street below pierced the cashmere-wrapped silence of the suite. Horns blared, brakes squealed, and engines growled. Trucks rumbled past and scooters buzzed like angry wasps.

Removing his Gauloises, he slid one from the pack, placed it between his lips, and struck a match.

Inhaling a cloud of leathery smoke into his lungs, he leaned forward against the wrought-iron railing and smiled. The view was perfect.

He was directly across the street from the Jardin des Tuileries.

From where he stood, he could look out over the entirety of the Terrasse des Feuillants—the area along the edge of the park where the Fête des Tuileries was in full swing, and where the attack would take place. He had the perfect front-row seat.

Like the Spanish coordinator in Santiago, Abdel would be close, just in case his men chickened out. He had the numbers of the cell phones attached to their vests programmed into his phone. If something happened, if they didn't go off at the appointed time, he would detonate them remotely.

That meant that the Moroccan would be someplace where he could watch the event unfold without attracting attention. Tursunov had no idea where. That was by design.

The less they knew about each other's movements, the better. The more compartmentalized they were, the less chance there was of the full plot being discovered.

It was a similar blueprint to what had been carried out in Spain. The only person who interacted with him was the head of operations for the country. The martyrs themselves never saw his face. They didn't need to. All that mattered was that they do their job.

After cutting the throat of the drug dealer, Tursunov had contacted Abdel and arranged to meet.

The Moroccan didn't want to believe that his nephew was involved in a drug ring, but based on what Tursunov explained to him, he had no choice.

Sharing his concern that the chemist's apartment, phone, and email communications were being monitored, the Tajik laid out a very specific course of action he wanted Abdel to follow. Then he handed him a stack of banknotes and a clean cell phone.

It hadn't taken long for the dead lieutenant's body in the men's room to be discovered. As soon as the police were called, the undercover officers following the chemist and his two drug-cooking cohorts descended on the café. After initial questioning at the scene, all three were taken in for further interrogation.

It was an attempt to get the trio to admit to what the police already suspected them of—drug manufacturing. They knew the young men were not involved in the murder. The victim was part of the gang they cooked for. There was also a trail of partial bloody footprints that led out the back of the café.

Having been a cop for many years, Tursunov knew what kind of exculpatory evidence to leave behind. As long as the chemist and his colleagues didn't have blood on their shoes, which they didn't, and there was nothing else incriminating on them, there was only so long that the French police would be able to hold them.

When they were released, that was when the chemist was going to have to make his move. That was what Tursunov had prepped the uncle for.

Because he was family, Abdel could approach the young man without drawing interest from the police. The immigrant grapevine being what it was, the authorities wouldn't think twice about an uncle showing up in the wake of a nephew's having been at a murder scene and having undergone police interrogation.

Neither would the police find it unusual that an angry uncle would arrange for his nephew to get out of Paris and away from a bad circle of friends for a while.

With a murder and a potential gang war on its hands, the French authorities would need all the manpower they could muster. They'd be glad not to have to waste resources on surveilling the chemist any longer.

So Tursunov had taken the second step in helping his chemist disappear. The third step would come tonight.

CHAPTER 51

Mafioso Carlo Ragusa lived with his wife and five children in a well-fortified home on the outskirts of Palermo. The grounds were patrolled by dogs and plenty of men with guns.

Could Harvath, with Gage and Haney out of the fight, have breached the Sicilian compound and gotten to Ragusa? With enough surveillance and planning, he was confident that he could pull anything off. But in their race against the clock, Libya had stolen much more time than it should have.

Anxiety was running high back home. In the wake of two deadly terrorist attacks, Americans wanted answers and Washington wanted results. Both of those wants fell on Harvath's shoulders. There had to be another way to get to Ragusa, and he pressed Lovett, the one with all the Italian connections, to find it.

To her credit, she did. A counterterrorism contact of hers in the Carabinieri's elite Special Operations Unit known as the Raggruppamento Operativo Speciale, or ROS for short, owed her a favor—a big one. She had allowed him to see intelligence the CIA was building on a suspect who had made multiple trips back and forth between Italy and Tunisia. While he couldn't cite it directly to his bosses, it had been the final piece in the puzzle he needed, and had helped roll up a burgeoning terrorist network outside Turin. The information he shared in return would prove just as useful.

Street racing of horses was a brutal and highly illegal sport in Sicily. It brought in over half a billion dollars annually, and Carlo Ragusa was right in the middle of it.

The horses were forced to race on asphalt or cobbles. To minimize accidents, roads that sloped uphill were chosen. To minimize the pain of running on such hard surfaces, the nerves in the horses' hooves were surgically severed.

Wagers could range from hundreds to thousands of dollars. In the past, angry mobs had stoned losing horses to death.

Spectators on scooters and motorbikes, yelling and honking, rode behind the terrified animals, frightening them into running faster.

The horses involved in the Palermo races were kept in deplorable conditions in dilapidated garages and storage units throughout the city's old town.

The races were normally held at dawn, just as the police shifts were changing. The location was kept secret until the very last moment. When the race was run, the road was closed down and residents were threatened with violence if they didn't stay indoors.

Harvath had no desire to try to snatch Ragusa from such an event. Lovett, though, told him she didn't think it would be necessary anyway.

The night before a race, men were known to stay out the entire evening. According to her source, Ragusa used the races as an excuse to see his mistress.

She was a tall, beautiful, twenty-two-year-old Nigerian named Naya. The Mafioso had put her to work as a bartender in one of his clubs in the old town. There, he could keep his eye on her. She lived in an apartment above.

The club was called Il Gatto Nero and no doubt a cretin like Ragusa enjoyed keeping his black mistress at an establishment called the Black Cat.

"Do they have the apartment under surveillance?" Harvath asked.

"My guy says *no*."

"Do you believe him?"

"I do," she replied.

Harvath nodded and Lovett continued the briefing.

Once it was complete, they returned to her vehicle and went to talk to the team.

The men listened and when Harvath was finished, Staelin asked, "So what's the plan?"

"I'm still working on it. I'll know more when we get there."

"That's my favorite kind of plan," the Delta Force operative responded. "Count me in."

Harvath looked at Barton, the short, red-bearded SEAL.

"I was in as soon as I heard *hot bartender*," the man replied.

Morrison laughed. "Harvath said hot, *tall* bartender. Maybe we should bring phone books so you can put them on one of the stools."

Barton feigned that he was about to laugh, then shot the Marine his death stare.

Turning to Lovett, Harvath said, "Looks like we're going clubbing."

•   •   •

Leaving the base at Sigonella, there were multiple signs that warned not to transport any weapons off-post.

"Oops!" Staelin said from the back of the SUV. "There's another one I didn't see."

Because of who they were and what their assignment was, all of their security checks had been waived. The weapons they had brought out of Libya had accompanied them to Sicily.

They were violating multiple local laws, as well as international agreements with Italy. The Italians didn't care for covert operations being conducted on their soil.

If Harvath and his team were caught, there was no doubt that the Italians would vigorously prosecute them. That was an inherent risk in any assignment they conducted abroad. *Don't get caught* was the unspoken, number-one rule. The key word in black ops was *black* for a reason.

The drive from Sigonella to Palermo took a little over two hours. The medieval old town area was a labyrinth of narrow streets and alleyways.

It became apparent rather quickly that they were driving the worst kind of vehicle possible.

Finding a parking space as close as they could, they then walked the rest of the way in on foot. Their first order of business was to get a look at Il Gatto Nero.

But not knowing how they were going to handle things later at the club, Harvath didn't want them seen together in the area in one big group. He instructed them to split up and surveil the club separately.

Lovett suggested a local restaurant where they could meet up, eat, and compare notes afterward. They all agreed to rendezvous there in an hour.

Harvath moved through the colorful, awning-covered, open-air market on the Via Ballarò. Blood oranges, lemons, tomatoes, garlic, lamb, beef, octopus, clams, cuttlefish, capers, olives, and chicory were all artfully displayed on tables, in crates, bowls, barrels, as well as atop mountains of ice. And all of it hawked by loud shopkeepers in a cacophony Sicilians called *abbanniate*.

The architecture of the old town was a reflection of Sicily's having been ruled over by many different cultures. Traces of Greek, Roman, Arab, French, and Spanish influences could be seen throughout.

Right before the end of the Via Ballarò, he came to the Via Rua Formaggi, took a right, and slowly walked down past the Black Cat.

It was housed in a four-story building, the first floor of which was painted a burnt tangerine. It had a black awning, with potted palms in the street, blocking any parking out front. A brown metal gate covered the door. Brown wooden shutters covered what looked to be an expanse of floor-to-ceiling windows that opened up onto the sidewalk.

The main entrance to the apartments above appeared to be adjacent to the entrance of the club. If there was a bouncer, which any club worth its salt would have, that was going to be a problem. There was no way they'd get through that door without being seen. Not without creating a major distraction. He'd have to come up with another way in.

Walking down to the next corner, he turned left and pulled out his phone. He had no problem at all looking like a tourist. It would only help his cover as he continued his surveillance.

Opening up Google Maps, he pinpointed his location. Then, he clicked the satellite view and zoomed in on the neighborhood from overhead.

For as many narrow passageways as the old town had, he'd pulled the short straw in this section. Buildings were built side by side and back to back. There were no alleys, no rear exits. There was, however, something interesting.

Behind the Black Cat was a group of adjoining buildings surrounding an enormous inner courtyard.

Palermo was famous for its palazzos. Harvath figured that's probably what the adjoining buildings originally were. That, or a convent. But now, with the concrete of the courtyard painted like a soccer field, he figured it was probably a school of some sort.

Along the north side of the complex, the roof was flat and lined with solar panels and hot water tanks. From there, it was a short scramble to get up onto the roof of the Black Cat building. Harvath decided to take a closer look.

Walking up to the Via Giuseppe Mario Puglia, he hung a left. Half a block down, he saw something that made him smile. *Scaffolding*.

The old town was just that, *old*. And during his short walk through the neighborhood, he had seen a ton of renovation projects. He made a mental note to look into investing in a Sicilian scaffolding company. But as quickly as the thought entered his mind, he got rid of it. If the Mafia here was anything like it was back in the U.S., the construction industry was the last place he'd want to put his money.

Crossing the street, he held his phone up and pretended to be trying to get a signal. As he did, he took a video of everything he saw.

The narrow cobbled street was quiet. As best he could tell, it was residential—no shops, no cafés. There was very little traffic.

It was perfect. He had found his way in.

Checking his watch, he saw that he had enough time to search for potential places to reposition their vehicle before he'd have to head back and meet the rest of the team at the restaurant.

CHAPTER 52

Staelin was the first to arrive at Osteria Ballarò. It was a Sicilian restaurant built in the stables of an old grand palazzo. He had taken a table in back, had his book out, and was reading when everyone else arrived.

Harvath noticed he also had a beer in front of him. "Having a good time?" he asked.

The Delta Force operative looked up from his book and drew Harvath's attention to the rest of the restaurant. "When in Palermo."

Harvath looked around. Everyone had a cocktail or a bottle of wine going.

He didn't mind drinking. In fact, he enjoyed it. Just not before an operation.

That said, his team didn't exactly look like teetotalers. They looked every muscled inch the intense ass kickers they were. To not have at least one drink on the table would have raised eyebrows.

More important, his guys were professionals. They had trained with alcohol in their systems and knew its limiting effects. He decided to allow it.

Morrison ordered a beer as well. Barton asked for a glass of Chianti. Harvath and Lovett joined him.

As soon as the waiter had left to go get their drinks, they began discussing what they had noticed while surveilling the nightclub.

They all agreed that getting up to the apartment unseen via the street entrance was a nonstarter. By the time the club opened, there'd be too much going on.

That also meant that getting Ragusa out of the apartment in order to interrogate him at another location was out of the question. The interrogation would have to happen there.

They assumed that the Mafioso would be traveling with bodyguards and could call upon nightclub security for backup if needed.

The Black Cat was equidistant between two of the busiest police stations in the old town. If a call went out to law enforcement, response time was likely to be fast.

The team had done an excellent job of mapping CCTV cameras, potential escape routes, choke points, and alternate rally locations if they were forced to split up.

When it came to breeching the apartment itself, they were in agreement with Harvath. They would have to come in from the roof.

The waiter delivered their drinks and asked if they were ready to order. Lovett asked him in Italian to give them a few more minutes.

"Show me your shoes," Harvath said after the waiter had left.

"My shoes?" she replied.

He motioned for her to do it and she complied. Turning in her chair, she slid one of her feet from beneath the table and showed it to him.

"You flew in from Rome. Where's your bag?" he asked.

"In the back of the truck."

"You have any other shoes in there?"

Lovett nodded. "My running shoes. Why?"

"Because I don't know if this Ragusa character speaks English. In case he doesn't, you're going to be my terp. You'll go in via the roof with us. Running shoes will do."

"Full disclosure. I'm not very good with heights."

"You'll be fine," he assured her.

"What about the rest of us?" Morrison asked. "How's this all going to break down?"

Taking out his phone, Harvath opened up Google Maps and showed the Force Recon Marine a large Baroque church, the Chiesa del Gesù, a block over from the nightclub.

Because it was built on an angle, back from the street, it created an area that opened up extra parking.

"You should be able to park right on the edge," Harvath explained. "As long as you don't leave the truck, it won't get towed."

"No offense, but why me?" Morrison asked.

"Because Haney's not here and I trust you. That's why."

Morrison didn't look convinced.

"Listen," Harvath continued. "If I'm a Palermo cop, and I roll up on you, I'm not going to get a bad vibe. You're obviously an American and he's probably going to peg you for military. Just smile and tell him you're waiting for a legit spot to open up so you can join your friends for drinks."

"Why not have Barton do it?"

"Because he's incapable of smiling. Nobody would believe him."

"That's true," the SEAL said from across the table, giving Morrison his death stare.

"Also," Harvath said, tightening in on the satellite image of the rooftops, "I think he's about the right size to go into the apartment via the skylight."

"And him?" Morrison asked, looking at Staelin.

"He's going to be our eyes and ears on the ground." Waiting a beat, Harvath added. "We all good then?"

They all nodded, except for Staelin.

"What's up?" Harvath asked.

The Delta Force operative slid his phone over to him. On it, a weather app was open.

Harvath hadn't thought to check the forecast. That was a mistake. And it was on him. He knew better.

Not that it would have made a difference. Their options were what they were.

Rain or not, they were going into that apartment and they were going to get Carlo Ragusa.

CHAPTER 53

The Le Meurice restaurant was the most beautiful restaurant Tursunov had ever seen.

Inspired by the Salon de la Paix at Versailles, it was beyond opulent. Gold coated the moldings, bifurcated the mirrors, and dripped from the crystal chandeliers. Silver coated the chairs, the lamps, and even the serving buffets.

But the pièce de résistance was the massive fresco painted on the ceiling. Floating above the dining room, it beckoned patrons into a lush spring landscape populated with alluring mothers and rosy-cheeked infants.

The restaurant's most desirable feature, however, was its view of the Tuileries across the street.

He could have watched the events unfold from his balcony, but he preferred to be here. He wanted to bathe in people's immediate reaction. He wanted to immerse himself in it.

This would be the closest he had been to any of his bombings, ever. His heart was pounding with excitement. He willed himself to be calm. Being seen was not a problem. Being remembered was.

As he was dining alone, the concierge had booked him a small table in the corner. With apologies for not being able to place him closer to the window, he explained that the hotel was quite full. Tursunov had smiled, thanked the man, and given him a generous tip.

A table near the window would have been excellent, but just being in the restaurant served his needs.

Up in his room, he had showered, shaved, and performed his prayers. After a cigarette on the balcony, he had descended to the lobby, where he'd had a ginger ale with lime in the wood-paneled bar, as he kept to himself.

Then, at the appointed time, he paid his bill and stood up. But instead of going right into the restaurant, he decided to step outside.

He wanted to take in the early evening air; to breathe one last breath of Paris before everything changed. His table wasn't going anywhere.

Pushing through the revolving door, he descended the short flight of stone steps and walked out onto the pavement.

"Taxi, Monsieur?" a doorman asked politely.

Tursunov shook his head.

The doorman nodded and shifted his attention to the guests behind him.

Across the street was the wrought-iron fencing of the Tuileries with its bright gold points. Through it, he could see and hear the outdoor carnival. It was packed and in full swing, just as he had known it would be.

Savoring the air, he took in a deep breath and closed his eyes. *The calm before the storm*, he thought to himself.

Exhaling, he stepped away from the front of the hotel, lit a cigarette, and had a quick smoke.

When he was done, he returned inside.

As he was shown to his table, the dining room looked like a sea of ornate ships under crisp, white linen sails.

The maître d'hôtel asked if he cared for a cocktail. Blaming jet lag, Tursunov ordered an espresso. With an understanding smile, the man disappeared to place his order.

For dinner, Tursunov began with scallops from Normandy and chose silk grain veal with smoked eel and olives for his main course. He had his eyes on the iced chestnut delight for dessert.

In his mind's eye, he envisioned the men preparing to martyr themselves. He envisioned how they had spent their last day, ritually cleansing and preparing themselves to enter Paradise. They would have read from the Qur'an, finding courage, comfort, and strength within its passages.

They would approach from different directions, their large soccer jerseys concealing the vests they wore beneath. Each man would carry a soccer ball. Cleated shoes would be worn over a shoulder or around the neck.

As they entered the garden, they would make their way to their appointed areas—guaranteeing that the force of their explosions and the tsunamis of shrapnel would be spread as widely and as efficiently as possible.

Turning his mind back to his food, he decided that the scallops had been quite good, but they were nothing compared to his first bite of veal. It was like an exquisitely flavored butter that melted in his mouth. He had never eaten like this before. *Never.* For a moment, he forgot where he was.

Trimming another piece of the delicately cooked meat, he raised the fork and opened his mouth. But the second bite of veal never made it to his lips.

Outside, there was an intense explosion. Its blast wave shattered the restaurant windows and covered many diners in glass.

Tursunov was spared only by virtue of having been seated away from them, farther back in the restaurant.

Some patrons had been knocked to the floor. Those who were not, were now up and running for the door. Many of them were screaming.

None of them could have known for sure what had happened, but instinct had taken over. *Get away from the danger.*

Tursunov himself didn't know what had happened. It was too early and the blast too close. Either Abdel had changed the attack, or one of the martyrs had chosen to go early. Perhaps he had been confronted by police, or by French security services.

The one thing he did know was that he couldn't sit at his table pretending nothing had happened. Calmly, he stood and followed the other patrons out of the dining room.

In the lobby, curious guests were pressing up against the windows and pushing through the doors to get outside, in order to figure out what had happened. Tursunov headed for the stairwell.

He took the stairs two and three at a time, hoping to get to his room and out onto the balcony before anything else happened.

Halfway there, he heard a second explosion, followed by a third, and a fourth.

All of the martyrs were detonating now. It was the protocol. Even if one went early, they were to get to their targets and detonate immediately.

Taking a deep breath at his landing, he opened the stairwell door, stepped out into the hallway, and walked calmly toward his room.

Once inside, he rushed to the balcony, threw open his still-intact French doors, and stepped outside.

As he looked out over the slaughter and destruction below, he excitedly repeated one phrase under his breath.

Allahu Akbar. Allahu Akbar. ALLAHU AKBAR.

CHAPTER 54

"I got here as quickly as I could," said Lydia Ryan as she entered the Director's wood-paneled conference room. She had always been in awe of this space. It had a tremendous amount of history, not the least of which being that this was the room where the bin Laden raid had been run. All of the monitors were tuned to live feeds from Paris.

A group was seated at the end of the long conference table. Several rolling suitcases were lined up against the wall. The Director waved her over.

"We're sending over a team?" she asked, as she removed a laptop from her briefcase.

"FBI too," McGee replied. "They're going to need all the help they can get." He then turned to a young analyst and said, "Bring Deputy Director Ryan up to speed."

The young man nodded and, picking up a remote, stated, "We got this video from French Intelligence twenty minutes ago. It was shot by one of their people, just after the bombs went off. I've got to warn you, it's bad."

All bombing aftermaths were bad, especially when civilians were involved. Either this person was new, or this really was on a different level. Taking a breath, she signaled for him to roll the footage.

As soon as the video started, she realized he had not been exaggerating. Amidst helicopters hovering overhead and the klaxons of emergency vehicles rushing to the scene, all you could hear were people screaming. The sound was horrible—like animals being slaughtered. The images were even worse.

Victims' limbs had been sheared off. Bodies lay, missing heads. Torsos had been torn open, their internal organs spilling out. There was blood absolutely everywhere.

As the French Intelligence officer walked his camera through the carnage, Ryan noticed people at the conference table turn their eyes away. They had already viewed the video. She tried to steel herself for whatever was coming up.

In addition to ripping through people, the bombs had ripped through the carnival stalls. The destruction was unlike anything she had ever seen. But these weren't the scenes her colleagues couldn't bear to watch. As soon as she saw the smoldering carousel, she knew what was coming.

Ryan was reminded of how ISIS had attempted to detonate a suicide bomber inside Kidsville—the children and family camp at Burning Man.

Even though one bomber had detonated in another part of the festival, stopping the Kidsville attack had been considered the greatest win of the operation. But seeing what she now saw, none of that mattered anymore.

The tiny bodies lay everywhere. Their injuries were just as horrific as the adults', but they were even more heart-wrenching due to their age.

The bomber had struck inside the part of the carnival geared toward the youngest attendees. Mixed with the wreckage of the carousel animals were actual ponies, some barely alive and still tethered to the rigging that allowed children to ride them in circles. Their screams of pain, mixed with those of parents and children, were unbearable.

A police officer could be seen approaching one of the animals and drawing his pistol, only to be stopped by a colleague for fear of creating a panic that a shooter was loose somewhere.

The French Intelligence officer seemed to have ice in his veins as he proceeded calmly through the rest of the carnival, documenting everything he could.

But when he reached the end, when there was nothing more to document, the phone dropped from his hand and the man could be heard throwing up.

The analyst paused the video there.

"Why don't we take ten minutes," Director McGee said. "I'd like to speak with the Deputy Director alone."

As the attendees pushed back from the table and filed out of the room, he picked up the remote and turned off the monitors.

Once the last person had exited and the door had shut behind them, he turned to Ryan and said, "The death toll is going to exceed Spain."

She shook her head at the grim news. "How many Americans?"

"We've got our people at the Embassy working on it. We know of eighteen already, but we expect the number to go higher."

"Suicide bombers, or were the explosives planted?"

"We're digging into the surrounding CCTV footage," said McGee, "but the working hypothesis right now is suicide bombers. At least six. One appears to have gone off prematurely and the rest followed not long after."

"Why do we think one went off *prematurely*?"

"Because it happened on the edge of the carnival, not inside, where the explosion would have done much more damage. French police reportedly approached a man in a soccer jersey shortly before the first explosion. We're trying to run that down."

"What can I do to help?" she asked.

"Get Harvath to move faster. Whatever it takes. I don't care."

"I'll reach out to him. In the meantime, what about my request?"

McGee leaned back in his chair, closed his eyes, and pinched the bridge of his nose. "Access to the Malice program."

"It's a big ask. I under—"

"Especially right now."

"I understand, but the more Reed and I have discussed this, the more concerned I've become. Somebody might be trying to smother us in the crib."

The Director didn't respond.

"The whole idea," Ryan continued, "is for us to assemble a lifeboat for the Agency. If there are people out there attempting to drill holes in it, we have to know."

He thought about it for a moment more before replying. "If I agreed, how would it play out?"

Ryan had wargamed it as best she could. Her plan wasn't perfect, but she felt she had come up with a pretty good idea. Remaining as brief as possible, she laid it out for him.

McGee let it all sink in. It *was* a big ask. And it involved a lot of risk for the CIA. If it went sideways, even the President wouldn't be able to save them.

Point by point, he went through his concerns. And point by point, she addressed them.

Finally, he only had one question left. "How are you going to get him in without anyone seeing him?"

Looking over at the suitcases along the wall, she replied, "I think I have an idea."

CHAPTER 55

Within minutes of the Paris attack, everyone's phones started going off in the restaurant. As the notification chimes rang, Harvath called the waiter over and paid their bill. He wanted to get to a television. Their waiter suggested an Irish bar a few blocks away.

Entering the pub, they saw the TV sets were tuned to several English-language stations including CNN and BBC. The team ordered coffee and energy drinks. They had a lot to get done this evening and things had just taken an even more serious turn.

The men were not shy about how they felt. Not even with Lovett in their midst.

"Fucking cocksuckers," Morrison growled as he watched the bloody footage from the Tuileries.

There were already preliminary reports coming through of how many dead and wounded, as well as the victims' countries of origin. France, Germany, Japan, the United States, Mexico . . . the crawl on the bottom of the screen seemed to just keep going.

"Religion of peace, my ass," said Barton, all but convinced he knew who and what was behind the attack.

Staelin and Harvath both watched the footage in silence, studying it for clues.

"Same group as Spain?" the Delta Force operative wondered aloud after several moments.

"And Burning Man," Harvath replied quietly.

"Were we supposed to stop this?"

Harvath nodded solemnly. It was why they had been put on the trail of the dead ISIS chemist. It had taken them first to Libya, and now Italy. The attacks were connected. He was sure of it.

They went back to watching the TVs in silence.

Everyone in the bar was in a state of shock. No one could speak. There was genuine fear in every single face.

Harvath knew what they were thinking. *How long until attacks like this start happening in Italy?*

The barman, a redheaded transplant from Dublin named Carey, was pouring complimentary shots of Irish whiskey. He wanted everyone in the pub to raise their glasses out of respect for the dead and wounded.

Harvath politely declined, explaining his team had to compete in the morning. Carey didn't ask in what. Instead, he retrieved five Red Bulls from the cooler and handed them to him.

When the time came, the team raised their drinks along with everyone else in the pub as the barman led them in a quick farewell to the deceased and a prayer for those who remained.

Harvath didn't think the attack in Paris would change Carlo Ragusa's plans, but he raised the subject with Lovett anyway.

"Mount Etna could erupt tonight," she stated, referencing the volcano on the east coast of the island, "and this horserace would still go in the morning."

"Then we'd better get started."

• • •

Lovett's contact had emailed her a picture of Naya, the Nigerian bartender at the Black Cat, and once more she showed it around.

After going over the plan one last time, Harvath organized the team into waves. As Morrison's job was to reposition the SUV, he sent him first.

His instructions were simple: Go in, sit at the bar, and send a text as to whether Naya was working.

Because their radios were so bulky, there was no way they could hide them under their street clothes. They were lucky enough simply to conceal their pistols.

If Ragusa was coming to see his mistress this evening, Harvath figured it would happen in one of two ways. Either the Mafioso would spend the bulk of his evening at home with his wife and family before heading out, or he would get to his mistress's apartment early and expect her to cook for him.

With the little he knew about Sicilians, he doubted Ragusa was going to trade his wife's cooking for his Nigerian mistress's. Plus, there was no way he was going to take Naya out to dinner. That wasn't how men in the Cosa Nostra operated. It was likely a very closely held secret that he was seeing the bartender.

Harvath assumed that Naya would work her shift until Ragusa showed up. Once he arrived, or let her know he was on the way, she'd punch out and head upstairs.

Fifteen minutes later, they had their answer. Harvath read the text aloud. "Naya and another woman tending bar. Club less than half full. Music sucks."

"Remind him to smile," Barton said.

"How's the mood?" asked Staelin. "Any TVs on in there?"

Ignoring Barton, Harvath texted back Staelin's question.

"No TVs," came the response. Harvath read it aloud.

"Good," Staelin replied. "We want everybody having a real good time."

"Let's just hope it's loud," Harvath remarked.

"Don't worry," the Delta Force operative stated. "It's an Italian nightclub. It'll be plenty loud."

Harvath then looked at Barton. "You're up."

"Don't forget to smile," Staelin added as the SEAL headed out.

Walking away, Barton gave him the finger over his shoulder.

"He's sweet," the Delta Force operative said as he took a sip of his Red Bull.

Harvath texted Morrison to let him know Barton was inbound. Then, turning to Lovett, he said, "Time to go."

Standing up, he looked at Staelin, who was eyeing two attractive young women who had just entered the pub. "See you there?" he asked.

"Yeah," the man replied, taking a beat longer than Harvath would have liked. "See you there."

Shaking his head, he gestured for Lovett to go first, and then followed her out the door.

As soon as they stepped outside, he caught the look on her face. "Don't worry," he said. "He'll be there."

"That's not what I'm worried about," she answered.

He was about to respond when he felt the first drops of rain begin to fall.

CHAPTER 56

The rain wasn't bad at first, but then it started to come down hard. Harvath and Lovett took refuge in a nearby doorway.

Based on what they had seen on the radar, it didn't look as if it would hang around for long.

Lovett got back to what had been bugging her when they were on their way out of the pub. "Have you figured out what you're going to do with Ragusa if he doesn't want to talk?"

"Don't worry," Harvath replied. "He'll talk."

"But what if he doesn't?"

"We'll burn that bridge when we come to it."

Was that supposed to be a joke? she wondered. This was serious. "If anything happens to him," she stated, "I'm the one who's going to get a call from the Carabinieri."

Harvath appreciated the spot she was in, but he didn't really care. They had a job to do. They were going to get the information out of Ragusa no matter what.

"How long have you been in Italy?" he asked.

"Almost two years. And before you say anything, I'd actually like to finish out my time here. I'd also like to be able to continue my career and have a nice long retirement without a Red Notice from Interpol hanging over my head."

This was exactly what was wrong with the CIA, and it pissed him off. "There were probably a lot of people at Burning Man, and in Spain and Paris, also hoping for long retirements with plenty of travel."

"Ouch," she replied.

Harvath didn't respond.

"Listen," she continued. "I didn't mean it to sound—"

"The rain's letting up," he said, stepping out of the doorway. "Let's move."

. . .

They walked in silence back to the repositioned SUV. As Lovett pulled her running shoes from her bag and put them on, Harvath texted Barton and Staelin. Naya was still behind the bar and Staelin was en route to take Barton's place.

Once she had changed her shoes, they headed off for the street behind the Black Cat, Via Giuseppe Mario Puglia.

Lovett had wanted to clear the air. When they stopped at the corner and Harvath pretended he was checking his messages while he checked out the street, she spoke.

"I want you to know that I'm committed to this assignment. I understand what's at stake."

"Good," he replied, scanning for anything out of the ordinary.

"I also want you to know that I've worked very hard to get where I am. I don't want it blown needlessly."

That got his attention. "What's that supposed to mean?"

"It means you've got a reputation. You're known for being a cowboy. A lot of china gets broken when you're around."

"And?"

"I like my job," she said. "I'm good at it. I'd like to keep it."

"That makes two of us," he responded, as he tucked his phone back in his pocket and turned to walk down the street. "Just do what I say and you'll be fine."

. . .

They did two passes of the building with the scaffolding in front. A very long time ago, it had been a school. Now, it was being renovated into apartments.

There were bars over the lower windows and heavy wooden doors on the ground floor.

"Why can't we go in through one of these?" she asked, nodding at one.

"Lever locks," Harvath replied, pointing at the hardware. "I don't have the right tools. Even if I did, they take too long to pick."

Lovett looked up at the scaffolding and resigned herself to the fact that she was going to have to climb.

"It's wet, so be careful," said Harvath.

She nodded.

The scaffolding was wrapped in gray plastic netting to make it less of an eyesore. Combined with the dimly lit street, it would help hide their ascent.

Orange plastic webbing had been wrapped around the base, ostensibly to keep people from doing exactly what they were about to do.

When Harvath was sure no one was watching, he untied a portion of it and climbed inside. Filled with trepidation, Lovett followed.

There were no ladders and no stairs. They had to scale the scaffolding itself.

As soon as she started, her heart began to pound and she began to perspire. She reminded herself not to look down.

A few narrow boards pushed up against the facade marked each floor. They bowed under their combined weight as Harvath tried to wrench open the metal shutters, all of which had been locked from the inside of the building. The only windows without shutters were on the very top floor.

The farther up they climbed, the more her muscles felt like hardening cement. It was getting tougher to get handholds as her fingers froze in midclench. She was dizzy and her legs felt as if they were made of lead.

"Almost there," Harvath reassured her. "You got this."

Lovett wasn't so sure. Her pace slowed even more. She hated being a slave to her fear, but she couldn't help it.

"I can't," she finally admitted.

"*Can't* what?"

"I can't climb any higher."

"Stay right there," he whispered. "I'm coming back down."

Beneath them in the street, they could hear the hum of a motor scooter approaching.

Harvath waited for it to pass and then climbed down to her. Slowly, he helped her descend to the last set of boards she had been on.

"Wait here," he said.

"Where are you going?"

"Don't worry. I'll be back."

And with that, he began climbing upward again.

Standing on the wobbly boards, she gripped the metal pipes of the scaffolding as hard as she could and pressed her face against the cool stone of the building's facade.

She stood there for what felt like forever before she heard a noise to her right. It sounded like a bolt being pulled, followed by the grating of metal on metal.

Opening her eyes, she saw a shutter had been opened. Standing on the other side of the window was Harvath.

"Give me your hand," he said, as he reached out for her.

She took his hand and he helped her climb inside the musty old building.

CHAPTER 57

O nce they were safely inside, Harvath took out his phone and texted Barton. A couple of seconds later, he received a response. Barton was on his way.

Lovett sat on a stack of tiles and tried to catch her breath.

"You going to be okay?" Harvath asked.

She nodded.

"Good. I'm going to take a look at the courtyard in back. Wait here."

She nodded and watched as he exited the room and disappeared into the darkness out in the hallway.

Using the low beam of his flashlight so as not to give away his presence in the building, he navigated to the rear stairwell. On the second floor, he came to a steel fire door and, first making sure it wasn't actively alarmed, inched it open and stepped outside.

He was on the flat roof at the north end of the complex. An eight-foot-high wall ran along it, separating it from the building next door. Hopping up onto one of two hot water tanks, he peered over the edge. It was a straight drop, two stories down. They were going to have to go to the end of the flat roof and then scramble up and over another roof system to get to Naya's apartment atop the Black Cat.

Climbing down from the hot water tank, he retraced his steps back inside and rejoined Lovett. Seconds later, Barton appeared at the window.

"Knock, knock," he whispered.

Harvath offered him a hand and helped him climb through.

Once the SEAL was in, Harvath looked at Lovett. "Ready to move?"

Her mouth was dry and her stomach was still in knots, but the dizziness had passed and her heart rate had come down. Nodding, she stood up and followed Harvath out of the room. Barton brought up the rear.

The trio proceeded to the staircase and down to the second floor. When they reached the steel door, Harvath texted Staelin for a final SITREP before they exited.

"Naya is still behind the bar," he texted back. "Music is plenty loud. You're good to go."

Harvath shared the message with Barton and Lovett, opened the door, and led them outside.

At the end of the flat roof, they squeezed past a set of solar panels and reached another pair of hot water tanks.

Turning to Lovett, he said, "I'm going to go first and you're going to come right behind me, okay? Keep your eyes on me the entire time. Don't look at anything else. You're going to be great."

She forced a smile, and when Barton flashed him the thumbs-up, he began his climb.

Leaping onto the hot water tanks, he then pulled himself up onto the roof of the building next to the Black Cat.

It wasn't terribly steep, but it was covered with curved, terra-cotta tiles. They were very hard to walk on. Now, slick from the rain, they were even more difficult.

Harvath waited for Lovett to climb up onto a water tank and then held out his hand to help her onto the roof. As soon as Barton had joined them, Harvath began walking.

He chose his steps very carefully. They were three stories above the street. One wrong move and it would all be over. Once you started sliding, there wasn't anything to stop you from going over the edge.

He walked near the roof's seam, testing each tile with only part of his weight before fully committing. Every couple of steps, he looked over his shoulder to see how Lovett was doing. Though the fear was etched across her face, she kept moving. So did Harvath.

He was only fifteen feet away from the end of the roof when he heard a tile crack and break away behind him.

He turned just in time to see not Lovett, but Barton lose his footing and go down.

Before he could get even two steps, Lovett had dropped to her stomach, reached out her hand, and grabbed him.

Her rescue, though, was short-lived as he began sliding toward the edge and pulling her with him. Barton was just too heavy and the roof too wet to stop it from happening.

Harvath moved as fast as he could. He could hear Lovett grunting under the strain of trying to hold on to him.

"Don't let go!" Harvath ordered her.

"I can't hold him!"

Harvath picked up his pace and as he did, he slipped and almost went down.

"I'm losing him!"

Feet away, Harvath lunged just as Lovett lost her grip. He came down hard on the tiles and there was a *slap* as his hand wrapped around the SEAL's wrist.

Slowly, he helped pull Barton back up.

Had Lovett not done what she had, Barton would have gone over the edge. She had saved his life.

"Thank you," he said to her. And then turning to Harvath, he also offered his thanks.

"You're welcome. We'll talk about starting you on a diet tomorrow. Right now, we've got to get to that apartment."

"Roger that," he said, as he raised himself onto his feet.

Lovett did the same and flashed Harvath the thumbs-up. The fear he had seen in her face moments ago was gone. In its place was a determination to finish this task and get off the rooftops.

Taking up the lead, Harvath began walking again and gave them the signal to follow.

Cautiously, they fell into step behind him.

CHAPTER 58

A t the end of the roof was another wall. Scaling it, they were able to get onto the roof of Naya's apartment.

The bartender lived on the fourth and very top floor of the building. The challenge now was getting inside.

She had a small balcony off the back, but an awning obscured most of it. With a much steeper roof, and drop-offs on both sides, only as an absolute last resort would they try to jump down onto it. And even then, trying to do it in the dark would only up the risk. That's why Harvath had wanted to use the skylight.

"It's locked," Barton said when they finally reached it.

Harvath wasn't surprised. There was a lot of crime in Palermo. "Let me take a look," he responded, pulling out his flashlight.

The skylight was over the bathroom and it was a piece of junk. Whoever had constructed it had used wired glass. One of the biggest myths on the planet was that the wire made it stronger, and therefore better for security purposes. In fact, the opposite was true. The inclusion of wire actually weakened the glass. It was good in fire situations, but that was it.

The skylight was old and in lousy shape. Pushing on it, he could feel it give. The wood around it was soft and rotten. Pulling out his knife, he tried to wedge it underneath without any luck. They desperately needed to get off the rooftop and into the apartment.

Motioning Barton and Lovett to move back, he put his knife back in his pocket and took out his pistol. Turning it in his hand, he drew his arm back and smashed the weapon into the skylight.

The entire pane of wired glass not only shattered, but fell out of the frame and crashed into the bathroom below.

Harvath raked the moldy edges of the skylight opening to make sure no glass or pieces of wire had been left behind and then got into position to cover Barton as he made the entry.

It was an easy drop—only about five feet. Barton had aimed to land on the toilet. He hit his target, but there was just one problem. The lid was as cheap as the skylight. One of his boots ended up punching right through and into the bowl.

Harvath had never seen the SEAL move so fast. His foot had barely touched the water before he leapt up, almost straight out of the skylight.

"Fuck," Barton whispered, as he simultaneously pulled his pistol and tried to shake the water off his boot. Stepping over to the bathroom door, he peered into the apartment and then signaled for Lovett and Harvath to come down.

Even on the top floor, they could hear the dance music throbbing from the club downstairs. The apartment smelled like cigarettes and cheap perfume.

Quickly, they cleared the rest of the rooms, and, confident no one was home, they cleaned up the glass in the bathroom and began to get everything they needed pulled together.

Forty-five minutes later, Harvath's phone vibrated with a message from Staelin. Naya had received a text and was now divvying up tips with the other bartender. When she handed her register drawer to one of the managers, Staelin pinged him again and told Harvath to expect company.

Because of the music, they couldn't hear any movement coming up the stairs. But soon enough, there was the unmistakable sound of a key in the lock.

When the door opened, Naya stepped inside. She was very tall and very pretty.

She closed and locked the door behind her, then pulled off her boots and tossed them in the corner.

Next, she pulled off her top and threw it through her open bedroom door onto the bed. She did the same with her skirt. She wasn't wearing a bra or panties.

Walking naked into her bathroom, she reached behind the curtain and started the shower. At the sink, she squeezed some toothpaste onto her toothbrush and began brushing her teeth.

It was then, as she looked in the mirror, that she noticed the hole in the roof above the toilet behind her.

Instantly, she spun around, and when she did, she saw the woman at her bathroom door with a gun pointed at her.

"Be calm," Lovett told her in Italian. "We're not here for you. Do everything we say and nothing bad will happen."

CHAPTER 59

Securing Naya in the bedroom, they dimmed the lights and got ready. Lovett had read the text on the bartender's phone and knew that Ragusa would be there shortly.

Half an hour later, Harvath received a message from Staelin. "He just pulled up. Two bodyguards with him. Get ready."

Harvath relayed the information to his team and everyone got into position.

Naya had informed Lovett that Ragusa always came upstairs alone. His men would either wait in the car, have a drink in the bar, or stand at the front door and chat with the bouncer until it was time to leave.

It sounded plausible, but all the same, Harvath didn't trust her. Yet whether the mobster came to the door by himself or with his two goons didn't matter. The team would be ready.

According to the bartender, Ragusa had his own key to her apartment. He expected her to be in bed, naked, and waiting for him when he arrived. So that's where they had put her. And though Harvath was glad to have the cover of the loud music from downstairs, he hated not being able to judge how many people were headed toward them by noise from the staircase.

The seconds dragged into minutes.

Finally, Harvath's phone vibrated again. "Goon One just sat down at the bar," Staelin texted. "Goon Two is talking with the bouncer. Target is unaccompanied. All yours."

Harvath passed it along. Moments later they heard Ragusa's key in the lock.

They had no idea how many times the Mafioso had been to the apartment to see the young Nigerian bartender, but enough that he had a routine. And if he had a routine, especially one that involved leaving his security downstairs, he hadn't arrived expecting trouble—anything but, in fact.

Ragusa had come expecting a good time with his mistress. After this visit, he was going to take his security very seriously. That was if Harvath let him live.

He had been racking his brain, trying to come up with a way so that there'd be no blowback for Lovett. But so far, he hadn't been able to come up with anything.

Depending on what information they got out of the mobster, they might not be able to let him go. The last thing Harvath wanted was for him to report back to ISIS that he'd been interrogated by an American team. Even worse—that the team was interested in knowing the destination of a Tunisian chemistry student who had drowned while being smuggled across the Mediterranean Sea.

The only way to keep him quiet would be to kill him or ghost him to a black site facility like the Solarium back on Malta. Either way, once he went missing, Lovett was going to be on the short list of suspects. Her antiterror contact at the Carabinieri would be all over her.

That wasn't Harvath's problem, though. Working at the CIA meant you had to be willing to take risks. It wasn't about covering your ass and hanging on for twenty years until you could collect a pension. The closer you got to the tip of America's spear, the more dangerous things became. As far as Harvath was concerned, the only measure that mattered was whether you did everything within your power to achieve the mission you had been sent to perform.

Right now, everything revolved around Ragusa and his interrogation. How cooperative or uncooperative he was, and what kind of information they got out of him, would dictate what they would do next.

As he watched the knob turn, Harvath's whole body tensed. He couldn't wait to get his hands on Ragusa.

The only other group he hated as much as terrorists were mobsters. This was one interrogation he was going to take extreme pleasure in.

The door began to open, and as it did, he could feel Ragusa on the other side. A thick, menacing energy radiated from him.

Harvath was so preoccupied with it that he almost didn't notice how slowly the Mafioso was opening the door. *Had he sensed Harvath as well?*

His question was answered as soon as he saw the muzzle of the man's pistol.

Sliding his foot forward, so that Ragusa couldn't slam the door into his face, Harvath grabbed the barrel of the weapon and yelled, "Gun!" as he wrenched the weapon sideways out of his grasp.

Barton leapt from where he had been hiding, grabbed Ragusa by his jacket, and wrestled him into the apartment. The two men landed in a tangled pile on the floor.

Though he was taller and much heavier, the Mafioso was no match for the younger and stronger SEAL. A fan of mixed martial arts, Barton liked nothing more than going to the ground. In no time flat, he had Ragusa in a submission hold, and, demoralized, the man gave up.

Getting him to his feet, they marched him into the kitchen where they duct-taped him to a chair.

Harvath had already unloaded the man's Beretta pistol and had placed it on top of the refrigerator. Emptying his pockets, he placed his keys, wallet, cash, and cell phone on the counter.

Pulling up a chair, he swung a leg over and sat on it backward. He rested his arms on the back of the chair as he studied Ragusa. Anger simmered all over the Sicilian's face.

As soon as Harvath asked him if he spoke English, the Mafioso began cursing at him in Italian.

Spittle collected in the corners of his mouth. He went on and on, no doubt unpacking everything he was going to do to his captors once this was all over. Harvath let him get it out of his system.

Then, giving him one last chance to admit whether he spoke English, he called in Lovett.

CHAPTER 60

Even though Harvath was addressing Lovett, he looked directly at Ragusa as he spoke. "Who is this?" he asked, holding up his phone with a picture of Mustapha Marzouk, the deceased chemistry student.

"He says he doesn't know," she replied.

"Tell him to look harder."

"Same answer. He claims he doesn't recognize the man."

"Ask him about Festus Aghaku, the water taxi driver for the Black Axe."

Lovett did and waited for his reply. It came back the same. Ragusa claimed he had no idea who they were talking about.

Harvath was losing his patience.

Holding the picture back up, he said, "Six weeks ago, you sent Festus Aghaku and his crew out into a storm to meet a boat from Libya. On it was the man in the picture. Who is he and who told you to pick him up?"

He burned holes into the man's eyes with his own as Lovett spoke. When the man responded, Harvath didn't need a translation. It was the same answer he had been giving since the beginning.

"Tell him I know everything about him. I know about his wife. I know about his five children. I know where he lives. And tell him that I know all about the men and the dogs he uses to protect his house and his family. None of which will stop me from getting to them."

As Lovett translated, Harvath watched as the anger and rage returned to the man's face. She hadn't even finished speaking before he went off on another tirade of curses and threats.

When Lovett began to translate, Harvath shook his head. He had gotten the gist of it.

"Let me be perfectly clear," he stated, once the man had finished. "You will tell me everything I want to know. The only question is how much pain you want to experience in the process."

This time when the man started cursing at him, Harvath didn't let it go. Cupping his hand, he hit Ragusa on the left side of his head.

It was the same technique he had used on the satellite phone salesman in Libya. It forced a painful stream of pressurized air into the ear canal, which could cause dizziness and even nausea.

Harvath had learned it as a SEAL, and he liked it for two reasons. One, it didn't risk breaking any bones in the hand the way a punch could. And two, it didn't leave any marks—unless you struck the subject so hard that you ruptured the eardrum. Out of respect for Lovett, he was trying to be as measured as possible.

He waited for the man to shake the stars from his head before continuing.

Once he felt the Mafioso had recovered enough, he spoke very slowly and explained, "As a Sicilian, I know honor is important to you. So, if you do not cooperate with me, I'm going to make sure that your body is found right here with your Nigerian girlfriend. But that's not all.

"I'm going to make it look like you both overdosed on drugs. And I will stage a scene that leaves no doubt that in your relationship, Naya was the man and you, Carlo Ragusa, were the woman. Understand?"

He understood all right. When Lovett finished translating, the mobster exploded. It was his angriest reaction yet. Harvath had found his button.

"I will make sure that your wife and children know exactly how and where your body was discovered, and I'll make sure all of your enemies know. And when word spreads, I'll make sure that there are plenty of pictures, which will live forever, on the Internet. In fact, when people in Sicily hear the name Ragusa, I promise you that's the only thing they'll think of."

Yet again, the Sicilian went ballistic. But when Harvath raised his hand to slap him, he stopped.

For a second, he wondered if they were making progress. Holding his phone back up and showing the mobster the photo of Mustapha Marzouk, he asked, "Where was he going? Where were you supposed to take him?"

Shaking his head, Ragusa smiled and repeated his same stale line in Italian, "I don't know what you're talking about."

Harvath smiled back. "Do you like being in the smuggling business, Carlo? Do you like smuggling terrorists and being responsible for helping to drown countless people?"

Lovett listened to him and then said to Harvath, "He says he's not a smuggler. He owns a few nightclubs, but his real business is in growing lemons and tangerines."

Harvath looked at her and replied, "Tell him we're done talking."

He then nodded at Barton, who stepped into the kitchen from behind and pulled a pillowcase over the Mafioso's head. Tying it tight at the base of his skull, he tipped the man's chair back onto its rear legs and dragged him into the bathroom.

There, he set him down with his back to the half-filled tub. When Harvath nodded, Barton tipped the chair backward, so that it rested against the edge of the tub and Ragusa's head was suspended over the water.

Anticipating what was about to happen, the mobster began to struggle. Barton held the chair firm.

"Drowning is a terrible way to die," said Harvath. From the doorway, Lovett translated.

Now, Harvath was really done talking and he signaled for Lovett that she could go. She shook her head. *No.* She intended to stay. That was fine by him.

Grabbing the plastic pitcher sitting on the side of the tub, Harvath filled it with water and without any warning, began to slowly pour it over Ragusa's nose and mouth.

CHAPTER 61

The mobster sputtered and coughed as he thrashed back and forth in his chair trying to escape the water. But there was no escape. Harvath kept slowly pouring. It took forty seconds, but it must have felt like a lifetime to Ragusa. When the pitcher was empty, Harvath refilled it.

He paused to let the Mafioso just begin to catch his breath and then, as soon as he began to inhale, began the process all over again.

It had been his experience that if he stopped right after the first round, subjects tried to hold out longer. But immediately going into a second round scrambled their brains. They became panicked.

So Harvath poured from the pitcher once more. Halfway through, Ragusa began to vomit.

Harvath untied the pillowcase and had Barton lean the chair forward, back onto all four legs.

He let him get it all out of his system, and then nodded for Barton to lean him back against the tub.

Right away, the mobster began to protest. Harvath refilled the pitcher and started again from full.

Ragusa thrashed even more violently this time. Harvath decided to stretch his pour a few extra seconds. By the time he was done, the mobster had been broken.

Harvath motioned Lovett all the way into the bathroom so that she could hear what Ragusa was saying. The CIA operative tried to step around the mess. The floor was disgusting and the smell was growing unbearable.

She had Ragusa repeat what he had been mumbling and then translated for Harvath. "He says he knows the man in your picture."

"What's his name?" Harvath replied.

Lovett presented the question to him in Italian, and then said, "He doesn't remember the name. Something Muslim. But he does remember the man's face."

"Tell him he's going to have to do a hell of a lot better than that."

She did, and then waited while Ragusa spoke. Finally, she replied, "He was important. A VIP."

"VIP to whom?"

"He doesn't know."

Harvath looked at her. "What does he mean *he doesn't know*? Who paid him?"

Lovett repeated the question to the Mafioso and waited for him to answer. As he spoke, she translated. "This wasn't a usual job. He did it as a favor."

"For whom?"

"He says he can't reveal the name. If he does, it will start a war."

Harvath rolled his eyes and, looking at Barton, said, "He obviously wants more. Tip him back over."

"No! No! No!" the man implored. The word was the same in English as it was in Italian.

While he screamed, Harvath filled a new pitcher of water. Just as he began to pour, the man yelled out another detail.

"Roma!"

"Who the hell's Roma?" Harvath asked, but Lovett held up her hand for him to be quiet.

After a quick back-and-forth with Ragusa, she said, "It's not a person. It's the city. *Rome*. That's where they were taking the chemist."

"What were they supposed to do once they got him there?"

The CIA operative asked the mobster and then replied, "Apparently, he had his own people there who would get him the rest of the way into Europe."

"Bullshit," said Harvath as he began pouring the water over Ragusa's face.

Again, the man cried out, pleading with him to stop. Harvath didn't until his pitcher was empty. Then he filled it back up.

"*Per favore.* No," he begged.

"Tell him I want to know who he did the favor for. Who asked him to smuggle Mustapha to Rome?"

"Marzouk!" the Sicilian interjected, screaming the man's name. "Mustapha Marzouk."

If he was hoping that was going to get him off the hook, he was sorely mistaken. Lovett explained as much to him.

They went back and forth until Harvath once more lost his patience. Filling the pitcher, he told Lovett to stand back.

Ragusa began to beg.

"Give me a name."

"No. *Per favore. Basta,*" he insisted.

Harvath let the water flow.

"La Formícula!" the mobster cried as he choked. "La Formícula! *Per favore, basta!*"

Harvath stopped and looked at Lovett, who began questioning Ragusa. Soon enough, he gave up a name."

"Antonio Vottari," she said. "Also known as La Formícula or the Ant."

"Who is he?"

"Mafia from Calabria. They're called the N'drangheta."

Harvath knew Calabria. If Italy was a boot, it was the part that made up the toe and looked like it was kicking the island of Sicily.

He was about to ask her another question when his phone vibrated. Pulling it from his pocket, he read the message. It was a text from Staelin.

"What is it?" Lovett asked.

"I don't know," he replied, signaling Barton to keep an eye on Ragusa. "A whole bunch of cars just pulled up outside."

Walking to the front of the darkened apartment, Harvath moved the curtain only a matter of millimeters so he could look out.

Down on the street, he saw a string of three black sedans, a black SUV, and a black, windowless van.

As he watched, someone opened the front passenger door of the lead vehicle and stepped out. *Were these Ragusa's people?*

The man standing in the street took out a cell phone, pressed a button, and raised it to his ear.

Seconds later, Harvath heard a ring coming from the kitchen where they had left the mobster's cell phone.

Instantly, Harvath's mind began to turn, figuring out how they were going to get the hell out of there without getting in a gunfight.

But then he heard Lovett answer the call, *in English*. Turning around, he saw her holding her own cell phone.

"It's the Carabinieri," she stated. "They say they have men on the roof and the building is surrounded."

CHAPTER 62

In the aftermath of the Paris attack, it had been all hands on deck. People had been in and out of the Central Intelligence Agency all afternoon. Director McGee hadn't been able to reach out to Lydia Ryan until after five o'clock. He had asked his assistant to summon her back and tell her to come "ready to travel."

When she arrived in the Director's Conference Room, McGee was waiting for her. "Any problems?" he asked.

"None," she replied, as she set her rolling suitcase upright and unzipped it. "I appreciate you sending your team down to meet me at the car."

Extending her hand, she helped Nicholas climb out.

He thanked her and then turned and shook hands with the Director.

"I apologize for the subterfuge," said McGee.

"That's the business you're in," Nicholas responded. "Besides, how many people can say they were smuggled into the CIA in a piece of luggage."

McGee smiled. "Hopefully, you're the only one."

"And as we agreed," Ryan reminded him, "this isn't a story you're ever going to tell."

"Agreed," the little man conceded. "That is our arrangement."

Getting down to business, the Director asked, "How much time do you think you're going to need?"

"It depends on how the Malice source code is structured. I only need a piece of it, but we'll have to test it and make sure it works."

"Is Jake good with all of this?" Ryan asked.

McGee nodded. Jake Fleischer was a brilliant hacker and IT specialist. In the CIA's Directorate of Digital Innovation, his expertise in cyber threats and cyber security were second to none.

Fleischer could have been running the Agency's Center for Cyber Intelligence. He was eminently qualified. But he didn't want the headache. Fleischer wanted to be on the cutting edge, pushing the boundaries of what the CIA could do when it came to cyber espionage.

"Jake's on board," said the Director.

"How much did you have to tell him?"

"I told him this was important, that he needed to trust me, and that he'd be the only person in this room with a computer."

Nicholas looked from Ryan to McGee. "I don't understand. How am I supposed to get what I need?"

"You're going to work with Jake," the Director replied. "Every string of code you need, he's going to get it for you."

"It would be a lot faster if—"

McGee cut him off. "It's not personal, Nicholas. It's business. I'm not giving you unfettered, unsupervised access to the Agency's cyber arsenal. This happens my way, or it doesn't happen at all."

The little man nodded. He understood. While the Carlton Group was building an ark to save America's intelligence capabilities, McGee had taken an oath to faithfully serve his country and execute his duties as the Director of the CIA.

"How confident are we that what happens in this room will stay in this room?" asked Ryan. "Even as Deputy DCI, I don't have any history with Fleischer."

"A large part of what I've been doing," McGee replied, "is identifying core personnel who are mission critical as we move forward—people who believe in the Agency's mission and are absolutely dedicated to it. Jake's one of them.

"He knows that something very serious is going on, but that the details of what he's being asked to do cannot be fully explained. He also understands he isn't allowed to talk to anyone about this."

Ryan smiled. "Real cloak and dagger. That's what everybody here signs up for, right? And on top of that, it's an assignment from the Director himself. What else could he have said, but *yes*?"

"He's a good man," McGee added as he turned and looked at Nicholas. "He also understands that there are some unorthodox components associated with this."

"Meaning me," the little man stated.

The Director nodded as the phone in front of him rang.

Picking it up, he listened to his assistant and said, "Okay. Thank you." Turning to Ryan and Nicholas, he said, "Jake's here."

CHAPTER 63

"You lied to me, Paolo," Lovett stated.

They were in a safe house in Albergheria, the oldest of the four *mandamenti*, or historical districts, that made up the old city of Palermo.

Paolo Argento stood in front of a table where his men had arrayed the weapons taken from the Americans. "You lied to me as well."

Argento was a handsome, fit man in his early fifties. He was tan, with spiked gray hair and a neatly trimmed gray beard. He wore black jeans, black boots, and an untucked, black button-down shirt. His sleeves were rolled up to his elbows. On his left wrist was a black Panerai diver's watch.

The Carabinieri operated under the Italian Ministry of Defense and the Raggruppamento Operativo Speciale was the Carabinieri's main investigative unit. The number-one goal of the ROS was taking down organized crime and terrorist networks.

They conducted a tremendous amount of undercover work, as well as high-risk assault operations. They reported directly to the Carabinieri General Command.

Of all the elite special units in Italy, theirs was given the most operational freedom. As a highly successful and highly respected commander, Argento was able to call most of his own shots. And this was one of those times.

"You should have told me you had the bartender's apartment wired," Lovett insisted.

Argento smiled. "If I had, you would have chosen someplace else to snatch Ragusa. This was the safest way. It was a contained environment. He didn't have his bodyguards. No one got hurt."

They were standing in the safe house's large living room. Peeling frescoes, hundreds of years old, covered the walls.

Standing near one of the windows, Harvath asked, "So, now what?"

Morrison, Barton, and Staelin were one floor below, being watched over by Argento's men. They weren't officially under arrest, but no one was free to leave.

Ragusa, Naya, and Ragusa's two bodyguards had been placed in restraints and were being held in a different part of the building. Under Italian law, Argento could hold them for seventy-two hours without charging them. Harvath had a feeling he could probably hold them a lot longer than that if he wanted to. Ragusa might not like it, but he knew the ROS had the upper hand and there was nothing he could do about it.

Argento turned his attention to Harvath. He had a slow, confident voice, and spoke excellent English. "What would you do," he asked, "if an Italian intelligence officer, along with four paramilitary operatives, entered the United States, held two people hostage, and tortured one of them?"

"If they'd come to interrogate an organized crime figure connected to terrorism? I'd probably hand them each a medal and ask what else I could do for them," Harvath replied.

"Your bosses might not like that."

"My bosses might not ever need to know."

"*Ecco*," the Italian said with a grin. *Fair enough*.

"I want you to understand," Harvath explained, pointing to Lovett, "that she was acting on my instructions."

"So you are in charge then?"

Harvath nodded.

"None of you are carrying passports, credit cards, or any sort of identification. I assume you left everything at Sigonella?"

Neither Harvath nor Lovett responded.

"Don't look so surprised," Argento said, as he winked at Lovett. "I ran a trace on your cell phone. I know what towers it was pinging off of."

"*Piove sul bagnato*," Lovett replied. *When it rains, it pours.*

Argento's grin spread into a smile. *"Tanto va la gatta al lardo che ci lascia lo zampino,"* he said. *When the cat goes to steal the lard, it always leaves a footprint.*

Harvath didn't speak Italian and had no idea what they were talking about.

Argento noticed the look on his face. "The best-laid plans of mice and men often go awry. No?"

Harvath nodded. "If it can go wrong, it often does."

The Italian shifted gears and walked toward him. "You don't remember me, do you?"

It was so abrupt that Harvath's defenses immediately shot up. His mind went into overdrive trying to place how the two knew each other.

"Relax," the Italian said, aware that he had put him on guard. Raising his hands, he framed his eyes, blocking out the rest of his face. "It was a decade ago. But you were with another beautiful blonde American. My team and I picked you up in—"

"A helicopter," Harvath replied, as it all came back to him. "A fast one. An Augusta."

The woman Argento was referring to was Meg Cassidy, a hijacking survivor he had teamed up with to track down a terrorist hell-bent on igniting war in the Middle East. The target had been a peace summit hosted by Italy.

With the help of the Italians, Harvath had prevented an attack on one of the delegations, designed to look as if the Israelis had been behind it.

"You were part of the Rapid Reaction Force," said Harvath.

Argento nodded. "I was the team leader. We picked you up in Rome and flew with you out to Frascati. With my helmet and balaclava, I don't blame you for not recognizing me."

Harvath smiled.

Lovett looked at them both. "Wait. You two know each other?"

Argento nodded. "Unfortunately, bad actors have brought us back together."

"Speaking of which, what can you tell us about Antonio Vottari?" Harvath asked.

The Italian held up his hand. "First, you're going to tell me everything you know about Mustapha Marzouk. Then, we'll have a discussion about La Formícula."

CHAPTER 64

H arvath's team was given a place to sleep. One of Argento's men made coffee. It was after midnight when they got down to business.

Harvath shared everything he knew. There was no sense in holding back. The Italians were aware that American Intelligence had been looking for Mustapha Marzouk. They were also aware of chatter about impending terror attacks in Europe. What they didn't know was how the two were connected.

From how the laptop of doom had been discovered and what it contained, to everything that had gone down at Burning Man and in Libya, he walked Argento through all of it.

The Italian listened intently, interrupting only occasionally to ask a question or probe for more information.

When Harvath had finished, he set his coffee cup down on the table and leaned back on the couch.

Argento had his laptop out. On it was the audio they had recorded from the bartender's apartment. He listened to it several times, smoking a cigarette and making notes as he did.

There were several things he wanted Ragusa to clarify, and he ran his list of questions by Harvath. As any good investigator would, he wanted all the details, no matter how small. How was the mobster planning to get Marzouk to Rome? Where was the drop-off? Was he supposed to provide him with new identification documents? Was he supposed to provide a phone or a new SIM card? Money? Clothing? The list went on.

Once he had written down everything he could think of, he handed the questions to one of his ROS operatives and sent him to interrogate Ragusa.

Then, he turned the conversation to La Formícula, Antonio Vottari, and the Calabrian Mafia known as the N'drangheta.

Having seen the barbarity of organized crime up close, Argento despised it every bit as much as Harvath did. He made no secret of his contempt. But like any wise, experienced warrior, he also respected his enemy—especially what they were capable of.

Like the Cosa Nostra of Sicily and the Camorra of Campania, the N'drangheta of Calabria were ruthless.

So thoroughly capable was the Mafia of getting to anyone who stood in its way that Carabinieri were required to work outside their home region for eight years before they could be trusted to apply for a transfer to come back.

It was said that 70 percent of the Carabinieri came from the four Italian regions most plagued by organized crime. Faced with a choice between good and evil, they chose good. They chose to side with law and justice. They were noble men and women engaged in a tough, dangerous fight.

And nobody knew that better than Paolo Argento.

"Okay," he said, opening a folder on his laptop and bringing up a photo. "Let's talk about Antonio Vottari."

Harvath and Lovett moved closer to each other so they could see.

"Antonio is the nephew of Franco Vottari. The Vottaris are one of the most powerful families in the Calabrian Mafia. The N'drangheta is considered one of the richest and most powerful organized crime groups in the world.

"They are known for their extreme violence. Of all its families, the Vottaris are considered one of the most brutal. Antonio, like his uncle Franco, is known for his savagery.

"He's small. That's how he received his nickname."

"La Formícula," said Harvath. "The Ant."

"Exactly," replied Argento as he clicked through pictures of Antonio, as well as bloody crime scene photos. "But make no mistake, he's extremely dangerous. Deadly even.

"The N'drangheta have their hands in everything—they traffic in drugs, weapons, prostitution, fraud, extortion, political corruption, contract killing, even black market artifacts looted out of North Africa and the Middle East. If there's money to be made in something illegal, you'll find them there."

Harvath was trying to connect all the dots. "So ISIS pays Umar Ali Halim to smuggle Marzouk from Libya to Italy. Members of the Black Axe, under Ragusa's control, are sent out to meet him near the island of Lampedusa and bring him to shore. Once Marzouk's feet are dry, Ragusa is supposed to smuggle him to Rome, where he has people who will get him to his final destination. All of which, Ragusa is doing as a favor for Antonio Vottari. Why?"

"Good question," Argento answered. "The different Mafia networks have been known to work together, but there's always something in it for them. Ragusa wasn't helping La Formícula out of the kindness of his heart. There had to be some sort of transaction."

"And what's the Vottari–ISIS connection?" Lovett asked.

"Also a good question and probably even easier to answer. Obviously, ISIS didn't have a smuggling relationship in Italy. They did, apparently, have a relationship with Vottari and asked him to arrange a smuggler to get Marzouk into Italy and up to Rome.

"Was this a relationship based on looted artifacts? Drugs? Weapons? All of those are possible. ISIS has been making strong inroads with different Mafia groups in southern Italy."

"If you had to guess," asked Harvath, "which would you pick?"

Argento shrugged. "Drugs or stolen artifacts make the most sense. That's all ISIS really has to offer, unless they're buying weapons."

"Which could be paid for with artifacts, drugs, or cash."

"Correct."

"They could have also been buying explosives. The attacks in Spain and Paris might end up leading right back to Vottari."

"Or they could have come from another source entirely," the Italian responded. "In this case, Vottari may be nothing more than a middleman. ISIS needed a smuggler and he made the introduction to Ragusa."

Harvath was growing frustrated. There had to be something. Something he was missing. "What if Vottari was lying to Ragusa?" he asked.

"About what?"

"About Mustapha Marzouk having his own people in Rome—people who would get him to his final destination," said Harvath.

"Why would he lie about that?"

"I can think of two reasons. The one that makes the most sense is for operational security purposes. The less Ragusa knew about Marzouk's final destination the better."

Argento nodded. "Agreed. What's the second reason?"

Harvath was a lot less sure of number two, but he shared it anyway. "What if Rome *was* Marzouk's final destination? What if that's where the attack was supposed to take place?"

Lovett felt a chill run down her spine as a terrible thought took hold of her mind. "Oh my God," she uttered.

Both men turned to look at her.

"What is it?" asked Harvath.

"What if the attack is still on? What if ISIS has already found a replacement chemist?"

Before anyone could say another word, Argento pulled out his phone and dialed a highly classified number.

CHAPTER 65

The best time to make a getaway was in the midst of chaos—when authorities didn't know who, or what, they were looking for.

In the wake of the Tuileries bombings, Paris was in a panic. Emergency vehicles fought to get to and from the scene. The streets were in gridlock.

People were terrified about a second round of attacks. No one felt safe.

Joining the wave of guests fleeing the city, Tursunov dropped his room key at the front desk of Le Meurice and exited the hotel.

Out on the street, he had no need to pause. He had taken in the full spectacle from the balcony of his room. Whatever had caused the first bomber to detonate early was not worth worrying about. As far as he was concerned, the attack had been a success.

Cutting across the Pont de la Concorde, he walked to the Boulevard Saint-Germain and took a left.

Emergency vehicles continued to speed past, their klaxons blaring and lights flashing. Pulling his rolling suitcase behind him, he was careful to take detours in order to make sure he wasn't being followed. Though this was extremely unlikely, it was good tradecraft.

At the Pont de Sully, in the shadow of the Arab World Institute building, he turned onto the Quai Saint Bernard. The walk from Le Meurice to the Gare d'Austerlitz took a little over a half hour.

The station took its name from a town in the Czech Republic where

Napoleon had defeated a far superior force. There might have been some irony for him there if Paris wasn't full of such monuments.

Checking his watch, he saw he had time to stop nearby for a coffee. The train wasn't leaving until 9:22. The less time he spent inside the station, the better. It would only be filled with nervous police and anxious soldiers, suspicious of everything and everyone.

He kept walking until he found a café with an open terrace where he could also enjoy a cigarette. Taking a seat, he pulled out his Gauloises and called the waiter over.

He ordered *un serré*, lit his cigarette, then watched the faces of the people who passed by.

Their expressions were the same as he had seen up and down the Boulevard Saint-Germain—shock, sadness, terror. It was all Tursunov could do not to smile.

The French, always so quick to participate in bombing runs of Muslim lands, had been served a stern rebuke.

From his table, he could also see the TVs on inside. It reminded him of how he sat, just days ago, in the tiny café in Reggio di Calabria, watching the aftermath of the bombing in America.

All of the televisions were broadcasting video from the Tuileries. The dead and injured were there in full, high-definition glory for the world to see. The attack had been more than successful; it had been spectacular.

The message from ISIS had been delivered, loud and clear: You may advance upon us in Iraq, Libya, or Syria, but you will never, ever defeat us.

When his coffee came, he savored it. It was made sweet by the pained face of every passerby. ISIS had indeed won a massive victory, but it was nothing compared to what was in store.

Paying his bill, Tursunov struck out in search of a small grocery. He wanted to pick up some edibles for his overnight train ride.

When conducting operations, there was rarely anything the Tajik ever looked forward to. Traveling overnight to Nice was an exception.

While recuperating from plastic surgery in Pakistan, he had had very little to do. There was only local television and a small shelf with a handful of books.

One of those books was about overnight train travel by a British author named Andrew Martin.

Over the course of his life, Tursunov had taken many trains. He had even slept on some of them, but only by sitting upright in an uncomfortable seat. He had never known the luxury of a proper sleeping compartment. The book by Martin had opened his eyes to what he had been missing. So, while planning the operation, he had decided to make his escape from Paris via the overnight train to Nice.

The author had talked about duplicating a railway "dinner basket" for the ride, as a character in Agatha Christie's *The Mystery of the Blue Train* had done for the journey. Having managed only one bite of his main course before the explosions had begun, Tursunov thought it a good idea.

At the grocery, he bought pasta salad, cheese, bread, smoked fish, some fruit, and bottled water. And while he would have enjoyed the old-fashioned romance of a picnic hamper, he satisfied himself with the plastic grocery bag provided by the shop.

It was a short walk to the station, and it proved to be everything the author had described. There were sparrows in the rafters and a complimentary piano in the large hall, which anyone could sit down and play.

A young man of university age began playing "La Marseillaise." A day, or maybe even a few hours later, he might have roused some of his fellow countrymen to sing in a defiant show of patriotism. But as it stood, no one joined him. People were still in shock.

With a newspaper tucked under his arm, and wearing a business suit, the Tajik kept his head down as he walked to his platform. Neither the police nor the soldiers paid him much attention. They were looking for Muslim terrorists and knew one when they saw one. He didn't fit the profile.

Climbing aboard the train, Tursunov found his compartment. It wasn't much bigger than a walk-in closet. He had paid extra in order to have it all to himself. The lower two bunks had been folded down and turned into beds.

White pillows in plastic wrappers sat atop thin, gray duvets that resembled sleeping bags. The walls were scuffed and the floor was dirty. A bathroom was at the end of the carriage, just after the vending machines. It was a far cry from the famed Orient Express.

After removing a few things, he put his suitcase on the luggage rack, sat down on one of the beds, and opened the paper.

At exactly 9:22, he felt a shudder beneath him as the enormous engine at the head of the platform came to life and the train began moving.

He watched through the window as the train left the station and made its way through the city.

Once the conductor had come by to check his ticket, he locked the door, unpacked his impromptu dinner basket, and assembled his meal.

The fish, unfortunately, was too salty, the pasta salad too oily, and the cheese entirely too strong. Had it not been for the fruit and bread, he would have been at the mercy of the vending machine.

After cleaning up his meal, he undressed, got into bed, and extinguished the light. The ride was smooth and quiet. It didn't take long for him to fall asleep.

CHAPTER 66

The Tajik awoke and raised his window shade as the train was passing through the coastal village of Cassis. It was just as the British author had described—cascading with red bougainvillea.

After saying his prayers and doing a light round of exercises, he dressed and made a small meal of what remained of his palatable food. Then, he spent the next two hours watching the turquoise water and pastel-colored buildings of France's decadent Riviera pass by his window.

At 8:37 a.m. the train came to a stop at the Gare de Nice-Ville. As Tursunov stepped off the train, he listened for the good-bye from the conductor. He remembered from reading the book in Lahore that it would be different here.

And indeed it was.

Instead of wishing departing passengers the typical Parisian *"bonne journée," have a good day*, he wished them a *beautiful "belle journée."*

The Tajik tipped his head politely as he passed the conductor and headed out in search of coffee and breakfast. He had exactly an hour and a half until his next train and he needed to make the most of it.

As he pulled his suitcase behind him, he noticed a heavy security presence here as well. Nice was no stranger to being attacked. After what had happened in Paris, he was not surprised to see the increase in vigilance.

Near the station, he found a small café. It was a warm, sunny morning and he sat on the terrace outside where he could have a cigarette while he waited for his food.

Removing one of the "burner" cell phones he had purchased for the operation, he powered it up and waited for it to get a signal.

Once it had, the message tone chimed. Tursunov checked his texts. There was just one.

Opening it, he saw a poor camera phone photo of a strip of grass. It was a code. *The chemist had made it to the Nice train station.* The Tajik powered off the phone.

Taking a drag on his cigarette, he watched the people as they passed. The mood in the South of France was better than it had been in Paris, but not much.

That was to be expected, he supposed. While the inhabitants along the Riviera despised the Parisians, they still shared a national identity as Frenchmen. As far as Tursunov was concerned, they could all go to hell.

After finishing his breakfast, he took his time smoking another cigarette. That was one of the few things he liked about the French. Even if you consumed only one coffee, the price entitled you to sit at the table all day if you chose.

When the allotted time had come, he paid his bill and rolled his suitcase back to the station.

The chemist had not been told that they would both be on the same train. The Tajik didn't want him to know. He wanted to watch him from afar. He wanted to make sure he didn't have any surveillance following him.

When he entered the station, it was even more crowded than it had been before. Seeing the lines at the ticket windows, he was glad he had purchased everything in advance in Paris. That was one of the other things he liked about the French. There was at least some semblance of organization in their rail system.

Because he had purchased the tickets himself and had delivered one set to Abdel, to be given to his nephew, he knew which train car the chemist would be in and exactly where he would be sitting.

Finding the platform for the train to Milan, he lingered where he knew the young man would board.

Ten minutes before departure, Younes El Fassi—the nephew of Abdel and son of Aziz the lion—arrived.

Tursunov watched and waited.

The only person to enter the car besides Younes was a woman with two children.

When the conductor gave the final call, the Tajik climbed aboard.

Stowing his suitcase, he made his way toward his seat. He was two rows back and on the other side of the aisle from Younes. He could see the young chemist, but the young chemist couldn't see him.

As the train pulled out, he made himself comfortable and settled in for the almost five-hour ride to Milan.

. . .

The trip was uneventful, though plenty of people had been stealing furtive glances at Younes. It was the curse of being a young Arab male in the wake of an Islamic terror attack. Tursunov was confident that ISIS would have already claimed credit for what had happened in Paris.

During the hour between trains in Milan, he kept a distant eye on the young chemist. Once again, he didn't detect any surveillance.

He wasn't surprised. Not only did the French authorities not have the resources to follow him all the way to Nice and then on to the border with Italy, the Italians had no actionable reason to take interest in him.

Boarding the new train, they found their seats. The Tajik hadn't seen anyone that gave him any cause for concern. Nevertheless, he continued to scan for any hint of trouble.

At precisely four o'clock, the high-speed Alta Velocità train exited the central Milan station. The trip to Rome's Termini station would take just under three hours. Then, provided Antonio Vottari had delivered his merchandise, the final step of the operation would begin.

Allah willing, it would be the biggest attack the world had ever seen.

CHAPTER 67

An Augusta AW109 transported Harvath and his team from Palermo back to Sigonella Air Base.

They stayed only long enough to pick up their gear and for Harvath to stop in the hospital to wish Haney and Gage a safe trip back to the United States. As soon as that was done, they climbed back on board and took off.

Argento and one of his lieutenants were with them. The rest of his men had been divided. Half had stayed at the safe house to watch over Ragusa, Naya, and the two bodyguards. The other half had flown on ahead to a different safe house in Calabria.

"We can make one, maybe two passes of La Formícula's house, depending on our altitude," Argento said over his headset. "Anything more than that and he's going to know something is wrong."

Harvath flashed him the thumbs-up. "If we can get it in one, let's do it that way."

The Italian nodded and said something to his lieutenant, who was seated next to the window with a large digital SLR camera. On the opposite side, Morrison also had a camera. Lovett sat next to Harvath with a map, Barton had his eyes closed, and Staelin was reading a new book.

Harvath looked at the title—*The Obstacle Is the Way* by an author named Holiday. Tapping it, he asked, "What's this one about?"

"It's about two hundred pages," the Delta Force operative replied.

Harvath just shook his head.

Staelin looked up and smiled. "Stoicism," he explained. "Turning obstacles into opportunities."

"Any good?"

"I don't know. My biggest obstacle right now is that my boss keeps asking me questions and won't let me read it."

Argento translated for his lieutenant and they both laughed.

Harvath shook his head once more and turned to look out the window.

The pilots raced up the Sicilian coastline, past the dramatic edifice of Mount Etna—the tallest active volcano in Europe—and crossed over the Strait of Messina to Calabria at the toe of Italy.

It was little moments like these that Harvath tried to savor. He hadn't gotten much sleep and probably should have had his eyes closed like Barton, but it wasn't every day you got a ride like this.

He could only imagine what it would have cost to privately hire a helicopter for this kind of tour. For the first time in a while, he thought of Lara. She would have loved it. He also thought about Reed Carlton. He would have loved it too.

In fact, the flight reminded Harvath of a story he used to tell. It was about Sicily and the CIA's precursor, the OSS, and drew a stark contrast between the two.

The story centered on Max Corvo, an Italian immigrant to the United States who joined the Army in 1942. Corvo had excellent ideas on how to defeat the Axis Powers in Italy, but it looked as if he was going to end up being a Quartermaster and not see any action. Instead of being quiet, Corvo wrote up his plan for intelligence gathering and covert operations in Italy.

The young private quickly came to the attention of the OSS, who gave him a command position in its Italian section. He was dispatched to North Africa to prepare for the invasion of Sicily. But when Corvo arrived, he found next to no resources. Undeterred, he begged, borrowed, or stole whatever he could get his hands on that would make the invasion a success.

Within a month of arriving in North Africa, he had recruited his own boat squadron and had planned, trained, staffed, equipped, and executed the first covert OSS operation to the highly dangerous, Gestapo-infested island of Sardinia.

There, the OSS linked up with partisan and pro-Allied forces and began to lay the groundwork for an organized resistance that would be critical in the taking of Italy.

What the Old Man loved about the story was not only the risk-taking, but the win-at-all-cost mentality. The OSS fostered creativity and bravery. To them, no mission was impossible. The organization stood behind you, it didn't get in your way. What they cared about most were results.

They had one mantra, and it came straight from the founder of the OSS, Wild Bill Donovan. *If you fall, fall forward.*

If the CIA bureaucracy were to have a mantra today, it could very well be, *Don't fall.* Or better yet, *Don't do anything that might result in a fall.*

That wasn't the Old Man's style. And it certainly wasn't Harvath's. For both of them, success was the only option.

As a SEAL, Harvath had had it drilled into him that the only easy day was yesterday. He had been trained to expect things to get worse and when they did, to persevere. No matter what happened, you were never out of the fight. No matter what happened, you *never* quit. You always found a way to successfully complete the mission.

It was a philosophy that called for quick and sometimes unorthodox thinking. It required dedication and a willingness to do whatever it took.

In air-conditioned offices across Washington, it was a mindset and steadfast determination most politicians and bureaucrats couldn't understand. It was one of the biggest reasons the country was in the position it was.

Fortunately, there were just enough people in D.C. who did understand. The question, though, was whether there was enough time to still pull things together.

As the helicopter banked and headed north, the pilot radioed that they were five minutes out from Vottari's.

Argento told his lieutenant and Morrison to get their cameras ready. They were going to want to take as many pictures as they could during the flyby. He wasn't feeling very comfortable about the possibility of a second pass. The clouds were going to require them to fly lower than he would have liked.

Harvath watched as the landscape sped by beneath the helicopter.

Vottari lived outside a small rural town in the foothills of the Aspromonte mountain range called Oppido Mamertina.

According to Lovett, the older members of N'drangheta tried to stay under the radar. They didn't flash their massive wealth. They tried to blend in. The newer generation, Mafiosi like Vottari, were the opposite. They drove flashy cars, wore expensive clothes, and lived in big houses.

The older members blamed the change on television and social media. Everybody wanted to be a celebrity. Everyone wanted to flaunt what he had. They swore it would be the younger generation's undoing. They warned them to tone it down, but very few listened.

The one area in which the younger generation respected tradition was in where they lived. They didn't run off and move to big cities. They stayed local, often residing in the same towns or villages where they had grown up. The result was that the flashy ones stood out like sore thumbs.

As they neared Vottari's house, Harvath didn't need to be shown which one it was. He could spot it from the air. It was enormous.

Forrest surrounded it on three sides. There was a long, straight drive that came up the front. On either side of the drive were cultivated fields with rows and rows of olive trees. There were a multitude of outbuildings.

Argento's lieutenant and Morrison snapped photo after photo as they flew by. People on the property stopped what they were doing and looked up.

Harvath had seen all that he needed to see. There was no reason to make a second pass.

What mattered now was coming up with a plan—something Argento and his team would go along with. But that would be a lot easier said than done.

Harvath had a bad feeling that the Carabinieri weren't going to like any of the ideas he was considering.

CHAPTER 68

The helicopter dropped them off on the private aviation side of the airport at Reggio Calabria. Two unmarked SUVs were waiting for them.

The ROS safe house was about twenty minutes up the coast in a town called Villa San Giovanni. It marked the closest point between mainland Italy and Sicily and was the main embarkation point for the ferries that went back and forth to the island.

With so much oceanfront, Harvath had hoped the safe house would be near the water. It wasn't.

The safe house was in a residential neighborhood, several blocks up from the docks and the main train station.

It was built on a hill and its rooftop deck provided a view of the town and the ocean. The outer courtyard was walled, could fit four vehicles, and had a heavy, reinforced gate to deter any would-be thieves.

There were citronella candles everywhere and netting over the beds. Apparently, mosquitoes were a problem.

Unloading the gear from the vehicles, Argento showed everyone to their rooms. The rest of his team was already there and had opened the doors and windows to get air moving through.

Harvath dropped his gear on his bed and then walked back to the living room. Argento was uploading the pictures from both cameras onto his laptop.

"Hungry?" he asked, as Harvath walked in.

They had eaten a late breakfast in Palermo, but nothing since.

Harvath nodded and Argento looked at his watch. "Most places won't be open for dinner until later, but I know one place we can try. It's near the water."

"Good," Harvath replied. Looking to get to work on a plan as quickly as possible, he added, "Bring your laptop."

. . .

Ristorante Glauco in neighboring Scilla wasn't just near the water, it was built right at its very edge. Its upstairs, open-air terrace extended out over the bay and provided one of the most incredible vistas Harvath had ever seen.

Sailboats bobbed in the water beneath the dramatic Ruffo Castle, an old fortress perched atop a rocky peninsula that jutted out into the sea.

A hodgepodge of Mediterranean buildings in all shapes and sizes were stacked side by side and one atop the other up the steep, terraced hillside.

Looking out over the deep blue Strait of Messina, Argento explained that this was the location Greek mythology attributed to Scylla, the famed sea monster.

After the helicopter ride and now this dramatic location for dinner, Harvath joked that the Italian needed to get out of terrorism and into tourism.

Argento smiled and asked if he could order for their table. Harvath looked at Lovett, and when she nodded, he told the man to go ahead.

As he ordered, Harvath glanced over at the next table, where Staelin, Barton, and Morrison were sitting with Argento's men, several of whom spoke decent English.

Satisfied that they were in good hands, he turned his attention back to what lay in front of them.

Argento opened his laptop and Harvath and Lovett adjusted their chairs so they could see the photos. As he clicked through them, every once in a while, Harvath would ask him to zoom in, or go back to the one they had just seen.

He was trying to get a thorough feel for the property; probing, looking for weak points that they could exploit. To his extreme relief, he didn't see any dogs.

"Vottari's property is set up much different than Ragusa's," Harvath said.

Argento nodded. "It's a different mentality in Sicily. Everyone wants a fortress. In Calabria, it's anonymity that protects you."

"He doesn't look very anonymous to me."

"No. He doesn't," the Italian agreed.

"Do we know anything about his routine?" Harvath asked. "Anything that might provide us an opportunity to get to him?"

"Nothing like Ragusa and the bartender."

"A restaurant he likes to go to? Does he visit his mother on a regular basis? How about going to see the uncle?"

Argento waved his hand in the air as if he was doing mini karate chops. "We don't want anything to do with the uncle. No way."

Harvath understood. "What kind of protection does Vottari normally roll with? Lots of men? Just a couple? What are we looking at?"

"Four to six men."

"Armed?"

"We should assume so."

Harvath reached over to the computer and clicked back to a previous photo of the property. "What kind of a security presence at night?"

Argento opened another folder, found the information Harvath wanted, and read him the answer. "Two men outside the house. Two men inside. Definitely armed. Semiautomatic rifles."

"Do we know anything about his perimeter security? Ground sensors? Anything like that?"

The Italian scrolled through the file and then shook his head. "We don't know."

"Alarm system on the house? Safe room? Pets?"

Again, Argento scrolled through the file. "No idea regarding the first two and as far as pets go, I assume you are asking about any dogs. None have been seen."

Harvath nodded.

There were always some question marks, no matter what the operation was. The less time you had to get ready, the more of them there usually were. Having access to Vottari's file was a real benefit.

"Before we start talking about a plan," said the Italian, "I want to go over a few ground rules."

Harvath looked at him. "Such as?"

Argento drew a deep breath, and the moment he did, Harvath knew they were in trouble.

CHAPTER 69

"You've got to be kidding me," Harvath stated.

"I'm not kidding you," said Argento.

"Why don't we just save ourselves the time? We can walk right up to the front door and ask them to shoot us."

"I think you're overreacting."

Harvath shook his head. "If I was overreacting, you'd know it. Trust me. What I'm giving you is the truth.

"Which is exactly what I have given you," the Italian countered. "I don't like it any more than you do. It is what it is."

"What it is, is bullshit."

"You need to listen to me. My men and I didn't join the Carabinieri to be the same as the Mafia. We joined because we are *better* men. We don't want to beat them by their rules. We want to beat them by ours."

"With all due respect, sometimes you need to re-evaluate the rules."

Argento didn't disagree. "I don't mind bending a few here and there," he said. "But as bad as those men are, they are *still* Italian citizens. The law exists to protect all Italians. Even the worst of us."

Harvath liked Argento. He was a good guy. But here, he was totally wrong. "And if I ignore the ground rules?"

"Come on, don't be stupid."

"I'm serious. What happens if I ignore them?"

"The CIA snatched a Muslim Imam off the streets of Milan and rendered him to Egypt, where he was tortured. Every CIA operative involved was tried in absentia and found guilty. Prison terms and big money judgments were handed down. What do you think the Italian courts will do to you if you harm Vottari or any of his people?"

"Define *harm*," said Harvath.

"Shoot," the Italian replied. "What do you think will happen to you and your team if you shoot even one of them?"

"No one even knows that we're here."

"I know you're here," Argento stated. "My men know you're here. My pilots know."

"So?"

"So who do you think I called last night from the safe house in Palermo? Where do you think my file on Vottari came from? I had to call the lead N'drangheta prosecutor himself to get that. I woke him up in the middle of the night and everything."

Harvath was right back in the position he had been earlier with Lovett, vis-à-vis Ragusa. To climb to the next rung of the ladder, someone else had to become involved. As soon as that happened, the operation, not to mention its operators, were exposed. It was no longer fully covert.

"Then you tell me," said Harvath. "How do we make this work?"

"Believe me, that's all I have been thinking about. If Vottari or any of his men turn up dead, I'll be the first person they look at. Same thing if he goes missing."

"And yet you didn't have any trouble pulling Ragusa, his girlfriend, and the two bodyguards off the street for a little while."

"Because he had already given up Vottari," Argento replied. "He's never going to admit to what happened. He'll scare the woman into silence and his men have no clue what went on in the apartment. Even if they did, they wouldn't say anything or he would have them killed. I don't have to worry about him running to the press or trying to file an action against me."

"Let's figure out then," said Harvath, "how to put La Formícula in the same position."

"There is no getting to La Formícula, though, if you and your team cannot agree to abide by the ground rules."

"Every operation has to have rules of engagement. I understand that.

I also understand that your ass is on the line with this. But so is mine. I am responsible for my team. I can't put them in a situation where they are unable to protect themselves. That's just not going to happen."

Harvath was at his wit's end.

"May I?" Lovett asked, pointing at Argento's computer.

The Italian nodded and slid it the rest of the way toward her. Turning to Harvath, he said, "You understand that this is not personal. I have much discretion in the execution of my missions. But this is one area in which I do not."

Harvath did understand. If their situation were reversed, he'd probably be taking the exact same position. Unless you were operating completely on your own, absolutely unaccountable, there were going to be restrictions you had to deal with.

These, though, were a little extreme, if Harvath did say so himself. With these rules of engagement, they were never going to make any headway against the Mafia. They'd always be left behind, trying to catch up.

Glancing over at Lovett, he saw that she had pulled up a bunch of additional photos from Vottari's file and had them side by side.

"What are those?" he asked.

"Pictures from his Facebook account," she replied.

"The Ant is on Facebook?"

"Yup. Even uses his real name."

Harvath shook his head. Everybody was on social media. Why not a mobster in his thirties?

The pictures showed Vottari partying with friends and pretty women, having a good time.

Looking closer, he noticed something. "Do the couches in these photos look similar to you?"

Lovett increased the photo size. "They do actually."

The photos had not been full screen captures. Harvath wanted to see them in their original state—the way Vottari had posted them.

Turning to Argento, he asked, "Do you have Facebook on your computer?"

"I don't do Facebook," the Italian replied.

"Done," Lovett replied, handing her cell phone to Harvath. She *did* do Facebook.

Via the app on her phone, she had pulled up Vottari's account. Harvath scrolled through the photos until he found the one he wanted. La Formícula had even been kind enough to tag the location in his post.

"Ever heard of a place called The Beach Club in Reggio Calabria?" he asked.

Argento nodded. "It's a big disco, not far from where we were at the airport."

Harvath handed the phone back to Lovett. "That's where we're going to nail him."

"How do we even know when he'll be there?" the Italian replied. "There's nothing in his surveillance that suggests a pattern."

"We're going to bait a shiny hook and put it right in front of him."

"How?"

Harvath smiled. "Don't worry. I have the perfect guy for it."

CHAPTER 70

Nicholas had just climbed out of his vehicle when Lydia Ryan pulled into Reed Carlton's driveway behind him. Following her was a blacked-out van.

Walking around to the gray Mercedes's cargo door, he let the dogs out and grabbed his backpack. Even from where he stood, he could tell not only that something was wrong, but that Ryan was very angry.

"What's going on?" he asked as she stepped out of her car and began giving orders to the team in the black van.

"This," she responded, handing him a tiny surveillance camera. "They were all over my fucking house. My car was wired too. There was even a tracker on it."

"Not good," he exclaimed. "Who do you think is responsible?"

"I'll let you know as soon as we do a full sweep inside. Until then, do me a favor and wait out here."

Nicholas nodded and Ryan escorted her personnel inside.

Forty-five minutes later, the team re-emerged. After sweeping Nicholas's vehicle, as well as those of Carlton's security detail, they packed up their van and drove off.

Giving his dogs the command to walk with him, he entered the house and found Ryan and Carlton at the dining room table. Scattered across it were all of the surveillance devices that had been found in the house.

"Really not good," Nicholas remarked, setting down his bag. "Are any of those still hot?"

Ryan shook her head. "All the power sources have been removed. None of them are transmitting."

"Even so," he said. "Wait here."

Moments later, he returned with a trash bag. With her help, they cleared the table. He then tied a knot in the top of the bag, tossed it in the garage, and returned to the dining room.

"FYI," stated Ryan, "your vehicle was clean."

"Thanks for having them check. What about the security team?"

"Their vehicles had been compromised. Trackers and wired for audio."

Nicholas shook his head. "What tipped you off?"

"As CIA Deputy Director, I get swept on a regular basis. Something didn't feel right, so I asked them to move up my next appointment. Call it intuition."

"How'd they get into your place?"

"Same way they got in here. They waited for me to go to work or for Reed to go to a doctor's appointment, and that's when they acted. They could come back and do any vehicles overnight. Judging by the sophistication of their equipment, they know what they're doing."

Reed Carlton glanced at her. "Somebody is obviously very interested in what we're up to."

"The same somebody," she replied, "who put the bounty on our email accounts."

"Speaking of which," said Nicholas. "I have an update on that. But I don't want to say anything if we're not safe to talk here."

Ryan nodded. "I had my team install some active countermeasures. We're safe, but your cell phone isn't going to work inside."

"I don't bring mine to these kinds of meetings anyway."

"Good. Then let's get started," Carlton ordered. "What do you have?"

The little man pulled some papers out of his backpack and spread them across the table. "Whoever is behind all this is smart. *Really* smart. In fact, I'm more than a little upset that I didn't think of this myself."

"What are you talking about?" asked Ryan.

"Per the agreement," he continued, "I was instructed where to upload all of your emails, once I had accessed them. The site is a dark web version of DropBox. Anyway yesterday, once I had the strings of Malice code I needed, I got right to—"

"What's Malice?" Carlton broke in.

Nicholas's heart sank. The man's ability to hold on to new pieces of information was getting worse. "It's a computer program I needed," he said politely, as if they had never before discussed it. "I was able to get the CIA to part with a piece of it."

"Excellent job. Sorry I interrupted. Keep going."

"No apology necessary," he replied. "Bottom line is that once I had it, I was able to embed it in the email data. I uploaded it all last night."

"And?" Ryan asked.

"And early this morning, someone downloaded it."

"Someone who?"

"I don't know the who," said Nicholas, "but I've got the *where*. As soon as those files were accessed, Malice activated its silent beacon."

"So where was it accessed from?"

"Cedars-Sinai Medical Center in Los Angeles."

Ryan was now just as confused as Carlton. "*Cedars-Sinai?*" she replied. "I don't get it."

"Do you know what HIPAA is?" the little man asked.

"Vaguely."

"It stands for Health Insurance Portability and Accountability Act. Basically, it's a law regulating data privacy and security provisions for medical information. The government takes it very seriously."

"So what," she answered.

"So Cedars-Sinai is one of the busiest, most technologically advanced hospitals in the world. Because of HIPAA, they have some of the most secure computer systems available. If you could get on the inside of their system, not only would your data be secure, but if you were a bad actor, you'd have the added benefit of being in one of the last places the government would ever think of, or dare to look for you. It's brilliant."

"Can you hack it?"

"With enough time and resources, I can hack anything. Here's the problem," he stated, as he pushed one of his pieces of paper across to her. On it was what looked like a flowchart of some sort. "Based on what I got back from Malice, I don't think the people we're looking for are keeping their data on the actual Cedars-Sinai system."

"What are they doing then?"

"They're using the system for cover and then offloading the data to a different system."

"Do you have any idea where that other system is?" Ryan asked.

Nicholas nodded. "I think it's right there in the hospital."

"What would you need to be absolutely sure?"

"I'd need to go there and see it for myself in person."

Ryan looked at Carlton. Any expression of confusion he might have had moments ago was gone. In its place was a focused look of determination.

"Put a team together," he ordered, "get the plane ready, and get him out to LA, ASAP."

• • •

After wrapping up all the details, Nicholas picked up his backpack and with the dogs by his side, exited the house.

Back in his van, he put on his seatbelt and grabbed his phone. One text had come while he was inside. It was from Scot Harvath.

URGENT: Need big favor. Fast.

CHAPTER 71

T he last thing Harvath wanted to do was head out to a dance club, but it was Thursday night, the place was going to have a decent crowd, and they might get lucky. At the very least, they'd get a feel for how it was laid out and could begin to get their arms around how they were going to snatch La Formícula.

Harvath's plan had been pretty straightforward. He kept within Argento's "ground rules" as best he could, but there were certain things he simply couldn't promise. Life, especially in their line of work, was full of surprises—many of them extremely dangerous.

As they ate dinner, Harvath sent two texts, stepped outside to field several phone calls, and compiled a list of things he needed Argento and his team to track down for him.

When they arrived back at the safe house, he headed to his room to grab a shower and close his eyes for an hour.

At the appointed time, both teams met in the living room and Harvath went over the plan, with Argento translating to make sure everyone was on the same page.

To a person, they all agreed that the biggest wild card was going to be Vottari's protection detail. They weren't professionals by any stretch. And because they weren't professionals, their behavior was unpredictable. Anything could happen. That was where the greatest danger lay.

In essence, the men "protecting" Vottari were thugs. They came from his village, or another close by. They would be fiercely loyal to him. When it came time to throw down, these boys wouldn't think twice.

That part didn't bother Harvath. He had them outmanned. In fact, even without Argento and his team, Harvath's men could handle La Formícula's crew. They just needed to bring the right tools for the job.

Someone raised the issue of security at The Beach Club and what should happen if they decided to jump in. Harvath had already discussed that possibility with Argento, and he let him inform his men. If they had to play the Carabinieri card, that was going to be the moment to do it.

With all of their questions answered, they piled into their vehicles and headed out.

It had been decided that the teams would go in separately and not acknowledge each other inside the club. The Americans were first.

Having pulled a stack of cash from his messenger bag, Harvath was ready to play the big-spending American. If The Beach Club had a VIP section, which it very likely did, that was where Vottari would be and Harvath wanted to be in it.

Unlike the restaurant where they'd eaten dinner, The Beach Club was actually built on a part of the coast with a long sandy beach. From its website, it looked like something you might have seen in Miami in the 1950s—lots of outdoor tables, chaise lounges, cabanas, and even a pool.

The building itself had a retractable roof and a full glass wall that opened up onto the outside. There were three bars, a huge dance floor, and some nights there were even fireworks. It was one of the hottest clubs in Calabria.

When they walked up to the entrance, Harvath wasted no time. He greased both bouncers, each with a hundred-dollar bill. As soon as that happened, word spread like wildfire that there was a big spender in the house.

The Beach Club did indeed have a VIP section, and Harvath and his team were shown right to it.

After being handed a hundred-dollar bill, the man at the velvet rope leaned in and told Harvath that it was five hundred to get in, but that included a bottle of champagne. Harvath discreetly peeled off four more notes and placed them in the man's hand.

With a smile, the man then undid the rope and allowed the team to enter. An attractive young waitress showed them to their own seating area with bright white couches like the ones in Vottari's Facebook photos.

"Well done," said Lovett as they all took a seat.

It was just after ten and the club had barely come alive, but you wouldn't have known it from the music. It was loud and thumping—as if the place was at max capacity on a Friday night.

Harvath took out his phone and texted Argento to let him know that they had made it inside. He then took a quick video of what he could see from the VIP section and sent it to Nicholas. The more he knew about the place, the better he'd be at pulling off his assignment.

A few minutes later, their waitress returned with a tray full of glasses. Right behind her was a busboy carrying an ice bucket. In it was their VIP bottle of champagne that came with their five-hundred-dollar entrance fee.

She showed the label to Harvath. It was a brand he'd never heard of before. It probably wasn't worth more than twenty dollars. With a big smile, he thanked her and tried to make small talk over the music as she opened it.

Her English was terrible, but that was a good thing. The less she knew about him and the people with him, the better. All he wanted was for her to remember that he was a great tipper, and to hope that he came back.

As soon as she had poured champagne for everyone, he handed her a hundred-dollar bill.

"*Grazie,*" she replied. *Thank you*. Then, holding up the bottle she had emptied by filling five glasses, she asked, "More?"

Harvath smiled. "Later."

She smiled back, and then left to take care of another group of customers.

"To pretty women," Barton said, raising his glass.

Raising his glass, Morrison added, "Present company included."

"I guess I'll have to drink to that," Lovett replied, and raised her glass as well.

Harvath and Staelin picked up theirs and everyone clinked glasses. About fifteen minutes later, the Italian team arrived.

Sticking to the plan, Harvath ignored them. Staelin, though, subtly raised his champagne glass and, from the comfort of the VIP section, tilted it in their direction.

Argento's lieutenant, with equal subtlety, placed his hand under his chin and flicked it at the American as he walked past. Harvath tried not to smile.

• • •

Over the next two hours, they roamed the club getting to know its ins and outs. They ordered drinks, took photos, and continued to tip heavily.

They checked out exits, got to know other members of the security team, and developed backup plans for their backup plans. When he felt they had seen enough, Harvath called it a night.

As they left, every staff person they had come in contact with encouraged them to come back again the following night. The head of the VIP room offered to reserve the same seating area for them and the bouncers out front told them not to even worry about the line, but to come directly up to the door and see them.

A little money had gone a long way.

With the skids greased, they returned to the safe house in Villa San Giovanni.

Harvath was ready to turn in, but he still had a couple of items to check off his to-do list.

Once he had written up a brief for McGee, returned several important emails, and uploaded the rest of the photos and video for Nicholas, he was ready to call it a night.

Getting undressed, he slid into bed and turned out the light.

Normally, even when he was on operations, he fell asleep pretty fast. Tonight wasn't one of those nights. His brain kept jumping from one topic to another. *What if the entire reason the CIA had sent him to investigate Mustapha Marzouk had been a waste? What if ISIS had already found a chemist to replace him? Would Rome be their target? And if it was, what kind of attack would they need a chemist for? What if they couldn't get Vottari to The Beach Club? What if Vottari didn't know anything?*

When Harvath started questioning whether he should have moved to Boston to be with Lara, and whether now he should move back to D.C. to run a Special Operations Group for the Old Man, he knew he was overtired.

Slowing his breathing, he picked one thing to focus his mind on. He tried to make it the view from the house he was renting overlooking the Charles River in Boston. That image slowly morphed into one he knew much better and felt much more comfortable with—the dock at his old house and its view over the Potomac.

With that image in his mind, and memories of how many times he'd sat there with a six-pack, decompressing after coming home from assignments just like this, he finally fell asleep.

CHAPTER 72

At precisely 6:55 p.m. the high-speed train from Milan pulled into Rome's Termini station. Tursunov had stood up early and had positioned himself at the door so he could be one of the first people from his carriage to exit. He wanted to make sure he was in the best possible position to observe the chemist.

Stepping down onto the platform, he walked to the far side and removed his cigarettes. The fines for smoking in Italy were outrageous. If you lit up in the wrong place, you could be ticketed for three hundred Euros or more.

He had thought about just holding a cigarette in his mouth until he could get outside to the street and light it up, but that might attract unwanted attention from the police, so he slid the pack back into his pocket.

Pretending to check the messages on his phone, he waited for Younes to disembark. When the young man appeared, he followed him.

As instructed, the chemist had tied a white handkerchief around the handle of his bag. Slowly, he made his way to the station's main hall.

He stopped in the McDonald's, chose the longest line, and when he got to the front, ordered a hamburger and fries to go. Once he had his meal in hand, he headed toward the station's side exit. Tursunov kept his eyes on him the entire time. There was no sign he was under surveillance.

Near the exit, Younes was approached by a gypsy cab driver. The young man had a goatee and wore jeans along with an AC/DC T-shirt. He offered to drive Younes anywhere he wanted to go.

The chemist turned him down by saying he expected Uber Rome to be just as good as Uber Paris.

When the driver professed to be a great tour guide with a cousin who could get him into the Colosseum for free, their coded introduction was complete. Younes handed over his bag and the pair exited the station.

The Tajik trailed behind and watched. The driver led the chemist a block down to his "taxi," where he placed his bag in the trunk, the chemist got into the backseat, and the car drove away. There was no one behind them.

Relieved, Tursunov gave a short prayer of thanks to Allah and walked to his hotel.

He had chosen a small, unremarkable hotel not far from the station, just as he had upon arriving in Paris. It was the kind of place that saw so many guests in a year that the faces were a blur for the staff.

After checking in, he conducted his ablutions, prayed, and unpacked.

Removing a razor from his shaving kit, he slit the hem of his suit jacket and exposed the edge of the lining.

Folding the jacket over his arm, he left the hotel and headed for the tram. His destination was a suburb on the eastern side of the city called Tor Pignattara.

Tor Pignattara was Rome's version of Aubervilliers—a predominantly Muslim enclave that had been left to atrophy. Throughout it and the surrounding neighborhoods, Italian authorities, citing building codes and safety concerns, had been shutting down Islamic cultural centers that had turned into mosques.

With no local places to congregate and pray, the faithful had taken to commandeering garages and empty storefronts. Shutting such places down over "safety" concerns had created a lot of ill will with local residents. Violence had broken out more than once and threatened to again.

And while Tursunov didn't like to see his Muslim brothers and sisters denied places to worship, heightened tensions served his ends. Tor Pignattara had quietly become known among police as a "no-go" area. In other words, if they showed up, they had better bring backup. The place was a powder keg and cops were doing whatever they could to avoid the area.

With this kind of hands-off mentality, ISIS was able to recruit, plan, train, and operate with little fear of discovery.

There were the occasional arrests, usually of idiots communicating with and supporting ISIS elements abroad. The local members were much more careful. Anyone who looked like he could end up being a problem was turned away on the spot. They had too much at stake to allow people in who could bring everything crashing down.

Exiting the tram, Tursunov walked for several blocks. It was a warm, sticky night.

Cars and motorbikes whizzed by. Women wearing the hijab passed, pushing strollers, their husbands or other male family members nearby. Men sat at small tables outside stores playing cards or dominoes. There were more signs in Arabic than in Italian. He felt as if he could have been in Amman, or Cairo, or Najaf.

Up ahead, he finally saw his destination. It was a small tailor's shop. The lights were still on, but the sign on the door read *Chiuso*, *closed*. Underneath was the same word in Arabic. A balding, middle-aged man sat at a table repairing a pair of trousers with a needle and thread.

Tursunov approached the glass door and knocked. When the man at the table looked up, the Tajik held out his jacket so he could see the damage.

Setting down his needle and thread, the man stood and came to unlock the door.

Opening it a crack, he said, "I'm closed."

"Indeed," the Tajik replied, quoting the Qur'an, "Allah, peace be upon Him, is with those who are of service to others."

"As He is with those who are righteous and those who do good."

Tursunov smiled. "The reward of goodness is nothing but goodness."

The tailor smiled and opened the door for his guest to enter. *"As-salāmu 'alaykum,"* he offered. *Peace be upon you.*

"Wa 'alaykum al-salaam," the Tajik responded.

The tailor's name was Hamad Sarsur. He was Syrian by birth, but had fled his nation more than twenty-five years ago. When ISIS had raised the call to jihad, he had answered, but he had done so while remaining in Rome.

Sarsur was an extremely gifted tailor. He had worked for multiple fashion houses in Milan and several high-end boutiques in Rome. All the while, he had never given up his shop in Tor Pignattara.

He was far more wealthy than appearances would suggest. And wealthy Muslims tended to know other wealthy Muslims. There was no one better at raising money in Italy than Sarsur.

But more important, he was a deeply pious Muslim. His knowledge of the Qur'an and the Hadith was without equal. He could have been one of the most revered Imams in all of Europe, but that was not the purpose Allah had chosen for him. Allah had selected Sarsur to help coordinate the efforts of ISIS in Italy and ultimately to strike right at the heart of the infidel.

Closing the door behind his guest, he said, "I am honored to have you in my shop, brother."

"The honor is mine," Tursunov replied. "Where may we speak?"

The tailor locked the front door and then led the Tajik into a back room that functioned as his office. On a hotplate was a kettle. "Tea?" he asked.

"Do you have coffee?"

Sarsur nodded, removed a jar of instant coffee from a cabinet, and selected a cup. Spooning in the granules, he drowned them with hot water and then stirred.

Handing the cup to his guest, he apologized, "I'm sorry, it's all I have."

"That's quite all right," the Tajik replied, taking the cup. He hated instant coffee.

Sarsur made himself a tea and then the two men took chairs at his desk.

"Everything is in place," said the tailor.

Tursunov took a sip of the coffee and immediately set it down. "The weapons were delivered?"

Sarsur nodded.

"Any problems with changing the location?"

The man shook his head.

"Did your men examine the crates as I instructed?"

The tailor nodded again, and, this time, he smiled.

Reaching into his desk, he retrieved his phone, opened the photo app, and showed the Tajik what his people had found.

"What did they do with those once they found them?" the Tajik asked.

Sarsur took a sip of his tea and responded, "We sent them out to sea."

Tursunov was pleased with his colleague's answer. "Well done," he replied. "Is everything else ready?"

"The chemist has arrived, the weapons are in place, and now, like the Italians say, the meal will cook itself."

He smiled in reply. "Where I am from, we also have a saying. The cook who doesn't watch his stove loses his house."

Sarsur looked confused. "I don't understand."

"We are going to go over all of it," he said. "All night if we have to. I want to cover every single step, every single millimeter. Until I am convinced that *everything* is absolutely perfect, we will do nothing else. Is that clear?"

The tailor nodded.

"Good," said Tursunov, as he picked up his cup and poured the contents into the pail next to the desk. "You can start by finding me some decent coffee."

CHAPTER 73

Despite being told to get a "good night's sleep," almost everyone was up early at the safe house in Villa San Giovanni.

Barton and Morrison joined several of Argento's men for a run. Lovett left to pick up some things she needed in town. Staelin was up on the roof drinking coffee and reading his book. Harvath was the last person to stumble into the kitchen.

"*Buon giorno,*" said Argento. He was standing at a press, wearing only a pair of workout shorts, juicing oranges. "Ready for breakfast? Let Roberto know how you like your eggs."

Standing at the stove, similarly dressed, was Roberto. Stopping what he was doing, he turned to look at Harvath.

Harvath, who was wearing a pair of Under Armour boxer briefs and a Parliament-Funkadelic T-shirt, replied, "Scrambled."

"*Strapazzate,*" Argento translated, as he continued to squeeze oranges.

"Is there any coffee?"

The Italian nodded toward the dining table. Grabbing a cup from the counter, Harvath walked over and poured himself some.

"How are you doing on my list?" he asked as he walked back into the kitchen.

"*Essere pane per i propri denti.*"

"What does that mean?"

Argento shrugged. "There's a degree of difficulty involved. Some things I can get. Some things are illegal."

Harvath laughed out loud. "Paolo, you're a cop—and a serious one at that. You can get anything you want."

"*Ecco,*" he relented, "but—"

"But nothing," Harvath said, cutting him off. Pointing to his laptop, he said, "May I?"

The Italian nodded.

On their drive from the airport to the safe house, Harvath was looking to build rapport and they had talked movies. Like any red-blooded Italian male, Argento loved American movies, especially the movies of Robert De Niro.

"You saw *The Untouchables*, right?" Harvath asked, as he pulled up YouTube.

"Robert De Niro and Kevin Costner. Of course. Directed by Brian De Palma; another Italian."

"Do you remember the scene when Kevin Costner and Sean Connery are in the church together?"

Argento stopped juicing and looked at him to see if he was being serious. "It's one of the best scenes in the movie. *That's,*" he said, mimicking Connery's Irish accent, "*the Chicago way.*"

"That's the first time I have ever heard an Italian speak English with an Irish accent," said Harvath.

"And?"

"You shouldn't do it again."

The Italian threw his hands in the air. "*Levati dai coglioni!*" he exclaimed, laughing. *Get off of my balls.*

"I'm serious. It was really bad. But that's not the point. Come here," he ordered. "Watch this."

Argento wiped his hands on a dishtowel and walked over. Harvath hit the Play button. Together, the two of them watched the scene.

When it was over, Harvath pointed at the computer and asked, "Who's me and who's you in the movie?"

"No contest," the Italian replied. "I'm older and much better looking, so I'm Sean Connery."

Harvath chuckled. "Wrong. You're Kevin Costner. *You're* Eliot Ness. You're the guy who wants to do everything by the book, no matter how dirty your opponent plays. *I'm* Sean Connery. I'm the guy trying to talk some sense into you. I'm the guy asking, what are *you* prepared to do in order to get Capone?"

Argento was about to respond when Roberto announced from the stove, *"Colazione!" Breakfast.*

Turning back to his oranges, Argento handed Harvath the pitcher and directed him to put it on the table.

With the shout of *"Colazione,"* everyone else who was in the house materialized in the kitchen for food. Somehow, even up on the roof, Staelin had heard the call and had come down too.

Scooping eggs, potatoes, and sausages onto their plates, the men shuffled into the dining room and sat down at the table. Those who couldn't find a seat carried their plates into the living room.

Staelin had grabbed the chair next to Harvath's. "So," he asked. "Are we going to be good for tonight?"

"Fingers crossed," Harvath replied as he reached for the orange juice.

"What are the odds we're going to get Vottari there?"

"If anybody can do it, Nicholas can."

"How?"

Harvath filled his glass, set the pitcher down, and took a bite of scrambled eggs before responding. "He hacked Facebook's algorithm."

"He what?"

"He had already stolen a couple of big ones from Google and someone bet him he couldn't hack Facebook, so he did. Can you pass the salt, please?"

Staelin handed him the shaker. "So how does that play into getting Vottari to The Beach Club?"

"All the photos and video I shot there last night go into a program. With it, Nicholas can access any social media post that has ever been done based on that club.

"He compares those against what Vottari reacts to on social media. Then, knowing what Vottari likes, he creates a bunch of fake accounts and starts drumming up a groundswell of posts about how tonight is a not-to-miss night at The Beach Club.

"Nicholas is smart, though. He doesn't push it directly at Vottari. He pushes it through other people Vottari knows and trusts on SnapChat, Instagram, et cetera. They repost it and it keeps showing up in his feeds. That's it."

Staelin shook his head. "That's pretty fucking manipulative."

Harvath shrugged as his phone chimed. "That's social media for you. There's a reason the intelligence community loves it so much."

Looking down, he read the text message. Addressing Argento, he said, "That's my VIP. He's got a plane on standby. He wants to know if we're a go for tonight."

A silence settled over the table. Everyone waited for Argento's response. Slowly, he nodded.

Harvath, though, wanted to make absolutely sure. "We're all good to go?"

Once more, Argento nodded. "Let's get Capone."

CHAPTER 74

Dressed in her pantsuit, meeting their plane on the tarmac at Sigonella, Lovett had been stunning. But now, totally dressed to the nines, she was unbelievably gorgeous.

"What do you think?" she asked as she turned in a circle for Harvath.

"I don't like your hair."

For a moment, she couldn't tell if he was joking. Then, realizing that he was, she shot him a look.

Laughing, he admitted, "You look fantastic."

"There were a lot of pretty, twenty-something Italians running around in that club last night. We'll see how it goes."

"Don't worry," he replied. "You're going to be a huge hit."

Lovett smiled. "Thank you."

"Do you want to go over it again?"

"Only if you want to. I've got it nailed down."

"I'm good too," he stated, glancing at his watch. "At this point, it's up to Argento."

At that moment, the front door opened and the Italian and two of his men walked in.

"*Sei bellissima,*" he exclaimed as he took in Lovett all made up, ready to hit the club. *You're beautiful.*

Her hair and makeup were perfect, but it was the very short black dress she had purchased that was the real showstopper.

"*Grazie,*" she said with another smile.

"Have you got something for me?" Harvath asked.

"Let's go in the back," Argento replied.

They walked down the hall to Harvath's room and closed the door. The Italian didn't want the rest of his team to see what he was giving him. Two of his guys had just gone out with him to get it, and everyone else knew what the plan entailed, but Argento was a good cop and hated drugs.

"Here," he said, handing an envelope filled with pills to Harvath.

"Jesus, Paolo," he responded, laughing as he felt how many were inside. "We're not taking out a soccer team."

The Italian wasn't laughing. "Whatever you don't use, just flush down the toilet."

Harvath opened the envelope and studied the tablets. "Did you have one of your guys pop one to make sure they work?"

"Of course not," Argento replied.

Harvath smiled. "I'm just kidding."

The Italian didn't find it funny. "The dealer knows what will happen if these don't work. That's all the certification I need."

"You have a history with this guy?"

"He's an informant. He lets us know when the Cosa Nostra moves drugs on the car ferry from Messina. The only reason he's still in business is that we allow him to be."

Folding the envelope and putting it in his pocket, Harvath replied, "That's the kind of informant I like."

Argento was nervous. "Have you ever used Rohypnol on a subject before?"

"Never needed it. I usually rely on debutante heroin."

"*Debutante heroin?*" the Italian asked.

Harvath winked at him. "Chardonnay."

Argento cracked a smile.

He was glad to see him loosen up. "This is all going to work out. Trust me."

"I am trusting you," the Italian stated. "All of my men are trusting you too. If things go bad, we're in big trouble. All of us."

CHAPTER 75

B y the time the teams were ready to leave the safe house, there was little doubt La Formícula was going to be at The Beach Club tonight. Not only had he been "liking" every single post that popped up in his feed, but according to Nicholas, he had been exchanging private messages with friends about what time he planned to be there.

Harvath and Argento had walked everyone through the plan a final time, explaining how everything would work and making sure there were no questions. There weren't any. Everyone understood what they had to do.

Tonight, instead of the American team going first, the Italians did. They wanted to get in before it got too crowded.

Harvath, though, wasn't worried. After the money he had dropped last night, the fire marshal could be outside turning people away and the staff still would have found a way to get him inside.

It was just after eleven o'clock and the club was packed. The lights were lower and the music louder than the night before. Both of those developments were going to work in their favor.

After tipping the bouncers, they were shown to the crowded VIP section. There, Harvath tipped the man behind the velvet rope and they were led to their seating area. The man removed the *Riservato* sign from their table and said the waitress would be right over.

As they sat down, Harvath noticed there was only one seating cluster left. It too had a *Riservato* sign on the table. He hoped that it had been reserved for La Formícula.

Because Vottari accessed all of his social media accounts through his phone, Nicholas had been able to hack into his "find my phone" feature. Harvath was getting regular updates on his progress.

Looking down at the latest, he saw that the Mafioso was less than twenty minutes away. He could also see who he had been messaging with. There appeared to be five or six friends of his already in the club.

Pulling up their avatars, he did screen shots and sent them in a group text to the rest of the team. It would be important to know who Vottari's friends were.

The one thing Harvath didn't have was a drone overhead. Before La Formícula even left his estate, it would have been helpful to know how many men he was traveling with and how many vehicles they were bringing.

Argento guaranteed him that they had the next best thing, Roberto—the ROS operator who had cooked breakfast that morning. He would be outside when La Formícula arrived and then would relay all the information, including whether any drivers were remaining with vehicles.

Another of Argento's men, Naldo, would be parked down the road with the engine running, ready to move as soon as Harvath gave the command.

The rest of the Italians were inside the club. Already, Harvath had been able to pick out a couple of them. The club was so dark and so crowded, though, that almost the moment he saw them, they were gone.

The pretty waitress with limited English skills brought over a tray of glasses and was followed by the busboy carrying the ice bucket and champagne.

Opening the bottle, the waitress poured glasses for everyone and, having drained it, asked, "More?"

Harvath smiled, handed her a tip, and responded the same way he had last time, "Later. *Grazie*."

She thanked him for the tip and walked over to another table.

This time it was Staelin who gave the toast. "May our sons have rich fathers and beautiful mothers!"

"I'll definitely drink to that," said Lovett, who had turned every single head when she had walked in.

They clinked glasses and all took a drink of champagne.

Harvath then instructed, "Time to make some new friends."

He wanted it to look as if they were here to have a good time. The more fun they were having, the less threatening they'd appear.

Besides, Harvath knew his team all too well. They were Alpha dogs. If there weren't any pretty girls for them to mix it up with, they'd end up shooting death stares at Vottari and his men. That would only end badly.

With their pockets full of cash, Morrison and Barton headed toward the main bar. Staelin, though, didn't budge. Instead he just sat there, texting on his phone.

"Tick tock," Harvath said, urging him to get going.

The Delta Force operative ignored him.

Harvath looked at Lovett, but she didn't have a clue what he was doing.

Finally, Staelin locked his screen and put his phone back in his pocket.

"Are you done?" asked Harvath. "Ready to go to work now?"

The Delta Force operative smiled, but it wasn't at Harvath. He was smiling past him.

Raising his hand, he gestured to the man at the velvet rope.

Harvath turned just as the man unclipped the rope and allowed two very pretty women into the VIP section. As they came closer, he noticed one of them was one of the women Vottari had been messaging with.

"What the hell?" Harvath asked.

Staelin tapped the phone in his pocket as he stood to greet the approaching ladies. "Tinder," he said, leaning over so Harvath could hear him. "Never leave home without it."

A hookup app? He had to hand it to him. While Morrison and Barton were trying to buy drinks and get women to dance with them, Staelin hadn't even gotten off the couch.

As the women arrived at the table, Staelin introduced himself, kissed them each on both cheeks, and then introduced Harvath and Lovett.

As they all sat down, the waitress materialized and asked what they wanted to drink. They ordered vodka Red Bulls and as soon as she was gone, began to flirt and pepper Staelin with questions. Their English was pretty good.

They wanted to know who he was, where he was from, and what he did. Having come up with a cover story the night before, he was ready with answers.

The team had decided that if anyone asked, they would say they were scouting locations for an extreme fitness competition similar to the Iron Man race. The key was to keep it simple.

When the drinks came, the ladies managed only a quick sip before Staelin dragged them both out onto the dance floor.

"He's one hell of an operator," Lovett remarked, as she watched the trio leave.

Harvath was about to agree when his phone illuminated. Picking it up, he read the message.

"Vottari just pulled up," he said. "Two vehicles. Four men in total with him. It looks like they're all coming in together."

As Lovett discreetly adjusted her dress, Harvath sent out a group text, notifying the team of the details.

It was time to heat the place up.

CHAPTER 76

La Formícula walked into the club dressed all in white—white linen trousers, a white linen shirt, and white shoes. His black hair was slicked back and on his small right wrist was an enormous Rolex in rose gold.

The entourage was admitted right into the VIP section and, sure enough, was guided to the last remaining seating area. The man's cologne was so strong, Harvath could smell it from where he sat.

Vottari took a spot on one of the white couches, while his bodyguards took up strategic positions nearby.

As the Mafioso's eyes swept the room, Harvath pretended to be absorbed in his phone. He wanted La Formícula to stare as long and as hard as he pleased at Lovett.

Soon enough, a pair of Vottari's friends arrived and he stood up to greet them.

"Did he get a good look?" Harvath asked, still interacting with his phone.

"And then some," said Lovett. "I don't think I had a stitch of clothing left by the time he got done. I feel like I need a shower."

Harvath smiled. "I get it. Women look at me like that all the time. It's degrading."

Lovett rubbed her thigh with her middle finger. Harvath laughed.

Over in Vottari's seating area, a few more friends had arrived, as had the waitress with glasses and two busboys toting ice buckets and champagne.

Soon enough, corks were flying and everyone was having a good time.

Morrison and Barton had met up with a pair of sisters. After drinks and some dancing they brought them back to the VIP section and made introductions. Harvath ordered another bottle of champagne.

Not too long after, Staelin and his lady friends came back. But instead of returning to sit with his teammates, he allowed the women to drag him over to meet Vottari and his gang of friends. The guy was amazing.

When Harvath's new bottle of champagne was opened, Barton raised his glass and said, *"Cent'anni!"*

The two sisters were delighted that he could toast in Italian. "Where did you learn it?"

"From *The Godfather*," he replied proudly.

"The film?" they asked in unison. When he nodded, they all began laughing.

Harvath knew the toast too. And he'd learned it the same way. It was a wish for one hundred years of good luck.

His wish, though, was that Barton would stop quoting from Mafia movies while they were sitting across from one of Calabria's most vicious mobsters.

Just looking at him, it was hard to believe that Vottari was so dangerous. But he knew that looks could be deceiving. The crime scene photos Argento had shown him had been disgusting.

Focusing his attention back on his group, he joined in as Morrison made a toast with some bawdy Irish limerick and everybody cracked up.

Out of the corner of his eye, he saw Staelin having a terrific time laughing and telling jokes with La Formícula. Moments later, the Delta Force operative waved the entire team over.

Picking up their drinks, they walked across the VIP section and joined them. Staelin made introductions and before Harvath knew what was happening, Vottari had given his bodyguards orders to move the furniture.

The large men walked back to Harvath's seating area, lifted the couches, chairs, and even the table and repositioned them so the two groups could sit together. As soon as they were done moving everything, they returned to their positions.

"Antonio is in the olive oil business," Staelin said, raising his voice so he could be heard above the music. "He's going to get us a case of his best stuff."

"Extra virgin," Vottari promised. "Absolutely the best."

Harvath flashed him the thumbs-up as the man leaned in to ask Staelin something.

"They only *work* together," The Delta Force operative replied, nodding at Harvath and Lovett. "In America, we say that he's her *work* husband. They're not married. She's totally single."

Harvath wasn't the jealous type. Not by a long shot. He was more protective than anything else, but with that said he really didn't like the vibe this guy was putting out toward Lovett. If she sensed it, which he knew she had to, she was doing an amazing job keeping it under wraps. Vottari was disgusting.

They made small talk as another bottle of champagne made the rounds and everyone's glasses were topped off.

Just then, a song came on and all of the Italians went wild.

Standing up, Vottari reached for Lovett's hand. "Number-one song all summer in Italy," he shouted. "Come dance!"

One of the women with Staelin grabbed Harvath and pulled him with her as the entire VIP section emptied onto the dance floor.

It was so crowded, you could barely move. Harvath did his best to keep Lovett and Vottari in sight.

The bodyguards had stayed behind, and he hoped that Lovett had noticed. This might be her only shot.

La Formícula was a real internationalist on the dance floor. He had Russian hands and Roman fingers all over Lovett. Harvath wanted to knock him out right there and then.

As the song picked up speed, the crowd got wilder and wilder. They knew the lyrics by heart and were belting them out.

The DJ, reading the room the way only a good DJ can, went from the big summer anthem into another huge European hit.

A cheer rose from the dance floor as people recognized the new song, and the energy in the club kicked up to a new level.

Lasers, choreographed to the music, slashed across the room, strobes popped, and fog machines roared to life.

The DJ was on a roll and continued to mix one dance hit into another. The crowd absolutely loved it and showed no sign of slowing down.

The woman Harvath was dancing with was ecstatic—grooving and whipping her hair from side to side. If he had turned and left the floor right at that moment, he doubted she would have even noticed.

Which, as it turned out, was a good thing, because when he looked back over at Vottari and Lovett, they were gone.

CHAPTER 77

After a solid twenty minutes of dancing, Lovett convinced Vottari that they should step outside for some air. Considering how welcoming she had been to all his advances on the dance floor, he was all for it.

They walked out onto a large terrace and headed for the round, outdoor bar.

"What would you like to drink?" he asked.

"Whiskey sour," she replied.

Once he got the attention of one of the bartenders, he ordered whiskey sours for both of them.

Vottari's shirt was soaked through with sweat. Grabbing a few napkins off the bar, he wiped his face, then his armpits, and tossed the napkins on the ground.

"What hotel are you staying at?" he asked.

The question took her by surprise. She didn't know any of the hotels in the area. "Airbnb," she said. She had to lean in to be heard over the music being pumped through the speakers above the bar.

La Formícula took her movement as an invitation, and he put his hands on both her hips. "At my house, I have a swimming pool *and* a hot tub. You like hot tubs?"

"They're okay," she replied as the bartender arrived with their drinks. Vottari needed his hands to pull out his wallet to pay for them.

"Let's go see the water," she suggested, tilting her head toward one of the tables near the beach.

Vottari nodded and motioned for her to lead the way. She knew he hadn't done it to be a gentleman and that he just wanted to check out her ass. The man was an absolute sleazebag.

The tables were counter-height with barstools and umbrellas made of palm fronds. Just as they arrived at the one she had picked out, he changed his mind.

"Where are you going?"

"This way," he said, heading toward the cabanas out on the sand.

Shit, she thought. Inside a canvas tent, with no one else around was about the last place she wanted to be with this guy. But if she didn't go with him, she might not get another chance to slip the Rohypnol into his drink. Reluctantly, she followed.

"Look how nice," he said when they had arrived.

There was a loveseat, two additional chairs, and a small table with thick, white candles in hurricane lamps. It was quite lovely, and in almost any other circumstance, might have even been romantic.

There was a small *Riservato* sign on the table and Lovett pointed at it. "Reserved," she said.

Vottari walked over, picked up the sign, and tossed it aside. "Not anymore. Come, sit," he replied, leading her over to the loveseat.

When she joined him he raised his glass and clinked it against hers. "Cheers."

"Cheers," Lovett responded, taking a sip of her cocktail.

As soon as she began to lower the glass, he took it from her and set it next to his on the table. That was when he pounced.

He was quite strong for a man of his size. Pushing her backward on the loveseat, he grabbed her wrists and pinned her down as he buried his face between the tops of her breasts and then ran his tongue up the side of her neck.

Lovett struggled to get free. "Wait a second," she said. "Stop."

Vottari, though, wasn't interested in hearing that word and kept going, nibbling her earlobe and then pushing his tongue inside.

"Stop!" she insisted, much more forcefully. This time, she got his attention.

"What is it?"

Over his shoulder, she could see their whiskey sours sitting on the table. Beyond was the entrance to the cabana. "What if someone sees us?"

Vottari smiled and bent down to kiss her. His overpowering cologne made her want to throw up. She turned her face to the side, frustrating him.

"Close the flaps," she said softly.

"The what?"

"The door. Close the door. I don't want anyone to see."

Figuring he was in for a very good time, Vottari's smiled widened. Lifting himself off her, he went to close the cabana's flaps.

The moment he turned his back, Lovett sat up and shot her hand into her bra.

Damn it, she worried. *Where are they?*

She had placed the tablets in her bra, where she thought she could easily get to them. But with having had his hands, and even his face, all over her, they must have shifted.

Come on. Come on. Come on. She was starting to freak out. *Where the hell were they?*

Just then, she felt the first tablet, and then the second. Her fingers closed around them like a vise and she slid them from her bra.

Looking up, she could see only Vottari's silhouette outside. He had already unfurled one flap and was working on the other.

Snapping the first tablet so that it would dissolve faster, she dropped it into his drink.

She was in the process of snapping the second when it popped out from between her fingers and landed on the table.

Without a moment to lose, she picked up her glass with the cocktail napkin underneath, set it atop the pill and pressed down, crushing it.

Then, setting her glass aside, she grabbed Vottari's. Sweeping the pieces into his glass, she gave it a swirl to mix everything up, and then she set it down.

Reclaiming her own glass, she leaned back against the loveseat and that's when she saw him.

He was standing in the entrance, glaring at her, his mind moving from passion to rage.

Finally, he spoke. "What the fuck did you just do?"

CHAPTER 78

Vottari advanced into the cabana. "What did you just put in my drink?"

Lovett's immediate instinct was to convince him that he had not seen what he had just seen. "What are you talking about? I didn't put anything in your drink."

"You lying bitch."

"You know what?" she said, starting to stand up. "We're done here."

"No we're not," the man replied, removing something from his pocket. "We're just starting."

As soon as she heard the distinctive *click* of a blade locking into place, she knew he had pulled a knife. In a flash, all of her training came flooding back.

Kicking the table over, she sent the candles and glass hurricane lamps hurtling at him.

It wasn't much, but it gave her enough time to get on her feet.

Snatching a cushion off the loveseat, she used it to blunt his attack. He came in fast, though, driving her backward.

She was so focused on the knife that she didn't see the chair, and went tumbling over it.

The moment she hit the ground, he was on top of her, the blade pressed tightly against her throat. She didn't dare move.

Putting his lips against her ear, he whispered, "Like I said, we're only getting started."

She could feel his other hand under her skirt. He was rough and pushed it up the inside of her thigh. When he got to her panties, he stopped. Then, with a snap, he ripped them off.

His hand was suddenly out from under her skirt and was unzipping his fly. She tensed. *He was going to rape her.*

Sensing she was about to do something stupid, he applied even more pressure to the knife.

Lovett felt the edge of the blade biting into her skin. When his free hand came up to his mouth and she saw him wet it with saliva, she knew she had to do something—even if that something was just to scream—in the hopes that someone would hear her.

She opened her mouth to yell, but as soon as she did, he punched her in the side of her face.

She saw stars. She had to fight with everything she had not to black out. She knew if she didn't, it would be all over.

He had remoistened his hand and was trying to force it between her legs. Summoning all of her strength, she fought to deny him.

Angered, he withdrew his hand and pulled it back to punch her again. That was when it happened.

Like a pair of pythons, two strong arms snaked around Vottari's throat and behind his neck.

Squeezing his shoulders back, her savior cut off the blood supply to the man's brain and within seconds, he passed out.

"Are you okay?" Harvath asked as he dropped Vottari to the ground and kicked his knife out of the way.

Lovett couldn't speak, she could only nod.

"Toss me your underwear," he said as he fished a set of flex-cuffs out of his pocket. "It's right there to your left."

It was a strange request, but she did as he asked.

Someone who has been choked out doesn't stay out for long. It was only a matter of seconds.

Securing Vottari's wrists behind his back, Harvath shoved Lovett's underwear in his mouth and covered it with a piece of duct tape he had wrapped around the flashlight in his other pocket.

He then gestured toward the overturned furniture. "Unzip one of those throw pillows, pull out the stuffing, and bring me the cover."

As she did that, Harvath removed his cell phone and sent another group text.

When she brought him the cover, he dialed a number and handed her his phone. "Tell Naldo where we are and that he needs to come get us *right* now."

Lovett took the phone and relayed the instruction in Italian as Harvath put the cover over Vottari's head as a makeshift hood.

Ninety seconds later, with all of his lights out, Naldo pulled up on the beach outside.

"Move, asshole," Harvath ordered, yanking the hooded Vottari to his feet.

When the man tried to break free of his grasp and run, Harvath hit him in the kidney so hard, he was sure to be pissing blood for a week.

Dragging him to the back of the SUV, Naldo helped toss him into the cargo area. Harvath leapt in behind him, forced him to lie down, and then kept him pinned to the floor.

As soon as Naldo and Lovett were in, he said, "Okay, let's go."

The ROS operative put the vehicle in gear, stepped on the gas, and raced down the beach.

Pulling his phone back out, Harvath sent his final group text.

Within seconds of its being received, Harvath's team began slipping out of the club.

Argento and his men stayed only long enough to make sure their American counterparts had gotten out without incident. Once that was confirmed, they too made their exit.

By the time any of La Formícula's bodyguards were concerned enough to go looking for him, the teams that had snatched him were long gone.

CHAPTER 79

Andrew Jordan pulled the MacBook Air out of his briefcase and pushed it across Paul Page's dining room table.

"Ever heard of a thumb drive?" Page asked, accepting it.

"That's what I said, but Susan Viscovich is spooked."

"You used Viscovich to hack Carlton and Ryan?"

Jordan nodded. "She's the best and I know you didn't want to waste any time."

"What did it cost us?"

"Don't ask."

Part of Page really didn't want to know. A job like this must have been exorbitantly expensive. "Why the laptop, though?"

"She said it was for our safety," Jordan replied. "She had to put out a contract for the hack. They scanned the files up and down for malware and didn't find anything, but she's paid to be suspicious. She wanted to make sure we were able to review all of the material on a computer stripped of any ability to connect with the Internet."

"How'd she get the information onto the laptop?"

Jordan shook his head. "No clue. And to tell you the truth, I don't really care."

"So what did she come up with?"

"The personal email accounts for Reed Carlton and Lydia Ryan."

Page was impressed. "That was quick."

"Like I said, she's the best. The emails go back quite a way, and there's lots of them."

"Did you also hire her for the rest of the surveillance?"

Jordan nodded. "That, though, didn't go as well."

"What do you mean?"

"Ryan wasn't scheduled to have her place swept for another two weeks. The plan was to get in and get out before the CIA came through, but for some reason, she had them come in early. They found everything."

Page was not happy. He was even less happy when Jordan added, "They found all the surveillance at Carlton's too."

"Son of a bitch," he cursed. "Now they know we're on to them."

"They know someone is on to them. They don't necessarily know who."

Page looked at his partner. "The Deputy Director of the CIA and Reed fucking Carlton found out their homes were wired. You don't think they're going to move heaven and earth to get to the bottom of it?"

"Viscovich has assured me that absolutely none of the equipment she used can be traced back."

"Well she wouldn't be the *best*," he replied, making air quotes with his fingers, "if it could. But I'm not worried about the equipment giving her away. I'm worried about whoever installed it. She does tons of fucking contract work for the Agency. If word gets out about this, her installers may start spilling what they know."

"She has assured me that won't happen."

"Well that's fucking great, Andrew. I'm glad you're willing to gamble everything on a promise from Susan Viscovich." Page paused and then added, "Are you fucking her?"

Jordan laughed, "Now that *would* be worth risking everything over."

Page was pissed off and didn't like his cavalier attitude. "She's a weak link. You need to fix this."

"Fix this?" Jordan said, with another laugh. "Fix it how?"

"Kill her."

"You're fucking crazy, you know that?"

"Kill her," Page instructed, "and kill the installers."

"Is that all?"

"You don't seem to understand how serious this is."

Jordan looked at him. "And you don't seem to understand how insane you sound."

"What exactly do you think is going to happen when Reed Carlton comes after us for this? Have you thought about that?"

"Frankly, Paul, he's your obsession. Not mine. I was just trying to do you a favor. And apparently, no good deed goes unpunished."

"We're *both* going to get punished if we don't get out in front of this."

"I'm not killing anybody," Jordan stated. "Full stop. Not going to happen."

"That's too bad," said Page, as he removed the suppressed .22 Walther pistol mounted under his dining room table and fired into his partner's left temple, killing him. "Now, I'm going to have to do all the work."

CHAPTER 80

When the teams arrived back at the safe house, Harvath's VIP was already set up and waiting for him.

As the vehicles pulled into the courtyard, Dr. Vella stood in the doorway. In his hand was a very special black hood. He wanted to get it on their subject as quickly as possible.

Once Naldo had backed their SUV in, Harvath opened the hatch and waved Vella over. No one said a word. They operated in total silence.

Using his flashlight to blind Vottari so he couldn't see where he was or what was going on, Harvath yanked the pillow covering off Vottari's head and Vella replaced it with the hood he had brought from the Solarium in Malta.

Morrison and Staelin then dragged the Mafioso into the house.

In the room that had been outfitted for his interrogation, they patted Vottari down, relieved him of all his personal effects, and secured him to a chair. All of the other furniture had been removed.

Heavy black moving blankets had been affixed over the windows, halogen lights rested on adjustable stands, and three video cameras sat atop tripods at different angles. The room looked like it had been set up for a terrorist video.

There was also a large medical bag and five plastic Storm cases of varying sizes that contained the rest of Vella's equipment.

It was now time for the doctor to take over.

After making sure Vella had everything he needed, Harvath stepped into the kitchen for a cup of coffee. He had a feeling it was going to be a long night.

Because of the nature of the operation, Harvath and Argento had agreed to a very specific division of labor. Argento and his men would be responsible for the security of the safe house and Harvath and his men would be responsible for securing Vottari. This way, the Italians could ostensibly deny knowledge of what had taken place. Technically, none of them had even seen La Formícula's face outside the nightclub.

While Barton pulled security outside the interrogation room, Staelin and Morrison had already turned in. Most of Argento's men had too.

Filling a mug, Harvath grabbed his backpack and headed upstairs to the roof. He wanted to get some work done. Back at Langley, McGee would be expecting an update.

Stepping outside, he saw Argento sitting at a table. He had lit a few of the Citronella candles to keep the mosquitos away, had his feet up, and was smoking a cigarette. When he saw Harvath, he motioned for him to join him.

Setting his backpack on the table, he pulled out a chair and sat down. The view of the town, all lit up at night, reminded him of a lot of the time he'd spent in Greece.

The Italian offered Harvath a cigarette. Harvath declined.

"So, how long will the interrogation take?" Argento asked as he exhaled a cloud of smoke.

"Hard to say."

"Does he always travel with a hood?"

Harvath nodded. "It's a designer hood."

"What's so special about it?"

"There's a pocket in the front that holds strips of cloth soaked in a unique chemical. It's supposed to make subjects more cooperative."

"Does it work?"

"Vella thinks so."

"Have you ever tried it?" Argento asked.

"I watched him do one interrogation with it and it worked. The one time I tried to do it in the field, it didn't work."

"What happened?"

"The subject had a heart attack. I haven't tried it again since then," said Harvath. "That's why I wanted to bring Vella in to do this."

The Italian nodded and took another drag on his cigarette. When he exhaled, he asked, "Your tech people blocked La Formícula's phone, correct? None of his people can trace it here?"

"Correct. I texted my guy as soon as we grabbed him. There's no trail. It's as if Vottari's phone never left The Beach Club," replied Harvath.

"And there will be no marks on him, correct? No needle punctures. No bruising."

"Just as we agreed."

Argento seemed content and had no further questions. He went back to smoking his cigarette and looking up at the stars. Harvath took out his laptop and began typing up an update for McGee.

After it was complete, he powered up his encrypted satellite phone, attached it to the computer, and sent the update back to the United States.

With that task checked off his list, he put his feet up as well and relaxed as he sipped his coffee.

Though Lovett might not agree, nor would he blame her, they had gotten off easy tonight. He had planned for a much more difficult extraction of Vottari. Argento's men had been armed with Tasers to take out the bodyguards and Harvath and his team had smuggled in flashbangs and smoke grenades to create a diversion in order to smuggle out the Mafioso during the chaos.

Looking at his watch, he saw that it was well after midnight, which meant that locally, it was Saturday. He couldn't believe that it had been only a week ago that he met with McGee and Ryan at the blue lockhouse.

Eight days ago, the attack at Burning Man had happened. Since then, the Spain and Paris attacks had happened. So many people were dead and so many more were wounded.

Quietly, he hoped that the attack at the Tuileries was the big one that the CIA had been worried about. He hoped that whatever ISIS had been planning that required a chemist, had been stopped dead in its tracks when Mustapha Marzouk had drowned.

He knew better than that, though. He knew that ISIS hadn't gone to this much trouble over a chemist for nothing. Whatever they had planned, they were going to keep pursuing it, no matter what the cost.

Harvath also knew that if he didn't figure out what it was, and find a way to stop it, many more people were going to die.

•   •   •

For the next two hours, Harvath sat on the roof, not thinking about anything. He spent most of that time with his eyes closed, giving his mind a rest and trying to recharge his batteries.

When he suddenly heard footsteps on the roof, his eyes snapped open and he was wide awake.

Turning in his chair, he saw Vella with a tablet in his hand. "What's going on?"

"Vottari broke," the doctor replied. "You need to see this."

"What is it?" Argento asked.

Vella set the tablet on the table in front of them. The portion of the interrogation he wanted them to view was already cued up. Tapping the Play icon, he then took a step back.

Harvath and Argento watched. The horror of what Vottari had done built with each passing second of his confession.

Before La Formícula was even finished speaking, Harvath was already scrambling for his satellite phone.

CHAPTER 81

The *Grande Senegal* was a Grimaldi Lines container ship that had left Rome's Civitavecchia Port en route to Baltimore, Maryland. The ship was almost two and a half football fields long and, according to Vottari, was carrying crates containing two cases of fragmentation grenades, six Russian mortars, and twelve binary chemical weapon shells designed for mixing highly deadly sarin gas in flight.

Ever suspicious of his ISIS clients, Vottari admitted to having hidden RFID tags in the weapons' crates to make sure the contraband material did in fact leave Italy. There was an app on his cell phone actively tracking the tags.

"But your ISIS contact told you that the final destination for Mustapha Marzouk, and the weapons, was outside Italy, somewhere in Europe," Vella had pressed during the interrogation.

"They lie," Vottari had responded. "It's what they do."

The fact that ISIS had intended to smuggle the weapons out via the Port of Rome was also reinforced in the interrogation when Vottari admitted that his ISIS contact wanted the weapons delivered to a warehouse in Civitavecchia.

So thorough was the security at the Port of Rome that after an initial investigation, Vottari's people had told him it was too dangerous. So Vottari had negotiated a different, safer location for the weapons to be delivered to.

For Harvath, everything was coming together. Via the Italian Mafia, ISIS had purchased Russian weapons, capable of delivering sarin gas. Those weapons were to be smuggled to Rome, along with an ISIS chemist.

ISIS had then lied about the final target, evidently intending to put the weapons and the chemist on a cargo container bound for the United States. According to the app on Vottari's phone tracking the RFID tags he had hidden in the crates, the weapons were on their way. If Lovett's assumption back in Palermo had been right, then so too was a new ISIS chemist.

The good news, though, was that the United States knew exactly where the Grimaldi Lines' *Grande Senegal* was and a U.S. Navy SEAL Team had already launched from a ship in the western Mediterranean.

Sitting on the rooftop of the ROS safe house in Villa San Giovanni, Harvath and Argento watched as a video feed of the interdiction was beamed to Harvath's laptop via his satellite phone.

A drone had been dispatched to shadow the ship and send back reconnaissance information.

Once the SEALs launched, they did so via two Sikorsky SH-60 Seahawk helicopters.

All of the SEALs were wearing miniature cameras that would provide real-time video of the assault.

Half of the team was responsible for locating the weapons, including any chemical components. The other half of the team was responsible for securing all crew and passengers. After which, they would conduct an investigation to determine if anyone aboard was an ISIS member or sympathizer.

Knowing what was at stake, the SEALs went in, not only expecting the chemist to be on the ship, but also expecting that he might be traveling with protection.

When the teams fast-roped out of the helos, Harvath's screen split in two and he received video feeds from each team leader.

As Alpha team—armed with an RFID scanner that let them zero in on the frequencies of Vottari's tags—headed for the containers, Bravo team headed for the bridge.

It took about twenty minutes for the bad news to start flooding in. First came a report from Alpha team. They had found the RFID tags, all thrown together in a plastic grocery bag. There were no weapons and no chemicals in the container.

Then came Bravo's SITREP. All passengers and crew were accounted for. Unless there were stowaways that nobody knew about, they were it.

Bravo team's leader held the passports up to his camera, so everyone watching the feeds could see them. Back at Langley, the CIA ran the names and photos through all of their databases. None of them were on any lists, nor were they affiliated with any known or suspected terrorist, terrorist supporter, or terrorist organizations.

The entire interdiction—all of that work—had been a bust. Harvath was back to square one.

But then, reflecting on the RFID tags, he abruptly realized that being back to square one was exactly where they needed to be.

CHAPTER 82

"If I hadn't seen it with my own eyes," Nicholas said over the secure uplink, "I never would have believed it. In addition to having their own covert servers, they've hidden an entire SCIF right inside Cedars-Sinai."

"How the hell is that possible?" Ryan replied.

"They won a legitimate contract to encrypt patient medical records. As part of the agreement, they have office space at the hospital. Inside that office space is a raised-floor computer room. Except the floor wasn't raised just so cables and a cooling system could run underneath. The entire room has been shielded to TEMPEST specifications."

TEMPEST was the code name for the NSA's data security guidelines. It set the standard for protecting highly sensitive information from being intercepted.

"You said 'they' won a legitimate contract. Who are *they*?"

"In putting out the contract for bid, priority was given to veterans, women, and minority-owned businesses. The winning bid came from a company called Blue Pine Technologies."

"Never heard of them," replied Ryan.

"Me neither. I had to work my ass off to track down their bid package. Apparently, they ticked all three boxes. Blue Pine is owned by two women, both IT whizzes. One of them is of Asian descent. The other is an Army veteran."

"And?"

"The Army veteran worked in Army Intelligence. Then she went to work for the NSA."

It just so happened that the CIA contracted a certain amount of off-the-books surveillance to a group run by a woman who had worked both in Army Intelligence and at the NSA. Ryan didn't believe in coincidences.

"What's her name?" she asked.

"Susan Viscovich."

• • •

Doing jobs for the branch of the CIA responsible for clandestine intelligence collection meant taking meetings at interesting times in interesting places. A lockhouse in the C&O National Historical Park on a Friday night definitely ranked toward the top of Susan Viscovich's "most interesting" list.

Upon arrival, she saw a lone Lexus sedan parked outside. It seemed a little bit odd, but then again, what had she expected? *A column of blacked-out Suburbans?* That probably wasn't how the Director of the Clandestine Service rolled—especially not when he was meeting to discuss such a sensitive surveillance case.

She figured the meeting had to do with her surveillance of Lydia Ryan and Reed Carlton. Was she going to get her ass chewed for the fact that the cameras, microphones, and vehicle trackers had been discovered? Maybe.

She had reached out to Andy Jordan to get a heads-up on what was going on, but her calls went right to voicemail. He hadn't responded to any of her texts either. *Whatever.*

Sometimes surveillance assignments got blown. It happened. She had, though, delivered on the emails, and maybe that was what she was being asked in to discuss.

Nevertheless, it was weird for her to be having a Director-level meeting. Perhaps they had discovered something highly sensitive and they wanted to dot all their *i*'s and cross their *t*'s before confronting Lydia Ryan. There was only one way to find out.

Parking her Volvo next to the Lexus, she got out, walked up the short flight of steps, and knocked on the blue door.

A moment later, it opened. But instead of seeing the Director of the Clandestine Service, she saw the Director of Central Intelligence.

"Thank you for coming," said Bob McGee.

Shocked, she looked deeper into the room and saw the Deputy Director, Lydia Ryan, sitting at a table near the fireplace.

Opening the door the rest of the way, the Director motioned for her to come inside.

What the hell was going on? For a moment, Viscovich thought about turning around and leaving. In fact, a voice in the back of her mind told her not only to leave, but to leave as fast as she could.

The rational part of her, though, maintained control. She wanted to know what this was all about. Taking a deep breath, she stepped inside.

•   •   •

Two hours later, realizing she had been lied to by Andrew Jordan, and that he had even forged the finding from the Director authorizing her to surveil Lydia Ryan and Reed Carlton, Viscovich exited the lockhouse, climbed back into her Volvo, and headed home.

The Director of Central Intelligence had given her a new directive. Until she heard from him personally, she was to do nothing and to speak with no one, including Andrew Jordan.

Before she had even exited the park, McGee and Ryan were formalizing what their next step would be.

The only question was whether it should be run through the CIA or whether they should use the anonymity of the Carlton Group to carry it out.

CHAPTER 83

Argento had a private jet waiting for them at the Reggio Calabria airport. The flight to Rome took less than an hour. A pair of helicopters was on the tarmac when they arrived, rotors hot, ready to take them the rest of the way.

From a public safety standpoint, the ROS wanted to hit the warehouse in the port at Civitavecchia as quickly as possible. From a media standpoint, Harvath wanted to hit it while it was dark and everyone was still asleep. The last thing they needed was a TV news crew showing up, or someone with a camera phone posting video to the Internet. The less the bad guys knew about what they knew, the better.

Patching Nicholas directly into Vottari's phone via satellite, they had been able to retrace where the RFID tags had been.

La Formícula's men had handed over the weapons near Cerveteri— a town northwest of Rome. From there, the ISIS men had driven to a warehouse in Civitavecchia, where there had been no movement since the tags were placed upon the cargo ship *Grande Senegal* shortly before it headed out to sea.

Harvath had no doubt that the target was somewhere in Rome. If ISIS had been planning on using the weapons someplace else in Europe, they would have had them, and Mustapha Marzouk, delivered much farther north—possibly Turin or Milan. What good is an illicit underground railroad if you don't follow it as far as it will take you?

The helicopters landed well north of the target, where an additional ROS team met them.

As the team leader spoke to Argento, Lovett translated for Harvath.

"The warehouse has been under surveillance for the last hour and a half. There have been no signs of any activity. The lease is only a couple of months old and, according to the landlord, is held by a trading company out of Panama. Probably a shell corporation.

"The ROS Hazmat unit out of Rome is two blocks away from the target. They have been watching the surveillance feeds and are ready to make entry as soon as Argento gives the order."

There was some back and forth between the men that got somewhat heated. Lovett waited until it was resolved before explaining it.

"Apparently, there's some disagreement about whether the neighborhood should be evacuated. It's largely an industrial area, but some of the businesses run overnight shifts."

"Argento won the argument?" Harvath asked.

"For now."

Once Argento and his colleague had finished going over the plan, everyone climbed into waiting vehicles and they took off for the target.

The command post had been established three blocks upwind of the warehouse. If sarin or any other hazardous chemicals were present, they wanted to be outside the immediate zone.

In addition to the ROS team outfitted with respirators and CBRN suits and prepared to make entry, hazardous incident response units from the Italian Department of Civil Protection had also been activated and were staging nearby.

Argento had taken great pains to keep the operational footprint as small as possible. Unfortunately, with so much at stake, this was as small as the situation would allow.

Pulling up at the staging area, Harvath and Lovett hopped out and followed Argento into the mobile incident command post, which was housed inside a climate-controlled tractor-trailer.

Staff in military green flight suits sat in front of computer screens, while large monitors bolted to the walls fed back a series of images, including footage from two drones that were observing the warehouse from overhead.

After a quick discussion, Argento gave the order to send the ROS team into the building.

Moments later, two black vans appeared on two different monitors. One approached the warehouse from the front, another from the rear. Each came to a stop only long enough to drop off its occupants before moving on.

Even wearing the bulky chemical, biological, radiological, and nuclear protection suits and respirators, the armed men moved with speed and dexterity. At both entry points, the lead operatives used fiber-optic cameras to make sure the doors weren't booby-trapped before calling up their breachers.

Just like the SEALs who had raided the cargo ship, the ROS operators were wearing individual cameras. When the breachers opened the doors and the teams flooded in, all eyes in the command post went from watching the drone footage to the individual POVs coming off the teams' helmet cams.

The men crowded in, their weapons up, scanning for threats. In the center of the empty warehouse was a large shipping container.

Carefully, the team approached. The lead operators stepped forward, fiber-optic cameras in hand, and attempted to snake the thin devices inside. There was just one problem. The container was so tightly sealed they couldn't find a way in.

Knowing it would take forever to get a portable X-ray machine on site, the team leaders made a decision.

Sending their men out of the building, they decided to risk opening the container's doors.

After unlocking the hardware, they counted to three, and then swung the heavy metal doors outward.

CHAPTER 84

Inside the container was a rough but fully functional laboratory. In addition to the chemistry area, with all its beakers, tubes, and Bunsen burners, there was a workbench with large vises and shelves full of tools.

It was the empty jugs of chemicals, though, that Harvath was most interested in. As the ROS operatives picked them up, Harvath read the labels aloud.

"Methylphosphonic dichloride. Hydrogen fluoride. Isopropyl amine. And isopropyl alcohol," he said. "They're making sarin."

Sarin was a tasteless, odorless nerve agent that was banned by the Chemical Weapons Convention, but that had been used in the Tokyo subway attack in the 1990s and, more recently, in horrific attacks in Syria that garnered international condemnation.

Sarin was considered a weapon of mass destruction. Just a drop of it could kill a healthy person. It was easily transformed from liquid to gas and could remain on clothing for over a half hour, thereby creating additional casualties by affecting many of those who came in contact with it.

Because sarin was so dangerous and had such a short shelf life, ISIS had purchased what were called "binary" artillery shells. The shells were essentially a delivery device with two separate compartments. On one side, methylphosphonyl difluoride, made from reacting methylphosphonic dichloride and hydrogen fluoride, was added. On the other, a mixture of isopropyl amine and isopropyl alcohol was added. In between them was a "rupture" disk that broke down in flight and allowed the compounds to mix and become sarin.

When the device detonated, it sent a cloud of sarin gas into the air, killing everyone who breathed it in or whose skin it touched. Sarin was considered twenty-six times more lethal than cyanide. Whatever attack ISIS had planned, it was going to make everything up to this point look like amateur hour.

"I need to go to the building," Harvath said.

Argento looked at him. "What for?"

He held up his phone. "I need to identify the nearest cell tower."

The Italian asked one of the containment specialists if it was safe to go in. Until testing had been completed, he warned them against it.

Argento, though, came up with a compromise. Hopping in one of the ROS vehicles, they drove the three blocks to the warehouse.

After pulling up in front, turning his phone off and then on again, Harvath and Argento drove around to the back and did the same thing. Harvath then reached out to Nicholas.

A half hour later, back at the command post, his cell phone rang. "Six brand-new phones were turned on last night for the first time. All six pinged off your tower in Civitavecchia," the little man stated. "Then they were all turned off."

"What about since then?" asked Harvath.

"They all popped up just once more. Each sent a one-word text later in the evening. It was likely a code of some sort. The texts all went to the same number."

"Do we know where they are now?"

"Negative," said Nicholas. "After the one-word text, they all went dark. Whether the signal is purposely being blocked, or they tossed them in a bathtub, I can't tell."

"When they did pop up that one time, where were they?"

"I'll text you the coordinates."

"And the number that received the text messages?" Harvath asked.

"That one also went dark, but I'll send you its tower location as well."

Asking Nicholas to keep an eye out for any activity on the phones, Harvath hung up and waited for the text to come in.

When it did, he read the information to Argento, who had one of his people pull the locations up on a map. All were in random spots around Rome.

The maximum effective range of a comparable American mortar was almost sixty-five hundred yards, or nearly six kilometers. With that kind of reach, you could hit anything in the city, regardless of which cell tower you were closest to.

"Connect the towers," said Harvath.

Argento relayed the command and everyone watched as a red circle appeared on the screen.

At that moment, everyone's eyes were drawn to what sat right in the middle—the Vatican.

CHAPTER 85

I t was a beautiful morning, sunny and warm. Tursunov had risen early, performed his ablutions, recited his prayers, exercised, and showered.

As he had done in Santiago de Compostela and Paris, he wanted to pay a preattack visit to the site he would strike next.

Dressed in a pair of khaki trousers, a white shirt, and blue blazer, he looked every inch the upscale Western visitor to the Eternal City. Not a single person he passed had any notion of the hatred he harbored for Rome and everything it represented.

It was the heart of Christendom. It was the enemy not only of ISIS, but of all true believers of Islam worldwide. Its conquest was a key ISIS objective.

The Prophet Mohammed himself had prophesied that two great Roman cities would one day fall to Islam—Constantinople and Rome. Constantinople, now Istanbul, had been conquered by Muslims. Rome was next.

And after Rome, Israel would fall. And after Israel, the United States and the rest of its allies. Armageddon would descend and a final battle between good and evil, Muslim against non-Muslim, would take place. With the help of the Muslim messiah known as the Mahdi, Islam would emerge victorious.

And here he was, walking the streets of the enemy, about to help make the Prophet's revelation come true. The pain he was about to inflict on

Rome would be felt around the world. It would demonstrate Islam's superiority over Christianity and rally even more to their cause.

Allahu Akbar, the Tajik whispered to himself. *Allahu Akbar.*

• • •

As he walked, he kept his eyes peeled for a *tabaccheria.* It was still early, though, and many stores were not open yet.

Smoking the last of his French cigarettes, he savored the taste and tried to make it last. When he had smoked it down to the filter, he made sure there were no police within view and tossed the butt into the gutter.

Exhaling his last draw of smoke, he thought about everything he had put in place for tomorrow. It was his most ambitious operation ever.

Shaheed willing to martyr themselves for the cause were easy enough to come by. Intelligent, competent, battle-tested men were something else entirely.

To winnow that pool down to experience with a certain weapons system, and then to hone that experience into expertise, was an undertaking like nothing else he had ever attempted.

He had taken twelve men, divided them into two-man teams, and convinced the leadership of ISIS that, given the right mathematical information, they could hit their target, sight unseen.

The leadership had challenged him to prove it. On a training range in the Syrian desert, with stakes and colored pieces of surveyor's tape to represent the target, he had done just that.

And he did it not just once, but over and over again. His mortar teams were that good.

The part the leadership loved most about using mortars was that there was no device to defend against them. Once they had been fired, there was no stopping the attack.

They had the added benefit of not needing a martyr to get right up to a target before engaging. At a distance from the target, there was less chance of being discovered and the attack being disrupted. Once the pieces were in place, it was impossible to stop.

The shells had been loaded with their chemicals, and the mortar teams dispatched with their equipment to their designated locations. As instructed, they had activated their new cell phones long enough to confirm they were in place.

Unlike at Santiago de Compostela and Paris, here he would not be observing the attack up close. He would watch it unfold via webcam from the safety of his hotel room.

Before that, though, he wanted to walk where so many infidels would die tomorrow. And while there, he had something very special to retrieve.

CHAPTER 86

The Pope's public schedule was posted on the Internet and known months in advance. When in Rome, he usually put in two public appearances a week.

On Wednesdays, he conducted a general public audience in St. Peter's Square, which drew tens of thousands of people. Being driven in the famous "Pope Mobile" through St. Peter's, he was known to stop to bless various people and kiss babies before presiding over a service given in multiple languages.

On Sundays, he gave an address and a blessing from a window of the papal apartments known as the Angelus. Though not as widely attended as the general audience, the Angelus still drew thousands of tourists and the faithful.

This Sunday, though, was the last Sunday of the summer season. Because travel would take him away for many Wednesdays throughout the fall, he had decided to change things up and conduct a general public appearance.

As soon as Argento had confirmed the event via the Vatican's website, they not only knew what the ISIS target was, but when the attack would take place.

When their helicopter landed at the heliport in the Vatican gardens, it was met by the Carabinieri's liaison to the Holy See, as well as a man in a dark suit and tie who identified himself only as Josef.

As they were being led to a waiting Mercedes limousine, Harvath whispered, "Who's the guy in the suit?"

"*L'entità,*" said Argento.

Lovett translated. "The Entity. Vatican Intelligence."

Sliding into the vehicle, Harvath didn't ask any further questions. It was obvious they were taking the threat very seriously.

A short drive through the immaculate gardens brought them to a large wrought-iron gate that automatically opened. Driving through, they soon came to a dramatic fountain and waterfall. Behind was a long building of cream-colored brick, its rooftop studded with satellite dishes and an enormous antenna that belonged to Vatican Radio.

"Monastery of Mater Ecclesiae," said Argento as they approached. "It used to belong to the Vatican police. Now it houses *cloistered nuns*."

The way Argento said it, it sounded as if he didn't believe it. And based upon the arrays of satellite dishes on the roof, Harvath didn't know if he should believe it either. It looked like a lot more was going on here than just a monastery coupled with a radio tower.

The Mercedes came to a stop moments later beneath an arched portico. Josef opened the rear door and instructed everyone to follow him. Inside, to their left, an elevator was waiting, its door open. There were no buttons, only a slot.

Once they were all in, Josef removed a keycard and inserted it. The doors closed and the elevator began to descend.

When the doors opened again, they were below ground. How many stories was anyone's guess.

If it weren't for the mosaic floor with the white dove of peace, a large crucifix suspended upon the far wall, and a portrait of the Pope, they could have been in any number of highly classified facilities run by the NSA, the CIA, or the FBI.

"Follow me," Josef ordered.

They walked down a long hallway and were interrupted at one point by a group of nuns who came out a door, carrying stacks of files. Harvath managed to get a peek inside the room they had just exited and saw rows of cubicles staffed by even more nuns.

Josef kept moving.

They ended up at another, similar door, and Josef waved his keycard in front of its handle to unlock it. When the lock released, he pushed the door open and held it so that everyone could enter.

It was a war room.

There was a long conference table and several workstations. The flag of Vatican City stood in a brass stand next to a map of the world highlighting all of the Church's holdings and interests. A blue, digital clock with six time zones ran above it. Opposite, was a large video wall surrounded by independent monitors.

Standing in the center of it all was a man dressed exactly like Josef, but a good twenty years older.

He was a tall, handsome man in his midsixties, with gray hair and green eyes. Stepping forward, he extended his hand and introduced himself simply as Carl. Whoever these guys were, they were not big on last names, or formalities.

Notepads and bottles of water had been set up at each place. There were pots of hot coffee in the center of the conference table and an espresso machine off to the side. Carl invited everyone to help themselves.

When everyone was seated, the man asked, "So. What do we have?"

Harvath let Argento do the talking, and he was kind enough to do it in English. On the rare occasion he had trouble with a word, he said it in Italian and either Lovett or Carl helped him out.

Once the ROS operative was done, Carl looked at Harvath. "I understand you protected the President of the United States at one point," he said.

"I did," Harvath replied.

"If you were me, what would you do with this information?"

"That depends. I don't know exactly know who you are."

Carl smiled. "I am in charge of protecting His Holiness and Vatican City. If I am involved, it is because a threat has been deemed substantial and very real."

"If you're asking what I would do, as a Secret Service officer, to protect the American President, I would cancel his public schedule. I would probably even go so far as to concoct a cover story. I'd have an ambulance arrive this evening to take him to the hospital. I'd leak to the press something about an illness or a fall."

Harvath's voice trailed off and the Vatican intelligence officer noticed. "But?"

"But that only postpones the attack. The weapons are here in Rome and so are the terrorists. If they are well funded, which we should believe they are, they might be able to stick it out—to wait until the Pope returns. Or . . ."

"Or what?"

"They pick another target and people still die."

"To protect the Pope and our visitors to St. Peter's Square, though, I would need to call everything off," said Carl.

Harvath nodded. "But to catch the terrorists and eliminate this threat altogether, you would need to act as if everything was still on."

The Vatican intelligence officer looked at the digital clock above the map. "I can give you eight hours. After that, we're going to cancel His Holiness's public schedule."

CHAPTER 87

For the same reason Harvath wouldn't use the Wi-Fi at the ROS safe house in Villa San Giovanni, he didn't want to use the Vatican intelligence service Wi-Fi either. Allies spied on each other. It was just the nature of the game.

Securing a temporary keycard from Josef, Harvath slung his backpack over his shoulder, walked back out to the elevator, and headed upstairs to use his phone.

Argento, who was dying for a smoke, joined him.

Reaching ground level, they exited the elevator and stepped outside onto the cobbled driveway.

The Vatican gardens covered fifty-seven acres, seven and a half of which were forest. From where they stood, Harvath thought he smelled gardenias, but as it was so late in the season, it had to be something else.

He took another breath, trying to place the scent, but it was interrupted by Argento, who lit up, and then promptly exhaled a cloud of steel-gray smoke.

He was about to make a joke about his smoking in the cleanest place in all of Rome when the Italian's cell phone rang.

Harvath listened as an animated conversation took place. When it was finished and Argento had disconnected the call, he turned to Harvath and said, "The ISIS man. The one who bought the mortars from La Formícula? We have his picture."

"From where?"

The Italian smiled. "Your man Vella has been hard at work. He had Vottari tell him everything, every single step from the beginning. Apparently, La Formícula set up a meeting. There is a bar in a rough neighborhood of Reggio Calabria. He told the ISIS man to go there and wait to be picked up. When he was there, he had to do something specific with a newspaper and order a Negroni so that they knew it was him. Once he did that, the bar owners reached out to Vottari."

"And there was a camera inside the bar?"

Argento nodded. "Outside too. Like I said, it is in a rough neighborhood."

"Has Vottari confirmed the picture?"

"Yes. Vella just showed it to him."

This was a huge break. "Send it to me," said Harvath as he reached for his phone and dialed Vella to confirm.

"He says it's him," the doctor stated from the ROS safe house.

"But he doesn't have any identifying information we can use to track him down?"

"All of their conversations were through an encrypted chat room."

"Okay," Harvath relented. "Keep working on him."

Turning back to Argento, he asked, "Did you send the still frame?"

The Italian nodded and moments later, he had it. Right away, he sent the photo along to Nicholas. Within a few seconds, the phone rang.

"This is the guy?" the little man asked.

"According to La Formícula, yes."

"Okay, I'm on it. No idea how long this will take."

"See if you can place him in Rome. If he's the guy who arranged the weapons, he may be connected to those six brand-new cell phones we're tracking."

"Roger that. Keep your ringer on," Nicholas replied.

And before Harvath could tell him where he was, and that he couldn't get a signal underground, the little man had hung up.

Crushing out his cigarette, Argento asked, "Back downstairs?"

"I have to wait for a call," Harvath replied, holding up his phone.

The Italian looked at him. "The Pope has Wi-Fi, you know."

"It's not the Pope I'm concerned about."

"Understood," said Argento. "It's too beautiful a day to spend in a dungeon. We should be outside. I'm going to get an espresso. What can I bring you?"

"Espresso sounds good," he responded, handing over his keycard so he could access the elevator.

As the Italian went back inside, Harvath leaned against the side of the building and turned his face up toward the sun.

It felt warm against his skin and it was good to close his eyes. He had only been able to snatch small slices of sleep here and there.

A lot of his body was still sore from Libya. That sore part wanted him to reach down and fish the bottle of Motrin out of his pack so he didn't forget to take some. The rest of his body didn't want him to move. It not only felt good just the way he was, but ever since Argento had put out his cigarette, it also smelled good. When was he ever going to get another chance to close his eyes and just relax in the Vatican gardens?

He stood there like that for several moments until a sound broke his reverie. It was off in the distance, but coming closer.

He opened his eyes and focused. He could distinctly make out a car, traveling at a high rate of speed.

Moments later, he could see it—a black, unmarked Fiat sedan, speeding up the driveway toward him. He didn't know what to make of it until Argento burst back outside, slinging his pack over his shoulder.

As the car came skidding to a halt atop the cobblestones, he could see a young Carabinieri officer inside behind the wheel.

"One of the phones just went active," Argento shouted. "We've got a fix on its location."

"Where is Lovett?" Harvath asked as the Italian opened the passenger door and hopped in.

"Downstairs," he replied. "She can't go tactical here. Now that she's brought the Ambassador up to speed, he wants her to stay put."

All Harvath could do was shake his head. He hated bureaucracy. Opening the rear door, he tossed his pack on the seat and jumped in.

Before he had even closed the door, the driver activated his lights and klaxon and took off.

CHAPTER 88

The terrorist's cell phone had been traced to a rooftop apartment overlooking the Campo de' Fiori, just south of the Piazza Navona. From the apartment's outdoor terrace, a mortar would have a straight line of travel over the Tiber River and into St. Peter's Square.

The Carabinieri officer turned off his lights and klaxon two blocks away from the building. Half a block from the entrance, he pulled over and stopped so Argento and Harvath could get out.

A tactical team was en route, but it would be another five minutes before they arrived. "Come watch the door," Argento told the young officer in Italian. "Don't let anyone in or out. Understand?"

The young man nodded and as he did, Harvath and Argento took off down the street.

Stepping inside the vestibule of the centuries-old apartment building, the ROS operator rang for the concierge. She appeared seconds later, a tough-looking woman in her seventies. Argento showed her his credentials and spoke with her in rapid-fire Italian. When they finished, the woman disappeared back inside.

Argento explained to Harvath what was going on. "She says the rooftop apartment is owned by a couple from Florence. She doesn't see them much. They rent the place out online to tourists."

"Who's in it now?"

"Two men."

"What do they look like?" asked Harvath.

"According to the concierge, Arabs. More than that, she doesn't know. They've been here for a week and have kept to themselves."

"Where'd she go?"

Argento was about to reply when the concierge returned and handed him a key. Holding open the main door, she stood back and allowed the men to step inside.

A wide staircase wound its way all the way up to the fifth floor. In the center was an ancient, cage-style elevator. Neither man needed to discuss which they were going to take. They both headed for the stairs.

Halfway up, they stopped and removed their weapons from their bags, then they climbed the rest of the way. Just shy of the final landing, they stopped to catch their breath.

When they were good to go, they nodded at each other and crept up the last handful of stairs.

Moving quietly down the hall, they found the door they were looking for and Argento stopped to listen. He pressed his ear against it for several moments. He looked at Harvath and shook his head. There was no sound from inside. Harvath got himself ready and then motioned to the Italian to open the door.

Cautiously, Argento slid the key inside the lock and, without making a sound, slowly turned it. When it was unlocked, he counted backward from three.

On "one," he quietly pushed the door open and Harvath slipped inside.

The door opened into a narrow hallway with wood floors. At the end of it, he could see windows, a small kitchen, and part of a dining room. Closing the door, Argento brought up the rear.

Moving forward, Harvath strained his ears for any sound. There was nothing. He wondered if maybe the phone had been left behind, or if the two occupants were out on the rooftop deck.

Creeping forward, Harvath stepped on a board that groaned beneath his foot. Instantly, he froze.

In the quiet apartment, the noise sounded like an air horn. Technically it wasn't as loud, but it had the same effect of trumpeting their arrival.

Suddenly, a man appeared from around the corner with an AK-47.

Harvath depressed the trigger of his suppressed H&K and fired, hitting him in the chest. He followed up with another round to the chest and one to the head.

The man fell over backward, his weapon clattering across the kitchen floor. *One down.*

Moving forward, Harvath swept into the living area. It was clear, as were the kitchen and dining room. Looking through the windows, he didn't see anyone on the deck outside

With Argento right behind, he moved into the bedroom. There was another AK-47 propped up in the corner. Argento checked the closet and under the bed. Both were clear. That left only one place to look.

Before he even reached the bathroom door, he could hear someone on the other side. The closer he got, the more he could begin to smell him. Someone was in gastric distress.

Kicking open the door, Harvath found the other terrorist pale and sweaty, sitting on the toilet, sick as a dog. The stench was overwhelming.

Clutching a garbage can, which he had been vomiting into, the man had to undergo an extreme balancing act when Harvath told him in English and Arabic to raise his hands over his head.

After making sure the man didn't have any weapons, Harvath released Argento to go check outside.

A few minutes later, he came back in, issuing orders over his cell phone. Pausing his call, he offered to watch the prisoner while Harvath went out onto the deck to review the evidence.

Backing out of the bathroom, and grateful for the fresh air, Harvath stepped onto the terrace. There, beneath the tarp Argento had pulled halfway back, was the Russian mortar and a crate with two chemical shells.

One team down, five more to go, thought Harvath.

When the tactical team arrived, there was nothing for them to do but secure the scene. Close on their heels was an explosive ordnance unit, as well as a chemical containment team.

An ambulance had been dispatched as well, the big fear being that the terrorist on the toilet had been exposed to a hazardous chemical, perhaps something currently leaking inside the apartment or from the shells out on the deck.

As it turned out, the man had food poisoning and was severely dehydrated. His partner had turned their cell phone on in hopes of reaching their handler and receiving instructions on how best to deal with the situation. The handler had never replied.

The medical team wanted to start an IV on the man. With Argento's help, Harvath pushed them and everyone else back out of the bathroom and out of the bedroom. He wanted to see what kind of information he could extract from him.

To a large degree, what he was able to get was useless. The man knew nothing about the other cells, their locations, or the location of the handler. Everything had been compartmentalized. He knew the other mortar teams because he had trained with them in Syria, but they had all entered Italy via different means and he had no idea where they were now. Harvath believed him.

The one thing the terrorist was able to do was confirm the identity of his handler. Holding up the picture of the man in the bar in Reggio Calabria that Argento's men had uncovered, the terrorist nodded. *That was him.*

The terrorist only knew him by his nom de guerre. Harvath had yet to meet a true jihadist who hadn't taken on an assumed name for engaging in combat. It was a time-honored Islamic tradition.

Allowing everyone back in the room, Harvath stepped outside to get more fresh air. Argento was standing off to the side, smoking a cigarette. *So much for fresh air.*

"Did he give you anything?" he asked.

Harvath shook his head. "Not much. Just confirmed the picture from earlier. No name or location, though."

"What did he say about the phone?"

"They were only supposed to use it in case of emergency. They have a communication window every eight hours. The man is so sick, his partner was afraid he might not make it. That's why they activated the phone and sent a message. They were hoping the handler might check in early."

"When is the next window?" Argento asked.

Harvath checked his watch. "Not for six more hours."

"That's a long time."

Nodding, he leaned against the parapet and looked out over the rooftops of Rome. *Where the hell are you?*

Finishing his cigarette, Argento flicked the butt off the roof as his cell phone rang.

At almost the same moment, Harvath's rang as well. Looking at the caller ID, he saw that it was Lovett.

"You need to get back here right away," she said, as he activated the call.

"What's going on?"

"That picture Argento gave you? The ISIS middleman who bought the weapons from Vottari? We've got him on camera. He just walked through St. Peter's Square forty-five minutes ago."

CHAPTER 89

Returning to the operations center back at Vatican City beneath the Monastery of Mater Ecclesiae, Harvath asked Carl to roll the footage for them.

"Coming up," Carl said, as he scrolled through. "Okay, that's him entering Vatican City. Blue blazer, tan khakis."

Freezing the shot, he zoomed in.

Harvath looked at it, and then at the picture on his phone. It was definitely the same guy. "How'd you find him?"

"We ran the photo through facial recognition. The computer did the rest."

"Unfreeze it," said Harvath. "Show me where he goes."

The Vatican intelligence officer did as asked.

Everyone in the room watched as he strolled St. Peter's Square and then headed through security and over to the bronze doors of the basilica. There, he began speaking with a pair of Swiss Guards.

"What's he doing now? Have you spoken with those two Swiss Guards?"

"Personally," said Carl. He was there to pick up a ticket for tomorrow's papal audience."

"Did he show any ID?"

"Yes. He had an Austrian passport and the ticket had been reserved ahead of time."

The Vatican intelligence officer handed Harvath a copy of the reservation.

"Why would he want a ticket?" Argento asked. "He's not going anywhere near St. Peter's Square tomorrow."

Harvath thought about it for a moment. "It could be a scalp. Just a sick souvenir. On the bin Laden raid, the SEALs allegedly found some 9/11 memorabilia in his house in Abbottabad."

The answer seemed to satisfy Argento, and they watched the rest of the footage. It lasted right up until the man left Vatican City. Stepping out onto the Via della Conciliazione, he eventually disappeared into the throng of morning tourists.

"Rome has a billion CCTV cameras. You can't follow him through those?" Harvath asked.

"My authority ends at the walls of Vatican City."

Harvath looked at Argento, who was already dialing a number on his cell phone. "I'm on it," he said.

As great as the ROS operators had been, Harvath had no idea who would be put in charge of sifting through the CCTV footage to try to locate their subject. For all he knew, it was some twenty-year-old kid, working for the City of Rome, who had been out all night partying and had showed up to work with a hangover and no sleep. Every second counted.

"Carl, could I get a copy of your footage?" Harvath asked.

"I don't see why not. How do you want to receive it?"

Harvath scrolled through his phone and pulled up a DropBox account he used with Nicholas. The Vatican intelligence officer took the information down and went to have one of his IT people copy and upload the footage.

Picking up a mug, Harvath filled it with coffee, added a shot of espresso, and after asking Argento for the keycard back headed upstairs to make a few phone calls.

Stepping outside, he wandered into the garden, where he found a small, shaded bench. Setting his pack down next to him, he fished out his satellite phone, extended the antenna, and fired it up.

When Nicholas answered, he filled him in on everything that had transpired. After describing what their target was wearing, Nicholas agreed that there'd be lots of people dressed like that in Rome today. He also agreed that the Italians were going to have a tough time finding that needle in such a large haystack.

"That's why I need you to hack into their CCTV system. There's already footage from Vatican City being uploaded to my DropBox account. Use it as a baseline and then apply the gait algorithm to all the cameras in Rome."

The gait algorithm was a program that could run concurrently with facial recognition software. But instead of studying faces, it studied how people walked. Your gait was unique, almost like a fingerprint. Once the program knew what it was looking for, it could race through footage until it located and identified its target.

"That could take a while," the little man replied.

"I need it as soon as possible," said Harvath, and before Nicholas could respond, he had already disconnected the call and was on to his next.

He called Staelin, who, along with Barton and Morrison, had stayed behind to help Vella continue his interrogation of Vottari. After bringing him up to speed, he asked for an update on their end. Staelin put Vella on the phone.

The doctor explained that he was coming to the end of what he could do in the field. He might be able to extract more back at the Solarium, but he doubted it. He was pretty confident they had wrung everything of value out of the Mafioso.

Harvath thanked him for the SITREP and told him he'd be back in touch as soon as he could.

Now came the hard part. Picking up his mug, he prepared to wait. Stretching out his legs, he was about to take a sip of coffee when something about the CCTV footage hit him.

Grabbing his pack, he ran back inside.

CHAPTER 90

It wasn't that they hadn't been asking the right question about the CCTV cameras. It was that they had only been asking one—*where was the man going*? No one had thought to ask *where had he been*?

Focusing on the moment the man had arrived at Vatican City, Argento's contact with the City's cameras had been able to work backward. Even though the man had disappeared into a crowd as he left St. Peter's, his arrival had been via quiet, uncrowded streets.

As soon as the City's computer system had locked in on him and had begun piecing his route together, Argento and Harvath had hopped back in the Fiat sedan and had given the driver directions on where to go.

Over his cell phone, Argento's contact continued to update him until the trail led to video of the man leaving a hotel near Rome's Termini station. Once the ROS operator had that information, he called the tactical team back at Campo de' Fiori and told them to get there as quickly as they could.

Stopping a block up, the Carabinieri officer pulled over and dropped Argento and Harvath off. With their backpacks slung over their shoulders, they walked down to the hotel and entered the lobby.

As Argento approached over to the front desk, Harvath kept an eye on the front door, along with everything else.

In under two minutes, the ROS operator had the man's room number and a pass key. The young lady working the desk this morning had been working the desk when he checked in two nights ago. She prided herself on remembering guests.

At Argento's request, she had called up to the room. There was no answer. *They had beaten him back to the hotel.*

Hustling up the stairs, they stepped out into the hallway and walked
down to the room. The man, who had used an Austrian passport at the
Vatican, had checked into the hotel under a Ukrainian passport.

Drawing their weapons, they took position on either side of the door
as Argento knocked. There was no answer.

Identifying himself as hotel security, he knocked again, but there
was still no answer. He dipped the card into the reader, the light flashed
green, and he pushed open the door.

The room and its contents were unremarkable. There were clothes in
the closet, a few things in the dresser, and toiletries in a shaving kit in the
bathroom. The only thing that caught Harvath's eye were the two different types of phone chargers on the desk. Other than that, there was nothing in the room that would give the man away as a terrorist.

They went through his clothes and his suitcase, looking for any hidden compartments or things that might have been sewn into the lining.
They found nothing.

They then turned the room upside down, looking under drawers, in
air vents, and behind draperies. Still nothing.

After putting the room back together, they had a decision to make.
Stay and wait him out, or try to pick up his trail out in the city?

Without a solid lead, Harvath wasn't keen on driving around Rome,
hoping to get lucky. All the man's belongings were in this room. They
had every reason to believe he was coming back. Whether that was in five
minutes or five hours there was no way to tell.

In the meantime, though, they could begin moving guests and isolat-
ing this end of the hotel. Already the room next door and the one across
the hall were empty. If there was a shootout, or worse, they'd be glad they
had minimized collateral damage as much as possible.

While Harvath remained in the room, Argento went back downstairs
to speak with the desk clerk and wait on the tactical team.

Pulling out his phone, Harvath scrolled through to see if he had received any messages. There was one from Haney, letting him know that
he and Gage had made it back to the United States and . . .

Harvath's thoughts were interrupted by a sound at the door. Argento would have knocked. This was not a knock. It sounded as if someone had started to dip his room key into the card reader, had second thoughts, and had suddenly stopped.

Picking up his pistol, he began to move off the bed when a hail of bullets tore through the door. Rolling hard onto the floor, he returned fire.

He ran his H&K dry, ejected the spent magazine, and inserted a fresh one. Depressing the slide release, he focused on the door and waited for another round of incoming fire, but it didn't come.

Pulling the alarm clock off the nightstand, he yanked the cord out of the wall, tossed it at the door, and waited. *Nothing happened.*

Hugging the floor, he crawled over to the door. Reaching up, he released the handle and opened it just far enough to get his fingers in between the door and the jamb. Taking a deep breath, he pulled it the rest of the way open.

From the other end of the hall, there was another barrage of gunfire, but it all went high, where the man had expected him to be.

Harvath returned fire, hitting him in both legs. He heard him cry out and fall back into the stairwell.

Down in the lobby, Argento had to have heard the gunfire. Without radios, their cell phones were their only means of communication.

Harvath pulled his out to call him and tell him what was going on, but he saw that Argento had already texted him.

I'm coming up south stairwell.

He couldn't let him do that. That was where the injured shooter was. Argento would run right into him.

Pushing into the hall, he hit the Dial button on his phone as he rushed toward the south stairs with his gun up and ready.

Before he could get there, the whole building shook with two horrible explosions.

They had come from the stairwell. Without even opening the door and seeing the destruction, he knew what had happened—a pair of grenades had been detonated.

Bracing for gunfire, or even more grenades, Harvath flung open the stairwell door. One flight down, bleeding badly from both legs, was the man they had been chasing.

It took everything Harvath had not to finish the job and put a bullet in him right there. "Hands!" he yelled. "Show me your hands! Do it now!"

Slowly, the man complied.

With his gun trained on him, Harvath descended the stairs and kicked his pistol away. When he was sure he wasn't hiding a live grenade, ready to blow them both up, he rolled the man onto his stomach, flex-cuffed his hands behind his back, and searched him for other weapons.

Confident that he was clean, Harvath peered over the railing. There, halfway between floors, was Argento. The grenades had torn him apart. Harvath had no words.

From the ground floor, he could hear the tactical team, finally on scene, entering the stairwell.

CHAPTER 91

Rural Virginia
Three Weeks Later

Harvath stood at the windows of the Old Man's study and looked out. The weather was already changing. There wouldn't be an Indian Summer this year. Winter would be here soon, and by all accounts, it was going to be long, hard, and cold.

He had stayed in Italy long enough to clean everything up and attend Argento's funeral. Lovett put on a tough show, but it was obvious that his death disturbed her deeply.

If there was anything good that had come out of it, it was that the attack on St. Peter's had been averted. Once they had the cell phone used to communicate with the other mortar teams, the ROS waited for the next communications window to open up and then tricked the terrorists into leaving their phones on. While they thought they were awaiting further instructions about the attack, the ROS was zeroing in on their locations.

The terrorists did not go peacefully. Many of them fought and were killed. Three ROS operatives were injured. The number of lives that were saved, though, was incalculable.

Once Tursunov was stable, the Italians agreed to let Harvath have a short window to interrogate him. He flew Vella in and let him do the work. With the information they gleaned, they were able to roll up high-level ISIS members across Europe and even in the United States. He turned out to be full of useful information. They were even able to locate the chemist who had helped assemble the shells for the St. Peter's attack.

Harvath would have been happy to take any or all of them out, but they were considered of significant intelligence value. What's more, the countries in which many of them had committed their grisly crimes wanted them to stand trial.

The families and victims needed closure. He understood. Though, if they had known what he was willing to do, he was certain many of them would have quietly chosen to have him handle things.

Part of handling things his way had been to get Staelin, Barton, and Morrison to pump Vottari full of Rohypnol and leave him naked in a cheap hotel room on Sicily. It wasn't the justice he deserved, but that had been Harvath's agreement with Argento, and he intended to honor it.

After a seventy-two-hour hold, the ROS operatives in Palermo blind-folded Ragusa, Naya the bartender, as well as the two bodyguards and dropped them in the middle of the street in front of the Black Cat.

Upon returning home, Bob McGee and Lydia Ryan had requested a private debriefing with Harvath. They met, as they had previously, at the blue lockhouse.

After taking them through everything that had happened, Ryan then explained all that she and the Old Man had been wrestling with.

Susan Viscovich had spilled the beans on Andrew Jordan. Working with Jake Fleischer, Nicholas had been able to connect Jordan and a ton of offshore accounts to Paul Page and Page Partners, Ltd.

In fact, they had been able to identify two other sources inside the Agency that Page had been buying information from without Jordan's knowledge.

The problem, though, was that Jordan had gone missing. No one had heard from him and no one knew where he was. They suspected Page might have had something to do with it. Harvath had been tasked with getting to the bottom of it.

Once he did, though, Page's confession—secured under considerable duress—was absolutely inadmissible in court. Ryan and McGee were just happy to have recovered Jordan's body from the forest preserve where it had been buried, and to have closure. The possibility of a well-funded rogue CIA agent floating around wasn't something they wanted to add to their to-do list.

And while recovering Jordan's body and knowing Page had been responsible for his murder did provide closure, it didn't provide any sense of justice. That was where the Old Man had come in.

The moment Harvath had heard his idea, he had been one hundred percent onboard. It meant one more plane ride, but he was happy to do it.

Pumping Paul Page full of ketamine, he had flown with him to Malta. There, he had met up with Vella, who had provided him a vehicle and a ticket on the high-speed car ferry to Sicily. Argento's lieutenant, along with Roberto and Naldo, had met them upon arrival.

In the car trunk, "attempting to sneak into Italy," was Page. In his pocket was a key for a safety deposit box at a bank in Palermo. In the box was a passel of uncut diamonds, paid for with money drained from one of Andrew Jordan's offshore accounts.

It was a payday worth sneaking into Italy for. No matter what tall tale Page told about being smuggled into Italy against his will, no jury would ever believe him. Not only would he be expected to serve his full sentence for the kidnapping of the Milan Imam, but the diamonds would be forfeited and go toward paying off the fines levied against him in the case.

For a man suffering from Alzheimer's, Reed Carlton was still pretty sharp.

"I have good days and bad," he said, as he picked up his drink and joined Harvath at the windows. "The only thing I know for sure is that it's not getting better."

This was the visit Harvath had wanted to pay before he had left for Libya, but now that he was here, he wanted to be anywhere but. Knowing the Old Man was slipping away was more painful than having him suddenly taken.

The two of them were like family. Now, the father was looking to hand over the business to the son. The problem, though, was that the son didn't want it. Not fully. Not yet.

"I know you want me to run a Special Activities Division for you," he said, "but I've still got a lot of special activities I'd actually like to carry out. I don't want to sit behind a desk."

"What if you didn't have to?" Carlton asked. "What if it were a hybrid and you could do a little bit of everything?"

"There'd have to be a solid team in place, starting with a number two who knew what the hell he or she was doing."

"I hear you and Mike Haney get along pretty well. What about him?"

Harvath smiled. The Old Man was always up on everything. "Haney walks funny."

Carlton smiled back. "That might be permanent. Time will tell. Nevertheless, he's interested. If you are."

"You already talked to him?"

"Of course. I don't have a lot of time to pull this succession plan together."

Harvath loved the Old Man, and also loved his offer, but there was a reason he had left D.C. and moved to Boston. "I have a plan I'm trying to pull together too. I can't do that from here."

"What if you didn't have to?" said a voice.

He turned to see Lara standing in the doorway of the study. He didn't know if he should hug Carlton or hit him. He had always been a resourceful yet manipulative spy. For the moment, Harvath decided to ignore him.

Crossing over to Lara, he took her in his arms and hugged her. He had missed her. "What are you doing here?"

"Lydia Ryan called me."

"Against my wishes," said Carlton.

"She cares about both of you," Lara continued, "and she thinks you should take this position."

Harvath laughed. "I'm sure she does. It'd make her job a lot easier having me around."

"So do it. Take the position."

"But what about us? What about Boston?"

"We'll figure it out," she replied. "Right now, though, there are a lot of people who need you here. The *country* needs you here. Not in Boston."

"And you and Marco?" he asked.

"You made the move for us and I love you for that. But maybe we should have made the move for you. Maybe the right answer for all of us is here."

Harvath kissed her. This was what he wanted. This was exactly where he wanted to be.

Looking over at Carlton, he saw the Old Man smile.

ACKNOWLEDGMENTS

The best part (for an author) of finishing a novel is getting to the acknowledgments and saying thank you to all the people so important to the process.

At the top of my list are you, my amazing **readers**—old and new. Thank you for making the career I love possible. Thank you for all the wonderful reviews. Thank you for all the great word of mouth. I work for you, and I have the best employers in the business.

Next, a BIG *thank-you* to all the sensational **booksellers** across the globe who sell my thrillers. You are gateways to adventure, excitement, and escape. We romanticize what you do, even though we know so much hard work goes into it. Always know how much this author (and book buyer) appreciates you.

Thank you, **James Ryan**, for your help on this one. While you're out there doing it, I'm at my desk writing it. You continue to inspire me to improve myself in every area of my life. Knowing I can reach out to you day or night is invaluable.

This year, while going through some old photographs, I found a picture of me and **Sean F** when we were little, little kids. I framed a copy and gave it to him for Christmas. It was a token not only of our friendship, but of my thanks for what he has given to this country and for the help he has provided me on my books. Thank you, Sean, for everything.

Speaking of photographs, I am indebted to **Greg Hammonds** for the pictures and fascinating, firsthand information he shared with me about Tajikistan.

Through thick and thin, **Rodney Cox** is someone I truly value. His advice is always excellent, and I appreciate his hard-won experience forged in some of the darkest corners of the world. Thank you, my friend, for everything.

J'ro—that was the best bottle of whiskey I ever consumed. A late, late evening indeed, but the information was invaluable. Thank you for that and so many other things.

Thomas Williams was a big help on and off the page. Thank you, brother—from the entire family.

Soon to be a newly minted thriller author himself, **George Petersen** was extremely gracious in answering a wide array of questions. No detail was ever too small. Thank you, George. I appreciate all of it.

Pete Scobell, **Morgan Luttrell**, and **Paul Craig** are good buddies and exceptional Americans. They helped in key places throughout the book, and I am grateful for their assistance. Next time we're all in the same town, dinner's on me.

Rome-based journalist **Barbie Latza Nadeau** couldn't have been more generous with her time. Her writing on the refugee crisis in Europe, human smuggling, and the ISIS-Mafia connection is top-notch. If you'd like to learn about any of those subjects, make sure to check out her work. Thank you, Barbie.

My thanks also go to **Chad Norberg**, **Jon Sanchez**, **Robert O'Brien**, **Peter Osyff**, **John Schindler**, and **Jeff Boss**. America isn't good because it is great, it is great because it is good. The selfless service these men have rendered to our great nation continues to humble me. I am honored to know them and to be able to call on them for help in writing my novels. Thank you.

As many people as I can name, there are also those whom I cannot. To those **selfless warriors** out there taking the fight to the bad guys each and every day, thank you.

Debra Lovett and **Susan Viscovich** helped contribute to two wonderful causes near and dear to my heart. These are two absolutely amazing ladies worthy of a novel all their own. I hope they enjoy their namesakes herein, and maybe—just maybe—we'll see a return appearance in the future. I thank you both.

The publishing world's equivalent of Scot Harvath is the magnificent **Carolyn Reidy**. You could not ask for a better champion on your side. Thank you for everything, Carolyn, and here's to many more years of excitement and success together.

The outstanding **Judith Curr** and the marvelous **Louise Burke** take such good care of me. If there's an issue that needs handling, I only need to ask, and they're on it. I am thankful for all that you have done and continue to do for me. I am extremely fortunate to be working with you both.

All of my novels have been with **Simon & Schuster**, and I want to thank everyone in the entire magnificent organization. A more wonderful group of people you will never meet. I am honored to be a part of the family. Thank you.

My absolutely brilliant editor and publisher, **Emily Bestler**, deserves more thanks than I could ever give her here. There isn't a single part of the process that she isn't involved with—and all are made so much better because of her involvement. Simply put, there is none better. Thank you, Emily, for your wisdom and unending well of talent.

So, I have this unbelievable guy from Frank Sinatra's hometown in New Jersey who can make *anything* happen. You could write the best book in the world, but if no one knew about it, where would you be? That's where the tremendous **David Brown** comes in. He is the publicists' publicist. Thank you, D—for every single thing.

When you have **Cindi Berger** and **PMK-BNC** on your team bringing additional PR heat, it's like having the Avengers on speed-dial. They are super people and super professionals. Thank you.

My entire **Atria**, **Emily Bestler Books**, and **Pocket Books** family is very important to me and I want to thank them for everything they do all year long. You are the best.

I want to also thank the incomparable **Michael Selleck**, **Gary Urda**, and **John Hardy**, as well as the astounding **Colin Shields**, **Adene Corns**, **Lisa Keim**, **Irene Lipsky**, **Lara Jones**, **Alison Hinchcliffe**, the **Emily Bestler Books/Pocket Books sales team**, **Albert Tang** and the **Emily Bestler Books/Pocket Books Art Departments**, **Al "Don't worry, Brad, I got this" Madocs** and the **Atria/Emily Bestler Books Production Department**, **Chris Lynch**, **Tom Spain**, **Sarah Lieber-**

man, **Desiree Vecchio**, **Armand Schultz**, and the entire **Simon & Schuster audio division**.

One of the best days of my personal and professional life was the day I met my astonishing agent, **Heide Lange** of **Sanford J. Greenburger Associates**. I owe Heide more thanks than I will ever be able to convey. Thank you, Heide. You mean the world to me.

As James Bond has Q, Heide (and I) have the incredible **Stephanie Delman** and **Samantha Isman**. I thank you both for everything you do for me on a daily basis. And to that, let me also thank everyone else at **Sanford J. Greenburger Associates** for such wonderful assistance throughout the year.

In a word, **Yvonne Ralsky** is marvelous. The key to being successful is surrounding yourself with great people and letting them do what they do best. Yvonne, you are one of the greatest. My thanks to you and your wonderful family for being part of the team.

Every year, I thank my awesome entertainment attorney and dear friend, **Scott Schwimer**. He's not only a superstar in Hollywood, but he's also one of the best people I have ever met. Thank you, my friend.

Finally, my biggest thanks of all go to **my spectacular family**. If it weren't for you, this book would not have happened. Ours truly is a "family business." You do more for me than I can list here. No father or husband could ever ask for more supportive people in his life. I love you and I thank you from the bottom of my heart.

In closing, please visit my website. I not only create a lot of bonus content for the novels, but I also put out a fun, fast, free newsletter each month that includes a terrific prize. Swing by BradThor.com and check it out.

Now, with the novel complete and everyone thanked, I am off on my next adventure!

RESOURCES

I spend a lot of my time between books reading and doing research. Material ends up piled all around my office, taped to the walls, etc. Picture the movie *A Beautiful Mind* and you're about halfway there.

In writing *Use of Force*, a few resources stand out, and I would like to share them with you:

No Easy Day by Mark Owen with Kevin Maurer
No Hero by Mark Owen with Kevin Maurer
Fearless by Eric Blehm
Beyond Repair by Charles S. Faddis
Fair Play by James M. Olson

As I mentioned in the acknowledgments, I also highly recommend the reporting of Barbie Latza Nadeau on ISIS, the Mafia, and the European refugee crisis.

Scott Onstott's blog at secretsinplainsight.com provided fascinating information about sacred geometry and patterns of distance between major world landmarks.

Burningman.org and burners.me are excellent resources for anyone wanting to learn more about the Burning Man celebration.

For the writers out there, Angela Ackerman and Becca Puglisi put out a great series of books covering character expression, flaws, and attributes. If you're looking for insight into why people do what they do, this is a great place to start.

Finally, in order to satisfy the time constraints of the novel, I took artistic liberty with the start/stop dates of the Burning Man festival and the Fête des Tuileries in Paris. In all other areas, I worked to be as accurate as possible.

Any mistakes in the novel are on me, and I take full responsibility for them.

Thank you for reading *Use of Force*.